HARRAP'S

Moriarty

A[illegible]Y
H[illegible]OROWITZ

First published in Great Britain in 2014
by Orion Books,
an imprint of the Orion Publishing Group Ltd,
Carmelite House, 50 Victoria Embankment,
London EC4Y 0DZ

An Hachette UK company

ISBN 978 2 81 870 444 8

About the author

Anthony Horowitz may have committed more (fictional) murders than any other living author. As a TV screenwriter[1] he created both *Midsomer Murders* and the BAFTA-winning[2] *Foyle's War*. Other TV work includes *Poirot* and the widely acclaimed[3] mini-series *Collision* and *Injustice*. He is also the author of a string[4] of bestselling children's books, including the Alex Rider series, which has sold over nineteen million copies worldwide[5]. His ingenious adult novel, *The House of Silk*, spent a fantastic seven weeks in the *Sunday Times* Top 10. He has often claimed Sir Arthur Conan Doyle to be an inspiration for his work, ever since encountering the Holmes canon, aged sixteen[6]. He currently[7] lives in Clerkenwell.

Find out more at www.anthonyhorowitz.com or follow him on Twitter @AnthonyHorowitz

1. scénariste
2. qui a reçu la récompense BAFTA [équivalent britannique des César, pour cinéma et télévision]
3. célèbres
4. série
5. qui s'est vendue à plus de 19 millions d'exemplaires dans le monde
6. depuis le jour où, à 16 ans, il a découvert les aventures de Holmes
7. aujourd'hui

DIRECTION DE LA PUBLICATION : Carine Girac-Marinier

DIRECTION ÉDITORIALE : Claude Nimmo

DIRECTION ÉDITORIALE ADJOINTE : Julie Pelpel-Moulian

NOTES EN MARGE : Aurélie Devillers

RÉVISION DES NOTES : Valérie Katzaros

RELECTURE : Nathalie Abdallah

INFORMATIQUE ÉDITORIALE : Philippe Cazabet, Marie-Noëlle Tilliette

CONCEPTION GRAPHIQUE : Uli Meindl

FABRICATION : Rebecca Dubois

Mot de l'Éditeur

Vous aimeriez lire en langue originale, mais le vocabulaire, les expressions figurées ou la syntaxe vous arrêtent parfois ?

Cette collection est faite pour vous !

Vous trouverez en effet, en note dans la marge, une traduction de certains mots et expressions qui vous permettra d'avancer facilement dans votre lecture.

Nous n'avons pas cherché à vous donner une traduction littéraire de l'ouvrage et nous nous sommes parfois écartés du sens littéral pour vous fournir le sens qui convient le mieux à l'histoire. Aussi les mots sont-ils traduits dans le contexte du texte original.

Les expressions figées anglaises sont, bien entendu, rendues par une expression équivalente en français.

Les allusions à des réalités culturelles du monde anglo-saxon sont expliquées également dans la marge, pour vous aider à mieux comprendre la trame de l'histoire.

Vous aurez ainsi, en regard du texte original, tout le savoir-faire d'un dictionnaire rien que pour vous et adapté à ce livre !

Notre objectif est de vous mener jusqu'au mot FIN en vous donnant les clés nécessaires à la compréhension du récit.

Laissez-vous gagner par l'angoisse, l'humour et le suspense qui règnent chez les maîtres de la littérature anglo-saxonne.

Lire en VO ? You can indeed!

For my friend, Matthew Marsh
And in memory of Henry Marsh, 1982-2012

Coup de pouce pour vous aider à bien comprendre le début de l'histoire...

Nous sommes en Suisse, près des chutes du Reichenbach, dans lesquelles Sherlock Holmes et son grand ennemi Moriarty auraient tous deux plongé et trouvé la mort, il y a quelques jours à peine. L'inspecteur Athelney Jones, dépêché par Scotland Yard, et le détective Frederick Chase, envoyé par l'agence Pinkerton de New York, se rendent sur les lieux. Ensemble, ils vont mener l'enquête sur les circonstances de la disparition du célèbre détective et du professeur, enquête qui les conduira à Londres...

From *The Times* of London
24th April 1891

HIGHGATE BODY FOUND

Police have no explanation for a peculiarly brutal murder that has come to light[1] close by Merton Lane in the normally pleasant and quiet vicinity[2] of Highgate. The deceased[3], a man in his twenties[4], had been shot in the head[5] but of particular interest to the police[6] was the fact that his hands had been tied prior to the killing[7]. Inspector G. Lestrade, who is in charge of the enquiry[8], inclines to the belief[9] that this dreadful act[10] took the form of an execution and may be related to recent unrest[11] in the streets of London. He has identified the victim as Jonathan Pilgrim, an American who had been staying[12] at a private club in Mayfair and who may have been visiting the metropolis for reasons of business[13]. Scotland Yard has been in contact with the American legation but so far[14] no address has been found for the dead man and it may be some weeks[15] before any relatives come forward[16]. The investigation continues.

1. qui a été découvert
2. les environs habituellement calmes et agréables
3. défunt
4. d'une vingtaine d'années
5. avait été tué d'une balle dans la tête
6. ce qui a particulièrement intéressé la police
7. avant d'être abattu
8. l'enquête
9. tend à penser
10. acte ignoble
11. des troubles récents
12. logeait
13. était peut-être de passage dans la métropole pour affaires
14. pour le moment
15. il se passera peut-être plusieurs semaines
16. avant qu'un membre de la famille se manifeste

ONE

The Reichenbach Falls

Does anyone really believe what happened at the Reichenbach Falls? A great many accounts[1] have been written but it seems to me that all of them have left something to be desired[2] – which is to say, the truth[3]. Take the *Journal de Genève* and Reuters, for example. I read them from start to finish, not an easy task for[4] they're both written in that painfully dry manner[5] of most European publications[6], as if they're reporting the news because they have to[7], not because it's something they want you to know. And what exactly did they tell me? That Sherlock Holmes and his foremost adversary[8], Professor James Moriarty, of whose existence the public were only now learning[9], had met and that both of them died. Well, it might as well have been[10] an automobile accident for all the excitement those two authorities[11] managed to put into their prose[12]. Even the headlines were dull[13].

But what really puzzles me[14] is the narrative[15] of Dr John Watson. He describes the entire affair in *Strand Magazine*, starting with the knock on the door[16] of his consulting room on the evening of April 24th 1891 and continuing with his

1. De très nombreux comptes rendus
2. ont omis quelque chose
3. la vérité, pour ainsi dire
4. ce qui est une tâche pénible car
5. dans le style terriblement aride
6. propre à la plupart des publications européennes
7. ils y sont obligés
8. plus grand adversaire
9. dont l'existence venait tout juste d'être révélée au public
10. il aurait tout aussi bien pu s'agir de
11. à voir le peu d'enthousiasme que ces deux grands noms
12. avaient réussi à instiller à leur prose
13. gros titres étaient ennuyeux
14. ce qui me déconcerte le plus
15. récit
16. en commençant par des coups frappés à la porte

journey[1] to Switzerland. I yield to no one in my admiration for[2] the chronicler of the adventures, exploits, memoirs, casebooks[3] and so on of the great detective. As I sit at[4] my Remington Number Two improved model typewriter (an American invention, of course) and begin this great labour[5], I know that I am likely to fall short[6] of the standards of accuracy[7] and entertainment that he maintained to the end[8]. But I have to ask myself – how could he have got it so wrong[9]? How could he have failed to notice inconsistencies[10] that would have struck even the most obtuse police commissioner as glaringly obvious[11]? Robert Pinkerton used to say that a lie[12] was like a dead coyote. The longer you leave it[13], the more it smells. He'd have been the first to say that everything about the Reichenbach Falls stank[14].

You must forgive me if I seem a touch over-emphatic[15] but my story – *this* story – begins with Reichenbach and what follows[16] will make no sense without a close examination of the facts. And who am I? So that you may know whose company you keep[17], let me tell you that my name is Frederick Chase, that I am a senior investigator with the Pinkerton Detective Agency in New York and that I was in Europe for the first – and quite possibly the last – time in my life. My appearance? Well, it's never easy for any man to describe himself but I will be honest and say that I could not call myself handsome[18]. My hair was black, my eyes an indifferent shade[19] of brown. I was slender[20] and though only in my forties I was already too put-upon by the challenges life had thrown my way[21]. I was unmarried and sometimes I worried that it showed in my wardrobe[22], which was

1. voyage
2. Personne n'admire plus que moi
3. recueils de cas pratiques
4. Tandis que je m'assois devant
5. grande entreprise
6. je risque de ne pas être à la hauteur
7. précision
8. jusqu'à sa mort
9. se fourvoyer à ce point
10. ne pas remarquer des incohérences
11. que même le plus obtus des commissaires de police aurait jugées évidentes
12. mensonge
13. Plus vous le laissez traîner
14. puait
15. un brin trop catégorique
16. ce qui suit
17. Afin que vous sachiez à qui vous avez affaire
18. je ne pouvais prétendre être beau
19. nuance quelconque
20. mince
21. très atteint par les épreuves que la vie m'avait fait subir
22. cela se voie dans mes tenues vestimentaires

perhaps a little too well worn[1]. If there were a dozen men in the room I would be the last to speak. That was my nature.

I was at Reichenbach five days after the confrontation that the world has come to know as[2] 'The Final Problem'. Well, there was nothing final about it, as we now know, and I guess that just leaves us with the problem[3].

So. Let's take it from the start[4].

Sherlock Holmes, the greatest consulting detective who ever lived, flees England in fear of his life[5]. Dr Watson, who knows the man better than anyone and who would never hear a word said against him[6], is forced to admit that at this time Holmes is at less than his best[7], utterly worn out[8] by the predicament[9] in which he finds himself and which he cannot control. Can we blame him? He has been attacked no fewer than three times[10] in the space of just one morning. He has come within an inch[11] of being crushed by a two-horse van[12] that rushes[13] past him on Welbeck Street; he has almost been hit by a brick that falls or is thrown from a roof[14] on Vere Street – and, right outside Watson's front door, he finds himself attacked by some good fellow who's been waiting with a bludgeon[15]. Does he have any choice but to flee[16]?

Well, yes. There are so many other choices available to him[17] that I have to wonder what exactly was in Mr Holmes's mind. Not, of course, that he's particularly forthcoming[18] in the stories, all of which I've read (without ever once guessing the solution, for what it's worth[19]). To begin with, what makes him think he will be safer on the Continent than he will be closer to home[20]?

1. usées
2. que l'on connaît depuis sous le nom de
3. mais c'était bien un problème
4. Reprenons depuis le début
5. fuit l'Angleterre car il craint pour sa vie
6. est son plus ardent défenseur
7. n'est pas au mieux
8. complètement épuisé
9. situation difficile
10. pas moins de trois fois
11. a failli
12. calèche
13. passant à toute vitesse
14. lancée depuis un toit
15. matraque
16. d'autres choix que la fuite
17. qui se présentent à lui
18. bavard
19. sans jamais en deviner la solution, d'ailleurs
20. plus en sécurité sur le Continent qu'en Angleterre

London itself is a densely knit, teeming[1], city which he knows intimately and, as he once confided, he has many rooms ('five small refuges', Watson says) scattered around the place, which are known only to him[2].

He could disguise himself. In fact he *does* disguise himself. Only the next day, after Watson has arrived at Victoria Station, he notices an aged Italian priest in discussion with a porter and even goes so far as to offer him his assistance[3]. Later, the priest enters his carriage[4] and the two of them sit together face to face for several minutes before Watson recognises his friend. Holmes's disguises were so brilliant that he could have spent the next three years as a Catholic priest without anyone being the wiser[5]. He could have entered an Italian monastery. *Padre Sherlock*... that would have thrown[6] his enemies. They might even have let him pursue some of his other interests[7] – beekeeping[8], for example – on the side[9].

Instead, Holmes goes haring off on a journey[10] that seems to have nothing that resembles an itinerary[11] and he asks Watson to accompany him. Why? The most incompetent criminal will surely work out[12] that where one goes, the other will quite probably follow[13]. And let's not forget that we are talking here about a criminal like no other, the master of his profession, a man who is equally feared and admired by Holmes himself. I don't believe for a minute that he could possibly have underestimated[14] Moriarty. Common sense tells me[15] that he must have been playing another game.

Sherlock Holmes travels to Canterbury, Newhaven, Brussels and Strasbourg, followed every step of the way[16]. At Strasbourg, he

1. dense, grouillante
2. un peu partout dans la ville et connues de lui seul
3. va même jusqu'à lui offrir son aide
4. voiture
5. sans que personne ne se doute de rien
6. ça aurait bien désarçonné
7. se livrer à ses autres centres d'intérêt
8. apiculture
9. en parallèle
10. file, se lançant dans un voyage
11. qui semble improvisé au jour le jour
12. aura sûrement compris
13. que si l'un va quelque part, l'autre le suivra à coup sûr
14. sous-estimé
15. Il me semble logique
16. sans jamais semer ses poursuivants

receives a telegram from the London police informing him that all the members of Moriarty's gang have been captured. This is, as it turns out[1], quite false. One key player has slipped through the net[2] – although I use the term ill-advisedly[3] as the big fat fish that is Colonel Sebastian Moran has never been anywhere near it[4].

Colonel Moran, the finest sharpshooter[5] in Europe, was well known to Pinkerton's[6], by the way. Indeed, by the end of his career, he was known to every law enforcement agency[7] on the planet. He had been famous once for bringing down[8] eleven tigers in a single week in Rajasthan, a feat[9] that astonished his fellow hunters as much[10] as it outraged[11] the members of the Royal Geographical Society. Holmes called him the second most dangerous man in London – all the more so in that[12] he was motivated entirely by money. The murder of Mrs Abigail Stewart, for example, an eminently respectable widow shot through the head as she played bridge in Lauder, was committed only so that he could pay off his gambling debts[13] at the Bagatelle Card Club. It is strange to reflect that as Holmes sat reading the telegram, Moran was less than a hundred yards away, sipping herbal tea[14] on a hotel terrace. Well, the two of them would meet soon enough[15].

From Strasbourg, Holmes continues to Geneva and spends a week exploring the snow-capped hills[16] and pretty villages of the Rhone Valley. Watson describes this interlude as 'charming', which is not the word I would have used in the circumstances but I suppose we can only admire the way these two men, such close friends[17], can relax in each other's company[18] even at such a

1. Ceci s'est avéré
2. est passé entre les mailles du filet
3. bien que le terme soit mal choisi
4. ne s'est jamais approché du filet de près ou de loin
5. tireur d'élite
6. était bien connu de l'agence Pinkerton
7. toutes les forces de police
8. avoir abattu
9. exploit
10. qui avait impressionné ses camarades chasseurs tout autant
11. qu'il avait scandalisé
12. d'autant plus que
13. à la seule fin de rembourser ses dettes de jeu
14. à siroter une tisane
15. bien assez tôt
16. collines enneigées
17. l'amitié entre ses deux hommes
18. tellement à l'aise ensemble qu'ils parviennent à se détendre

time as this[1]. Holmes is still in fear of his life, and there is another incident. Following a path close to the steel-grey water[2] of the Daubensee, he is almost hit by a boulder[3] that comes rolling down from the mountain above. His guide, a local man, assures him that such an event is quite commonplace[4] and I am inclined to believe him[5]. I've looked at the maps and I've worked out[6] the distances. As far as I can see, Holmes's enemy is already well ahead of him[7], waiting for him to arrive. Even so, Holmes is convinced that once again he has been attacked and spends the rest of the day in a state of extreme anxiety.

At last he reaches the village of Meiringen on the River Aar where he and Watson stay at the Englischer Hof, a guest house run by a former waiter from the Grosvenor Hotel in London. It is this man, Peter Steiler, who suggests that Holmes should visit the Reichenbach Falls, and for a brief time the Swiss police will suspect *him* of having been in Moriarty's pay[8] – which tells you everything you need to know about the investigative techniques of the Swiss police. If you want my view[9], they'd have been hard pressed[10] to find a snowflake on an Alpine glacier. I stayed[11] at the guest house and I interviewed Steiler myself. He wasn't just innocent. He was simple[12], barely taking his nose out of his pots and pans[13] (his wife actually ran the place[14]). Until the world came knocking at his door, Steiler wasn't even aware of his famous guest's identity and his first response after the news of Holmes's death had been revealed was to name a fondue after him.

Of course he recommended the Reichenbach Falls. It would have been suspicious if he hadn't[15].

1. dans de telles circonstances
2. En longeant les eaux gris acier
3. bloc de roche
4. assez fréquent
5. je suis tenté de le croire
6. calculé
7. le devance largement
8. à la solde de Moriarty
9. mon avis
10. ils auraient été bien en peine
11. J'ai pris une chambre
12. un peu benêt
13. sortant à peine de sa cuisine
14. c'était en fait sa femme qui gérait l'établissement
15. Il aurait été étrange qu'il ne le fasse pas

They were already a popular destination for tourists and romantics. In the summer months, you might find half a dozen artists dotted along the mossy path[1], trying to capture the meltwater[2] of the Rosenlaui Glacier as it plunged three hundred feet down into that ravine. Trying and failing[3]. There was something almost supernatural[4] about that grim[5] place that would have defied the pastels and oils of all but the greatest painters[6]. I've seen works[7] by Charles Parsons and Emanuel Leutze in New York and maybe they would have been able to do something with it. It was as if the world were ending here in a perpetual apocalypse of thundering[8] water and spray rising like steam[9], the birds frightened away and the sun blocked out[10]. The walls that enclosed this raging deluge were jagged and harsh[11] and as old as Rip van Winkle[12]. Sherlock Holmes had often shown a certain fondness for melodrama[13] but never more so than here. It was a stage like no other to act out a grand finale[14] and one that would resonate, like the falls themselves, for centuries to come.

It's at this point that things begin to get a little murky[15].

Holmes and Watson stand together for a while and are about to continue on their way when they are surprised by the arrival of a slightly plump, fair-haired[16] fourteen-year-old boy. And with good reason. He is dressed to the nines[17] in traditional Swiss costume with close-fitting trousers tucked into[18] socks that rise up almost to his knees, a white shirt and a loose-fitting red waistcoat[19]. All this strikes me as a touch incongruous[20]. This is Switzerland, not a Palace Theatre vaudeville. I feel the boy is trying too hard[21].

1. postés le long du sentier couvert de mousse
2. d'immortaliser le spectacle de l'eau de fonte
3. Essayant en vain
4. surnaturel
5. sinistre
6. des plus grand peintres
7. des œuvres
8. rugissante
9. embruns s'élevant tel un nuage de vapeur
10. Faisant écran à la lumière du soleil
11. irréguliers et raides
12. [Personnage très âgé d'une nouvelle de Washington Irving]
13. manifeste un certain penchant pour le mélodrame
14. une scène sans pareille pour terminer l'histoire en apothéose
15. obscures
16. grassouillet, aux cheveux clairs
17. tiré à quatre épingles
18. rentré dans
19. gilet
20. Tout ceci me paraît quelque peu incongru
21. en fait trop

1. En tout cas
2. prétend venir
3. est tombée malade
4. médecin
5. improbable
6. resteriez là
7. On n'en apprend pas plus sur le jeune Suisse
8. il prend congé de Holmes et se dirige précipitamment
9. malavisé jusqu'au bout
10. pour ainsi dire
11. en ce qui concerne ce récit
12. déclarations
13. parvenaient à accumuler autant d'invraisemblances
14. le prendre pour argent comptant
15. qui tourne à mi-chemin des chutes
16. Holmes n'a aucun moyen de s'échapper
17. Il faut lui rendre justice
18. affronté ses peurs de front

At any event[1], he claims to have come[2] from the Englischer Hof. A woman has been taken ill[3] but refuses for some reason to be seen by a Swiss physician[4]. This is what he says. And what would you do if you were Watson? Would you refuse to believe this unlikely[5] story and stay put[6] or would you abandon your friend – at the worst possible time and in a truly infernal place? That's all we ever hear about the Swiss boy[7], by the way – although you and I will meet him again soon enough. Watson suggests that he may have been working for Moriarty but does not mention him again. As for Watson, he takes his leave and hurries off[8] to his non-existent patient; generous but wrong-headed to the last[9].

We must now wait three years for Holmes's reappearance – and it is important to remember that, to all intents and purposes[10], as far as this narrative is concerned[11], it is believed that he is dead. Only much later does he explain himself (Watson relates it all in 'The Adventure of the Empty House'), and although I have read many written statements[12] in my line of work, few of them have managed to stack up quite so many improbabilities[13]. This is his account, however, and we must, I suppose, take it at face value[14].

After Watson has left, according to Holmes, Professor James Moriarty makes his appearance, walking along the narrow path that curves halfway around the falls[15]. This path comes to an abrupt end, so there can be no question of Holmes attempting to escape[16] – not that such a course of action would ever have crossed his mind. Give him his due[17]: this is a man who has always faced his fears square on[18], whether they be a deadly swamp adder[1], a hideous poison that might drive you to insanity[2] or a hell-hound set loose on the moors[3]. Holmes has done many things that are, frankly, baffling[4] – but he has never run away.

The two men exchange words. Holmes asks permission to leave a note for his old companion and Professor Moriarty agrees. This much at least can be verified for[5] those three sheets of paper are among the most prized possessions[6] of the British Library Reading Room in London where I have seen them displayed[7]. However, once these courtesies have been dispensed with[8], the two men rush at each other in what seems to be less a fight, more a suicide pact, each determined to drag[9] the other into the roaring[10] torrent of water. And so I might have been[11]. But Holmes still has one trick up his sleeve[12]. He has learned *bartitsu*. I had never heard of it before but apparently it's a martial art invented by a British engineer, which combines boxing and judo, and he puts it to good use[13].

Moriarty is taken by surprise. He is propelled over the edge[14] and, with a terrible scream, plunges into the abyss. Holmes sees him brush against a rock[15] before he disappears into the water. He himself is safe … Forgive me, but is there not something a little unsatisfactory[16] about this encounter? You have to ask yourself why Moriarty allows himself to be challenged in this way. Old-school heroics are all very well[17] (although I've never yet met a criminal who went in for them[18]) but what possible purpose can it have served to endanger himself? To put it bluntly[19], why didn't he simply take out a revolver and shoot his opponent at close range[20]?

1. vipère des marais
2. conduit à la démence
3. chien démoniaque rôdant sur la lande
4. déconcertantes
5. car
6. parmi les objets les plus précieux
7. exposées
8. après cette échange de politesses
9. entraîner
10. rugissant
11. Et c'est ce qui aurait pu se produire
12. un tour dans sa manche
13. il en fait bon usage
14. poussé dans le vide
15. heurter un rocher
16. quelque chose d'un peu mal ficelé
17. Les actes de bravoure à l'ancienne, c'est bien joli
18. un criminel qui choisisse cette stratégie
19. À vrai dire
20. à bout portant

If that is strange,[1] Holmes's behaviour now becomes completely inexplicable. On the spur of the moment[2], he decides to use what has just occurred to feign[3] his own death. He climbs up the rock face[4] behind the path and hides there until Watson returns. In this way, of course, there will be no second set of footprints[5] to show that he has survived. What's the point?[6] Professor Moriarty is now dead and the British police have announced that the entire gang has been arrested so why does he still believe himself to be in danger? What exactly is there to be gained?[7] If I had been Holmes, I would have hurried back[8] to the Englischer Hof for a nice Wiener schnitzel and a celebratory glass of Neuchâtel[9].

Meanwhile, Dr Watson, realising he has been tricked, rushes back to the scene, where an abandoned alpenstock[10] and a set of footprints tell their own tale[11]. He summons help[12] and investigates the scene with several men from the hotel and a local police officer by the name of Gessner. Holmes sees them but does not make himself known[13], even though he must be aware of the distress it will cause his most trusted[14] companion. They find the letter. They read it and, realising there is nothing more to be done, they all leave. Holmes begins to climb down again and it is now that the narrative takes another unexpected[15] and wholly inexplicable turn. It appears that Professor Moriarty has not come to the Reichenbach Falls alone. As Holmes begins his descent – no easy task in itself[16] – a man suddenly appears and attempts to knock him off his perch[17] with a number of boulders. The man is Colonel Sebastian Moran.

1. Cela était déjà étrange, mais
2. Sur un coup de tête
3. feindre
4. escalade la paroi rocheuse
5. série d'empreintes de pas
6. Dans quel but ?
7. Qu'il y a-t-il à gagner ?
8. Je me serais hâté de rentrer
9. célébrer ma victoire avec un verre de Neuchâtel
10. [bâton d'escalade]
11. en disaient long
12. appelle à l'aide
13. ne se montre pas
14. son plus fidèle
15. prend à nouveau un tour inattendu
16. une tâche déjà peu aisée
17. tente de le faire tomber de la paroi

What on earth is he doing there? Was he present when Holmes and Moriarty fought, and if so, why didn't he try to help? Where is his gun? Has the greatest marksman[1] in the world accidentally left it on the train[2]? Neither Holmes nor Watson, nor anyone else for that matter, has ever provided reasonable answers to questions which, even as I sit here hammering at the keys[3], seem inescapable[4]. And once I start asking them, I can't stop. I feel as if I am in a runaway coach[5], tearing down[6] Fifth Avenue, unable to stop at the lights[7].

That is about as much as we know of the Reichenbach Falls. The story that I must now tell begins five days later when three men come together in the crypt of St Michael's church in Meiringen. One is a detective inspector from Scotland Yard, the famous command centre of the British police. His name is Athelney Jones. I am the second.

The third man is tall and thin with a prominent forehead and sunken eyes[8] which might view the world[9] with a cold malevolence and cunning[10] were there any life in them at all[11]. But now they are glazed[12] and empty. The man, formally dressed in a suit with a wing collar and a long frock coat[13], has been fished out of the Reichenbach Brook[14], some distance from the falls. His left leg is broken and there are other serious injuries to his shoulder and head, but death must surely have been caused by drowning[15]. The local police have attached a label to his wrist[16], which has been folded across his chest[17]. On it is written the name: James Moriarty.

This is the reason I have come all the way to Switzerland. It appears that I have arrived too late.

1. tireur

2. l'aurait accidentellement oublié dans le train

3. même à moi qui suis en train de taper ce récit

4. inévitables

5. une carriole incontrôlable

6. descendant au grand galop

7. feux de circulation

8. un front saillant et des yeux enfoncés

9. qui poseraient sans doute sur le monde

10. un regard froid, malveillant et fourbe

11. si tant est qu'il y brillât encore une étincelle de vie

12. vitreux

13. à col cassé et d'une longue redingote

14. a été repêché dans les eaux du Reichenbach

15. noyade

16. étiquette à son poignet

17. replié sur sa poitrine

TWO

Inspector Athelney Jones

1. tout à fait certain
2. mettons de côté
3. et examinons les indices
4. sa présence
5. correspond parfaitement aux faits dont nous disposons
6. au demeurant
7. Un seul corps a été retrouvé
8. privé
9. enterrement
10. perdurera
11. le sous-sol sombre et humide
12. que n'atteignait pas
13. le parfum
14. penché sur
15. les mains serrées
16. observant le cadavre de la tête aux pieds

'Are you sure it is really him?'

'I am as sure of it as I can be[1], Mr Chase. But setting aside[2] any personal convictions, let us consider the evidence[3]. His appearance and the circumstances of his being[4] here would certainly seem to fit all the facts at our disposal[5]. And if this is not Moriarty, we are obliged to ask ourselves who he actually is, how he came to be killed and, for that matter[6], what has happened to Moriarty himself.'

'Only one body was recovered[7].'

'So I understand. Poor Mr Holmes … to be deprived[8] of the consolation of a Christian burial[9], which every man deserves. But of one thing we can be certain. His name will live on[10]. There is some comfort in that.'

This conversation took place in the damp, gloomy basement[11] of the church, a place untouched by[12] the warmth and fragrance[13] of that spring day. Inspector Jones stood next to me, leaning over[14] the drowned man with his hands clasped tightly[15] behind him, as if he were afraid of being contaminated. I watched his dark grey eyes travel the full length of the cadaver[16], arriving at the feet, one of which had lost its shoe. It appeared that Moriarty had had a fondness[1] for embroidered silk[2] socks.

We had met, just a short while ago, at the police station in Meiringen. I was frankly surprised that a tiny village stuck in the middle of the Swiss mountains surrounded by goats and buttercups[3] should have need of one. But, as I've already mentioned, it was a popular tourist destination and what with the recent coming of the railway[4], there must have been an increasing number of travellers passing through[5]. There were two men on duty[6], both of them dressed in dark blue uniforms, standing behind the wooden counter[7] that stretched across the front room[8]. One of them was the hapless[9] Sergeant Gessner who had been summoned to the falls[10] – and it was already obvious to me that he would have been much happier dealing with[11] lost passports, train tickets, street directions[12] … anything rather than the more serious business of murder.

He and his companion spoke little of my language[13] and I had been forced to explain myself using the images and headlines of an English newspaper, which I had brought with me for that express purpose[14]. I had heard that a body had been dragged out of the water[15] beneath the Reichenbach Falls and had asked to see it, but these Swiss police were obstinate in the way of many a uniformed man[16] given limited power[17]. Speaking over each other, and with a great deal of gesticulation, they had made it clear to me[18] that they were waiting for the arrival of a senior officer[19] who had come all the way from England and that any decision would be his[20]. I told them

1. avait eu un faible
2. en soie brodée
3. boutons d'or
4. avec la récente arrivée du chemin de fer
5. de plus en plus de voyageurs passaient par ici
6. en service
7. comptoir
8. s'étendait sur toute la longueur de la pièce
9. infortuné
10. qu'on avait fait venir aux chutes
11. de prendre en charge
12. l'orientation des visiteurs
13. ne connaissaient que quelques mots d'anglais
14. dans ce but précis
15. sorti de l'eau
16. comme le sont souvent les hommes en uniforme
17. dans une position de pouvoir
18. m'avaient fait comprendre
19. officier supérieur
20. la décision lui reviendrait

1. étais venu de bien plus loin
2. jetai un coup d'œil
3. , la moitié de la matinée était perdue
4. le reste se passe de la même manière
5. sa silhouette découpée dans
6. qui lui retombaient sur le front
7. Il dégageait une impression de sérieux
8. il était impossible de ne pas le remarquer
9. complet-veston
10. pardessus
11. qui pendait librement
12. à sa pâleur et à ses traits tirés
13. canne
14. pommeau en argent
15. s'appuya
16. Pouvez-vous m'aider ?
17. sans essayer d'adopter
18. Je suis
19. de
20. remarquant ma présence et la mettant de côté

that I had travelled a great deal further[1] and that my business was quite serious too but that didn't matter. I'm sorry, *mein Herr.* There was nothing they could do to help.

I took out my watch and glanced[2] at it. It was already eleven o'clock with half the morning wasted[3] and I was afraid the rest of it would go the same way[4], but just then the front door opened and, feeling the breeze on the back of my neck, I turned to see a man standing there, silhouetted against[5] the morning light. He said nothing, but as he moved inside I saw that he was about the same age as me, perhaps a little younger, with dark-coloured hair lying flat on his forehead[6] and soft grey eyes that questioned everything. There was a sort of seriousness about him[7], and when he stepped into a room, you had to stop and take notice[8]. He was wearing a brown lounge suit[9] with a pale overcoat[10], which was unbuttoned and hung loosely[11] from his shoulders. It was evident that he had recently been quite ill and had lost weight. I could see it in his clothes, which were a little too large for him, and in the pallor and pinched quality of his face[12]. He carried a walking stick[13] made of rosewood with an odd, complicated silver handle[14]. Having approached the counter, he rested[15] on the stick, using it to support him.

'*Können Sie mir helfen?*[16]' he asked. He spoke German very naturally but with no attempt at[17] a German accent, as if he had studied the words but never actually heard them. '*Ich bin*[18] *Inspector Athelney Jones von*[19] *Scotland Yard.*'

He had examined me very briefly, accepting my presence and filing it away[20] for later use, but otherwise he had ignored me. His name, however, had an immediate effect on the two policemen.

'Jones. Inspector Jones,' they repeated, and when he held out his own letter of introduction they took it with much bowing and smiling[1] and, having asked him to wait a few moments while they entered the details in the police log[2], retired to an inner office[3], leaving the two of us alone.

It would have been impossible for us to ignore each other and he was the first to break the silence, translating what he had already said.

'My name is Athelney Jones,' he said.

'Did I hear you say you were from Scotland Yard?'

'Indeed.'

'I'm Frederick Chase.'

We shook hands. His grip was curiously loose[4], as if his hand were barely[5] connected to his wrist.

'This is a beautiful spot[6],' he went on. 'I have never had the pleasure of travelling in Switzerland. In fact, this is only the third time I have been abroad[7] at all.' He turned his attention briefly to my steamer trunk[8] which, having nowhere to stay, I had been obliged to bring with me. 'You have just arrived?'

'An hour ago,' I said. 'I guess we must have been on the same train.'

'And your business[9] ...?'

I hesitated. The assistance of a British police officer was essential to the task[10] that had brought me to Meiringen, but at the same time I did not wish to appear too forward[11]. In America, there had often been conflicts of interest between Pinkerton's and the official government services. Why

1. avec moult courbettes
2. entraient les détails dans le registre
3. disparurent dans un bureau à l'arrière
4. Sa poigne était curieusement molle
5. à peine
6. très bel endroit
7. à l'étranger
8. malle de voyage
9. la raison de votre visite
10. était cruciale pour accomplir la tâche
11. avoir l'air trop cavalier

should it be any different[1] here? 'I am here on a private matter[2] …' I began.

He smiled at this, although at the same time I saw a veil of something in his eyes that might have been pain[3]. 'Then perhaps you will allow me to tell you[4], Mr Chase,' he remarked. He considered[5] for a moment. 'You are a Pinkerton's agent from New York and last week you set off for England[6] in the hope of tracking down[7] Professor James Moriarty. He had received a communication which is important to you and which you hoped to find about his person[8]. You were shocked to hear of his death and came directly here. I see, incidentally[9], you have a low opinion of the Swiss police[10]—'

'Wait a minute!' I exclaimed. I held up a hand. 'Stop right there! Have you been spying on me, Inspector Jones? Have you spoken to my office? I find it pretty bad that the British police should have gone behind my back[11] and involved themselves in my affairs[12]!'

'You do not need to concern yourself[13],' Jones returned, again with that same strange smile. 'Everything I have told you I have deduced from my observation of you here, in this room. And I could add more[14], if you wish.'

'Why not?'

'You live in an old-fashioned apartment block[15], several floors up[16]. You do not think your company looks after you as well as it might[17], particularly as[18] you are one of its most successful investigators. You are not married. I am sorry to see that the sea crossing[19] was a particularly disagreeable one – and not just because of the very bad weather on the second or perhaps the third day.

1. Pourquoi les choses seraient-elles différentes
2. pour une affaire privée
3. passer dans ses yeux comme un voile de douleur
4. me permettrez-vous de le dire
5. réfléchit
6. vous êtes parti pour l'Angleterre
7. remonter la piste du
8. trouver en sa possession
9. incidemment
10. vous ne faites pas grand cas de la police suisse
11. agisse dans mon dos
12. se mêle de mes affaires
13. Nul besoin de vous inquiéter
14. continuer
15. vieil immeuble
16. à l'un des étages supérieurs
17. vous traite comme elle le devrait
18. étant donné que
19. votre traversée de l'Atlantique

You are thinking that your entire trip has been a wild goose chase[1]. I hope, for your sake[2], it is not.'

He fell silent and I stared at him as if seeing him for the first time. 'You are right in almost everything you say,' I rasped[3]. 'But how the devil you managed it[4] is quite beyond me[5]. Will you explain yourself?'

'It was all very straightforward[6],' he replied. I might almost say elementary.' He chose the last word carefully, as if it had some special significance.

'That's easy enough for you to say[7].' I glanced at the door that now separated us from the two Swiss policemen. Sergeant Gessner seemed to be on the telephone – I could hear his voice jabbering away[8] on the other side. The empty counter stretched out, a barrier[9] between them and us. 'Please, Inspector Jones. Will you tell me how you reached[10] these conclusions?'

'Very well, although I should warn you that it will all seem painfully obvious[11] once it is explained.' He shifted his weight on the walking stick[12], trying to find a comfortable position in which to stand[13]. 'That[14] you are American is evident from the way you speak and from your clothes. Your waistcoat in particular, striped[15] and with four pockets, would have been extremely difficult to find in London. I take note of your vocabulary[16]. Just now, you said, "I guess" where we would have said "I think". My knowledge of accents is limited[17], but yours would suggest[18] the East Coast.'

'My home is in Boston,' I said. 'I now live and work in New York. Please, continue!'

1. en pure perte
2. pour votre bien
3. dis-je, d'une voix rauque
4. quant à savoir comment diable vous l'avez deviné,
5. cela me dépasse complètement
6. simple
7. facile à dire pour vous
8. jacasser
9. formait comme une barrière
10. vous en êtes arrivé à
11. terriblement évident
12. reporta son poids sur sa canne
13. essayant de trouver une position confortable
14. Le fait que
15. à rayures
16. J'ai noté votre choix de mot
17. Je n'ai qu'une connaissance limitée en matière d'accents
18. le vôtre m'évoque

'As I came in, you were examining your watch and although it was partly covered by your fingers, I saw quite clearly the symbol engraved on the casing[1] – an eye with, beneath it[2], the words "We Never Sleep". This is, of course, the legend of the Pinkerton Detective Agency whose principal offices are, as I recall[3], in New York. That you embarked from there is evident from the New York Port Authority stamp[4] on your luggage.' He glanced a second time at my steamer trunk, which I had stood beneath the photograph of a scowling[5] man, presumably some local ne'er-do-well[6]. As for your disdain[7] of the Swiss police – why should you choose to look at your own watch when there is a perfectly good working clock[8] on the wall just to one side? They have, I can see, been less than helpful[9].'

'You are absolutely right, sir. But how do you know of my connection with Professor Moriarty?'

'What other possible reason could there be for you to have come here to Meiringen? I would wager[10] that, but for[11] the events of the last week, you would never have heard of[12] this unremarkable[13] village.'

'My business could have been with[14] Sherlock Holmes.'

'In which case you would have surely stayed in London and begun your enquiries[15] in Baker Street. There is nothing here but the dead body of a man, and whoever he is, he is certainly not Holmes. No. From New York, your most likely destination would have been Southampton – which is confirmed by the folded copy[16] of the *Hampshire Echo* protruding from your right-hand jacket pocket[17]. The date on the masthead[18], I see,

1. gravé sur le boîtier
2. en dessous
3. si je me souviens bien
4. cachet des autorités portuaires
5. renfrogné
6. fripouille
7. dédain
8. une horloge en parfait état de marche
9. ne vous ont été d'aucun secours
10. parierais
11. sans
12. n'auriez jamais entendu parler
13. bien ordinaire
14. J'aurais pu être venu pour consulter
15. recherches
16. l'exemplaire plié
17. dépassant de la poche droite de votre veste
18. l'encadré du journal

is Thursday the seventh of May which would suggest that you purchased[1] it at the dock and were then compelled[2] to travel at once[3] to the Continent. And what was the news that could have brought you here? There was only one story of interest that day. It *had* to be Moriarty.' He smiled. 'I am surprised I did not see you. As you say, we must surely have travelled on the same train.'

'You mentioned a communication.'

'There is nothing Moriarty can say to you. He is dead. It is unlikely[4] you could identify him – very few people have ever seen him face to face. Therefore it must be something he has that interests you[5], something you hope to find about his person – a letter or a parcel[6] sent from America. I presume that this is what you were discussing with the police when I arrived.'

'I was asking them to let me examine the body.'

'There is a little more to add.'

'The crossing?'

'You were forced to share a cabin—'

'How do you know?' I exclaimed.

'Your fingernails and teeth suggest to me that you do not smoke but I can still detect a strong smell of tobacco about you[7]. This tells me that although your employers must surely have chosen the best man[8] for whatever job this is – they have, after all, sent you halfway across the world[9] – they were not prepared to pay for a single cabin[10]. It cannot have been very pleasant for you, sharing with a smoker.'

'It was not.'

'And the weather made it worse.' He lifted a hand, waving away my question[11] before I could ask it. 'That is a nasty cut[12] on the side of your

1. acheté
2. contraint
3. immédiatement
4. peu probable que
5. vous devez être intéressé par un objet en sa possession
6. paquet
7. qui se dégage de vous
8. aient sûrement choisi leur meilleur homme
9. fait traverser un océan
10. disposés à vous payer une cabine individuelle
11. balayant ma question d'un revers de la main
12. vilaine entaille

1. J'éclatai de rire
2. Je dois ma position à mon assiduité et mes efforts acharnés.
3. Je n'ai jamais vu de telles méthodes de travail
4. étaient entraînés à raisonner ainsi
5. disons
6. ma situation personnelle et mes conditions d'hébergement
7. alliance
8. ne prouve rien en soi
9. pardonnez-moi
10. sortir avec des manchettes aussi tachées
11. auraient grand besoin d'être ressemelées
12. Quant à
13. tissu
14. est très usé
15. La seule explication possible est que vous avez l'habitude
16. de grimper plusieurs étages
17. en frottant
18. rampe
19. je le regardais
20. non dissimulée
21. si

neck. It cannot have been easy shaving at sea, particularly during a storm.'

I laughed out loud[1]. 'Inspector Jones,' I said, 'I am a simple man. I have achieved what I have achieved by diligence and hard work.[2] I have never come across techniques such as these before[3] and had no idea that British police inspectors were trained to use them[4].'

'Not all of us were,' Jones replied, quietly. 'But you might say[5] that I received special instruction … and I learned from the best.'

'There is just one last thing. You still haven't explained to me how you know of my status and my living arrangements[6] in New York.'

'You wear no wedding ring[7], which might not be conclusive in itself[8] but – you will forgive me[9] – no wife would permit her husband to leave with such stains on his cuffs[10] nor with shoes that cry out to be reheeled[11]. As to[12] the apartment, that is again simply a question of observation and deduction. I notice that the fabric[13] of your jacket – the right sleeve – has been quite worn down[14]. How could this have occurred unless you had become accustomed[15] to climbing several flights of stairs[16], rubbing[17] your arm against a metal banister[18]? I would imagine your office has an elevator. An old-fashioned apartment block might not.'

He stopped, and I could see that all the talking had tired him for he rested more heavily on his stick. For my part, I was gazing[19] with an admiration that I made no attempt to disguise[20] and might have stood there for a while longer had[21] the door not suddenly opened and the two police officers reappeared. They spoke rapidly in German and although the meaning was unclear, their tone was friendly enough, and I gathered[1] that they were now ready to escort the Scotland Yard man to wherever the body lay[2]. This proved to be the case[3]. Jones straightened up[4] and began to move towards the door.

'Can I have a word?' I said. 'I am sure you have your instructions, Inspector Jones, but it may just turn out[5] that I'm able to help you. Everything you said to me – that extraordinary demonstration just now[6] – was absolutely right. I've followed Moriarty here because of a communication that was made three weeks ago and which may have serious consequences for you and for me. It is true that I cannot identify him, but it is of the utmost importance[7] that I'm at least allowed to see the body.'

The man from Scotland Yard paused, his hand clenched around[8] the top of the walking stick. 'You understand, sir, that I am here following orders given to me by[9] my superiors.'

'You have my word[10] that I will not interfere in any way.'

The two Swiss policemen were waiting for us. Jones came to a decision[11] and nodded[12]. '*Er kommt mit uns*[13].' He turned to me. 'You can join us.'

'I am truly grateful[14] to you,' I said. 'And I give you my word that you won't regret it.'

We left my luggage at the police station and crossed the village, following the main road past a scattering of houses[15]. All the while[16] Jones and Gessner spoke in German, keeping their voices low[17]. At length we arrived at the church of St Michael, a queer[18] little building with its bright red roof and rather top-heavy bell tower[19]. The policemen unlocked the door for us and stood back as we stepped inside[20]. I bowed[21] my head in front of

1. j'en déduisis
2. à l'endroit où reposait le corps
3. C'était effectivement le cas
4. se redressa
5. il se pourrait bien
6. à l'instant
7. d'une importance capitale
8. serrée autour
9. sur les ordres de
10. Je vous promets
11. prit finalement sa décision
12. hocha la tête
13. Il vient avec nous
14. reconnaissant
15. quelques maisons éparpillées
16. Pendant tout ce temps
17. à voix basse
18. étrange
19. un clocher un peu trop massif
20. se reculèrent pour nous laisser entrer
21. J'inclinai

the altar[1] but Inspector Jones, I noticed, did not. We came to a flight of steps leading down to[2] the crypt and he indicated that he wished to continue with me alone. Gessner needed little persuasion[3]: even in the coolness of the church[4] with its thick stone walls, the smell of death was already apparent.

The body was as I have described it. When living, the man who lay stretched out in front of us[5] would have been unusually tall[6] though with stooped[7] shoulders. I could imagine him a librarian[8] or perhaps a lecturer[9] in a university, which, of course, James Moriarty had once been. His clothes, black and old-fashioned, clung to him like seaweed[10] – I fancied[11] they were still wet. There are many ways to die but few leave a nastier imprint on the human frame[12] than drowning[13]. His flesh was heavy and foul.[14] Its colour was hideous to describe.

'We cannot be certain that this is Moriarty,' I suggested. 'You were quite correct when you said that I could not identify him. But can you?'

Jones shook his head. 'I never set eyes on him[15]. Nor did any of my colleagues. Moriarty lived in the shadows most of his life and made a virtue of it[16]. It is possible that in due course[17] we will be able to find someone who worked with him in his capacity as a[18] professor of mathematics, and be assured that I will set about just such an investigation on my return[19]. For the present, however, I will say this much[20]. The man in front of us is the right age and the clothes he is wearing are undoubtedly English. You see the pocket watch[21]? It is silver-cased[22] and clearly marked, "John Myers of London". He did not come here for the pleasures of the countryside. He died at the same time as Sherlock Holmes. So I ask you again. Who else can he be?'

1. l'autel
2. un escalier descendant vers
3. accepta sans faire d'histoire
4. malgré la fraîcheur de l'église
5. étendu devant nos yeux
6. exceptionnellement grand
7. voûtées
8. Je le voyais bien en bibliothécaire
9. maître de conférence
10. l'enserraient comme des algues
11. me doutais
12. rares sont celles qui laissent sur le corps humain
13. une empreinte plus repoussante que la noyade
14. Sa chair était lourde et fétide.
15. posé les yeux sur lui
16. avait fait de cette nécessité une vertu
17. à terme
18. lorsqu'il occupait le poste de
19. lancer cette enquête dès mon retour
20. on peut déjà déduire plusieurs choses
21. montre à gousset
22. son boîtier est en argent

'Has the body been searched[1]?'

'The Swiss police went through[2] the pockets, yes.'

'And there was nothing?'

'A few coins. A handkerchief[3]. Nothing more. What is it you were hoping to find?'

I had been waiting for the question. I did not hesitate. I knew that everything, certainly my immediate future, hung on[4] my answer. Even now I can see us[5], standing alone in the dark crypt with the body stretched out[6] before us. 'Moriarty received a letter on the twenty-second or the twenty-third of April,' I explained. 'It was written by a criminal very well known to Pinkerton's, a man in every respect as wicked[7] and as dangerous as Moriarty himself, inviting him to a meeting. Although it would appear that Moriarty is dead, I still hoped I might find it about his person, or if not, then perhaps at his place of residence.'

'It is this man that interests you and not Moriarty?'

'He is the reason I am here.'

Jones shook his head. 'Sergeant Gessner was explaining to me as we came here that the police have already made enquiries and have been unable to discover where Moriarty was staying. He may have established his base[8] in a village nearby but if so he certainly used an assumed name[9]. There is nowhere outside here that we can search[10]. What makes you think he might have this letter on him?'

'Perhaps I'm grasping at straws[11],' I said. 'No, I'll admit it. I am grasping at straws.[12] But the way these people work … sometimes they use signs and symbols as a method of identification. The

1. fouillé

2. a passé en revue

3. Un mouchoir

4. dépendait de

5. Je nous revois encore aujourd'hui

6. étendu

7. à tous points de vue aussi malfaisant

8. établi son quartier général

9. nom d'emprunt

10. Nous n'avons aucune propriété à perquisitionner

11. Peut-être que c'est un coup d'épée dans l'eau

12. Non, c'est même sûr.

1. gardée près de lui
2. horrible besogne
3. gorgé d'eau
4. semblait complètement inhumain sous nos doigts
5. visqueux
6. Passant la main sous la veste
7. retroussée
8. la partie supérieure du corps
9. autre chose que les quelques objets
10. les arracher
11. je m'éloignai, pris de vertige, le cœur au bord des lèvres
12. les coutures autour de la poche de poitrine
13. couture
14. n'a rien à faire là
15. doublure

letter itself could become a passport – and if so, Moriarty would have kept it close[1].'

'If you wish, we can examine him one more time.'

'I think we must.'

It was a grisly task[2]. The body, cold and waterlogged[3], felt utterly inhuman in our hands[4] and as we turned it, we could almost feel the flesh separating itself from the bones. The clothes were slimy[5]. Reaching into the jacket[6], I found the shirt had been rucked back[7] and my hand briefly came into contact with dead, white skin. Although there had been no prior arrangement between us, I concentrated on the upper part of the body[8] while Jones busied himself with the lower. Just like the police before us, we found nothing. The pockets were empty. If they had contained anything more than the few items[9] Jones had mentioned, the rushing waters of the Reichenbach Falls must have brutally ripped them away[10]. We worked in silence. Finally, I reeled away, the gorge rising in my throat[11].

'There is nothing,' I said. 'You were right. It was a waste of time.'

'One moment.' Jones had seen something. He reached out and took hold of the dead man's jacket, examining the stitching around the breast pocket[12].

'I've looked,' I said. 'There's nothing there.'

'Not the pocket,' Jones said. 'Look at this seam[13]. This stitching has no business being here[14]. I think it has been added later.' He rubbed the fabric between his fingers. 'There might be something inside the lining[15].'

I leaned forward. He was right. A line of stitches stretched out a couple of inches below the pocket. 'I have a knife,' I said. I took out the jackknife[1] that I always carried with me and handed[2] it to my new friend.

Jones inserted the point into the seam and gently sliced down[3]. I watched as the stitches were cut through and the material came away[4]. There was a secret pocket in the dead man's jacket – and there was indeed something inside. Jones eased out[5] a folded square of paper. It was still wet and might have disintegrated had he not handled it with the greatest delicacy[6]. Using the flat blade[7] of the knife he laid it on the stone table next to the body. Carefully, he unfolded it, a single page covered in handwriting that could have been a child's[8].

We leaned over together. This is what we read:

HoLmES WaS CeRtAiNLY NOt A DIFFiCulT mAn to LiVe WItH. He wAs QuIeT iN HiS WAYs[9] and his hABiTS wErE REgulAr. iT wAs RARE fOR HIm To BE up[10] AfTeR TEN at nighT aND hE hAD INVariABLY breAKfasteD AND GoNE OUT BeFOrE i RoSe in The morNINg. SOMEtImEs He SPeNt hiS DAy At ThE ChEmiCaL lABoRatORY, SoMeTimes IN THE dIsSeCting ROoms And oCcAsionaLly iN lOnG WALKs whICH ApPeAREd TO taKE HIM INtO THE LOwEsT PORTioNs[11] OF thE CITy. nothINg COuld exCEeD HiS ENErgY WHeN tHE wORkING FiT WAs upOn HiM[12].

If Jones was disappointed[13], he didn't show it. But this wasn't the letter that I had described. It did not seem to be relevant[14] in any way at all.

'What do you make of it?[15]' he asked.

1. canif
2. tendis
3. la découpa doucement
4. l'étoffe se détachait
5. retira soigneusement
6. s'il ne l'avait pas manipulé avec la plus grande délicatesse
7. Utilisant le plat de la lame
8. écriture ressemblant à celle d'un enfant
9. C'était un homme paisible
10. encore debout
11. semblaient le mener dans les quartiers les plus sordides
12. une crise de travail le prenait
13. déçu
14. pertinente
15. Qu'en pensez-vous ?

'I … I do not know what to say.' I read the words a second time. 'I know this text,' I continued. 'Of course I know it. This is part of a narrative written by Dr John Watson. It has been copied from *Lippincott's Magazine*!'

'I think you will find it was actually from *Beeton's Christmas Annual*,' Jones corrected me. 'It is from Chapter Three of *A Study in Scarlet*[1]. But that does not make it any the less mysterious[2]. I take it[3] this is not what you expected to find[4].'

'It was the last thing I expected.'

'It is certainly very puzzling[5]. But I have been here long enough. I suggest we retreat[6] from this grim place and fortify ourselves with a glass of wine.'

I took one last look at the dead man on the slab[7] then turned and together we climbed back up, Jones limping[8] heavily.

1. *Une Étude en rouge*
2. ça ne la rend pas moins mystérieuse
3. J'imagine
4. ce que vous vous attendiez à trouver
5. déconcertant
6. quittions
7. dalle
8. boitant

THREE

The Midnight Watch

Athelney Jones had taken a room at the Englischer Hof and suggested that I do the same. We headed there together after we had parted company with[1] the Swiss policemen, walking through the village with the sun brilliant in a cloudless[2] sky and everything silent apart from our own footsteps and the occasional jangle[3] of a bell coming from the sheep or goats that were grazing in the nearby hills[4]. Jones was deep in thought[5], reflecting on the document we had discovered in the dead man's pocket. What on earth[6] was Moriarty doing with an extract from a Sherlock Holmes story hidden about him as he travelled to Switzerland? Had he perhaps been seeking some insight into his adversary's mind[7] before the two of them met at the Reichenbach Falls? Or was it actually the communication I had described, the reason for my long journey to Switzerland? Could it have some secret meaning unknown to both of us[8]? Jones did not address these questions to me[9] but I could see that they were plainly on his mind[10].

The hotel was small and charming with shapes cut into the wood[11] and flowers hanging around the windows[12]; the very image[13] of a Swiss chalet

1. après avoir pris congé des
2. sans nuage
3. tintement
4. qui broutaient dans les collines environnantes
5. plongé dans ses pensées
6. que diable
7. Cherchait-il peut-être à cerner l'esprit de son adversaire
8. signification secrète inconnue de nous deux
9. ne me confia pas ces questions
10. elles le préoccupaient
11. avec du bois sculpté
12. accrochées aux fenêtres
13. l'image même

that every English traveller might dream of finding[1]. Fortunately, there was room for me[2], and a boy was dispatched to[3] the police station to collect my luggage. Jones and I parted company at the stairs. He had the page in his hand.

'I would like, with your permission, to hold onto it a while longer[4],' he said.

'You think you can make some sense of it[5]?'

'I can at least give it my full attention and … who knows?' He was tired. The walk from the police station had not been a long one but, combined with the high altitude, it had almost drained him[6].

'Of course,' I said. 'Will we meet again this evening?'

'We can dine together. Shall we say eight o'clock?'

'That will suit me very well[7], Inspector Jones. Apart from anything else, it will give me time to walk to the famous Reichenbach Falls. I never thought I'd find myself in Switzerland[8] of all places[9], and this village – it's quite delightful[10], like something out of a fairy story[11].'

'You might perhaps ask about[12] Moriarty. If he didn't stay in a hotel or a guest house, he might have taken a room in a private home[13]. And someone may have seen him before he met up with[14] Holmes.'

'I thought the Swiss police had already made these enquiries[15].'

'Wachtmeister Gessner? An admirable man doing the best that he can. But it won't hurt[16] to ask again.'

'Very well. I'll see what I can do.'

1. rêve de trouver
2. de la place pour moi
3. envoyé à
4. la garder encore un peu
5. y comprendre quelque chose
6. cela l'avait presque épuisé
7. Ça m'ira très bien
8. Je n'aurais jamais cru me retrouver un jour en Suisse
9. , figurez-vous.
10. absolument charmant
11. on se croirait dans un conte de fées
12. interroger les gens sur
13. loué une chambre chez l'habitant
14. avant qu'il ne rejoigne Holmes
15. posé ces questions-là
16. mais ça ne fait pas de mal

I did as I was asked and strolled through[1] the village, talking to those inhabitants who spoke my language, not that there were many of them[2]. There were two words though[3] that they all understood: Sherlock Holmes. At the mention of his name[4], they became serious and animated[5]. That such a man[6] had visited Meiringen was extraordinary; that he had died here beyond belief[7]. They wanted to help. Sadly, though, none of them had seen Moriarty. No stranger had taken a room in their midst[8]. They had nothing to offer me but broken English and sympathy[9]. Eventually[10], I returned to my own room. On second thoughts[11], I had no desire to walk to the falls, which were at least two hours away. The truth was that I could not even think of them without shuddering[12] and visiting them would have told me nothing I did not already know.

Athelney Jones and I dined late that night and I was glad to see that he had recovered his strength. We sat together in the snug[13] hotel restaurant with the tables packed closely together[14], animal heads on the wall, and a roaring fire quite out of proportion to the size of the room. It was needed[15] though, for[16] with the darkness a torrent of cold air had come twisting through the mountain passes and settled on[17] the village. This was, after all, only May[18], and we were at an elevation of almost two thousand feet[19]. There were only a few other diners around us and we had chosen a table close to the inglenook[20] so that we could talk together undisturbed[21].

We were welcomed by a small, round-shouldered[22] woman wearing an apron dress with

1. me promenai dans
2. ce qui était rarement le cas
3. cependant
4. Dès que je prononçais son nom
5. ils s'animaient
6. Qu'un tel homme
7. défiait l'entendement
8. ne s'était installé parmi eux
9. qu'un anglais écorché et de la compassion
10. Finalement
11. À bien y réfléchir
12. sans avoir des frissons
13. douillet
14. rapprochées les unes des autres
15. nécessaire
16. car
17. s'était faufilé à travers les cols montagneux et abattu sur
18. Après tout, nous n'étions qu'en mai
19. six cent mètres
20. au coin de la cheminée
21. sans être dérangés
22. aux épaules rondes

puffed-out sleeves and a shawl[1]. She brought us a basket of bread and a pint of red wine served in a pitcher[2] and, setting them down[3], introduced herself as[4] Greta Steiler, the Swiss wife of our English host. 'We have only soup and roast meat tonight,' she explained. Her English was excellent and I hoped the cooking would be the same[5]. 'My husband is alone in the kitchen today and you are lucky we are only half full. If we had any more guests, I do not know how we would manage[6].'

'What has happened to your cook?' Jones asked.

'He went to visit his mother in Rosenlaui because she hasn't been well. He was due back almost a week ago[7] but we haven't heard from him[8] – and this after[9] he has been with us five years! And then we have this business[10] with the falls and with all the police and the detectives asking us their questions. I wait for Meiringen to be back as it was[11]. We do not ask for all this excitement[12].'

She bustled off[13] and I poured myself some wine but Jones refused, helping himself instead to water[14]. 'The document ...' I began. From the moment we had sat down, I had wanted to ask what he had made of it.

'I may be able to shed a certain light on the matter[15],' Jones replied. 'To begin with it is very likely that it *is* the communication of which you spoke[16]. It certainly seems to have been written by an American.'

'How can you possibly know?'

'I have examined the paper closely[17] and found it to be clay-coated groundwood[18] and therefore very probably American in origin.'

'And the content?'

1. une robe tablier avec des manches bouffantes et un châle
2. pichet
3. tout en les disposant [sur la table]
4. s'était présentée comme
5. que sa cuisine le soit autant
6. nous y arriverions
7. censé revenir il y a presque une semaine
8. pas eu de nouvelles
9. alors qu'
10. affaire
11. J'ai hâte que Meiringen redevienne comme avant
12. Nous n'avons pas besoin de toute cette agitation
13. s'éloigna d'un pas rapide
14. préférant se servir de l'eau
15. Je peux sans doute vous éclairer sur certains points
16. dont vous parliez
17. de près
18. une pâte à papier enduite d'argile

'We will come to that shortly[1]. But first, I think, we should reach an agreement[2].' Jones lifted[3] his glass. He swirled it round[4] and I saw the firelight reflecting in the liquid. 'I am here as a representative[5] of the British police. As soon as we heard that Sherlock Holmes was dead, it was felt[6] that one of us should attend upon the scene[7], if only as a matter of courtesy[8]. He had, as I am sure you are aware, been helpful to us on a number of occasions. And anything relating to[9] the activities of Professor James Moriarty was naturally of interest to us. What happened at the Reichenbach Falls seems straightforward enough[10] but even so there is clearly something afoot[11], as Mr Holmes was wont to say[12]. Your presence here and your suggestion that Moriarty was in contact with a member of the American underworld[13]—'

'Not just a member, sir. The master.'

'It may well be that we have mutual interests and should work side by side although I must warn you that, generally speaking, Scotland Yard has a certain reticence about dealing[14] with foreign detective agencies, particularly private ones. It may not be helpful, but that's how it is.[15] It follows that[16], if I am to make the case to[17] my superiors, I need to know more. In short, you must tell me everything about yourself and the events that have brought you here. You can do so in confidence[18]. But it is only on the strength of what you tell me[19] that I can decide what course of action I should take[20].'

'I will willingly[21] tell you everything, Inspector Jones,' I said. 'And I'll make no secret of the fact that I am greatly in need[22] of any help you and the British police can provide.' I broke off[23] as

1. J'y viens
2. nous mettre d'accord
3. leva
4. le fit tournoyer
5. en tant que représentant
6. nous avons cru bon
7. se rende sur place
8. ne serait-ce que par politesse
9. en rapport avec
10. assez évident
11. il se trame clairement quelque chose
12. avait coutume de dire
13. pègre
14. à collaborer
15. C'est regrettable, mais il en va ainsi.
16. en conséquence
17. plaider votre cause auprès de
18. en toute confiance
19. C'est en fonction de la solidité de vos arguments
20. quel plan d'action adopter
21. bien volontiers
22. je ne vais pas vous cacher que j'ai grandement besoin
23. m'interrompis

Frau Steiler returned to the table with two bowls of steaming soup and *Spätzle* – which was the word she used to describe the little dumplings[1] floating in a murky brown liquid[2]. It smelled better than it looked and, with the scent of boiled chicken and herbs[3] rising in my nostrils[4], I began my narrative.

'I was, as I have already told you, born in Boston, where my father was the owner of a very highly regarded law practice with offices[5] in Court Square. My childhood memories are of a family that was correct in every detail[6], with several servants and a black nanny – Tilly – who was very dear to me[7].'

'You were an only child?'

'No, sir, I was the second of two boys. My brother, Arthur, was quite a few years older than me and we were never close. My father was a member of Boston's Republican Party and spent much of his time surrounded by like-minded gentlemen[8] who prided themselves on the values[9] which they had brought with them from England and which they felt set them apart as a sort of elite[10]. They were members of the Somerset Club and the Myopia Club[11] and many others. My mother, I'm afraid, was fragile in her health and spent much of the time in bed. The result was that I saw very little of either of my parents and that might explain why, in my teens[12], I became quite rebellious in nature[13] and finally left home in circumstances which I still regret.

'My brother had already joined the family firm[14] and it was expected[15] that I would do the same. However, I had no aptitude for the law[16]. I found the textbooks dry[17] and almost indecipherable.

1. morceaux de pâte
2. liquide brun et épais
3. tandis que l'odeur du bouillon de poulet aux herbes
4. me montait aux narines
5. cabinet d'avocats très réputé situé
6. convenable en tous points
7. à laquelle j'étais très attaché
8. entouré d'hommes partageant sa tournure d'esprit
9. et qui s'enorgueillissaient d'un système de valeurs
10. à leurs yeux, faisait d'eux l'élite de la nation
11. [prestigieux clubs pour hommes fondés en 1926 et 1870]
12. à l'adolescence
13. d'un tempérament plutôt rebelle
14. rejoint le cabinet d'avocats familial
15. on attendait de moi
16. aucune prédisposition pour le droit
17. manuels ennuyeux

Besides, I had other ambitions. I cannot quite say what it was that first interested me in the criminal world … it may have been stories that I found in *Merry's Museum*. This was a magazine read by every child in the neighbourhood[1]. But there was also an incident I remember very clearly. We were members of the congregation at the Warren Avenue Baptist Church. We never missed a service[2] and it was the one place we were together as a family. Well, when I was about twenty, it was discovered that the sexton[3], one Thomas Piper, had committed a series of quite gruesome[4] murders—'

'Piper?' Jones's eyes narrowed[5]. 'I recall the name[6]. His first victim was a young girl …'

'That's correct. The story was widely reported outside America.[7] As for me[8], although my entire community felt nothing but outrage[9], I must confess that I was thrilled[10] that such a man could have concealed himself in our midst[11]. I had seen him often in his long black cape, always smiling and beneficent[12]. If he could be guilty of such crimes, was there anyone in our community who could genuinely claim to be above suspicion[13]?

'It was at this moment that I found my vocation in life. The dry world of the lawyer was not for me. I wanted to be a detective. I had heard of the Pinkertons. They were already legendary throughout America[14]. Just a few days after the scandal came to light[15], I told my father that I wanted to travel to New York to join them.'

I fell silent. Jones was watching me with an intensity that I would come to know well[16] and I knew that he was weighing my every word[17]. There was a part of me that did not wish to open

1. du voisinage
2. l'office
3. sacristain
4. absolument effroyables
5. Jones plissa les yeux
6. me souviens de ce nom
7. Les journaux étrangers ont beaucoup parlé de cette affaire
8. Quant à moi
9. alors que dans notre communauté l'indignation fut générale
10. absolument fasciné
11. se dissimuler parmi nous
12. bienveillant
13. véritablement prétendre être au-dessus de tout soupçon
14. à travers toute l'Amérique
15. ait éclaté au grand jour
16. qui me serait bientôt familière
17. soupesait chacun de mes mots

myself up to him in this way[1] but at the same time I knew that he would demand nothing less[2].

'My father was a quiet man and a very cultivated one,' I continued. 'He had never raised his voice to me[3], not in my entire life, but he did so on that day. To him, with all his sensibilities, the work of the policeman and the detective (for he saw no difference between the two) was lowly, disgusting[4]. He begged me to change my mind.[5] I refused. We quarrelled[6], and in the end I left with hardly more than a few dollars in my pocket and the growing fear[7] that, as my home slipped away behind me[8], I was making a terrible mistake.

'I took the train to New York and it is hard to convey[9] to you my first impressions as I left Grand Central Depot[10]. I found myself in a city of extraordinary opulence and abject poverty, of astonishing elegance and extreme depravity[11], the two living so close by[12] that I only had to turn my head to pass from one to the other. Somehow I made my way to[13] the Lower East Side, a part of the city that put me in mind of[14] the tower of Babel, for here there were Poles[15], Italians, Jews, Bohemians, all of them speaking their own languages and observing their own customs[16]. Even the smells in the streets were new to me. After my long, protected childhood, it was as if I were seeing the world for the first time.

'It was easy enough to find a room in a tenement[17]; every door carried an advertisement[18]. I spent that first night in a dark, airless place with no furniture[19], a tiny stove[20] and a kerosene lamp and I will admit that I was very glad to open my eyes and see the first light of dawn[21].

1. m'ouvrir ainsi à lui
2. n'en exigeait pas moins de moi
3. haussé le ton contre moi
4. sale et dégradant
5. me supplia de changer d'avis.
6. Nous nous disputâmes
7. crainte grandissante
8. disparaissait derrière moi
9. décrire
10. [nom de la gare ferroviaire de New York de 1871 à 1899]
11. d'une élégance époustouflante et d'une dépravation extrême
12. les deux se côtoyant de si près
13. Je ne sais comment, mais je me retrouvai dans
14. qui n'était pas sans m'évoquer
15. des Polonais
16. vivant selon leurs propres coutumes
17. immeuble
18. il y avait des annonces sur toutes les portes
19. endroit étouffant et sombre totalement dénué de mobilier
20. à l'exception d'un poêle minuscule
21. premières lueurs du jour

'I had considered applying[1] to the police force in New York, thinking that I would need some experience as a guardian of the law[2] before I could apply to the Pinkertons, but I soon discovered that such a course of action would be practically impossible. I had brought with me no letters of recommendation; I had no connections, and without preferment of one sort or another[3], it would be hard even to get a foot through the door[4]. The police were poorly resourced and corruption was rife[5]. Would the famous detective agency, "The Eye that Never Sleeps", even consider[6] a rash and inexperienced youth[7]? There was only one way to find out. I went straight to their office and applied.

'I was fortunate.[8] Allan Pinkerton, the most famous detective in America and the founder of the company, and his sons, Robert and William, were actively seeking recruits[9]. It may surprise you to learn that police experience was not a requirement[10]. In fact, it was the other way round.[11] Many senior police officers in America first learned their trade with[12] Pinkerton's. Honesty, integrity, reliability[13] … these were the qualities that counted and I found myself being interviewed along with former bootmakers[14], teachers and wine merchants, all hoping to better themselves[15] in the company. Nor did my youth count against me[16]: I was well presented[17] and I had a good knowledge of the law. By the end of the day I had been recruited as a special operative[18], working on a temporary basis for $2.50 a day plus bed and board[19]. The hours[20] were long and it was made clear to me that my employment could be termi-

1. postuler
2. gardien de la paix
3. aucun contact, et sans le moindre soutien quel qu'il soit
4. ne serait-ce que de passer le pas de la porte
5. avait peu de moyens et la corruption allait bon train
6. prendrait-elle au sérieux
7. un jeune homme impulsif et inexpérimenté comme moi
8. J'eus de la chance.
9. cherchaient justement de nouvelles recrues
10. prérequise
11. c'était plutôt l'inverse.
12. faisaient leurs armes
13. fiabilité
14. d'anciens bottiers
15. qui tous espéraient améliorer leur condition
16. Mon jeune âge n'était pas non plus un inconvénient
17. présentais bien
18. j'avais été recruté en tant qu'agent spécial
19. le gîte et le couvert
20. journées de travail

1. n'étais pas à la hauteur
2. à ce que ce ne soit pas le cas
3. remuai
4. éclata d'un rire bruyant
5. indigne à dire
6. Je vais passer rapidement
7. très intéressé
8. je suis monté en grade
9. pardonné
10. léguant son cabinet
11. petit pécule
12. bien que je ne m'en plaigne pas
13. Le travail de policier n'a jamais été bien rémunéré
14. répondit
15. enquêté sur des affaires d'escroquerie
16. de faux billets, de braquage de banques
17. monnaie courante
18. dont vous avez fait preuve
19. privilégie la ténacité. Je suis méticuleux.
20. dépositions
21. témoignages contradictoires

nated at any time if I was found wanting[1]. I was determined that it should not be[2].'

Briefly, I stirred[3] my soup with my spoon. A man at a table on the far side of the room suddenly broke into loud laughter[4], I think at his own joke. It struck me that he laughed in a way that was peculiarly Germanic, although perhaps it was an unworthy thought[5].

I began again. 'I am moving quickly forward[6], Mr Jones, because my own life story will be of little interest to you.'

'On the contrary, I am immersed[7].'

'Well, let me just say that my work was found to be more than satisfactory and that, over the years, I rose up within the ranks.[8] I will mention that I returned to Boston and that I was reunited with my father, although he never completely forgave[9] me. He died a few years ago, leaving his practice[10] to my brother and a small sum[11] to me. It has proved useful for, although I am not complaining[12], I have never been highly paid.'

'The enforcement of the law has never been particularly well remunerated[13] in any country, to my knowledge,' Jones returned[14]. 'I might add that criminality pays more. However, you must forgive me. I interrupt.'

'I have investigated fraud[15], murder, counterfeiting, bank robberies[16] and missing persons – all of which are prevalent[17] in New York. I cannot say that I have used the same methods, the same extraordinary intelligence that you demonstrated to me[18] this morning. I am dogged in my approach. I am fastidious[19]. I may read a hundred witness statements[20] before I find the two conflicting remarks[21] that will lead me to the truth.

And it is this, more than anything, which has led me frequently to success and brought me to the attention[1] of my superiors. Let me tell you, however, of one investigation that was entrusted to me[2] in the spring of 1889. Although I didn't know it at the time, it was this more than anything that was eventually to bring me here[3].

'We had a client, a man called William Orton, the president of Western Union. He had come to us because his company's lines[4] had been intercepted and a series of completely false and damaging[5] messages were being sent to the New York stock market[6] with devastating results. Several large companies had been brought to the very edge of bankruptcy[7], and investors found themselves with losses stretching into the millions[8]. The chairman of a mining company[9] in Colorado, receiving one of these wires[10], went up to his bedroom and shot himself. Orton thought it must be the work of an extremely malevolent and cold-hearted practical joker[11]. It took me three months and an endless[12] series of interviews to discover the truth. It was, in fact, a remarkable and completely original form of embezzlement[13]. A consortium of brokers[14], working out of Wall Street, were buying up the stocks[15] of the companies that had been affected – acquiring them, of course, at rock-bottom prices[16]. In this way, they were making a fortune. The operation required nerve[17], imagination, cunning and the bringing together of a great many criminal talents[18]. At Pinkerton's, we knew at once that we had never encountered anything quite like it[19]. Eventually, we arrested the gang – but the leader, the man who had

1. m'a permis de me démarquer auprès
2. m'a été confiée
3. qui finirait par me conduire ici
4. les lignes télégraphiques de sa compagnie
5. préjudiciables
6. la bourse de New York
7. s'étaient retrouvées au bord de la faillite
8. des pertes qui se comptaient en millions
9. Le président d'une exploitation minière
10. faux télégrammes
11. un farceur extrêmement malveillant et insensible
12. interminable
13. détournement de fonds
14. courtiers en bourse
15. achetaient ensuite toutes les actions
16. des prix très bas
17. du cran
18. de l'ingéniosité et la collaboration de nombreux
19. nous n'avions jamais rien vu de pareil

1. à l'origine de
2. nous a glissé entre les doigts
3. en tant que tel
4. à bien des égards
5. le non-respect de la loi
6. j'aurais pu m'y attendre
7. si elle n'avait pas été indispensable
8. des maisons closes, des salles de jeu
9. se retrouvaient pour se vanter ouvertement
10. les faussaires, les faux-monnayeurs
11. les myriades de coupe-jarrets
12. s'aventurer dans les rues
13. au vu et au su de tous
14. voleurs
15. ce qui nous sauvait la mise, si on peut dire
16. ils agissaient presque toujours seuls
17. étaient à la tête d'
18. une petite fortune
19. apparaissaient puis disparaissaient
20. un réseau criminel complet avec son propre code de conduite
21. une hiérarchie soigneusement établie

initiated[1] the whole enterprise, slipped through our fingers[2]. His name was Clarence Devereux.

'You have to understand that America is a young country and as such[3] it is still, in many respects[4], uncivilised. I was actually shocked by the lawlessness[5] that I found all around me when I first arrived in New York, although I suppose I might have expected it[6]. How else could a company like the Pinkerton Detective Agency have become so successful if it wasn't needed[7]? The tenement where I lived was surrounded by brothels, gaming places[8] and saloons where the criminal classes congregated and boasted quite openly[9] about their exploits. I've already mentioned forgers, counterfeiters[10] and bank robbers. To those I might have added the countless footpads[11] who made it dangerous to venture out[12] at night and the pickpockets who committed their crimes quite brazenly[13] in the day.

'There were criminals everywhere. A thousand thieves[14]; two thousand prostitutes. But – and this, you might say, was the saving grace[15] – they were disparate and disorganised, nearly always acting alone[16]. Of course, there were exceptions. Jim Dunlap and Bob Scott headed[17] an organisation that became known as The Ring and which stole three million dollars, an amazing sum[18], from banks across the country. Other gangs – the Dead Rabbits and the Bowery Boys – came and went[19]. There were the Plug Uglies over in Baltimore. I read all the files. But Clarence Devereux was the first man to see the advantages of a comprehensive criminal network with its own code of practice[20] and a fully worked-out chain of command[21]. We first heard of him at the time of the

Western Union business, but by then he had already established himself as[1] the most brilliant and most successful criminal of his generation.'

'And this man is the reason you are here?' Jones enquired. 'He is the author of the letter sent to the late[2] Professor Moriarty?'

'I believe so, yes.'

'Please, continue.'

I had not even tasted the soup in front of me. Jones was still watching me intently[3]. It was a strange meal, two foreigners in a Swiss restaurant, neither of them eating a thing[4]. I wondered how much time had passed since I had begun my tale[5]. Outside, the night seemed darker than ever[6] and the flames were crackling, leaping at the chimney[7].

'By now I had been promoted[8] to the role of General Operative[9],' I continued, 'and Robert Pinkerton made me personally responsible for[10] Devereux's arrest. I was given a special team – three investigators, a cashier[11], a secretary, two stenographers and an office boy[12] – and together we became known as the Midnight Watch[13], a reference to the long hours we kept[14]. Our office, tucked away in the basement[15], was jammed with correspondence[16] and not an inch of our four walls was visible beneath[17] the veritable rogues' gallery that we had pinned into place[18]. Reports from Chicago, Washington and Philadelphia were sent to us and slowly, methodically, we worked our way through hundreds of pages[19]. It was an exhausting business but by the beginning of this year, a face had begun to take shape[20] ... well, not so much a face, a presence.'

'Clarence Devereux.'

1. s'était déjà imposé comme
2. au défunt
3. attentivement
4. ne touchant ni l'un ni l'autre leur assiette
5. le début de mon récit
6. plus sombre que jamais
7. crépitaient, bondissant dans la cheminée
8. À l'époque, j'avais été promu
9. détective en chef
10. m'avait chargé personnellement de
11. trois enquêteurs, un comptable
12. garçon de bureau
13. les Veilleurs de Minuit
14. nos interminables journées de travail
15. enfoui au sous-sol
16. croulait sous le courrier
17. les quatre murs disparaissaient complètement sous
18. les photos des repris de justice que nous avions épinglées
19. épluchions des centaines de pages
20. commençait à se dessiner

'I cannot even be certain that that is his real name. He has never been seen. No illustration or photograph of him exists. It is said that he is about forty years of age; that he came to America from Europe, from a well-to-do family[1]; that he is charming, highly cultivated and philanthropic. Yes, I see you start[2]. But I know for a fact[3] that he has given substantial sums of money[4] to the New York Foundling Hospital[5] and to the Home for the Friendless[6]. He has endowed a scholarship[7] at Harvard University and he was one of the founding subscribers[8] of the Metropolitan Opera.

'And yet at the same time, I tell you, there is no more evil influence[9] in the whole of America. Clarence Devereux is a criminal like no other, utterly ruthless[10], as much feared by the villains who work for him as by the victims whose lives he has ruined. There is no form of depravity, no vice that is below him.[11] Indeed, he takes such pleasure in the organisation and execution of his various schemes[12] that we have been led to believe[13] that he commits his crimes as much to amuse himself as to benefit from any profits they might bring. After all, he has already made his fortune. He is a showman, a ringmaster[14] who brings misery to[15] everyone he touches, leaving his bloody fingerprints[16] everywhere he goes.

'I have studied him. I have pursued him. He represents everything that I loathe[17] and find most vile and to bring an end to his activities would be the crowning moment of my career[18]. And yet he remains out of my reach[19]. Sometimes I feel that he knows my every move; that he is toying with me[20]. Clarence Devereux is very careful about the way he operates, hiding behind his

1. famille aisée
2. je vois bien que vous êtes surpris
3. de source sûre
4. des sommes considérables
5. [Hospice pour enfants trouvés de New York]
6. [Célèbre orphelinat de Baltimore, dans le Maryland]
7. créé une bourse d'étude
8. donateurs historiques
9. nul n'a plus néfaste influence
10. sans la moindre pitié
11. Aucune forme de débauche, aucun vice n'est trop vil pour lui
12. multiples manigances
13. en sommes venus à penser
14. C'est une bête de scène, un maître de cérémonie
15. fait souffrir
16. empreintes ensanglantées
17. exècre
18. couronnement de ma carrière
19. hors d'atteinte
20. qu'il anticipe chacun de mes mouvements et se joue de moi

false identity. Never once will he expose himself or put himself in any danger. He will plan a crime – a bank robbery, a burglary[1], a murder; work out the details[2], recruit the gang, take the spoils[3] – but he himself will not come close. He remains invisible. He has, however, one trait[4] that may one day help me identify him. It is said that he has a strange psychological condition[5] called agoraphobia – which is to say, a morbid fear of open spaces. He remains indoors and travels only in a covered carriage[6].

'There is something else. As we continued our work, we were able to track down[7] three men who knew his true identity and who almost certainly worked for him: his closest lieutenants and bodyguards. They formed a satellite around him[8], all three of them vicious criminals in their own right[9]. Two of them are brothers – Edgar and Leland Mortlake. The third started life as a smatter-hauler[10], which is what we call a handkerchief thief, but soon graduated[11] to safe-cracking and grand larceny[12]. His name is Scotchy Lavelle.'

'Can you not arrest them?'

'We have arrested them – many times. They are all three of them graduates of[13] Sing Sing and the Tombs[14] but in recent years they have been careful to keep their hands clean[15]. They pretend to be respectable businessmen now and there is no evidence to prove otherwise[16]. Arresting them again would do no good[17]. The police have questioned them repeatedly but there is nothing in this world that would make them talk. They represent the new breed[18] of gangster, the one that we at Pinkerton's most fear[19]. They

1. cambriolage
2. planifier tout en détails
3. récupérer le butin
4. trait de caractère
5. trouble mental
6. voiture couverte
7. retrouver la trace de
8. un réseau autour de lui
9. des criminels endurcis à part entière
10. [terme victorien désignant un gang de voleurs de mouchoirs]
11. fut rapidement promu
12. à l'ouverture des coffres-forts et au vol qualifié
13. d'anciens détenus de
14. [prisons américaines de l'État de New York]
15. pris soin de garder les mains propres
16. il n'y a aucune preuve du contraire
17. ne servirait à rien
18. race
19. celle que nous redoutons le plus chez Pinkerton

1. se considèrent au-dessus de la loi.
2. de loin et à travers un grillage
3. Il m'a toujours semblé préférable
4. que l'on ne se rencontre pas
5. faire en sorte que j'ignore à quoi il ressemble
6. il me semble légitime de lui rendre la politesse
7. bûche
8. d'une chaleur étouffante
9. poursuivis mon récit
10. avons enquêté sur Devereux avec un succès mitigé
11. nous avons fait une découverte capitale
12. n'avait qu'une vingtaine d'années
13. et de par son enthousiasme et sa droiture morale
14. originaire de l'ouest du pays
15. brillant violoncelliste
16. lancer des balles
17. avait accompagné un troupeau de chevaux
18. [sur mille six cents kilomètres]
19. dans le transport fluvial
20. couleur paille

are no longer afraid of the law. They think themselves above it.[1]'

'Have you met them?'

'I have observed all three of them from a distance and from behind a wire mesh[2]. I always thought it best[3] that we should remain unacquainted[4]. If Devereux can keep his face a secret from me[5], it seems only fair to repay the compliment[6].' Mrs Steiler walked past and placed another log[7] on the fire although her restaurant was already sweltering[8]. I waited until she had left us and then finished my account[9]. 'For two years we investigated Clarence Devereux with little success[10], but then, just a few months ago, we had a breakthrough[11]. One of my investigators was a young man called Jonathan Pilgrim.'

'I know that name too,' Jones muttered.

'He was only in his twenties[12] when I first met him and in his enthusiasm and basic decency[13] he reminded me of myself at his age. He was a remarkable fellow who'd come to us from the west[14]. A fine cello player[15] and a baseball player too. I once saw him pitch[16] at Bloomingdale Park. When he was nineteen, he trailed a horse herd[17] a thousand miles[18] across the Texas plains and he'd had experience of ranches, mines – he'd even spent time working the riverboats[19]. He joined the team in New York and, working on his own, managed to get close to Leland Mortlake. Let's just say that the older of the two brothers had always enjoyed the company of a handsome boy and with his straw-coloured[20] hair and bright blue eyes, JP was very handsome indeed. He became Mortlake's secretary and travelling companion. The two of them dined together. They visited[1] the theatre and the opera and hung out at[2] the saloons. Well, in January, Mortlake announced that he was moving to London and he invited JP to go with him.'It was a brilliant opportunity. We had an agent right inside[3] the gang and although Jonathan never came face to face with Devereux – how much easier it would have made our task if he had![4] – he did have access to much of Mortlake's correspondence. Although it placed him in the greatest personal danger, he eavesdropped on conversations[5], kept an eye on[6] everyone who came and went and made extensive notes on the workings[7] of the gang. I used to meet with him secretly on the third Sunday of every month at the Haymarket, a dance hall[8] on Thirtieth Street. He would report everything that he had learned to me.

'From him, I gathered[9] that although Clarence Devereux exerted[10] almost total control over the American underworld, it still was not enough. He was turning his attention to England. He had been in communication with a certain Professor James Moriarty, exploring the possibility of what might be termed[11] a transatlantic alliance. Can you imagine it, Inspector Jones? A criminal fraternity[12] whose tentacles would extend all the way from the west coast of California to the heart of Europe! A worldwide confederation. The coming together[13] of two evil geniuses.'

'You knew of[14] Moriarty?'

'By name and by reputation[15], most certainly. Although it is unfortunately true[16] that Scotland Yard is not always co-operative in its dealings with[17] Pinkerton's, we still have our contacts within[18] the New York police – and for that mat-

1. fréquentaient
2. traînaient dans
3. infiltré dans
4. Si cela avait été le cas, combien notre tâche aurait été facilitée!
5. écoutait aux portes
6. surveillait attentivement
7. prenait des notes détaillées sur le fonctionnement
8. guinguette
9. Grâce à lui, j'en déduisis
10. exerçait
11. ce qu'on pourrait appeler
12. confrérie
13. L'union
14. connaissiez
15. De nom et de réputation
16. S'il est vrai, hélas,
17. n'est pas toujours très coopératif lorsqu'il s'agit des
18. nous avons toutefois des contacts dans

ter with the Rijkswacht[1] and the Sûreté. We had always been afraid that one day Moriarty might head west[2] but it now appeared that the exact opposite had occurred.

'Scotchy Lavelle, Leland Mortlake and Edgar Mortlake had all set themselves up[3] in London by the start of the New Year. Jonathan had gone with them and, a few weeks later, he sent us a telegraph to the effect[4] that Clarence Devereux had also joined them. It was exactly what we had been waiting for. There are not so many forty-year-old wealthy[5] Americans in London. His psychological condition, if true, could also help to identify him. At once[6], the Midnight Watch drew together[7] the passenger lists of every steamship[8] that had made the crossing from[9] America to England in the past month and although it was a huge task – there were hundreds of names – we still thought it possible to narrow them down.[10] Unless Clarence Devereux had somehow found a way to fly, he must be among them[11] and to find him we worked night and day.

While this was continuing, we received a second telegraph from Jonathan Pilgrim informing us that he had personally delivered a letter to Moriarty, arranging a meeting between him and Devereux. Yes! Our agent had actually met Moriarty[12]. The two of them talked. But the very next day, before he could tell us exactly what had taken place[13], tragedy struck[14]: Jonathan must have been discovered by the gang. Perhaps that last telegraph was the undoing of him[15]. At any event[16], he was brutally killed.'

'He was tied up[17] and shot. I remember the report.'

1. [gendarmerie belge]
2. puisse mettre le cap à l'Ouest
3. s'étaient tous installés
4. nous informant
5. fortunés
6. Immédiatement
7. ont rassemblé
8. tous les bateaux à vapeur
9. avaient fait la traversée
10. nous pensions quand même pouvoir réduire la liste
11. son nom devait s'y trouver
12. vu Moriarty en personne
13. ce qu'il s'était passé
14. une tragédie s'est produite
15. causa sa perte
16. En tout cas
17. ligoté

'Yes, Inspector – this was not so much a murder as an execution[1]. It is how New York gangs frequently deal with informers[2].'

'Even so, you followed him across the Atlantic.'

'I still believed it would be easier to find Devereux in London than it was in New York and it also occurred to me[3] that if I could pinpoint[4] this meeting between Devereux and Moriarty, why, it would be two birds with one stone[5]: the arrest of the two greatest criminals on the planet at one fell swoop[6].

'So you can imagine my dismay[7] when I disembarked from my vessel, stepping on English soil[8] for the first time, only to see the newspaper headlines[9] … Moriarty believed dead[10]. That was May seventh[11]. My immediate thought was[12] to come here to Meiringen, a village I had never heard of in a country I had never visited. Why? Because of the letter; if Moriarty still had it with him, it might lead me to Devereux. It even occurred to me that Devereux might be here and that his presence might be connected in some way to what had occurred at[13] the Reichenbach Falls. At any event, there was nothing to be gained by kicking my heels[14] in Southampton. I took the first train to Paris and then down to Switzerland and I was attempting to prise some sort of co-operation from the Swiss police[15] – without much success– this morning when you and I met.'

I fell silent. It was too late now to attack my soup, which had cooled in the long telling of my tale[16]. I took instead a sip[17] of wine, which tasted sweet and heavy[18] on my lips. Inspector Jones had listened to my long discourse as if the two of us had been alone in the room. I knew that

1. Ça tenait plus de l'exécution que du meurtre
2. indics
3. je me disais aussi
4. localiser
5. hé bien, ce serait d'une pierre deux coups
6. en un coup de filet
7. désarroi
8. j'ai débarqué, foulant le sol anglais
9. tout ça pour tomber sur les gros titres des journaux
10. présumé mort
11. le 7 mai
12. J'ai immédiatement décidé
13. pourrait être liée de près ou de loin avec les événements de
14. il n'aurait servi à rien de me tourner les pouces
15. d'obtenir de la police suisse une forme de collaboration
16. avait refroidi pendant que je racontais mon long récit
17. gorgée
18. épais

he had absorbed every detail, that he had missed nothing and would – if called upon[1] – be able to set down[2] almost everything I had said. And yet it was not without effort. I had already marked him as the sort of man[3] who sets the very highest standards for himself[4] but who achieves them only through perseverance and fortitude[5]. It was as if he were at war with himself[6].

'Your informant, Jonathan Pilgrim; do you know where he was staying?'

'He had rooms at a club – the Bostonian. I believe it is in a part of London called Mayfair. If he had one weakness as an agent,[7] it is that he was independently minded[8]. He told us very little and will, I am sure, have left nothing behind[9].'

'What of the others? The Mortlake brothers and Lavelle?'

'As far as I know, they are still in London.'

'You know them. You know what they look like. Can you not use them to reach Devereux?'

'They are too careful. If they ever meet, it is in secret and behind locked doors[10]. They communicate only through telegrams and secret codes.'

Jones considered what I had told him. I watched the flames devouring the logs[11] in the fireplace and waited for him to speak. 'Your story is of the greatest interest,' he said at length[12]. 'And I would see no reason not to offer you my assistance. However, it may already be too late.'

'Why is that?'

'Now that Moriarty is dead, why should this man, Clarence Devereux, wish to remain[13] in London?'

'Because it may be an opportunity for him; Devereux was suggesting some sort of partnership.

1. si on le lui demandait
2. mettre par écrit
3. J'avais déjà compris que c'était le genre d'homme
4. qui se fixe les objectifs les plus exigeants
5. et ne les atteint que grâce à sa persévérance et son courage
6. en guerre contre lui même
7. Il n'avait qu'un seul défaut en tant qu'agent,
8. c'est qu'il était indépendant de nature
9. n'aura rien laissé derrière lui
10. derrière des portes fermées à double tour
11. dévorer les bûches
12. au bout d'un moment
13. resterait-il

With Moriarty gone, everything can be his alone[1]. He can inherit[2] Moriarty's entire organisation.'

Jones sniffed at that[3]. 'We had arrested pretty much[4] the entire gang before Professor Moriarty reached Meiringen,' he remarked. 'And Sherlock Holmes himself had left an envelope containing the identities and the addresses of many of his associates. Clarence Devereux may have come to England in search of a business partner but he will have already discovered that his journey was in vain. The same, I fear, may be true for you.[5]'

'The note that we found in Moriarty's pocket – you said it would shed some light on the affair[6].'

'And so it does.[7]'

'You have solved it?'

'Yes.'

'Then tell me, for Heaven's sake[8]! Moriarty may be finished but Clarence Devereux most certainly is not[9] and if there is anything you or I can do to rid the world of this evil creature[10], we must not hesitate.'

Jones had finished his soup. He moved his plate aside, clearing a space[11], then took out the sheet of paper, unfolded it and laid it in front of me[12]. It seemed to me that the restaurant had suddenly become quieter. The candles were throwing dark, nimble shadows across the tables[13]. The animal heads craned towards us[14] as if trying to listen in[15].

Once again I read the extract with its jumble[16] of capital and small letters.

'It makes no sense to you?[17]' Jones enquired.

'None at all.[18]'

'Then let me explain.

1. tout cela pourrait être à lui

2. hériter de

3. fit une moue dubitative

4. quasiment

5. Je crains qu'il n'en soit de même pour vous.

6. pourrait éclaircir quelque peu les choses

7. Et c'est bien le cas.

8. pour l'amour du ciel

9. ne l'est en aucun cas

10. débarrasser le monde de cette créature malfaisante

11. poussa son assiette pour faire de la place

12. la posa devant moi

13. projetaient sur les tables des ombres noires et agiles

14. tendaient le cou vers nous

15. comme pour écouter notre conversation

16. fouillis

17. Cela n'a aucun sens pour vous ?

18. Absolument aucun.

FOUR

The Letter

HoLmES WaS CeRtAiNLY NOt A DIFFiCulT mAn to LiVe WItH. He wAs QuIeT IN HIS WAYs and his hABiTS wErE REgulAr. iT wAs RARE fOR HIm To BE up AfTeR TEN at nighT aND hE hAD INVariABLY breAKfasteD AND GoNE OUT BeFOrE i RoSe in The morNINg. SOMEtImEs He SPeNt hiS DAy At ThE ChEmiCaL lABoRatORY, SoMeTimes IN THE dIsSeCting ROoms And oCcAsionaLly iN lOnG WALKs whICH ApPeAREd TO taKE HIM INtO THE LOwEsT PORTioNs OF thE CITy. nothINg COuld exCEeD HiS ENErgY WHeN tHE wORkING FiT WAs upOn HiM.

'Do you really believe,' I said, 'that there is some sort of secret message contained on this page?'

'I not only believe it. I know it to be the case.[1]'

I took the paper and held it up to the light[2]. 'Could it be written in invisible ink?'

Jones smiled. He took the page back again and laid it between us on the white tablecloth[3]. For the moment, all thoughts of our dinner had been forgotten[4]. 'You may be aware that Mr Sherlock Holmes wrote a monograph[5] on the subject of codes and secret writings,' he began.

1. J'en suis absolument persuadé.
2. l'approchai de la lampe
3. nappe
4. nous avions oublié toute idée de dîner
5. [étude exhaustive portant sur un sujet précis]

'I was not,' I said.

'I have read it, as I have read everything that he has, generously, allowed to come to the public attention[1]. The monograph examines no fewer than[2] one hundred and sixty forms of concealed communication[3] and, more importantly, the methods by which he was able to bring them to light[4].'

'You will forgive me, Inspector,' I interrupted. 'Whatever the relevance of this letter[5], it cannot be in code. We both recognise the contents. You said as much yourself. It was written, word for word, by Dr John Watson.'

'That is indeed the case. But there is of course one peculiarity[6]. Why do you think it has been copied in this way? Why has the writer taken such care with[7] his presentation of the text?'

'I'd guess it's obvious, isn't it? To disguise his handwriting[8]!'

'I think not. After all, Moriarty knew who the letter had come from. There was no need for disguise. No. I believe the capital and the small letters go to the very heart of the matter[9] and there is nothing indiscriminate about them[10]. The moment I set eyes[11] on the passage, I saw that it had been written slowly and methodically. You can observe the heavy indentation[12] of the pen on the paper. This is more than an exercise in copying. It is a deliberate attempt to communicate something to Moriarty that will remain secret should it fall into the wrong hands[13].'

'So there is a code!'

'Exactly.'

'And you were able to crack it!'

1. dont il a généreusement accepté de faire profiter le public
2. pas moins de
3. messages secrets
4. de les révéler
5. Quel que soit l'intérêt de cette lettre
6. bizarrerie
7. mis tant de soin dans
8. écriture
9. sont au cœur du problème
10. n'ont pas été choisies au hasard
11. posai les yeux
12. l'empreinte profonde
13. s'il tombait entre de mauvaises mains

'Through trial and error[1], yes.' Jones nodded. 'I take no credit for it, mind.[2] Where Holmes has gone, I have merely followed.[3]'

'Then what does it say?' I glanced once again[4] at the page. 'What can it possibly say?'

'I shall explain it to you, Chase. I trust you will forgive the familiarity but I am beginning to think that you and I may be united in a common pursuit[5].'

'I very much hope so.'

'Very well. As you rightly say[6], the letters alone cannot mean anything for they are exactly as Dr Watson set them down[7]. We are therefore left with the seemingly random scattering of small and capital letters[8]. But let us suppose it is not random. There are three hundred and ninety letters on the page. That in itself is an interesting number in that it is exactly divisible by five. So let us begin by separating the letters into groups of that length[9]—'

'Wait a minute. It's also divisible by six.'

'Six would create far more combinations than are actually required[10].' He scowled.[11] 'Anyway, I tried six without success – trial and error[12]. I am no Sherlock Holmes and so it is sometimes necessary to take the long way round[13].' He took out a second sheet of paper and laid it beside the first. 'We must ignore the spaces between the words. We must ignore everything apart from the question of whether the letter is large or small[14]. And in that event, the text will look like this:

Ls[15]LsL LLsLL sLsLs LLLLL sLLLL LsLss LsLss sLsLs LLsLL ssLsL sLsLs LLsLL LLsss sssss LLsLL sLsLL LsssL ssLsL sLLLL sLLLL sLsLL ssLsL sLLLL sssss sLsLL sLsLL

1. En tâtonnant
2. Je ne m'attribue aucun mérite, cela dit.
3. Je me suis contenté de suivre les traces de Holmes.
4. jetai à nouveau un coup d'œil
5. unis par un même but
6. Comme vous le dites si justement
7. les a écrites
8. une poignée de lettres en apparence aléatoires
9. longueur
10. que nous n'en nécessitons
11. grimaça.
12. Il m'a fallu tâtonner
13. parfois il ne faut pas avoir peur de faire des détours
14. sauf la hauteur des lettres
15. [L pour « large », majuscule, s pour « small », minuscule]

LLLss sLLLL sssLL sssss LLLLL sLLLL LLsLL sLsLs LsssL sssss LLLsL LLLsL sLsLs LLsLs ssLLL sLsLs LLsLs sLsLs LLsLs sLLLL sLsLs sssLL LLLsL sLsLs sssLL sssLs ssLsL sssss LsssL sLsLL LLLss sLLLL sLsLL LsLLs sLLLL LLLsL LLLLL sLsLL LLLss LsLLs sLLLL sssss LLsLL sssss LLsLL sLLLL ssLLL sLsLL sLLsL LLLsL LLsss LsLsL

Jones had carefully written the groups of letters across the page. I stared at them.[1] 'It's the electrical telegraph system!' I exclaimed.

'It is something very similar,' the detective agreed. 'Morse code, with each group representing a single letter! And you will see, Chase, that certain groups repeat themselves. "sLLLL", for example, appears no fewer than eleven times.'

'A vowel?[2]' I suggested.

'Almost certainly, and "sssss" might be another, appearing seven times. But set out this way[3], the groups are confusing. My next step was to assign each one of them a number[4], making it simpler to see what it was in fact we had before us[5]. We are helped by the fact that only nineteen of the twenty-six letters of the alphabet have actually been used.'

He withdrew[6] a third sheet of paper. On this, he had written as follows:

1 2 3 4 5 6 6 3 2 7 3 2 8 9 2 10 11 7 5 5 10 7 5 9 10 10 12 5 13 9 4 5 2 3 11 9 14 14 3 15 16 3 15 3 15 5 3 13 14 3 13 17 7 9 11 10 12 5 10 18 5 14 4 10 12 18 5 9 2 9 2 5 16 10 19 14 8 1

'You understand,' he explained, 'that each number merely stands for[7] a group. So one equals LsLsL, two equals LLsLL and so on …'

'I see that. Yes.'

1. les regardai attentivement.
2. voyelle ?
3. disposés ainsi
4. d'attribuer à chacun d'eux un nombre
5. ce que nous avons sous les yeux
6. sortit
7. ne fait que représenter

'And what does it tell you?' This was a very different Athelney Jones from the one I had seen earlier, exhausted after the walk from the church[1]. There was no escaping[2] the energy and the sense of excitement that glimmered in his eyes[3].

'Each number now stands for a single letter,' I said. 'But there are a lot of numbers – nineteen, as you correctly say – and we are not helped by the fact that there are no spaces[4]. We have no way of telling[5] where one word ends and the next begins.'

'That is indeed the case,' Jones agreed. 'However, at the very least we can see[6] now which numbers – 3, 5 and 10, for example – crop up[7] the most frequently. These must be vowels or perhaps the more commonly used letters[8] such as T, R or S. Unfortunately, you are correct in saying that without spaces, we cannot spot the shapes[9] of common English words such as "the" or "a". That is very much to our disadvantage.'

'So how were you able to continue?'

'With a combination of diligence and good luck[10]: I began by asking myself if there might be a single word appearing in this communication which I would be able to recognise simply from its shape. Several came to mind.[11] SHERLOCK HOLMES, for example, was one. PINKERTONS was another. But in the end I settled on MORIARTY. If it was he for whom the message was intended, then it was surely not unreasonable[12] to suppose that his name might appear. I therefore searched for a sequence of eight digits[13] in which one – and only one – was repeated in the third and sixth position as is the case with the R in MORIARTY. For example, at the very begin-

1. épuisé par la marche depuis l'église

2. Il était impossible d'ignorer

3. qui brillaient dans ses yeux

4. l'absence d'espaces ne nous aide pas

5. n'avons aucun moyen de savoir

6. nous pouvons au moins voir

7. survient

8. les lettres les plus souvent utilisées

9. repérer les formes

10. Grâce à un mélange de ténacité et de chance

11. Plusieurs me vinrent à l'esprit.

12. il n'était sûrement pas insensé

13. une suite de huit nombres

ning of the message we come upon[1] 6 6 3 2 7 3 2 8 where the 3 might be an R. But that cannot be MORIARTY because of the double 6 and the repeated 2. Later on in the text we see 5 3 13 14 3 13 17 7 where the figure 13 might stand for R. But this time it is the repeated 3 that defeats us[2].

'In fact, in the entire message, the correct formulation appears only once – near the beginning of the first line we have 7 3 2 8 9 2 10 11. In this instance,[3] the number 2 stands for R and – as in the name itself – no other letter is repeated. And if we assume that this stands for MORIARTY, something very interesting happens. For if we then examine the letters that appear *before* it, this is what we read ...'

1 R O 4 5 6 6 O R

'It could be more than one word,' I said.

'But I do not think it is more than one word,' returned he. 'Look at the repeated R, the repeated O – and whatever letter is represented by the repeated 6. As far as I can tell, there is only one word in the English language with a shape like that. And consider also the context. This is a salutation to the receiver[4] of the message.'

'Professor!' I exclaimed.

'Exactly. Professor Moriarty – the first two words of the communication. And, using that information, many more of the letters contained in the code are revealed.

PROFESSOR MORIARTY – M E E T M E A T T 12 E 13 A F E R O Y A 14 14 O 15 16 O 15 O 15 E O 13 14 O 13 17 M A Y T 12 E T 18 E 14 F T 12 18 E A R A R E 16 T 19 14 I P

1. on peut lire
2. qui nous met en échec
3. À cet endroit,
4. destinataire

' "Professor Moriarty, meet me at … "' I began. My voice trailed off.[1] 'There is not very much more after that,' I said.

'I do not agree. "Meet me at" is followed by "T 12 E". What else can that be but "the"? You will see that the same formulation is repeated in the third line after MAY. And that provides us with another letter. 12 is H! And looking at the second line, you will see the letters ROYA all together. Again, the fifth letter is obvious[2]. It can only be one word.

'Royal?'

'Precisely. Meet me at the something Royal …'

'What can that be?'

'It can only be the Café Royal!' Jones explained. I looked blank[3] so he continued. 'It is a famous restaurant in the heart of London. Like yourself, Clarence Devereux might not have heard of it but it would be easy enough to find.'

'And what of the word that follows?' I asked.

'That is not so difficult. We now have the L. So – L O 15 16 O 15. The repeated 15 gives us another clue if we need it.'

'London,' I said. 'The Café Royal, London. It can be nothing else.'

'I agree. That is the meeting place. And now let us see what comes next.'

ONE O C L O C 17 MAY THE T 18 E L F T H

'It is perfectly obvious,' I cried. 'One o'clock, May the twelfth!'

'That is three days from now.[4] You see how quickly the code unravels itself[5]. But let us proceed to the end.[6]'

1. Ma voix s'estompa.
2. évidente
3. Je ne réagis pas
4. Soit dans trois jours.
5. se dévoile
6. Mais continuons jusqu'au bout.

W E A R A R E 16 T 19 L I P

'We are ...' I stopped, confused.

'It is not "we are". It is "wear a". From what you told me, it is almost certain that Moriarty and Clarence Devereux have never seen each other face to face. Both pride themselves on the fact that nobody knows their appearance. So Moriarty is being instructed[1] to wear something that will identify him. That something is contained in the last eight letters.'

RE 16 T 19 LIP

I said nothing and with a smile, Jones finished his work for me. 'It can only be a red tulip,' he said, 'a buttonhole[2]. And there you have it, Chase ...'

PROFESSOR MORIARTY. MEET ME AT THE CAFÉ ROYAL, LONDON. ONE O'CLOCK, MAY THE TWELFTH. WEAR A RED TULIP.

'We were lucky. Professor Moriarty was the key to the entire thing. Had the sender omitted[3] the salutation, we would have been stuck[4].'

'But you are remarkable, Inspector Jones! I cannot express my admiration strongly enough.[5] I wouldn't have known where to begin.[6]'

'Pshaw.[7] It was not so very difficult. I'm sure Mr Holmes would have achieved the same in half the time[8].'

'This is exactly what I had been hoping for,' I said. 'It's the vindication[9] of my long journey to Europe – and the costs involved, for that matter[10]. Clarence Devereux is coming to this place, the Café Royal, three days from now. He will ap-

1. On ordonne donc à Moriarty
2. boutonnière
3. Si l'expéditeur avait omis
4. coincé
5. Je ne sais comment exprimer l'admiration que j'ai pour vous.
6. n'aurais jamais su par où commencer.
7. Pfff.
8. atteint le même résultat en deux fois moins de temps
9. justification
10. et des dépenses engendrées, par ailleurs

proach a man wearing a red tulip and in doing so[1] he'll identify himself.'

'If he knows that Moriarty is dead, he will not come.'

'That's true.' I fell silent, then thought again. 'But suppose you were to issue a statement to the effect[2] that you believe Moriarty to be alive? After all, you were sent to enquire into what had taken place[3] at the Reichenbach Falls. You could easily say that you had found fresh evidence that Moriarty had not been involved[4] in the attack.'

'And the body in the crypt?'

I paused. 'Couldn't we pretend that it was somebody else?' At that moment, our hostess approached the table to remove the plates. 'Mrs Steiler,' I said. 'Can you tell me the name of the chef whose mother was ill[5]?'

'Franz Hirzel.' She looked at my soup, barely touched. 'Not good?'

'It was excellent,' I replied. I waited until she had gone back into the kitchen. 'There's the name for you, if you need one. The dead man can be our wandering chef[6]. He was on his way back[7], he got drunk and fell into the falls. It's just a coincidence that the two incidents occurred at about the same time[8]. Tell the papers that Moriarty is still alive and let Devereux walk into a trap[9].' Jones looked down with his lips tightly pursed[10], so I went on. 'I haven't known you very long and yet I can see you don't like the idea of doing something dishonest[11]. I feel the same. But trust me when I say that you have no idea what sort of disease has arrived in[12] your city. You owe it to your fellow citizens[13] to do everything you can to purge it[14]. Believe me, Inspector. With Moriarty gone, this

1. ce faisant
2. imaginons que vous fassiez une déclaration stipulant
3. on vous a envoyé enquêter sur ce qui s'est passé
4. la preuve que Moriarty n'était pas impliqué
5. dont la mère est souffrante
6. notre chef baladeur
7. sur le chemin du retour
8. se soient produits à peu près en même temps
9. tomber dans notre piège
10. avec les lèvres pincées
11. quelque chose de malhonnête
12. du véritable fléau qui est prêt à s'abattre sur
13. devez à vos concitoyens de
14. l'éradiquer

meeting is our only hope. We have to be there.[1] We have to see what comes of it[2].'

Mrs Steiler returned with the main course[3], two plates of roast lamb[4]. I picked up my knife and fork, this time determined to eat.

Jones nodded slowly.[5] 'You're right,' he said. 'I will send a telegram to Scotland Yard and we can leave tomorrow. If the trains are kind to us, we will just arrive in time.[6]'

I raised my glass. 'To the capture of Clarence Devereux,' I said. 'And – if I may – to the two of us, Scotland Yard and Pinkerton's, working together.'

We drank and in this way our association began[7]. And yet how bitter that wine might have tasted[8] and how reluctant we might have been to continue[9] if we had only known what lay ahead[10].

1. Nous devons absolument y être.

2. ce qu'il adviendra

3. plat principal

4. rôti d'agneau

5. hocha lentement la tête.

6. Si les trains sont avec nous, nous arriverons juste à temps.

7. c'est ainsi que nous scellâmes notre collaboration

8. Comme ce vin nous aurait paru amer

9. comme nous aurions été réticents à continuer l'aventure

10. si nous avions seulement su ce qui nous attendait

FIVE

At the Café Royal

Not many Americans have the opportunity to travel across Europe and yet[1] I cannot describe very much of what I saw. For much of the time I had my face pressed against the glass[2], gazing at the little farmhouses dotted over the hills[3], the rushing streams[4], the valleys with their early summer flowers, and yet I was ill at ease[5], unable to concentrate on what I saw. The train journey was a very slow business[6] and, in our second-class carriage[7], an uncomfortable one. My constant fear was that we would arrive too late for, as Jones had told me, we had a distance of some five hundred miles to cover[8] with four trains and the steam packet[9] from Calais to London Bridge. We couldn't afford[10] to miss even one of our connections.[11] From Meiringen we headed west, crossing Lake Brienz at Interlaken and then continuing up to Bern. It was from here that Jones sent the cable that we'd devised together[12], stating that Professor Moriarty had miraculously escaped from the catastrophe of the Reichenbach Falls and was believed to have returned[13] to England. The post office was some distance from the station and almost cost us our next train as Jones was unable to

1. pourtant
2. fenêtre
3. contemplant les petites fermes qui parsemaient les collines
4. vifs ruisseaux
5. mal à l'aise
6. traînait en longueur
7. voiture de seconde classe
8. une distance de près de 800 km à rallier
9. bateau à vapeur
10. ne pouvions pas nous permettre
11. de rater ne serait-ce qu'une correspondance
12. télégramme que nous avions composé ensemble
13. était probablement retourné

walk for any great length of time[1]. He was quite pale and clearly in discomfort[2] as we took our seats in our carriage.

We sat in silence for the first hour or two, each of us absorbed in our own thoughts. However, as we approached the French border[3] near Moutier, we became more talkative[4]. I told Jones something[5] of the history of the Pinkertons – he had a keen interest in[6] the methods of investigation practiced by foreign law enforcers, dull though they were compared to his own[7] – and I gave him a detailed account of their involvement[8] in the Burlington and Quincy Railroad strike[9] which had taken place a few years before. The agency had been accused of inciting riots and even murdering strikers[10], although I assured him that their role had only been to protect property and to keep the peace. That was their story[11], anyway.

After that, Jones turned away, immersing himself[12] in a printed pamphlet which he had brought with him and which turned out to be a monograph by Sherlock Holmes no less[13], this one on the subject of ash[14]. Apparently – or so Jones assured me – Holmes was able to differentiate between one hundred and forty different types of ash, from cigars, cigarettes and pipes, although he himself had only mastered[15] ninety of them. To humour him, I made my way to[16] the salon dining room and took a pinch of five different samples[17] from the mystified[18] passengers. Jones was extremely grateful[19] and spent the next hour examining them minutely with a magnifying glass[20] he had extracted from his travelling bag.

'How I would have liked to have encountered[21] Sherlock Holmes!' I exclaimed when he finally

1. pendant une durée prolongée
2. indisposé
3. frontière
4. loquaces
5. une partie
6. un vif intérêt pour
7. bien qu'elles soient fort insipides comparées aux siennes
8. lui fis un récit détaillé de leur implication
9. [célèbre épisode de grève dans les chemins de fer en 1888]
10. provoquer des émeutes et même d'assassiner des grévistes
11. leur version des faits
12. se détourna, se plongeant dans la lecture
13. rien de moins qu'une monographie de Sherlock Holmes
14. portant sur l'étude des cendres
15. lui-même ne pouvait en reconnaître que
16. Pour lui faire plaisir, je me rendis au
17. pris une pincée de cinq échantillons différents
18. déconcertés
19. reconnaissant
20. dans les moindres détails à l'aide d'une loupe
21. avoir rencontré

cast the ashes aside[1], dismissing them quite literally with a wave of his hand[2]. 'Did you ever meet him?'

'Yes. I did.' He fell silent and I saw, to my surprise, that my question had in some way offended him. This was strange as so much of what he had said in our brief acquaintance[3] had led me to believe[4] that he was an ardent, even a fanatical, admirer[5] of the famous detective. 'I actually met him on three occasions,' he continued. He paused, as if unsure where to begin[6]. 'The first was not exactly a meeting as I was only there as part of a larger assembly. He gave a lecture to a number of us[7] at Scotland Yard – it led directly to the arrest[8] of the Bishopsgate jewel thief[9]. To this day, I am inclined to think[10] that Mr Holmes relied more on guesswork[11] than strict logic. He could not possibly have known[12] that the man was born with a club foot[13]. The second occasion, however, was quite different and has been made public by Dr John Watson who actually mentions me by name. I cannot say it gives an account of me that is particularly kind[14].'

'I'm sorry to hear it,' I said.

'You have not read the investigation that came to be known as "The Sign of the Four"[15]? It was a most unusual case[16].' Jones took out a cigarette and lit it[17]. I hadn't seen him smoke before and he seemed to have forgotten the conversation we'd had when we first met. At the last moment, he remembered. 'I'm sorry to inflict this on you a second time,' he said, 'I occasionally indulge.[18] You don't mind?[19]'

'Not at all.'

1. se débarrassa enfin des cendres
2. les balayant littéralement d'un revers de la main
3. Lors de notre brève rencontre
4. m'avait poussé à croire
5. admirateur
6. comme s'il ne savait pas par où commencer
7. donnait une conférence à certains d'entre nous
8. qui conduisit directement à l'arrestation
9. voleur de bijoux de Bishopsgate
10. J'ai toujours pensé
11. s'appuyait plus sur des conjectures
12. n'aurait jamais pu deviner
13. que l'homme était né avec un pied-bot
14. qu'il dresse de moi un portrait particulièrement flatteur
15. nommé par la suite « Le Signe des quatre »
16. une affaires des plus inhabituelles
17. l'alluma
18. Je m'y adonne à l'occasion.
19. Cela ne vous dérange pas ?

He shook out the match and discarded it.[1] 'I had not been a police inspector for very long at the time,' he explained. 'I had only recently been promoted. Perhaps if Dr Watson had known this, he might have been a little more charitable. At any event, I happened to be in Norwood[2] one evening in September – this was '88[3] – investigating a trifling matter[4], a housemaid who had been accused by her mistress[5] of theft[6]. I had just finished interviewing her when a messenger arrived with the news of a murder that had taken place in a house not far away and, being the most senior officer present, it was my duty to attend[7].

'That was how I came upon[8] Pondicherry Lodge[9], a great white Aladdin's Cave of a place[10], standing in its own grounds[11] with a garden that could have been a graveyard, it was filled with so many holes. The owner was one[12] Bartholomew Sholto and I will never forget my first sight of him, sitting in a wooden armchair in a study that was more like a laboratory, up on the third floor, quite dead, with a hideous grin stamped across his face[13].

'Sherlock Holmes was there. He had broken down[14] the door to get in which by rights he shouldn't have[15] because this was a police matter. It was the first time I had seen the great man at close quarters[16] and in action too, for he had already begun his investigation. What can I tell you, Chase? He was taller than I remembered, with the leanness of an aesthete[17] as if he had deliberately starved himself[18]. This gave prominence to his chin, his cheekbones and above all to his eyes which never seemed to settle on anything[19] without stripping them of all the

1. secoua l'allumette et la jeta.
2. Quoiqu'il en soit, il se trouve que j'étais à Norwood
3. c'était en 1988,
4. pour enquêter sur une affaire des plus triviales,
5. maîtresse de maison
6. vol
7. de m'en charger
8. me retrouvai à
9. Villa
10. immense palais immaculé digne d'Aladin,
11. trônant dans une propriété
12. un certain
13. un rictus hideux imprimé sur le visage
14. enfoncé
15. ce qu'il n'était en aucun droit de faire
16. de près
17. une silhouette élancée digne d'un esthète
18. comme s'il s'affamait de son plein gré
19. qui semblaient ne jamais se poser sur quoi que ce soit

information they might provide[1]. There was an energy about him, a restlessness[2] that I had never encountered in any other man. His movements were brief and economical. He gave you the sense[3] that there was no time to be wasted. He was wearing a dark frock coat[4] and no hat. When I first saw him, he was holding a tape measure[5] which he folded away[6].'

'And Dr Watson ...?'

'I took less notice of him. He stood in the shadows at the edge of the room[7], a shorter man, round-faced, genial[8].'

'I do not need to describe the details of the case. You can read them if they are of interest to you. The dead man was, as I said, Bartholomew Sholto. It transpired[9] that he and his twin brother, Thaddeus, had been bequeathed[10] a great treasure by their father. They'd had trouble finding it, mind[11], hence all the holes[12] in the garden. But the facts of the case seemed quite straightforward to me. The two of them had argued[13] as men often will when confronted by unexpected wealth[14]. Thaddeus had killed his brother using a blowpipe[15] and a poison dart[16] – I should have explained that the house was full of Indian curiosities. I arrested him and also took in[17] his servant, a man called McMurdo, as his accomplice.'

'And were you right?'

'No, sir, as it turned out, I was wrong[18]. I had made a complete fool of myself[19] and although I was not the first to do so – I had colleagues who had been in exactly the same position as I – at the time it was small consolation.'

1. sans en soutirer toutes les informations possibles
2. Il dégageait une énergie, une fébrilité
3. l'impression
4. redingote
5. mètre ruban
6. repliait
7. dans l'ombre qui bordait la pièce
8. l'air avenant
9. Il s'avéra
10. avaient hérité
11. visiblement,
12. d'où les nombreux trous
13. s'étaient querellés
14. fortune soudaine
15. sarbacane
16. fléchette empoisonnée
17. interpellai
18. il s'avéra que j'avais eu tort
19. m'étais couvert de ridicule

He fell silent[1], staring out of the window[2] at the French countryside although, from the look in his eyes, I was sure he saw none of it.

'And the third time?' I asked.

'That was a few months later … the curious business of the Abernettys. I will not discuss it now, if you don't mind. It still annoys me. It began with what seemed to be, on the face of it[3], a burglary[4] – although a very unusual one. All I will say is that once again I missed everything of importance and stood idly[5] by while Mr Holmes made the arrest. It will not happen again, Mr Chase. I promise you that.'

Jones barely[6] spoke to me for the next few hours. We made our connection in Paris quite easily and it was the second time I had crossed the city without so much as glimpsing[7] the Eiffel Tower. But what did it matter? London lay ahead of us[8] and already I was uneasy[9]. I felt that a shadow had fallen over us[10] but to whom it belonged[11] – be it[12] Holmes, Devereux or even Moriarty – I dared not say[13].

And so to London.

It has been said that good Americans, when they die, go to Paris[14]. Perhaps the less saintly variety[15] would end up like me, dragging my steamer trunk[16] from Charing Cross Station with the drivers shouting, the beggar boys[17] circling, and the crowds streaming past[18]. For this was where Inspector Jones and I parted company[19]; he to return to his home in Camberwell, I to find a hotel that would suit[20] a general operative[21] travelling on a Pinkerton's budget. I had been surprised to learn that he had a wife and child. He had

1. interrompit son récit
2. regardant par la fenêtre
3. en apparence du moins
4. cambriolage
5. restais spectateur
6. à peine
7. sans même ne serait-ce qu'entrevoir
8. pointait à l'horizon
9. mal à l'aise
10. s'était abattue sur nous
11. l'ombre de qui
12. que ce fut
13. n'aurais su le dire avec certitude
14. [citation du « Portrait de Dorian Gray » d'Oscar Wilde]
15. les moins saints du lot
16. finiraient comme moi, à traîner une malle de voyage
17. mendiants
18. au milieu du flot des passants
19. mon chemin et celui de l'inspecteur Jones se séparaient
20. conviendrait
21. détective privé

struck me[1] as a single, even a solitary, man. But he had mentioned them to me in Paris and as we disembarked from our steamship at Dover he was clutching an India rubber ball[2] and a puppet of the French policeman Flageolet[3], which he had picked up near the Gare du Nord. The revelation troubled me but I said nothing until we reached the very end of our trip.

'You will forgive me, Inspector,' I remarked, as we were preparing to go our separate ways. 'I know it is not for me to say[4], but I wonder if you should not reconsider.'

'Reconsider what?'

'This entire adventure – by which I mean the pursuit of Clarence Devereux. I may not have made it clear to you quite how ruthless, how vicious this man is[5]. Trust me when I say that you would not choose to have him as your enemy. He left a trail of bloodshed[6] behind him in New York and if he is in London, as I believe, he will certainly do the same there. Look at what happened to poor Jonathan Pilgrim! It is my task to hunt him down[7] and I have no dependants[8]. The same is not true for you and I feel uncomfortable bringing you into imminent danger.'

'It is not you who has brought me here. I am merely pursuing the enquiry[9] that was given to me by my superiors at Scotland Yard[10].'

'Devereux will have no respect for Scotland Yard or for you. Your rank[11] and position will not protect you.'

'That makes no difference.' He stopped and looked up at the dull[12] afternoon sky, for London had welcomed us with clouds and drizzle[13]. 'If this man has come to England and plans to con-

1. Je l'avais pris pour
2. serrait entre ses mains une balle en caoutchouc
3. Flageolet [nom du gendarme dans le théâtre guignol]
4. cela ne me regarde pas
5. toute la cruauté, toute la malveillance de cet homme
6. suite de cadavres
7. le traquer
8. suis sans attaches
9. poursuis simplement l'enquête
10. [siège de la police londonienne]
11. grade
12. gris
13. crachin

tinue his criminal activities as you have suggested, then he must be stopped and that is my duty.'

'There are plenty of other detectives.'[1]

'But I was the one who was sent to Meiringen.' He smiled. 'I understand your sentiments, Chase, and I will say that they do you credit[2]. It is true that I have a family. I would not do anything that would threaten their well-being and yet the choice is not mine. For better or for worse, you and I have been thrown together[3] and that is how we shall remain. If it sets your mind at ease[4], I will add, in confidence, that I would not want Lestrade, Gregson or any of my other friends and colleagues stealing the credit for hunting this man down. But here is a cab[5] approaching. I must be on my way!'

I can still see him hurrying away[6] with the ball in one hand and the blue-uniformed doll hanging limply[7] over his arm. And I wonder now as I wondered then how Dr Watson could have turned him into such a fool in his own account[8]. I have read 'The Sign of the Four' since then and can say that the Athelney Jones in that adventure bears very little similarity to[9] the man I knew and who was, I would have said, unequalled by any[10] at Scotland Yard.

There were several hotels close to the station in Northumberland Avenue but their very names[11] – the Grand, the Victoria, the Metropole – warned me they would not fit the bill in any sense of those words[12] and in the end I found somewhere on the Embankment[13], close by the bridge … so close, in fact, that the whole place rattled every time a train went past[14]. Hexam's Hotel was grimy[15] and ramshackle[16]. The carpets were threadbare[17] and

1. Les inspecteurs ne manquent pas.
2. ils sont tout à votre honneur
3. nous sommes dans le même bateau
4. Si cela vous tranquillise
5. fiacre
6. s'éloigner d'un pas pressé
7. pendant mollement
8. avait pu en faire un tel imbécile dans son récit
9. n'a pas grand-chose en commun avec
10. sans égal
11. rien que leurs noms
12. étaient bien trop pompeux pour tenir sur ma note
13. [digue et artère de Londres]
14. chaque train qui passait ébranlait tout le bâtiment
15. crasseux
16. tombait en ruines
17. élimés

the chandeliers lopsided[1]. But the sheets were clean, it only cost two shillings[2] a night, and once I had wiped the soot off the window[3], I was rewarded with a glimpse[4] of the river and a coal ship gliding slowly past[5]. I had dinner in the hotel's restaurant, alone but for[6] a scowling maid and a disgruntled Boots[7], then sat reading in my room until midnight when I eventually fell into a troubled sleep[8].

Inspector Jones and I had arranged to meet at twelve o'clock the following day outside the Café Royal on Regent Street, a full hour ahead of the assignation[9]. After much consideration – we had, after all, spent thirty hours together on the train – we had devised[10] a plan that seemed to cover every eventuality. I would wear the red tulip, posing as[11] Moriarty, while Jones would sit at a table, close enough to overhear any conversation that ensued[12]. We had both agreed that it was highly unlikely[13] that Clarence Devereux would appear in person. Apart from the unnecessary risk of his exposing himself to danger, there was the question of his agoraphobia that would make his journey down[14] Regent Street, even in a closed carriage[15], highly impractical[16]. He would surely send a confederate[17] and that person would expect to find Moriarty alone.

And then? There were three possibilities.

Hopefully[18], I would be met by someone who would escort me[19] to the house or to the hotel where Devereux was staying. In that event, Jones would follow quietly behind, to ensure my safety and also, of course, to make note of the address. Alternatively, Devereux's accomplice might know what Moriarty looked like. He would see imme-

1. penchés
2. [anciens centimes britanniques]
3. une fois que j'eus essuyé la suie sur la fenêtre
4. pus apercevoir
5. un bateau transportant du charbon qui passait lentement
6. à part
7. une domestique revêche et un groom à l'air renfrogné
8. finis par sombrer dans un sommeil agité
9. une bonne heure avant le rendez-vous
10. avions élaboré
11. me faisant passer pour
12. qui en résulteraient
13. fort improbable
14. sa traversée de
15. fiacre couvert
16. irréalisable
17. son lieutenant
18. Avec un peu chance,
19. quelqu'un se présenterait à moi et me conduirait

diately that I was a fake and walk out[1]. In this event, Jones would slip out of the[2] restaurant and follow him to wherever he had come from, which might at least give us a clue as to[3] where Devereux might be found. And finally, there was a chance that nobody would show up[4] at all. However, Moriarty's survival at Reichenbach had been widely reported in the London newspapers and we had every reason to hope that Devereux would suppose him alive[5].

I had purchased a red tulip from a flower stall[6] outside the station and was wearing it as I approached the Café Royal, located in the very epicentre[7] of the city. Chicago might have its State Street and New York the luxury of Broadway, but neither of them, I venture to say[8], came close to[9] the elegance and charm of Regent Street with its clean air and handsome classical façades. Carriages rolled past in both directions, sweeping round the curve[10] of the road in an endless stream[11]. The pavements were thronged with loungers and urchins[12], English gentlemen and foreign visitors but above all with ladies, immaculately dressed[13], accompanied by servants who struggled under the weight of their many purchases[14]. And what had they been buying? I passed windows[15] displaying perfumes, gloves and jewellery[16], vanille chocolates and ormolu clocks[17]. It seemed that there was nothing you could find here that was not expensive and very little that was actually necessary.

Jones was waiting for me, dressed in a suit, as ever leaning on his walking stick[18]. 'You found a hotel?' he asked. I gave him the name and the

1. repartirait aussitôt
2. s'esquiverait du
3. nous renseignerait sur le lieu
4. ne se montre
5. le croit toujours en vie
6. étal
7. en plein cœur
8. si j'ose dire
9. ne rivalisent avec
10. filant dans le virage
11. flot ininterrompu
12. étaient assaillis par les oisifs et les enfants des rues
13. à la toilette impeccable
14. bataillaient avec leurs lourdes emplettes
15. des vitrines
16. gants et autres bijoux
17. des pendules en bronze doré
18. appuyé sur sa canne, comme à son habitude

address. 'And you had no trouble finding this address?'

'It was only a short walk and they gave me excellent directions.'

'Good.'

Jones glanced doubtfully[1] in the direction of the Café Royal. 'This is a pretty place for a rendezvous,' he muttered[2]. 'How our man will even find you, I don't know. And following him without being observed is going to be difficult, to say the least[3].'

He had a point.[4] Even the entrance on Regent Street – three sets of doors set behind three pillars[5] – suggested too many ways in and too many ways out and once we'd entered it was unclear where we were supposed to meet as the building was a warren[6] of corridors and staircases, bars, restaurants and meeting rooms – some of them obstructed by mirrored screens[7], others partly concealed by great displays of flowers[8]. Nor did it help that[9] half of London seemed to have gathered[10] here for lunch. I had never seen such an assembly of the well-to-do[11]. Clarence Devereux and his entire gang could have already been there, planning their next murder or perhaps an armed assault on the Bank of England and we wouldn't have been able to spot[12] them. There was so much noise, we wouldn't have been able to hear them either.

We chose the café on the ground floor, which, with its high ceilings and bright, public atmosphere[13], seemed to be the most natural place for a meeting between two strangers. It was a beautiful room with turquoise pillars and gold ornamentation, top hats and billycocks hanging[14] every-

1. lança un regard dubitatif
2. grommela-t-il
3. c'est peu de le dire
4. Et il avait raison.
5. doubles portes, chacune masquée par un pilier
6. dédale
7. paravent en miroir
8. disparaissaient sous d'immenses compositions florales
9. Cela n'arrangeait guère les choses
10. semble s'être passé le mot pour se retrouver
11. un tel rassemblement de nantis
12. repérer
13. et l'animation qui régnait dans ce haut lieu de rencontre
14. des hauts-de-forme et chapeaux melons pendaient

where and people packed together at[1] marble tables while the waiters in their black tailcoats and long white aprons[2] fought their way through like circus performers[3], their overladen trays[4] almost seeming to float above their shoulders[5]. Somehow we managed to find two tables side by side. Neither Jones nor I had spoken since we came in. To anyone watching[6], it would appear that we were unaware of each other's existence[7]. I ordered a small glass of wine. Meanwhile, Jones had taken out a French newspaper and called to the waiter for a cup of tea.

We sat side by side, ignoring each other, watching as the minute hand of the clock[8] on the far wall climbed ever higher[9]. I could sense the detective growing more and more tense[10] as the hour approached. He had already persuaded himself that we were going to be disappointed and that our rush across the continent had been to no avail[11]. But at exactly one o'clock, I saw a figure appear at the doorway and scrutinise[12] the room, peering through the crowd[13]. Beside me, Jones stiffened[14] and his eyes – always serious – became suddenly alert.

The new arrival[15] was a child of about fourteen, smartly[16] dressed in the bright blue jacket and bowler hat[17] of a telegraph boy. He looked ill at ease, as if he were unused to the clothes[18] that he had been forced to wear and they certainly didn't fit him very well for the uniform was tight and trim[19] and he was the exact opposite. Indeed, with his plump stomach[20], short legs and round cheeks it struck me that he rather resembled the cupids[21] that ornamented the very room in which we sat.

1. agglutinés autour de
2. en queue de pie noire et longs tabliers blancs
3. fendaient la foule tels des acrobates
4. leurs plateaux surchargés
5. comme flottant au-dessus de leurs épaules
6. Un observateur extérieur
7. aurait été convaincu que nous nous ignorions totalement
8. suivant des yeux l'aiguille des minutes de l'horloge
9. tandis qu'elle poursuivait son ascension
10. je percevais chez l'inspecteur une tension grandissante
11. traversée du continent à la hâte avait été vaine
12. scruter
13. balayant le café bondé du regard
14. se raidit
15. nouveau venu
16. élégamment
17. casquette
18. comme si cette tenue ne lui était pas familière
19. étroit et ajusté
20. ventre protubérant
21. chérubins

1. d'un air entendu

2. se faufiler dans l'assemblée

3. Ce comportement en soi était une démonstration d'arrogance

4. indigne de sa fonction

5. en savait déjà trop pour son âge.

6. humides

7. comme s'ils n'avaient jamais rien vu d'autre que le mal

8. rauque

9. presque celle d'un homme

10. Peut-être que oui. Peut-être que non.

11. avec malice

12. Ça m'paraît pas utile

13. A quoi ça sert les noms, vu qu'on va pas vraiment s'connaître ?

14. Mais vous savez quoi ?

15. ne perdait pas une miette de notre conversation

16. tenait la page un peu plus bas

He saw me – or rather the tulip on my coat – and with a glint of recognition[1] began to make his way through the crowd[2]. He reached me and, without asking permission, sat down opposite me, crossing one foot over his knee. This in itself was a display of arrogance[3] that would have been unbecoming to his station[4] – but now that he was close, it was quite obvious that he had never worked for the telegraph office. He was too knowing.[5] There was something very strange about his eyes, which were moist[6] and empty as if they had never looked on anything that was not evil[7]. At the same time, his eyelashes were fine, his teeth white, his lips full – and the overall effect was that he was both very pretty and very ugly at the same time.

'You waiting for someone?' he asked. His voice was husky[8], almost that of a man[9].

'I might be,' I replied.

'Nice tulip. Not something you would see every day, mister, I would say.'

'A red tulip,' I agreed. 'Does it signify something to you?'

'It might do. It might not.[10]'

He fell silent.

'What is your name?' I asked.

'Do I need a name?' He winked at me, mischievously[11]. 'I wouldn't say I do[12], mister. What good is a name when one is 'ardly going to be hacquainted.[13] But I'll tell you what.[14] If you want to call me something, you can call me Perry.'

Inspector Jones was still pretending to read his newspaper but I knew that he was attending to every word that was spoken[15]. He had lowered the page a little[16] so that he could peek over the top[1] but at the same time his face was blank[2], showing no interest at all.

'Well, Perry,' I said, 'there was someone I was waiting to meet but I can say without doubt that it's not you[3].'

'Of course not, mister, my job is to bring you to 'im but first we 'ave to ascertain[4] that you is who you say you is. You got the tulip, sure enough[5]. But do you 'ave a certain letter that was sent to you by my master?'

I did indeed have the torn page[6] with the coded message. It was Jones who had suggested that I might be asked to present it[7] and so I had brought it with me. I drew it out[8] and placed it on the table.

The boy barely glanced at it[9]. 'Are you the professor?' he asked.

'I am,' I said, keeping my voice low.

'Professor Moriarty?'

'Yes.'

'Not drowned in the Reeking-back Falls?[10]'

'Why do you ask these foolish questions[11]?' This was surely how the real Moriarty would speak. 'It was your master who arranged this meeting. If you persist in wasting my time, I can assure you, you will suffer the consequences.'

But the boy was not to be intimidated[12]. 'Then tell me how many ravens flew out of the[13] Tower of London?'

'What?'

'The ravens. The tower. How many?'

It was the one eventuality we had most feared[14]. Turning over the plan[15] on our long train journey, Jones and I had discussed the likelihood of there being a recognition signal[16]. Two criminals of the

1. afin de pouvoir jeter un coup d'œil par dessus

2. neutre

3. je peux affirmer avec certitude que ce n'est pas vous

4. faut d'abord m'convaincre

5. pour sûr

6. page déchirée

7. que je puisse avoir besoin de la montrer

8. Je la sortis

9. la regarda à peine

10. Pas fini noyé dans les chutes de Riche-Barre ?

11. questions ridicules

12. ne se laissait pas intimider si facilement

13. combien de corbeaux se sont envolés depuis

14. la possibilité que nous avions le plus redoutée

15. Tournant et retournant le plan dans nos têtes

16. la probabilité qu'ils aient un signe de reconnaissance

1. envergure

2. ne se livreraient jamais l'un à l'autre

3. devinette

4. dont ils avaient dû convenir dans un autre message

5. J'esquivai la question.

6. Tu ne me feras pas croire l'inverse.

7. en hâte de partir

8. Il regarda en direction de la sortie

9. s'écarta de la table

10. et se leva

11. le saisis par le bras

12. et le maintins au sol

13. clients

14. bavardant joyeusement

15. tandis que se déroulait notre petite comédie

16. Pas la peine de se fâcher

17. mauvaise et menaçante

magnitude[1] of Clarence Devereux and Professor James Moriarty would not deliver themselves into each other's hands[2] without the certainty that they were safe. And here was the final precaution – a riddle[3] taking the form of an exchange of words which must have been agreed in a separate communication[4].

I waved the question aside.[5] 'Enough of these stupid games,' I said. 'I have travelled a long way to meet with Clarence Devereux. You know who I'm talking about. Don't pretend! I see it in your eyes.'

'You're mistaken, mister. I've never heard that name.'

'Then why are you here? You know me. You know of the letter. Don't try to pretend otherwise.[6]'

The boy was suddenly anxious to be on his way[7]. I saw him glance at the door[8] and a moment later he pulled away from the table[9], getting to his feet[10]. But before he could move, I grabbed hold of his arm[11], pinning him down[12].

'Tell me where I can find him,' I said. I was keeping my voice low, aware of the other diners[13] all around me, sipping their coffees and their wine, ordering their food, chatting animatedly[14] as they began their lunch. Athelney Jones was still sitting at his table, close to me and yet completely separate. Nobody in the room had noticed us. At that moment, as we played out our little drama[15], we were quite alone.

'There's no need to get nasty[16], mister.' Perry's voice was also low but it was ugly, filled with threat[17].

'I will not let you leave until you tell me what I want to know.'

'You're 'urting me![1]' Tears sprang to his eyes[2] as if to remind me[3] that he was, after all, only a child. But then, even as I hesitated, he twisted in my grasp[4] and suddenly I felt something pressing against my neck. How he had managed to produce it[5] with just one hand is beyond me[6] but I could feel it cutting through my skin even though he was barely exerting any pressure at all[7]. Looking down, I saw the weapon that he had withdrawn[8] from somewhere inside his jacket. It was a horrible thing – a black-handled surgeon's knife[9] with a blade that must have measured at least five inches[10]. He was holding it very carefully so that only he and I could see it although surely the gentleman at the next table might have caught sight of it[11] had he not, inexplicably, returned to[12] his French newspaper.

'Let me go,' the boy hissed[13], 'or by God[14], I'll cut your throat clean through, 'ere and now[15], and put all these nice people off their dinners[16], no mistake[17]. I've seen the blood shoot seven feet up[18] when I done it before. Come gushing out, it does.[19] Not the sort of thing you want to 'appen in a posh 'ouse like this.[20]' He pressed with his hand and I felt a trickle of blood run down the side of my neck[21].

'You're making a mistake,' I whispered. 'I am Moriarty …'

'No more fun and games, mister. You been done by them ravens.[22] I'm going to count to three …'

'There's no need for this!'

'One—'

'I'm telling you—'

'Two …'

1. Vous me faîtes mal !
2. Des larmes jaillirent dans ses yeux
3. comme pour me rappeler
4. il se dégagea de mon emprise
5. Comment il y était parvenu
6. cela me dépasse
7. n'exerçait aucune pression ou presque
8. qu'il avait dégainée
9. un scalpel à manche noir
10. une bonne dizaine de centimètres
11. l'aurait entrevu
12. s'il ne s'était pas inexplicablement replongé dans
13. souffla
14. sinon, Dieu m'en est témoin,
15. je vous trancherai la gorge moi-même devant tous ces messieurs-dames
16. de quoi leur couper l'appétit,
17. vous pouvez me croire
18. gicler jusqu'à 2 m de haut
19. Ça pisse à flots, pour sûr.
20. Pas le genre de scène à faire dans ce café chicos.
21. un filet de sang couler le long de mon cou
22. C'est les corbeaux qui t'ont trahi.

He didn't reach three. I let him go. He was a devil-child[1] and he had made it quite clear that he would happily commit murder[2], even in this public place. Meanwhile, Jones had done nothing, although he must have seen what was happening. Would he have stood by[3] and let the boy murder me in plain sight[4] to achieve his aim[5]? The boy hurried away, weaving through[6] the crowd. I snatched up a napkin[7] and held it against my neck. When I looked up again, Jones was on his feet, moving away.

'Is everything all right, monsieur?' A waiter had appeared, conjuring himself up from nowhere[8], and hovered over me[9], his face filled with alarm[10].

I took away the napkin and saw a smear of bright red blood on the linen[11]. 'It's nothing,' I said. 'A small accident.'

I hurried to the door but by the time I reached the street[12] it was too late. Both Inspector Jones and the boy who called himself Perry had gone.

1. C'était l'enfant du diable
2. qu'il n'hésiterait pas à tuer
3. Serait-il resté sans rien faire
4. à la vue de tous
5. pour parvenir à ses fins
6. se faufilant à travers
7. m'emparai d'une serviette
8. comme sorti de nulle part
9. restait campé devant moi,
10. le visage marqué par l'inquiétude
11. souillure de sang écarlate sur le linge
12. lorsque je gagnai la rue

SIX

Bladeston House

I didn't see Jones until the following day when he came hurrying into my hotel, full of the same nervous energy that I had witnessed when he was deciphering[1] the message taken from the dead man's pocket. I had just breakfasted when he arrived and sat down opposite me.

'This is where you're staying[2], Chase?' He looked around him at the shabby wallpaper[3] and the few tables positioned close to one another on the well-trodden carpet[4]. I had been kept awake half the night by a man with a racking cough[5] who, for some reason, had been given the room next to mine. I had expected him to join me in the breakfast room but so far he had not shown himself[6]. Apart from this one mysterious guest, I was alone at Hexam's and frankly I was not surprised. It wasn't the sort of accommodation[7] that Baedeker or Murray[8] would have recommended, unless it was to avoid[9]. Accordingly, we had the breakfast room to ourselves.[10] 'Well, I suppose it will do well enough[11]. Not quite the Clarendon[12] but things are proceeding apace[13] and with luck, it may only be a matter of weeks[14] before you are on your way back to New York.' He rested his

1. dont j'avais été témoin tandis qu'il décryptait

2. C'est l'hôtel que vous avez choisi

3. tapisserie défraîchie

4. tapis élimé

5. une toux à se râper la gorge

6. il ne s'était pas montré jusque-là

7. le type d'hôtel

8. [éditeurs de guides touristiques]

9. auraient mentionné, si ce n'est pour le déconseiller

10. En conséquence, nous avions la salle du petit-déjeuner pour nous.

11. cela fera l'affaire

12. [hôtel de standing]

13. l'affaire progresse à grands pas

14. ce ne sera l'affaire que de quelques semaines

stick against the table[1] and suddenly he was more solicitous[2]. 'You were not hurt, I trust[3]. I saw the boy produce[4] the knife and didn't know what to do.'

'You could have stopped him.'

'And given us both away?[5] From the look of him[6], he wasn't the sort to yield under pressure[7]. If I had arrested him, it would have achieved nothing[8].'

I ran a finger along[9] the mark that Perry had left on my neck. 'It was a close-run thing[10],' I said. 'He could have cut my throat.'

'Forgive me, my friend. I had to make a judgement. I had no time to think.'

'Well, I suppose you acted for the best[11]. But you see now what I was trying to tell you, Inspector. These are vicious people, utterly without qualms[12]. A child of no more than fourteen! And[13] in a crowded restaurant! It almost beggars belief.[14] Fortunately, he didn't hurt me. The more important question is, did he lead you to[15] Clarence Devereux?'

'Not to Devereux. No. It was a pretty chase across London[16], I can tell you. All the way up Regent Street to Oxford Circus and then east to Tottenham Court Road. I would have lost him in the crowd but we were fortunate[17] that he was wearing a bright blue coat. I had to keep my distance though and it was just as well I did[18] for he turned round several times[19] to ensure he was not being followed. Even so[20], I almost lost him at Tottenham Court Road. He had climbed onto an omnibus and I only just spotted him[21] as he took his place on the knife-board[22], up on the roof.'

1. Il appuya sa canne contre la table
2. fit soudain preuve d'une certaine sollicitude
3. j'espère
4. sortir
5. Au risque de nous trahir tous les deux ?
6. À le voir
7. céder sous la pression
8. cela n'aurait abouti à rien
9. passais un doigt sur
10. C'était un pari risqué
11. j'imagine que vous avez fait pour le mieux
12. totalement dénués de scrupules
13. Qui plus est,
14. Cela dépasse l'entendement.
15. vous a-t-il conduit jusqu'à
16. Une course-poursuite à travers Londres
17. c'était une chance
18. et j'ai été bien inspiré de le faire
19. parce qu'il ne cessait de se retourner
20. Malgré tout
21. et je l'ai seulement aperçu
22. [plate-forme découverte d'un omnibus à cheval londonien]

'You were fortunate, again, that he did not sit inside[1].'

'Perhaps. I flagged down a hansom that was heading the right way[2] and we followed. I must say I was glad not to have to walk much further[3], particularly when we began to climb up towards the northern suburbs[4].'

'That was where the boy went?'

'Indeed. Perry — if that was his name – led me to the Archway Tavern and from there he took the cable tramway[5] up to Highgate Village. I travelled with him, he in the front compartment[6], I in the back.'

'And then?'

'Well, from the tramway[7], I followed the boy a short way back down the hill and along[8] Merton Lane. The sight of it caused me some alarm[9], I will admit, for was it not here that the body of your agent, Jonathan Pilgrim, was discovered? At any event, he continued to a house completely surrounded by a high wall[10] on the edge[11] of the Southampton Estate and it was here that, finally, I lost him. As he approached his destination, he hastened his step[12]. You will have observed, Chase, that I do not enjoy the best of health[13], and I was still some distance away when I saw the boy disappear behind the wall. I hurried forward but by the time I had turned the corner, he had gone[14]. I did not actually see him go into the house but there could still be no doubt of it. At the back was an empty field with a couple of shrubs[15]. No sign of him there. A few more residences stood close by, but if he had been making for any of them[16], I would have surely seen him as he moved across[17]. No. Bladeston House

1. qu'il ne s'asseye pas à l'intérieur
2. J'ai hélé un fiacre qui prenait la même direction
3. j'étais soulagé de ne plus avoir à marcher
4. grimper en direction des faubourgs nord
5. tramway électrique
6. dans le wagon de tête
7. en descendant du tramway
8. qui est redescendu un peu de la colline et s'est engagé sur
9. Je n'étais pas tranquille en voyant ce nom
10. entourée de tous côtés par un haut mur
11. à la lisière
12. pressait le pas
13. je suis loin d'avoir une santé de fer
14. il avait disparu
15. bordé d'arbustes ici et là
16. mais s'il s'était dirigé vers l'une d'entre elles,
17. je l'aurais assurément vu traverser

1. Ça ne pouvait être que Bladeston House.
2. n'avaient sciemment rien fait pour y remédier
3. piques
4. Toutes les fenêtres ont des barreaux.
5. [serrure réputée incrochetable]
6. que seul le plus virtuose des cambrioleurs
7. crocheter
8. montai la garde
9. à l'aide d'un instrument qui s'est souvent révélé utile
10. le large pommeau en argent
11. se détachait pour former une paire de jumelles
12. ce qui m'inclinait à croire
13. qu'il n'était pas venu transmettre
14. Je brûlais de le faire.
15. que nous devrions y aller ensemble
16. C'est très délicat de votre part.
17. je ne suis pas resté oisif
18. au-dessus de tout soupçon
19. louent la propriété depuis six mois
20. En personne.

it had to be.[1] There was a gate set in the wall in the back. That must have been where he entered. It was locked.

'Bladeston House is not a particularly welcoming place and it is my opinion that the occupants had made it their business to keep it so[2]. A wall surmounted with metal spikes[3] surrounds it. Every window is barred.[4] There was a Chubb patent lock[5] in the garden door, which only the most accomplished burglar[6] would be able to crack[7]. Might the boy come out again? I retreated some distance and kept watch[8] using a device which I have often found useful[9] …' He gestured at the walking stick and for the first time I saw that the cumbersome silver handle[10] I had noticed earlier could unfold to become a pair of binoculars[11]. 'There was no sign of Perry, leading me to conclude[12] that he could not have been delivering[13] another message. He must surely live there.'

'You did not go in?'

'I very much wanted to.[14]' Jones smiled. 'But it seemed to me that we should do so together[15]. This is as much your investigation as mine.'

'You are very considerate.[16]'

'However, I have not been idle[17],' he continued. 'I have made certain enquiries which I think may be of interest to you. Bladeston House is the property of George Bladeston, the publisher, who died last year. His family is unimpeachable[18]. They rented the property out six months ago[19] to an American businessman who goes by the name of Scott Lavelle.'

'Scotchy Lavelle!' I exclaimed.

'The same.[20] This is undoubtedly Devereux's lieutenant, the man of whom you spoke.'

'And Devereux himself?'

'Lavelle can lead us to him. I see you have finished your breakfast. Shall we leave straight away? For I tell you, Chase, the game is very much afoot[1].'

I needed no further encouragement[2] and together we followed the same trail that the child Perry had set down for us[3] the day before, continuing through the heart of the capital, up into the suburbs, finally travelling on the cable tramway which pulled us effortlessly up the hill[4].

'This is a remarkable device[5],' I exclaimed.

'It's a shame I cannot show you more of the area. There are some fine views from the Heath, which is nearby. Highgate was once a village in its own right[6] but I fear it has lost much of its charm.'

'That happened the day Scotchy Lavelle arrived,' I said. 'When he and his friends have been dealt with[7], we will both enjoy the city more.'

We reached the house, which was just as Jones had described only grimmer[8], more determined to keep its distance from the world outside. It was not a handsome building, taller than it was wide and built out of dull grey bricks, more suited to[9] the city than the countryside. Its architecture was Gothic with an elaborate archway[10] constructed over the front door and pointed windows covered with tracery[11], gargoyles and all the rest of it[12]. Jones had certainly been right about the security measures. Gates, spikes, bars, shutters ...[13] the last time I had seen a building like this, I had been looking at a prison. Any casual visitor[14], or indeed a thief in the night[15], would have found

1. il se trame quelque chose
2. Il n'en fallait pas davantage pour me convaincre
3. avait tracée pour nous
4. qui nous hissa sans peine sur la colline
5. Quel remarquable engin !
6. à part entière
7. Une fois que nous nous serons chargés de sa joyeuse bande
8. si ce n'est plus sinistre encore
9. qui se prêtaient plus
10. agrémentée d'une voûte travaillée
11. de fenêtres ogivales ornées de remplage,
12. de gargouilles et le reste à l'avenant
13. Grille, piques, barreaux, persiennes...
14. Le visiteur qui se présente à l'improviste
15. comme le cambrioleur du beau milieu de la nuit

entrance impossible, but then knowing these people as I did I had expected nothing less[1].

We were not even able to approach the front door as there was an ornate metal gate set in the wall[2], separating the entrance from the street, and this too was locked[3]. Jones rang a bell for attention[4].

'Is there anyone in?' I asked.

'I see a movement behind the window,' he replied. 'We are being watched.[5] Suspicious minds, they must have here. Ah! Their man approaches …'

A footman[6], dressed all in black, walked to us at such a mournful pace[7] that he might have been about to[8] announce that no visit was possible because the master of the house[9] was dead. He reached the gate and spoke to us from the other side of the bars.

'May I help you?[10]'

'We are here to see Mr Lavelle,' Jones said.

'I am afraid[11] Mr Lavelle is not receiving visitors today,' the footman returned[12].

'I am Inspector Jones of Scotland Yard,' Jones replied. 'He will most certainly receive me.[13] And if you don't open this gate in five seconds, Clayton, you'll be back in Newgate where you belong[14].'

The servant looked up, startled[15], and examined my companion more closely. 'Mr Jones!' he exclaimed in quite a different voice. 'Lord, sir, I didn't recognise you.'

'Well, I never forget a face, Clayton, and it gives me no pleasure to see yours.' As the footman fumbled in[16] his pocket for the keys and opened the gate, Jones turned to me and said, in a low voice,

1. je n'en attendais pas moins
2. une grille richement décorée et intégrée au mur d'enceinte
3. elle aussi verrouillée
4. pour manifester notre présence
5. On nous observe.
6. valet de pied
7. d'un pas si lugubre
8. qu'il aurait tout aussi bien pu être sur le point d'
9. le maître des lieux
10. Puis-je vous aider ?
11. J'ai bien peur que
12. répliqua le valet
13. Il a plutôt intérêt à me recevoir.
14. à la prison de Newgate où tu aurais mieux fait de rester
15. leva les yeux, surpris
16. fouillait avec empressement

'Six months for dog-sneaking[1] the last time we met. It seems Mr Lavelle is none too fussy about the company he keeps[2].'

Clayton opened the gate and led us into the house, struggling to regain his composure with every step[3]. 'What can you tell us of your new master?' Jones demanded[4].

'I can tell you nothing, sir. He is an American gentleman. He is very private[5].'

'I'm sure. How long have you worked for him?'

'Since January.'

'I guess he didn't ask for a reference' I muttered[6].

'I will tell Mr Lavelle you are here,' Clayton said.

He left us alone in a vast, shadowy[7] entrance hall whose walls, rising high above us, were covered with wooden panelling of the gloomiest sort[8]. A massive staircase, uncarpeted[9], led up to the second floor which took the form of a galleried walkway open on every side[10] so that we could be observed from any one of a number of upper doorways[11] without knowing it. Even the pictures on the walls were dark and miserable[12] – winter scenes of frozen lakes and trees bereft of leaves[13]. Two wooden chairs had been set on either side of a fireplace[14] but it was hard to imagine anyone wishing to sit in them[15], even for a moment, in this gloomy place.

Clayton returned. 'Mr Lavelle will see you in his study.'

We were shown into[16] a room filled with books that had never been read – they had a musty, unloved look about them[17]. As we entered, a man glared at us from behind a monstrous Jacobean desk[18] and for a moment, I thought he was about to attack us. His appearance was that of a

1. Six mois pour trafic de chiens
2. n'est pas du genre regardant sur ses fréquentations
3. essayant de retrouver une contenance à chaque pas
4. le questionna Jones avec autorité
5. secret
6. murmurai-je entre mes dents
7. plongé dans la pénombre
8. ornés de boiseries des plus mornes
9. dépourvu de moquette
10. une galerie ouverte de part et d'autre
11. depuis l'une des nombreuses portes à l'étage supérieur
12. moroses
13. dépouillés de leurs feuilles
14. encadraient une cheminée
15. tenté de s'asseoir
16. Il nous introduit dans
17. ils donnaient une impression de renfermé et de délaissement
18. nous foudroya du regard depuis un immense bureau jacobin

1. Il avait l'allure d'un boxeur de rue
2. quand bien même il n'en portait pas la tenue
3. chauve
4. avec un nez retroussé
5. un costume à motif voyant
6. les pierres rivalisant de mauvais goût
7. tape-à-l'œil et assez dérangeant
8. s'étaient ratatinés pour tenter de tenir dans son col
9. je l'identifiai aussitôt
10. dans le décor d'une villa des faubourgs londoniens
11. nous interrogea-t-il, visiblement irrité
12. Et d'abord c'est qui, lui ?
13. Un ramassis de bons à rien et de traîtres.
14. le parler vulgaire des quartiers sud de Manhattan
15. et encore moins dans ma piaule, circulez y'a rien à voir
16. Je n'ai pas plus à faire avec vous.
17. l'un de vos comparses

prizefighter[1] even if he did not dress the part[2]. He was completely bald[3] with an upturned nose[4] and very small eyes that were set deep in his face. He was wearing a boldly patterned suit[5] that fitted him tightly and he wore a ring on almost every finger of both his hands, the gaudy stones fighting with each other[6]. One might have been acceptable but the overall effect was tawdry and strangely unpleasant[7]. The folds of his neck had bunched up as they sought a way to enter his collar[8] and I knew him at once[9]. Scotchy Lavelle. It seemed strange to be meeting him for the first time in the surroundings of a suburban house[10], thousands of miles from New York.

There were two seats opposite the desk and although he had given us no invitation, we took them. It signalled at least our determination to stay.

'Now what is all this?' he demanded[11]. 'Inspector Jones of Scotland Yard? What are you doing here? What do you want? I've got nothing to say to you.' He noticed me. 'And who's he with you?[12]'

'My name is Frederick Chase,' I replied. 'I'm with the Pinkerton Agency in New York.'

'Pinkerton's! A ragbag of bums and backstabbers.[13] How far do I have to go to be away from them?' He was using the coarse language of the lower Manhattan streets[14]. 'There's no Pinkerton's over here and I won't speak to you, not in my own crib, thank you very much[15].' He turned to Jones. 'Scotland Yard, you say! I have no business with you either.[16] I've done nothing wrong.'

'We are looking for an associate of yours[17],' Jones explained. 'A man called Clarence Devereux.'

'I don't know the name. I never heard it. He's no associate. He's nothing to me.' Lavelle's small, pugnacious eyes dared us to challenge him[1].

'You did not travel with him to England?'

'Didn't you just hear me?[2] How could I travel with someone I never met?'

'Your accent tells me that you are American,' Jones tried. 'Can you tell me what brings you to England[3]?'

'Can I tell you? Maybe I can – but I don't know why the blazes I should[4].' He jabbed a single finger[5] towards us. 'All right, all right. I'm a company promoter.[6] Nothing wrong with that! I raise capital.[7] I offer opportunities for investment. You want shares[8] in soap, candles, bootlaces or what have you[9], I'm your man. Maybe I can interest you in an investment, Mr Jones? Or you, Mr Pinkerton? A nice little gold mine in Sacramento. Or coal and iron in Vermissa.[10] You'll get a better return than a catch-pole's salary[11], I can promise you.'

Lavelle was taunting us[12]. We both knew the truth of his connection to Devereux and he was well aware of it. But with no evidence of any crime, planned or committed[13], there was little we could do.

Inspector Jones tried a second time[14]. 'Yesterday I followed a young man – a child – to this house. He was fair-haired[15], dressed in the uniform of a telegraph boy. Did you meet with him?'

'Why would I have done that?' Lavelle sneered. 'I may have received a telegraph. I may not.[16] I don't know. You'll have to ask Clayton,'

'I saw the boy come into the house. He did not leave.'

1. nous défiaient de remettre en cause ses dires

2. Vous êtes sourd ?

3. ce qui vous amène en Angleterre

4. y'a rien qui m'y oblige, parbleu

5. pointa un doigt menaçant

6. conseiller en investissement

7. Je lève des fonds.

8. des actions

9. les lacets, ou tout ce qui vous chante

10. Ou alors le charbon et le fer de Vermissa.

11. Ca offre plus de profits qu'un salaire de limier

12. nous provoquait ouvertement

13. Mais sans la moindre preuve d'un crime, ni planifié ni avéré

14. tenta une autre approche

15. blond

16. Il se peut que j'ai reçu un télégramme. Ou peut-être pas.

'Sitting there with your peeper, were you?[1] Measuring me?[2] Well, there's no squeakers here, telegraph or otherwise[3].'

'Who resides here?'

'What's it to you?[4] Why should I tell you that? I've already said. I'm a respectable businessman. You can ask about me at the legation[5], why don't you? They'll vouch for me.[6]'

'If you do not wish to assist us, Mr Lavelle, we can return here with a warrant[7] and a dozen officers. If you are as you say you are[8], then you will answer my questions.'

Lavelle yawned and scratched the back of his neck[9]. He was still scowling at us[10] but I could see that he had weighed up his options[11] and knew he had no choice but[12] to give us what we demanded.

'There are five of us[13],' he said. 'No, six. Myself and my woman, Clayton, the cook, the maid and the kitchen boy.'

'You said there were no children here.'

'He's no child. He's nineteen. And he's a ginger.[14]'

'We would still like to meet him,' I interposed[15]. 'Where is he?'

'Where do you think you'll find a kitchen boy?' Lavelle snarled[16]. 'He's in the kitchen.' He tapped the fingers of one hand against the desk, making the jewelled rings dance.[17] 'I'll fetch him for you.'

'We will go to him[18],' I said.

'Want to nosey around, do you?[19] Very well. But after that you can hop the twig.[20] You have no reason to be here, I tell you, and I've had enough of the both of you.'

1. Vous étiez venu me reluquer, c'est ça ?
2. Vous voulez mes mesures ?
3. y'a pas de squatteurs ici, ni télégraphe ni quoi que ce soit
4. Qu'est-ce que ça peut vous faire ?
5. Vous n'avez qu'à vous renseigner au consulat
6. Ils vous diront que du bien de moi.
7. mandat
8. Si vous êtes aussi respectable que vous le prétendez
9. bâilla et se gratta la nuque
10. nous regardait toujours d'un sale œil
11. soupesé ses options
12. qu'il n'avait d'autre choix que
13. Nous sommes cinq
14. Il est rouquin de toute façon.
15. objectai-je
16. aboya
17. faisant danser ses bagouses
18. C'est plutôt nous qui allons le trouver
19. Ca vous démange de fouiner partout, hein ?
20. débarrassez le plancher.

He rose up from behind the desk, the movement reminding me of a swimmer breaking the surface of the sea. As he revealed himself to us, he seemed to shrink in size, with the huge desk looming over him[1]. At the same time, it seemed to me that the lurid[2] colour and tight fit of his suit along with his surfeit of jewellery only diminished him further[3].

He was already moving to the door. 'This way!' he commanded.

Like supplicants who had just been interviewed[4] for a menial position in his household[5], Jones and I followed. We recrossed the hall and this time we were met by[6] a woman coming down the stairs, a great deal[7] younger than Lavelle and, like him, dressed extravagantly, in her case in swathes of crimson silk[8] that hugged her ample form rather too closely[9]. Her neckline was low enough to have caused a commotion[10] had she walked onto[11] the streets of Boston and her arms were bare[12]. A string of diamonds – real or paste[13], I could not say – hung around her neck.

'Who is it, Scotchy?' she asked. She had a Bronx accent. Even at a distance, I could smell soap and lavender[14] water.

'It's no one,' Lavelle snapped[15], doubtless annoyed that she had betrayed him by using the name by which he was known to myself and to many law enforcers[16] across America.

'I've been waiting for you.' She had the whining voice of a schoolgirl dragged unwillingly to class[17]. 'You said we were going out ...'

'Shut the potato trap and give the red rag a holiday.[18]'

'Scotchy?'

1. comparé au bureau dont l'imposante stature le dominait
2. criarde
3. et son étalage de bijoux le rabaissaient encore davantage
4. Tels des va-nu-pieds qui venaient de passer un entretien
5. pour un poste subalterne au service de la maisonnée
6. nous tombâmes nez à nez avec
7. bien plus
8. enveloppée, elle, de kilomètres de soie pourpre
9. qui épousaient d'un peu trop près sa plantureuse silhouette
10. décolleté était si plongeant qu'elle aurait fait sensation
11. si elle avait arpenté ainsi
12. nus.
13. Une rivière de diamants, véritables ou imitations
14. de lavande
15. asséna
16. policiers
17. voix plaintive d'une écolière traînée en classe à contrecœur
18. Boucle-la et épargne-moi tes jacassements.

'Just get upstairs and wait for me, Hen[1]. I'll tell you when I'm ready for you.'

Pouting, the woman hitched up her skirts[2], turned and ran up the way she had come.

'Your wife?' Jones enquired.

'My convenience.[3] What's it to you? I met her in a goosing slum[4] and brought her with me when I travelled. This way ...'

He led us across the hall and through a doorway into the kitchen, a cavernous room where three people were busily occupied. Clayton had laid out the silver[5], which he was polishing, each implement receiving the most careful attention[6]. The ginger-haired kitchen boy, a lanky, pockmarked lad[7] who did not resemble Perry in the least[8], was sitting in the scullery[9], peeling vegetables. A rather severe woman with grey hair and an apron[10] was stirring a large pot on the cooking range[11] and the whole room was filled with the smell of curry. Every surface in the kitchen had been scrubbed clean[12]. The floor, black and white tiles[13], was immaculate. Two large windows and a glass-panelled door looked out into[14] the garden, providing natural light, and yet, even so, I had a sense that this was a gloomy place[15]. As in the rest of the house, the windows were barred, the door locked. It would be easy to believe that these people were being held here against their will[16].

They stopped what they were doing when we came in. The kitchen boy got to his feet. Lavelle stood in the doorway, his broad shoulders almost touching the frames[17]. 'These men want to talk to you,' he muttered, as if no further explanation was required.

1. [diminutif]
2. La femme troussa ses jupes en faisant la moue
3. Ma commodité.
4. dans un claque
5. avait sorti l'argenterie
6. prêtant la plus grande attention à la moindre petite cuillère
7. un môme dégingandé à la peau grêlée
8. le moins du monde
9. arrière-cuisine
10. tablier
11. remuait le contenu d'une marmite sur le feu
12. avait été récurée à fond
13. carrelage
14. et une porte vitrée donnaient sur
15. je ne pouvais me défaire de cette impression lugubre
16. étaient retenus entre ces murs contre leur gré
17. cadre de la porte

'Thank you, Mr Lavelle,' I said. 'And as we know how busy you are, we will not ask you to stay. Clayton can show us out[1] when we are done.'

He wasn't too pleased about that, but went anyway.[2] Jones said nothing but I could see he was surprised that I had dismissed Lavelle in this manner[3] and it occurred to me that I had behaved, perhaps, a touch impetuously[4]. However, this was my investigation too, and as much as I looked up to Jones[5], I surely had a right to make my presence felt[6].

'My name is Inspector Athelney Jones,' my companion began. 'I am making enquiries about[7] a man called Clarence Devereux. Does that name mean anything to you?'

None of them spoke.

'Yesterday, shortly after two o'clock in the afternoon, I saw a boy enter this house. I had followed him here from Regent Street.[8] He was wearing a bright blue coat[9] and a hat. I see that the path leads directly to this room.[10] Were any of you here when he came in?'

'I was here all afternoon,' the cook mumbled[11]. 'There was only me and Thomas and we didn't see no one.'

Thomas, the kitchen boy, nodded in agreement[12].

'What were you doing?' I asked.

She looked at me insolently. 'Cooking!'

'Luncheon[13] or dinner?'

'Both!'

'And what are you cooking now?'

'Mr and Mrs Lavelle are going out today. This is for tonight. And those vegetables ...' she nodded

1. nous escortera vers la sortie

2. Cette perspective ne l'enchantait guère, mais il partit.

3. de me voir congédier Lavelle sans plus de formes

4. j'avais fait preuve, peut-être, d'une certaine impulsivité

5. j'avais beau admirer profondément Jones

6. d'affirmer ma présence

7. J'enquête sur

8. l'ai suivi jusqu'ici depuis Regent Street.

9. veste bleu vif

10. Je constate que l'allée mène directement à cette pièce.

11. marmonna la cuisinière

12. hocha la tête en signe d'approbation

13. Pour le déjeuner

1. elle fit un signe de tête en direction de Thomas
2. interjeta Clayton
3. Pour le peu de visiteurs qu'on reçoit de toute façon.
4. n'a pas utilisé l'entrée principale
5. Elle est verrouillée des deux côtés.
6. Pourquoi donc ?
7. Vous faites ce qu'on vous dit et puis c'est tout.
8. traîna des pieds jusqu'au buffet
9. à côté, un tableau sur lequel pendait une dizaine de clés
10. la tournant dans l'une des myriades de serrures compliquées
11. qui assuraient la sécurité de la villa
12. car ils avaient été autrefois bien entretenus
13. mais semblaient d'ores et déjà à l'abandon
14. et Jones qui fermait la marche en claudiquant
15. un loquet avec un second verrou sur la face intérieure
16. qui bloquait la porte contre le chambranle

at Thomas[1], '... is for tomorrow. And then we'll start work on the day after!'

'No one came to the house,' Clayton cut in[2]. 'If they had rung the bell, I would have answered it. And we don't get many callers here.[3] Mr Lavelle don't encourage 'em.'

'The boy didn't come in the front way[4],' I said. 'He entered through the garden door.'

'That's not possible,' Clayton said. 'It's locked both sides.[5]'

'I would like to see it.'

'To what purpose?[6]'

'I don't think it's your business to ask questions, Clayton. It is simply to do as I say.[7]'

'Very well, sir.'

He put down the fork that he had been polishing and lumbered over to the dresser[8], an oversized piece of furniture that dominated an entire wall. I had noticed a panel with a dozen keys hanging beside it[9] and he carefully selected one, then used it to open the kitchen door, turning it in yet another of the complicated locks[10] that lent themselves to the security of the house[11]. The three of us – Jones, Clayton and myself – stepped into the garden. A curving path led to the wooden gate at the bottom with lawns and flowerbeds on either side. I suspected these had been planted by the former residents, for they had once been neat[12] and symmetrical but were already in a state of some neglect[13]. I led the way, with Clayton next to me and Jones limping behind[14]. In this way we came to the door that we had observed from outside and saw that, as well as the Chubb lock, there was a metal hasp with a second lock on the inside[15], securing the door to the frame[16]. It would have been very difficult to scale the wall[1], which was topped with sharp spikes[2] and which would, furthermore, be in full sight of the house. Nor could anybody have jumped down. They would certainly have left footmarks in the lawn.

'Do you have the key to this lock?' Jones asked, indicating the metal hasp[3].

'I have it in the house,' Clayton replied. 'But this gate is never used, Mr Jones, despite what you and this other gentleman may say. We're very careful in this house. Nobody comes in except through the front door[4] and the keys are themselves kept in a safe place.' He paused. 'Do you want me to open it?'

'Two locks – one inside, one out. Both of them, I would have said, added recently[5]. What is it your employer fears?' I asked.

'Mr Lavelle does not discuss his affairs with me.' Clayton sneered at me[6]. 'Have you seen enough?' It struck me that his manner was deliberately impertinent. Although he had encountered Athelney Jones in his former life[7], he had no fear of me.

'I will not tell you what I have or have not seen,' I returned. But he was right. There was no reason to stay any longer.

We went back to the kitchen. Once again, I was the first to enter and I saw that the cook and the kitchen boy had returned to their work as if they had forgotten we had called[8]. Thomas was in the scullery and the old woman had joined him, selecting onions from a shelf one at a time[9] as if she suspected that they might be counterfeit[10]. Finally Jones arrived and the footman once more locked the door behind him and returned the key to its place. It was clear that there was nothing more to

1. d'escalader le mur
2. surmonté de piques aiguisées
3. en désignant le loquet métallique
4. Personne n'y entre autrement que par la grande porte
5. Les deux m'ont tout l'air d'ajouts récents.
6. rétorqua Clayton avec mépris
7. croisé le chemin d'Athelney Jones dans une vie précédente
8. notre visite
9. choisissant un à un les oignons sur l'étagère
10. comme si elle redoutait les contrefaçons

1. à la recherche du petit télégraphiste
2. mais à quoi bon
3. cachettes, et peut-être quelques panneaux coulissants aussi
4. laissés par un homme ou un garçon
5. d'après les preuves dont nous disposons
6. que le loquet ait été ouvert
7. dans l'anticipation de sa venue
8. Pour autant, prenez en compte ce qui suit.
9. à son insu
10. qu'il se soit rendu ailleurs
11. sa véracité, quoique improbable, ne saurait être ignorée
12. Alors, que faire ?
13. Il faut nous en remettre aux autorités compétentes

be said. We could perhaps have demanded to be allowed to search the house for the missing telegraph boy[1] but what would that achieve[2]? A place like this would have a hundred hiding places and possibly secret panels too[3]. Jones nodded at Clayton and we left.

'I do not think the boy came to the house,' I said as we stood, once more, on the other side of the front gate.

'Why do you believe that?'

'I searched around the garden door. There was no sign of any footprints, man or boy[4]. And he could not have opened the door from the outside as there was a metal hasp within.'

'I saw it myself, Chase. And I agree that, from the evidence[5], it would seem impossible for the boy to have entered, unless, of course, the hasp had been unfastened[6] in expectation of his arrival[7]. And yet consider this.[8] I followed him and, unwittingly[9], he brought me directly to the house of Scotchy Lavelle, a man familiar to you and a known associate of Clarence Devereux. This must have been where he came unless Devereux himself is living somewhere nearby and, as I told you, it is impossible that he went elsewhere[10]. When the evidence leads to only one possible conclusion, the truth of it, no matter how unlikely, cannot be ignored[11]. I believe the boy entered the house and I believe he may still be there.'

'Then what are we to do?[12]'

'We must seek the proper authority[13] and return to make a full search.'

'If the boy knows we are looking for him, he will leave.'

'Maybe so[1], but I would like to speak to that woman of Lavelle's[2]. Henrietta – was that her name? She may be more nervous of the police than he.[3] As for Clayton, he may be too afraid to talk for the moment, but I will make him see sense[4]. Trust me, Chase. There will be something in the house that will direct us along the next step of the way[5].'

'To Clarence Devereux![6]'

'Precisely. If the two men are in communication with one another, which they must be[7], we will find the link.'

We did return, as it happened, the very next day[8] – but not to make the search that Jones anticipated. For by the time the sun had risen once again over Highgate Hill[9], Bladeston House would have become the scene of a peculiarly horrible and utterly baffling[10] crime.

1. C'est bien possible

2. cette femme qui vit avec Lavelle

3. Elle est peut-être plus nerveuse face à la police que lui.

4. je vais le raisonner

5. qui nous mènera à l'étape suivante

6. Et à Clarence Devereux !

7. ce qui ne fait aucun doute

8. Nous y sommes bien retournés comme prévu le jour suivant

9. Car, quand le soleil se lèverait de nouveau sur Highgate Hill

10. tout à fait déconcertant

SEVEN

Blood and Shadows

It was the maid who discovered the bodies and who awoke the neighbourhood with her screams the next morning. Contrary to what her employer had told us, Miss Mary Stagg did not live in the house and it was for that simple reason that she did not die there. Mary shared a small cottage with her sister, who was also in service[1], in Highgate Village, the two of them having inherited it from their parents. She had not been at Bladeston House when we were there – it happened to be her day off[2] and she and her sister had gone shopping. She had presented herself the following morning, just as the sun was rising, to clear the hearths[3] and to help prepare the breakfast and had been puzzled to find both[4] the front gate and the front door open. Such an unusual lapse of security[5] should have warned her that something was seriously amiss[6] but she had continued forward, doubtless whistling a tune[7], only to encounter[8] a scene of horror she would remember to the end of her days.

Even I had to steel myself[9] as I climbed down from the barouche which had been sent to collect me[10]. Athelney Jones was waiting at the door

1. domestique elle aussi
2. il se trouve qu'elle était de repos
3. pour ôter les cendres des âtres
4. avait été troublée de trouver à la fois
5. Un tel manquement aux règles de sécurité
6. que quelque chose ne tournait pas rond
7. sifflotant sans doute un air
8. juste avant de découvrir
9. Moi-même, je m'efforçai de me préparer
10. du fiacre qu'on m'avait envoyé

and one look at his face[1] – pale and disgusted – warned me[2] that this was a scene of horror which he, with all his experience[3], had never encountered before.

'What snakepit have we uncovered[4], Chase?' he demanded, when he saw me. 'To think[5] that you and I were here only yesterday. Was it our visit that in some way, unwittingly, led to this bloodbath[6]?'

'Lavelle …?' I asked.

'All of them! Clayton, the ginger-haired boy, the cook, the mistress … they have all been murdered.'

'How?'

'You will see. Four of them died in their beds. Maybe they should be grateful.[7] But Lavelle …' He drew a breath.[8] 'This is as bad as Swallow Gardens or Pinchin Street – the very worst of the worst[9].'

Together, we went into the house. There were seven or eight police officers present, creeping slowly and silently in the shadows[10] as if they might somehow wish themselves away[11]. The hall, which had seemed dark when I first entered, had become significantly darker[12] and there was the heavy smell of the butcher's shop in the air[13]. I became aware of the buzzing of flies[14] and at the same time saw what might have been a thick pool of tar[15] on the floor.

'Good God![16]' I exclaimed and brought my hand to my eyes[17], half covering them whilst unable to avoid staring at[18] the scene that presented itself to me.

Scotchy Lavelle was sitting in one of the heavy wooden chairs that I had noticed the day before

1. un simple coup d'œil à son visage
2. suffit à m'avertir
3. malgré ces années d'expérience
4. Quel nid de vipères avons-nous découvert
5. Quand je pense
6. a, bien malgré nous, provoqué ce bain de sang
7. Ils devraient s'estimer heureux.
8. Il inspira profondément.
9. je n'ai jamais rien vu de pire
10. frôlant lentement les murs en silence
11. en espérant sans doute disparaître d'ici au plus vite
12. s'était encore sensiblement assombri
13. il était imprégné d'une odeur fétide de boucherie
14. du bourdonnement des mouches
15. ce qu'on aurait pu prendre pour une mare de goudron
16. Grands dieux !
17. plaçai ma main devant mes yeux
18. sans pouvoir pourtant m'empêcher de fixer

and which had been dragged forward expressly for this purpose[1]. He was dressed in a silk nightshirt[2] which reached to his ankles. His feet were bare.[3] He had been positioned so that he faced a mirror. Whoever had done this had wanted him to see what was going to happen.

He had not been tied into place. He had been nailed there.[4] Jagged squares of metal protruded from[5] the backs of his broken hands which even in death still clasped[6] the arms of the chair as if determined not to let go[7]. The hammer that had been used for this evil deed[8] lay in front of the fireplace and there was a china[9] vase, lying on its side. Nearby, I noticed two bright ribbons[10] which must have been brought down[11] from the bedroom and which were also strewn on the floor[12].

Scotchy Lavelle's throat had been cut cleanly and viciously in a manner that could not help but remind me of the surgeon's knife[13] that Perry had so cheerfully[14] used to threaten me in the Café Royal. I wondered if Jones had already leapt to the same, unavoidable conclusion[15]. This horrific murder could have been committed by a child … though not one acting alone[16]. It would have taken at least two people to drag Lavelle into place.[17] And what of the rest of the household?[18]

'They were murdered in their sleep,' Jones muttered, as if looking into my mind. 'The cook, the kitchen boy, the woman whose name was, perhaps, Henrietta. There is not a mark of any struggle on them.[19] Clayton slept in the basement[20]. He has been stabbed through the heart.[21]'

'But did none of them wake up?' I asked. 'Are you really telling me they heard nothing?'

'I believe they were drugged.'

1. avait été avancée dans ce seul but
2. chemise de nuit en soie
3. Il était pieds nus.
4. On ne l'avait pas attaché, mais bien cloué sur place.
5. Des carrés de métal saillants transperçaient
6. toujours agrippées
7. ne pas lâcher prise
8. office macabre
9. en porcelaine
10. rubans de couleur vive
11. provenaient sans doute
12. et qui gisaient également pêle-mêle sur le sol
13. qui me rappelait, malgré moi, le scalpel
14. de bon cœur
15. avait lui aussi déjà tiré la conclusion qui s'imposait
16. quoiqu'il n'ait pas agi seul
17. déplacer Lavelle.
18. Et qu'était-il advenu des autres occupants ?
19. Aucune trace de lutte.
20. au sous-sol
21. On l'a poignardé en plein cœur.

I absorbed this information and even as I spoke I knew Jones was ahead of me[1]. 'The curry!' I exclaimed. 'You remember, Jones? I asked the woman what she was cooking and she said that it was for dinner. They must have all eaten it, and whoever came here … it would have been easy enough to add some powerful drug, maybe powdered opium[2]. The curry would have disguised the taste[3].'

'But they would have had to reach the kitchen first,' Jones muttered.

'We should examine the door.'

We both circled the body, keeping our distance, for the blood and the shadows looked very much like one another[4] and we had to be careful where we placed our feet. It was only when we had reached the relative sanctuary of the kitchen[5] that we breathed again[6]. For a second time I found myself examining the spotless cooking range, the tiled[7] floor, the open door of the scullery with the shelves neatly stacked[8]. In the midst of all this[9], the cooking pot that had held the curry sat[10] dark and empty, like a guilty secret[11]. The one surviving maid was in this room, hunched up in a chair and weeping into her apron[12], watched over by a uniformed police constable[13].

'This is bad,' I said. 'This is very bad.'

'But who would do such a thing and why? That must be our first line of investigation.[14]' I could see that Jones, knocked off his feet by the ruthlessness of the murders[15], was struggling to regain the composure[16] that had been so much part of his nature when we were together in Meiringen. 'We know that Scott Lavelle – or Scotchy

1. m'avait devancé

2. de la poudre d'opium

3. aura masqué le goût

4. les traces de sang et les ombres se confondaient

5. le sanctuaire tout relatif que représentait la cuisine

6. que nous reprîmes notre respiration

7. carrelé

8. aux étagères minutieusement organisées

9. Au milieu

10. qui avait contenu le curry, trônait,

11. comme coupable d'un secret inavoué

12. courbée sur une chaise, sanglotant dans son tablier

13. sous l'œil d'un agent de police en uniforme

14. Il faut en faire la priorité de cette enquête.

15. bouleversé par ces crimes d'une cruauté sans nom

16. s'efforçait de reprendre contenance

1. mené par
2. mais il n'est pas dupe de l'imposture
3. Cela met fin à l'entrevue.
4. Pour eux, c'est ce que tout porte à croire.
5. originaires de deux pays différents
6. mais à dire vrai
7. Il n'en a plus le loisir à présent
8. me revint à l'esprit la large entaille qui balafrait sa gorge,
9. semblable à un sourire démoniaque.
10. Clayton avait verrouillée puis déverrouillée sous nos yeux
11. à l'aide d'une clé pendue à côté du buffet
12. poignée
13. ravi de sentir l'air frais
14. pelouse mal entretenue
15. que la porte extérieure
16. La serrure incrochetable avait été ouverte depuis la rue.

Lavelle – was part of a gang headed by[1] Clarence Devereux.'

'Of that there can be no doubt,' I said.

'He arranges to meet with Professor James Moriarty and to that end he sends a boy, Perry, to the Café Royal. A man pretending to be Moriarty is there but the impersonation fails[2]. The boy knows you are not who you say you are …'

'… because of the ravens in the tower.'

'So that is the end of the matter.[3] The boy makes the long journey to Highgate and reports back to the people who sent him. There will be no meeting. Perhaps Moriarty is dead after all. That is what these people are led to believe.[4]'

'And then we appear.'

'Yes, detectives from two separate nations[5]. We know about the boy. We ask questions – but the truth of it is[6], Chase, we make little progress. I imagine Lavelle was smiling when we left.'

'He's not doing so now[7],' I said, although I couldn't help but think of the great red gash in his throat[8]. It had the shape of a demonic smile.[9]

'Why has he been killed? Why now? But here is our first clue, our first indication of what may have taken place. The door is unlocked.'

Athelney Jones was right. The door that led into the garden, that we had seen Clayton fasten and unfasten[10] with a key from beside the dresser[11], was open. He turned the handle[12] and, grateful for the fresh air[13], I followed him out onto the ill-trimmed lawn[14] that we had crossed only the day before.

Together we walked down to the wall and saw at once that the far door[15] was also open. The Chubb had been unlocked on the outside.[16] A circular hole had been drilled through the wood[1], positioned exactly to reveal the inner lock[2]. This had then been cut through[3] and the metal hasp removed. Jones inspected the handiwork[4].

'The Chubb undamaged[5],' he said. 'If it was picked[6], then our intruders have shown skills beyond those of any common or garden burglar[7] – not that such a creature was involved, of that we can be sure. It is possible that they were able to lay their hands on a duplicate key[8]. We will see. The other lock, the one holding the hasp, is of particular interest[9]. You will see that they have cut a hole in the door, perhaps using a centre bit with two or three blades[10]. It would have made very little noise. But see where they have placed it!'

'The hole is level with the lock[11],' I said.

'Exactly. It has been measured to the inch.[12] A second drill has then been used to cut through the casing[13], exposing the wards[14]. It is a professional job – but it would not have been possible if the intruders had not stood where we are now[15] and made careful note of the exact position of the lock.'

'They could have been helped by someone inside the house.'

'Everyone inside the house is dead, apart from the maid. I am more inclined to think they acted on their own.'

'You speak of intruders, Inspector Jones. You are certain there was more than one?'

'Undoubtedly. There are tracks.' He gestured with his walking stick and, looking down, I was able to make out two sets of footprints[16], side by side, heading away from the wall and approach-

1. On avait percé un cercle dans le bois
2. de manière à exposer précisément la serrure intérieure
3. Celle-ci avait été percée
4. le travail d'orfèvre
5. intacte
6. si elle a été crochetée
7. nous n'avons pas affaire à de banals cambrioleurs
8. mettre la main sur un double de la clé
9. celle munie d'un loquet, en particulier, est digne d'intérêt
10. peut-être à l'aide d'une mèche à trois points
11. Pile au niveau de la serrure
12. Au millimètre près.
13. Une seconde mèche a été utilisée pour percer le chambranle
14. et dégager les fentes du mécanisme
15. ne s'étaient pas trouvés à l'endroit exact où nous sommes
16. je distinguai deux empreintes de pas distinctes

ing the house. 'A man and a boy,' he continued. 'You can see that the boy is carefree[1]. He almost trips along.[2] The man has left a deeper impression.[3] He is tall, at least six feet in height[4], and he was wearing unusual boots. You see the square toe?[5] He held back while the boy raced ahead.[6]'

'The boy had been here before.'

'It is true that his stride could suggest a familiarity with his surroundings[7]. Note also that he follows the most direct route to the kitchen. There was a moon[8], I believe, last night, but he had no fear of being seen.'

'He knew that the household was asleep.'

'Drugged and sound[9] asleep. There still remains the question of how he entered the house, but my guess is that he climbed a drainpipe[10] and entered by the second floor.' Athelney Jones unfolded the binoculars on his walking stick and used them to examine the upper part of the building. There was indeed a slender[11] drainpipe beside the kitchen door which would never have supported the weight of an adult[12] – perhaps it was for this reason that Lavelle had never considered it as a breach in his defences[13]. But for a child, it would have been a different matter entirely[14], and once he had reached the first floor …

'The windows are snibbed[15],' Jones continued. 'It would be easy enough to slide a knife inside the frame[16]. He would then have come down the stairs and opened the door to allow his accomplice in[17].'

'The boy of whom we speak … it must be the same,' I said.

'Perry? Undoubtedly.' Athelney Jones lowered the walking stick. 'I would not normally associ-

1. est insouciant
2. À croire qu'il sautille presque.
3. Les empreintes laissées par l'homme sont plus profondes.
4. près d'un mètre quatre-vingts
5. Vous remarquez le bout carré ?
6. Il restait en arrière tandis que le garçon courrait devant.
7. son pas décidé laisse penser qu'il connaissait les lieux
8. La lune était claire
9. profondément
10. gouttière
11. étroite
12. qui n'aurait jamais résisté au poids d'un adulte
13. une faille dans sa forteresse
14. cela n'aurait pas représenté le moindre obstacle
15. fermées
16. glisser la lame d'un couteau dans l'encadrement
17. pour permettre à son complice d'entrer

ate a child with crimes as gruesome as these[1], but I saw him with you. I saw the weapon he carried. He came here. I followed him myself. He entered through the garden door, came into the kitchen and saw the curry being prepared. It must have been then that he made his preparations[2], intending to[3] return at night with his colleague. But there still remains the one question. Why did Lavelle lie to us? Why did they all pretend the boy had not been here? They had sent him to meet us. There could be no other reason for him to have appeared in the[4] Café Royal. But when he returned, alone, what then occurred?'

'And why, if he was working for Lavelle, did he turn on his master and assist in his murder[5]?'

'I hoped you might shed some light on that[6]. Your work in America ...'

'I can only repeat what I have already told you, Inspector. The American criminal has no discrimination[7] and no sense of loyalty. Until Clarence Devereux came onto the scene[8], he worked in isolation, with no organisation or structure. Even afterwards, he remained vicious, treacherous and unpredictable[9]. Crime in New York was often as bloody as this and as incomprehensible. Brothers could fall out over the toss of a coin[10] and one of them – both of them – might end up dead[11]. Sisters too. Do you see now? I was trying to warn you. The events here at Bladeston House are only the start, the first warning signs of the poison[12] that has entered the bloodstream of your country[13]. Maybe Devereux was responsible. Maybe our visit here – for you can be sure that he will have received the intelligence[14] – was enough to persuade him that Lavelle had to be silenced[15]. I

1. un crime si effroyable

2. qu'il a dû concevoir son funeste plan

3. prévoyant de

4. Il n'avait aucune autre raison de se montrer au

5. trahir son maître et participer à son assassinat

6. que vous pourriez nous éclairer sur ce point

7. n'a aucun discernement

8. se fasse une place

9. il est toujours aussi cruel, fourbe et imprévisible

10. se brouillent pour un rien

11. si ce n'est les deux – risque d'y passer

12. les signes avant-coureurs d'un poison

13. qui s'est à présent insinué dans les veines de votre pays

14. qu'il en aura eu vent

15. devait être réduit au silence

don't know. It all makes me sick. But I fear a great deal more blood may be shed[1] before we arrive at the truth.'

There was nothing more to be gained by lingering in the garden[2] and reluctantly we re-entered[3] the charnel house, as it had now become[4]. The one survivor of the household, Mary Stagg, was still in the kitchen but she had little to tell us.

'I used to work for Mr and Mrs Bladeston,' she explained, between sobs[5]. 'And I'll be honest with you, gentlemen. I was much happier then. They were a good family. You knew where you were with them. But then Mr Bladeston died and they said they would be putting up the house for rent[6] at the start of the year and Mrs Bladeston persuaded me to stay. She said it would help her, knowing the place was being looked after[7].

'But I didn't like the American gentleman from the start. He had a wicked temper[8] and you should have heard his language[9]! It wasn't the sort of words a gentleman would use. The cook was the first to go.[10] She wasn't having any of it.[11] And then Mr Sykes decided he'd had enough[12] and he was replaced by Mr Clayton and I didn't very much like him either. And I was saying to Annie – that's my sister, sir – that I was thinking of handing in my notice too[13]. And now this![14]'

'Was the garden gate always kept locked?' Jones asked, once the maid had recovered her composure.

'Always, sir. Every gate, every window. The moment Mr Lavelle came here, he was very particular about it[15]. Everything had to be locked and shut down and all the keys in their right place. Nobody ever came to the door, not even the

1. que davantage de sang se répande
2. à s'attarder dans le jardin
3. nous regagnâmes, à contrecœur,
4. le charnier qu'était devenue cette villa
5. entre deux sanglots
6. Ils m'ont annoncé vouloir mettre la maison en location
7. de savoir que j'en prendrai soin
8. un vilain tempérament
9. et si vous l'aviez entendu parler
10. La cuisinière partit la première.
11. Elle ne le supportait en rien.
12. Puis M. Sykes en a eu assez
13. que j'envisageais moi aussi de quitter le service
14. Il ne manquait plus que ça !
15. Il se montrait très insistant sur ce point

delivery boy[1], unless Mr Clayton was there to greet them. We used to have such dinners and parties in Mr Bladeston's time. The house was a happy place then. But in just a few months, Mr Lavelle turned it into a sort of prison – with him as the main prisoner for he seldom went out[2].'

'Mrs Lavelle? Did you have any dealings with her?[3]'

The maid flinched[4], and despite everything she could not conceal the look of distaste that crept across her face[5]. At that moment I understood how difficult her position must have been[6] since Scotchy and his entourage had arrived.

'Begging your pardon[7], sir, but I'm not sure she was Mrs Lavelle. We just called her "madam" and a right proper madam she was too[8]. Nothing was ever right for her – but she did what Mr Lavelle told her. She never went out unless he said[9].'

'There were no visitors?'

'Two gentlemen used to come from time to time. I didn't see very much of them. They were tall, well-built[10] with dark hair and one of them with a moustache. Otherwise, they were as alike as peas in a pod[11]. Brothers, for sure.'

'Leland and Edgar Mortlake,' I muttered.

'Did you ever hear of a man called Clarence Devereux?' Jones asked.

'No, sir, but there was another man they talked about all the time, not that he ever came here[12], and when they spoke of him, they did so in a low voice[13]. I heard his name once and I never forgot it.' The maid paused, twisting her handkerchief in her hands[14]. 'I was passing the study and Mr Lavelle was talking to Mr Clayton … at least, I think it was he. I couldn't see and it wasn't my

1. pas même le livreur de journaux

2. dont il était lui-même captif car il sortait rarement

3. Aviez-vous affaire à elle ?

4. La bonne se contracta

5. l'aversion qui s'empara de son visage

6. la position délicate dans laquelle elle avait dû se trouver

7. Sauf votre respect

8. elle se prenait vraiment pour une grande dame

9. autrement que sur son ordre

10. bien bâtis

11. Sans ça, ils se ressemblaient comme deux gouttes d'eau.

12. mais on l'a jamais vu ici

13. ils baissaient toujours la voix

14. tortillant son mouchoir entre ses mains

place to eavesdrop[1]. But they were deep in conversation.[2] And that was when I heard them. "We must always be prepared for Moriarty." That's what Mr Lavelle said. I don't know why it made such an impression on me – only later on, Mr Clayton made a joke of it. "You shouldn't do that, Mary," he said to me once, when I left the door open, "or Professor Moriarty will get you[3]." It's a horrible name. I sometimes used to think of it when I was trying to get to sleep and it would turn over and over in my head. It seemed the whole house was afraid of this Moriarty, and with good reason[4], for you can see what's happened now!'

There was nothing more that Mary Stagg could tell us and, after warning her not to reveal what had taken place to anyone, Athelney Jones sent her home in the company of a constable[5]. The good woman clearly could not wait to get out of the house and I rather doubted she would ever return[6].

'Could Moriarty have done this?' I asked.

'Moriarty is dead.'

'He may have had associates, fellow criminals[7], members of his gang. You saw the way that Lavelle was killed, Inspector Jones. The way I see it, it's nothing less than a message[8], written in blood, perhaps sent as a warning[9].'

Jones thought for a moment. You told me that Moriarty and Devereux planned to meet, to create a criminal association …'

'That's right.'

'But they never did meet. We know that from the coded message that we found in Meiringen. As far as we can tell[10], they had no business together, so why would one wish to kill the other[11]?'

1. ce n'était pas mon rôle d'écouter aux portes

2. étaient plongés dans leur conversation.

3. sinon, gare au Professeur Moriarty

4. et non sans raison

5. la renvoya chez elle, escortée d'un agent

6. je doutais qu'elle y remette jamais les pieds

7. des complices

8. c'est un véritable message qu'il envoie

9. tracé au sang, peut-être pour nous mettre en garde

10. Pour autant que nous le sachions

11. alors pourquoi l'un voudrait éliminer l'autre

'Perhaps Devereux had something to do with what happened at the Reichenbach Falls.'

Jones shook his head wearily[1]. 'At the moment, nothing makes sense. I need time to reflect and to clear my thoughts[2]. But that will not happen here. For now, we must search the house and see what secrets, if any, the various rooms may reveal[3].'

And so we set about our grim task[4] – for it was as if we were exploring a catacomb. Each door opened upon another corpse[5]. We started with the kitchen boy, Thomas, who had closed his eyes one last time in a bare, shabby room[6] beside the scullery. The sight of him lying there, still dressed in the clothes he had worn to work, his bare feet resting[7] on the sheet, clearly affected Jones, and I was reminded[8] that he had a child who might only be a few years younger than this young victim. Thomas had been strangled.[9] The rope was still around his neck. Half a dozen steps led down to a basement room[10] where Clayton had lived and died. A carving knife[11], perhaps taken from the kitchen, had been plunged into his heart and remained there[12], almost seeming to pin him, like an insect in a laboratory, to the bed[13]. With heavy hearts, we made our way up to the attic room[14] where the cook – we now knew her name to be Mrs Winters – lay scowling in death as she had in life[15]. She too had been strangled.

'Why did they all have to die?' I asked. 'They may have worked for Lavelle but surely they were blameless[16].'

'Their assailants could not risk any of them waking up[17],' Jones muttered. 'And with Lavelle dead, they would have had no reason to hold

1. avec lassitude
2. me vider l'esprit
3. quels éventuels secrets ses différentes pièces renferment
4. nous nous acquittâmes alors de notre macabre office
5. s'ouvrait sur un nouveau cadavre
6. dans une pièce dépouillée et miteuse
7. reposant
8. et je me remémorai
9. avait été étranglé.
10. à une chambre au sous-sol
11. couteau à découper
12. toujours planté en plein cœur
13. semblait l'épingler au lit tel un insecte dans un laboratoire
14. nous montâmes jusqu'à une chambre sous les toits
15. avait le même air renfrogné dans la mort que de son vivant
16. ils n'avaient sûrement rien à se reprocher
17. que l'un des occupants se réveille

1. plus de raison de taire ce qu'ils savaient
2. Ainsi, ils sont réduits au silence.
3. il risquait davantage de se réveiller
4. n'ont rien laissé au hasard.
5. Quelle est la prochaine étape ?
6. femme à la crinière rousse
7. gisait négligemment sur un matelas de plumes d'oie
8. en batiste rose ornée de dentelle
9. l'avoir vieillie d'une décennie.
10. était en extension
11. comme tendu vers l'homme qui avait partagé sa couche
12. étouffée
13. oreiller
14. les hématomes
15. qui indiquent les points de pression
16. Mon regard se posa sur le côté où le lit était défait.
17. avait un faible pour
18. comme en témoignaient ses penderies qui croulaient sous
19. articles de toilette
20. [grand magasin de luxe à New York]

back what they knew[1]. This way, they are prevented from speaking to us[2].'

'The boy and the woman were strangled but Clayton was stabbed.'

'He was the strongest of the three of them, and although he had been drugged, he would have been the most likely to wake up[3]. The killers were taking no chances.[4] With him, they used a knife.'

I turned away. I had already seen enough. 'Where next?[5]' I asked.

'The bedroom.'

The flame-haired woman[6] whom Lavelle had addressed as 'Hen' lay sprawling on a goose-feather mattress[7], wearing a nightdress of pink cambric with ruffles[8] around her neck and sleeves. Death seemed to have aged her ten years.[9] Her left arm was flung out[10], reaching towards the man who had lain beside her[11], as if he could still bring her comfort.

'She has been smothered[12],' Jones said.

'How can you tell?'

'There are lipstick marks on the pillow[13]. That was the murder weapon. And you can see also the bruising[14] around the nose and mouth, where it was held in place[15].'

'Dear God in Heaven,' I muttered. I looked at the empty space where the bed covers had been thrown back.[16] 'And what of Lavelle?'

'He is the reason for all this.'

We made a quick search of the bedroom but it revealed little. 'Hen' had a fondness for[17] cheap jewellery and expensive dresses, the closets bursting with[18] silk and taffeta. Her bathroom contained more perfumes and toiletries[19] than the entire first floor of Lord & Taylor[20] on Broadway –

or so I remarked to Jones[1]. But the truth was that both of us knew that we were only delaying the inevitable[2] and, with a heavy heart, we made our way back downstairs.

Scotchy Lavelle sat waiting for us, a few police officers still lingering around him[3], wishing they could be anywhere but here[4]. I watched as Jones examined the body, leaning forward on his stick[5], being careful to keep his distance. I remembered the anger and the hostility with which we had been greeted[6] only the day before. 'Want to nosey around, do you?' Had Scotchy been more obliging[7], might he have escaped this fate?[8]

'He was carried here, half-conscious,' Jones muttered. 'There are many indications of what took place. First, the chair was moved and he was tied down[9].'

'The ribbons!'

'There is no other reason for them to be here. The killers must have brought them down from the bedroom for that express purpose[10]. They tied Lavelle to the chair and then, having assured themselves that everything was as they wanted, they dashed water into his face to wake him up[11]. It is hard to see with so much blood but I would have said the collar and sleeves of his nightshirt are damp[12] and anyway we have, as evidence, the upturned vase which was brought in from the kitchen[13]. I saw it there yesterday.'

'And what then?'

'Lavelle awakens. I have no doubt that he recognised his two assailants. Certainly the boy he must have met before.' Jones stopped himself. 'But I am wrong to describe it to you in this way. I am sure you have observed every detail for yourself[14].'

1. comme j'en fis la remarque à Jones

2. que nous ne faisions que retarder l'inéluctable

3. s'attardant près de lui

4. tout en souhaitant ardemment être ailleurs

5. se penchant en appui sur sa canne

6. avec lesquelles nous avions été accueillis,

7. Si Scotchy s'était montré plus coopératif,

8. aurait-il échappé à ce sort funeste

9. puis on l'a attaché

10. dans ce but précis

11. ils l'ont aspergé d'eau pour le réveiller

12. humides

13. le vase renversé qui provient de la cuisine

14. vous-même

1. je n'ai pas votre talent pour recomposer tout le tableau
2. Je vous en prie, poursuivez.
3. à leur merci
4. Et son calvaire ne fait que commencer.
5. exigent des informations
6. clouent
7. Je ne peux me résoudre à l'examiner de plus près
8. marteau
9. genou
10. Voyez plutôt comment pend le tissu de sa chemise de nuit.
11. Ils ont aussi brisé son talon gauche.
12. Des détails sur l'organisation dont il faisait partie.
13. considéra la question
14. S'il avait refusé de parler,
15. Ils l'ont tué malgré tout.
16. J'imagine qu'il a dû accueillir la mort comme un soulagement.
17. [série de crimes commis par Jack l'Éventreur]
18. qui me sont revenus à l'esprit
19. la préméditation de sang-froid

'Observed, yes,' I replied. 'But I don't have quite your facility for completing the picture[1], Inspector. Pray, continue.[2]'

'Very well. Lavelle is tied down and helpless[3]. Although he may not know it, his entire household has been killed. And it is now that his own ordeal begins.[4] The man and the boy require information[5]. They begin to torture him.'

'They nail[6] his hands to the chair.'

'They do more than that. I cannot bring myself to examine it too closely[7] but I would say that they used the same hammer[8] to break his knee[9]. Look at the way the fabric of his nightshirt lies.[10] They have also smashed the heel of his left foot.[11]'

'It is disgusting. It's horrific. What was it, I wonder, that they wished to know?'

'Matters relating to the organisation for which he worked.[12]'

'And did he talk?'

Jones considered.[13] 'It is almost impossible to tell but we must assume he did. Had he kept silent[14], his injuries would surely have been even more extensive.'

'And still they killed him.[15]'

'I would imagine that death would have come as a relief.[16]' Jones sighed. 'I have never encountered a crime like this in England. The Whitechapel Murders[17], which came straight to mind[18] when I arrived, were barbaric and vile. But even they lacked the cruelty, the cold-blooded calculation[19] that we have witnessed here.'

'Where next?'

'The study. That was where Lavelle greeted us and, if he had letters or documents of any interest, we will probably find them there.'

It was to that room that we returned. The curtains had been drawn back[1] allowing some light from the front to come through but it still seemed dark and abandoned without its owner, as if it belonged to a house that had been deserted long ago. Only one day before, the desk and the chair had been the stage from which our lead actor had played his part[2]. Now they were useless and the unread[3] books seemed more irrelevant[4] than ever. Still, we went through the drawers.[5] We examined the shelves. Jones was quite certain that Scotchy Lavelle would have left something of value behind.

I could have told him otherwise.[6] I knew that any organisation run by a man like Clarence Devereux would take no chances when it came to its own protection[7]. There would be no letters lying conveniently in wastepaper baskets[8], no addresses scribbled carelessly[9] on the backs of envelopes. This whole house had been designed specifically to guard its own secrets and to keep the world at bay[10]. Lavelle had described himself as a company promoter but there was not a scrap of evidence in the room to support this[11]. He was an invisible man with no background and no foreground[12], and plans, strategies and conspiracies[13] he would have taken with him to the grave[14].

Athelney Jones was struggling to conceal his disappointment[15]. All the papers we found were blank. There was a cheque book with no entries[16], a handful of receipts for trifling domestic matters[17], some letters of credit and promissory notes[18] that seemed entirely respectable, an invitation to a party at the American lega-

1. ouverts
2. l'acteur principal avait joué parfaitement son rôle
3. jamais lus
4. absurdes
5. Nous fouillâmes pourtant les tiroirs.
6. J'étais convaincu du contraire.
7. ne laisserait rien au hasard en matière de protection
8. jetées bien en vue dans la corbeille à papiers
9. négligemment griffonnées
10. maintenir le reste d'une monde à bonne distance
11. le bureau n'offrait aucune preuve pour étayer ses propos
12. sans passé, ni activité de façade
13. et autres cabales
14. tombe
15. cachait mal sa déception
16. chéquier sans mention sur les talons
17. quelques reçus pour des achats domestiques sans intérêt
18. billets à ordre

tion 'celebrating American and British business enterprise'. It was only when he was thumbing through[1] Lavelle's diary, turning one empty page after another, that he suddenly stopped and drew my attention to a single word and a figure[2], written in capital letters and encircled.

HORNER 13

'What do you make of that?[3]' he demanded.

'Horner?' I considered. 'Could it be referring to Perry? He was about thirteen.'

'I think he was older.' Jones reached into the back of the drawer and found something there. When he held out his hand, I saw that he was holding a bar of shaving soap[4], brand new, still wrapped in the paper[5]. 'It seems a strange place to keep such a thing,' he remarked.

'Do you think it has some significance?'

'Perhaps. But I cannot see what.'

'There is nothing,' I said. 'There is nothing here for us. I begin to regret that we ever found this house. It's shrouded in mystery and death[6] and leads us nowhere.'

'Do not give up hope,' Jones replied. 'Our path may be a murky one[7] but our enemy has shown himself[8]. The battle lines are at least engaged.[9]'

He had no sooner spoken than[10] we were interrupted by a commotion from[11] the hall. Someone had come in. The police officers were trying to prevent them moving forward[12]. There were voices raised in anger[13] and, among them, an accent that I recognised as American.

Jones and I hurried out of the study to find a slim, rather languid[14] man with black hair plas-

1. Ce fut seulement lorsqu'il feuilleta
2. assorti d'un chiffre
3. Cela vous évoque quelque chose ?
4. un savon à barbe
5. tout neuf et encore dans son papier d'origine
6. Elle est entourée de mystère et de mort
7. Je vous le concède, le chemin est trouble,
8. mais notre ennemi a dévoilé son visage
9. Voilà enfin chacun sur sa ligne de front.
10. À peine eut-il prononcé ses mots que
11. une agitation qui venait
12. tentaient de les empêcher de pénétrer davantage
13. Des voix furieuses s'élevaient
14. indolent

tered down in an oily wave across his forehead[1], small eyes and a well-cultivated moustache drooping over his lip[2]. If Scotchy Lavelle had exuded violence[3], this man presented more a sense of considered menace[4]. He would kill you – but he would think about it first. The many years he had spent in prison had left their mark on him, for his skin was unnaturally pale and dead-looking. It was made worse by the fact that he was dressed entirely in black – a tight-fitting frock coat and patent leather shoes[5] – and held a walking stick, also black, which he was brandishing[6] almost like a weapon, holding back the police officers who had rounded on him[7], pressing him back[8]. He had not come alone. Three young men had entered the house and stood surrounding him, hooligan boys from the look of them[9], aged about twenty with pale faces, ragged clothes, sticks and heavy boots[10].

They had all seen what had happened to Scotchy Lavelle. How could they have avoided it?[11] The man was staring at the corpse with horror but also with disgust, as if it were a personal insult that such a thing could be permitted[12].

'What the devil has happened here?[13]' he was demanding. He looked round as Jones emerged from the study. 'Who are you?'

'My name is Athelney Jones. I am a detective from Scotland Yard.'

'A detective! Well, that's very helpful. A little bit late, don't you think? Do you know who did this?' It was his accent I had heard. Less profane than Lavelle's[14], it was nonetheless clear that he too had come from New York.

1. des cheveux noirs plaqués en une mèche huileuse sur le front
2. une moustache élégamment taillée tombant sur la lèvre
3. Alors que Scotchy Lavelle avait exsudé la violence
4. représentait plutôt une menace raisonnée
5. des bottines en cuir verni
6. brandissait
7. qui l'avaient encerclé
8. pour le forcer à reculer
9. des petites frappes, cela ne faisait aucun doute
10. déguenillés, chaussés de gros souliers et munis de bâtons
11. Comment ne pas le voir ?
12. comme offusqué qu'il eut lui-même permis cela
13. Mais que diable s'est-il passé ici ?
14. Son langage était certes moins grossier que celui de Lavelle

'I arrived only a short while ago,' Jones replied. 'You know this man?'

'I knew him. Yes.'

'And who are you?'

'I'm not sure I'm minded[1] to give you my name.'

'You will not leave this house until you do, sir.' Athelney Jones had drawn himself up to his full height[2], propping himself on his walking stick[3]. He was looking at the American, eye to eye[4]. 'I am a British police officer,' he continued. 'You have entered the scene of a violent and inexplicable murder. If you have any information, it is your duty to share it with me[5] and if you refuse, I promise you will find yourself spending the night in Newgate[6] – you and the hoodlums with whom you surround yourself[7].'

'I know who he is,' I said. 'His name is Edgar Mortlake.'

Mortlake turned his little black eyes on me. 'You know me,' he said, 'but we haven't met.' He sniffed the air.[8] 'Pinkerton's?'

'How did you guess?'

'I'd know that smell anywhere.[9] New York? Chicago? Or maybe Philly[10]? Never mind. A little far away from home either way, aren't you, boy?[11]' The American smiled with a sense of confidence and self-control that was positively chilling[12]. He seemed to be unaware of the smell of blood and the sight of the broken and mutilated corpse sitting in the same room just inches from him.

'And what business brings you here?[13]' Jones demanded.

'My own business.' Mortlake sneered at him. 'And certainly none of yours.[14]'

1. Pas sûr d'être disposé à

2. s'était dressé de toute sa hauteur

3. ancré solidement sur sa canne

4. droit dans les yeux

5. vous êtes tenu de m'en faire part

6. je peux vous garantir que vous passerez la nuit en prison

7. la bande de voyous dont vous vous entourez

8. Il renifla dans ma direction.

9. Je reconnaitrais cette odeur entre toutes.

10. Philadelphie

11. Si loin de chez soi, on est perdu, mon garçon ?

12. qui donnait froid dans le dos

13. Et quelle affaire vous amène ?

14. Qui ne vous regarde en rien.

Jones turned to the nearest police constable, who had been watching this exchange with increasing alarm[1].

'I want you to arrest this man,' he said. 'The charge is obstruction.[2] I'll have him up before the magistrate this very day.[3]' The constable hesitated. 'Do your duty,' Jones said.

I will never forget that moment. There were Jones and Mortlake, standing face to face, surrounded by perhaps half a dozen police officers but with the hooligan boys in opposition[4]. It was as if a war were about to break out. And in the middle of it all, Scotchy Lavelle sat silently, the unwitting cause of all this[5] and yet, for the moment, almost forgotten.

It was Mortlake who backed down.[6] 'There's no need for this,' he said, forcing the faintest shadow of a smile to his death's-head face[7]. 'Why should I wish to interfere with the British police?[8]' He lifted his cane, gesturing at the corpse. 'Scotchy and I were in business together.'

'He said he was a company promoter.'

'Is that what he said? Well, he was many things. He invested in a little club I have in Mayfair. You could say we were co-founders.'

'Would that be the Bostonian?' I asked. I recalled the name.[9] It had been where Jonathan Pilgrim had stayed when he came to the country.

I had taken Mortlake by surprise, although he tried not to show it[10]. 'That's the one[11],' he exclaimed. 'I see you've been busy, Pinkerton. Or are you a member? We have a lot of American visitors. But then, I doubt you could afford us.[12]'

I ignored him. 'Is Clarence Devereux another partner in this little enterprise?'

1. avec une inquiétude grandissante

2. Pour entrave à la justice.

3. Je le ferai comparaître devant le juge aujourd'hui même.

4. Et à l'opposé, les petites frappes

5. cause involontaire de cette scène,

6. Mortlake recula le premier.

7. feignant l'ombre d'un sourire sur son visage de mort-vivant

8. Loin de moi l'idée d'interférer avec le travail de la police.

9. Le nom m'était revenu en mémoire.

10. bien qu'il tenta de le dissimuler

11. Tout juste

12. Ça m'étonnerait, nous sommes bien au-dessus de vos moyens.

1. Vous êtes mal informé.
2. Je perdais patience.
3. J'ai vu votre casier judiciaire.
4. Perçage de coffre-fort.
5. [prison de Manhattan]
6. fit quelques pas vers moi
7. rugit-il
8. et non de vous acharner sur moi
9. Tâche où vous avez lamentablement échoué
10. en ce qui concerne mon défunt associé.
11. Toute la maisonnée
12. sembla perdre sa contenance
13. et ses lèvres se tordirent de dégoût
14. Je vous laisse fureter à votre guise, messieurs.
15. il s'était esquivé
16. aussi effrontément qu'il avait fait son entrée
17. le suivirent de près
18. de former un mur vivant

'I don't know any Clarence Devereux.'

'I believe you do.'

'You're mistaken.[1]'

I'd had enough.[2] 'I know who you are, Edgar Mortlake,' I said. 'I have seen your record sheet.[3] Bank burglary. Safe-cracking.[4] A year in the Tombs[5] for armed assault. And that was only the most recent of your convictions.'

'You should be careful how you speak to me!' Mortlake took a couple of paces towards me[6] and his entourage circled him nervously, wondering what he was going to do. 'That was all in the past,' he snarled[7]. 'I'm in England now … an American citizen with a respectable enterprise, and it would seem that your job is to protect me, not to harass me[8].' He nodded at the dead man. 'A duty you have signally failed to carry out[9] where my late partner was concerned.[10] Where's the woman?'

'If you are referring to Henrietta, she is upstairs,' Jones said. 'She was also killed.'

'And the rest of them?'

'The entire household[11] has been murdered.'

Mortlake seemed to be thrown[12] for the first time. He took one last look at the blood and his lip curled in disgust[13]. 'There is nothing for me here,' he said. 'I will leave the two of you gentlemen to sniff around.[14]'

Before anyone could stop him, he had swept out again[15], as brazenly as he had come in[16]. The three hooligan boys closed in on him[17] and I saw that their primary concern was to protect him, to provide a living wall[18] between him and his enemies in the outside world.

'Edgar Mortlake,' I said. 'The gang is making itself known.[1]'

'And that may be helpful to us.' Jones glanced at the open door.

Mortlake had reached the bottom of the garden and passed through the gate. Even as we watched[2], he climbed into the carriage that was waiting for him, followed by his three protectors, and with the cracking of a whip he was off, back towards[3] Highgate Hill. It occurred to me[4] that if the murder of Scotchy Lavelle and his household had been designed to send a message[5] then it was one that had most definitely been received[6].

1. Le gang commence à se faire connaître.

2. Sous nos yeux

3. en un claquement de fouet, il avait disparu en direction de

4. Je me fis la réflexion

5. était supposé envoyer un message,

6. ses destinataires l'avaient, de toute évidence, reçu cinq sur cinq

EIGHT

Scotland Yard

If Hexam's had anything to recommend it[1] – and the list was not a long one – it was its close proximity to the centre of London. The breakfast room was once again empty and, after finishing my meal, I left the maid and the Boots[2] behind me and set off[3], intending to follow the Embankment, something that Jones had recommended the day before.

The Thames was glistening[4] on the other side of a long row of trees that graced[5] the boulevard. There was a fresh spring breeze blowing and as I stepped out of the hotel, a black-hulled river steam ship chuffed past on its way to[6] the Port of London. I stopped and watched it pass and it was at that moment that I had the strange feeling that I was being watched[7]. It was still early and there were few people around: a woman, pushing a pram[8], a man in a bowler hat[9] walking with a dog. I turned and looked back at the hotel. And it was then that I saw him, standing behind a window on the second floor, gazing out into the street[10]. It took me only a second to work out[11] that he occupied the room next to mine. This was the man whom I had heard coughing[12] through-

1. Si tant est que l'hôtel Hexam ait eu quoi que ce soit pour lui
2. garçon d'étage
3. sortis
4. La Tamise scintillait
5. égayaient
6. bateau à vapeur à coque noire haletait en filant vers
7. qu'on m'observait
8. landau
9. chapeau melon
10. observant la rue depuis une fenêtre du deuxième étage
11. pour comprendre
12. que j'avais entendu tousser toute la nuit

out the night. He was too far away – and the windows were too grimy[1] – for me to see him clearly. He had dark hair and wore dark clothes. He was almost unnaturally still.[2] It might have been my imagination but I would have said his eyes were fixed on me. Then he reached out with one hand and drew the curtain across[3]. I tried to put him out of my mind[4] and continued on my way. But I could no longer enjoy the walk as much as I had hoped. I was uneasy[5] without knowing why.

Another fifteen minutes brought me to my destination.[6] Scotland Yard, as it was already known (although in fact it was situated in Whitehall Place), was an impressive building that straddled the ground[7] between Victoria Embankment and Westminster. It was also a pretty ugly one, or so it seemed to me[8] as I crossed the boulevard and looked for the main entrance. It was as if the architect had changed his mind after construction had begun[9]. Two floors of austere granite suddenly yielded to[10] red and white brickwork, ornate casements[11] and Flemish-style tourelles, giving the impression of two quite separate buildings squashed one on top of the other[12]. There was something of a prison about the place too.[13] Its four wings enclosed a courtyard barely touched by the sun[14]. The inmates[15] of Newgate would probably enjoy their exercise[16] more than the unfortunate police officials penned up here[17].

Athelney Jones was waiting for me and raised a hand in greeting[18]. 'You got my message! Excellent. The meeting is to start very soon[19]. It is quite remarkable. In all my time here, I would say it is almost unique. No fewer than[20] fourteen of the most senior detective inspectors have come

1. crasseuses
2. Sa posture immobile manquait de naturel.
3. tira le rideau
4. le chasser de mon esprit
5. J'éprouvais un malaise
6. Un quart d'heure plus tard, j'arrivai à destination.
7. occupait tout l'espace
8. du moins il m'apparut ainsi
9. à mi-chemin de la construction
10. cédaient la place contre toute-attente à
11. des croisées ornementées
12. agglutinés
13. Sans compter que le tout avait des airs de prison.
14. encadraient une cour qui ne voyait quasiment pas le soleil
15. détenus
16. promenade
17. condamnés à travailler ici
18. me fit un signe de la main
19. ne va pas tarder à commencer
20. Pas moins de

together in response to[1] the Highgate murders. We won't have it[2], Chase. It is simply beyond the pale.[3]'

'And I am to be permitted to attend?[4]'

'It wasn't easy. I won't pretend otherwise.[5] Lestrade was against it – and Gregson too. I told you when we first met, there are many here who believe we should have no dealings[6] with a commercial detective agency such as Pinkerton's. In my view, it is foolish, this lack of co-operation[7] when we have the same aims[8]. Still[9], this time I have been able to persuade them of the importance of your presence. Come – we should go in.'

We climbed a set of wide steps[10] and entered a hall where several uniformed constables[11] stood behind tall desks, examining the letters of introduction[12] and passports of those who wished to enter. Jones had already prepared the way for me and together we fought our way up a crowded staircase[13] with uniformed men, clerks and messengers pushing past each other in both directions[14].

'The building's already too small for us,' he complained. 'And we have barely been here a year![15] They found a murdered woman in the basement[16] during the construction.'

'Who killed her?'

We don't know. No one has any idea who she was or how she came to be there. Do you not find it strange, Chase, that the finest police force[17] in Europe should have chosen to locate itself[18] at the scene of an unsolved[19] crime?' We reached the third floor and passed a series of doors, evenly spaced[20]. Jones nodded as we passed one of

1. ont joint leurs forces en réaction aux
2. ne le tolèrerons pas
3. Cette fois, ils ont dépassé les bornes.
4. M'autorise-t-on à y assister ?
5. ne vous ferai pas croire le contraire.
6. ne devrions jamais nous associer
7. cette absence de coopération est absurde
8. alors que nous avons des objectifs communs
9. Toujours est-il
10. volée de larges marches
11. agents
12. lettres de recommandation
13. tentâmes de nous frayer un passage dans l'escalier bondé
14. qui se bousculaient en se croisant
15. cela fait à peine un an que nous l'occupons!
16. sous-sol
17. la crème de la crème de la police
18. ait élu domicile
19. non résolu
20. espacées à intervalle régulier

them. 'My office. The best rooms have a view over the river.'

'And yours?'

'I look into the quadrangle.[1]' He smiled. 'Perhaps when you and I get to the end of this business[2], they'll think to move me. At least I am close to the records office[3] and the telegraph room!'

We had passed an open door and, sure enough[4], there were about a dozen men dressed in dark suits[5], sitting at tables or along a high counter[6], crouched over their telegraph sets[7] with papers and printed tape[8] all around them.

'How quickly can you contact America?' I asked.

'The actual message[9] can be sent in a matter of minutes[10],' Jones replied. 'The printing takes a while longer[11] and if there is too much traffic it can be days. Do you wish to communicate with your office?'

'I should send them a report,' I said. 'They've heard nothing from me since I left.[12]'

'In truth, you'd do better to apply to[13] the Central Telegraph Office in Newgate Street. You may find them more obliging[14].'

We continued through a set of doors and into a large, airless[15] room, the windows recessed in such a way that they seemed to hold back the light[16]. A vast table, curved at both ends[17], took up all the available space and seemed to have been fashioned not so much to bring people together as to keep them apart[18]. I had never seen such a great expanse of polished wood[19]. There were already nine or ten men in the room, one or two smoking pipes, talking amongst themselves in low voices. Their ages ranged[20], I would have said, from about twenty-five to about fifty. Their

1. J'ai une vue imprenable sur la cour.
2. viendrons à bout de cette affaire
3. salle des archives
4. justement
5. en costume sombre
6. devant un haut comptoir
7. penchés sur des télégraphes
8. bandes imprimées
9. message en lui-même
10. en l'espace de quelques minutes
11. L'impression prend plus longtemps
12. Je ne leur ai pas donné signe de vie depuis mon départ.
13. vous feriez mieux de vous adresser au
14. plus disposés à vous aider
15. qui manquait d'air
16. encastrées de manière à empêcher la lumière d'entrer
17. arrondie aux extrémités
18. conçue moins pour rassembler les gens que pour les séparer
19. une telle surface de bois ciré
20. allaient de

clothes were by no means uniform.[1] Although the majority were smartly dressed in frock coats[2], one man wore a tweed suit while another presented himself in the unusual attire of a green pea-jacket and cravat[3].

It was this man who first saw us as we came in and strode hastily towards us as if about to make[4] an arrest. My first impression was that it would be hard to imagine him as anything other than a police officer. He was lean and business-like[5] with dark, inquisitive eyes[6] that examined me as if I – and everyone else he met – must surely have something to hide. His voice, when he spoke, had an edge to it[7] that was almost deliberately unfriendly.

'Well, well, Jones,' he exclaimed. 'I take it[8] this is the gentleman of whom you spoke.'

'I am Frederick Chase,' I said, extending a hand[9].

He shook it briefly. 'Lestrade,' he said and his eyes glinted[10]. 'I would welcome you to our little gathering[11], Mr Chase, but I'm not sure welcome is the right word. These are queer times.[12] This business at Bladeston House … very, very bad. I am not sure what it portends.[13]'

'I am here to give you any help I can,' I said, heartily[14].

'And who is it that most needs help, I wonder?[15] Well, we shall see.'

Several more inspectors had entered the room and finally the door was closed. Jones gestured at me to sit[16] next to him. 'Say nothing for a while,' he said, quietly. 'And watch out for[17] Lestrade and Gregson.'

'Why?'

1. Aucun ne portait d'uniforme.
2. étaient élégamment vêtus de redingotes
3. détonnait avec un caban vert et un cache-col
4. fondit sur nous comme s'il allait procéder à
5. svelte et sérieux
6. regard inquisiteur
7. était tranchante
8. J'imagine
9. lui tendant la main
10. avec une lueur dans le regard
11. réunion
12. Nous traversons une période trouble.
13. Je ne saurais dire ce qu'elle présage.
14. avec chaleur
15. Et qui en a le plus besoin, je me le demande.
16. m'invita à prendre place
17. méfiez-vous de

'You cannot agree with one[1] without antagonizing the other.[2] Youghal over there is a good man but he *is still finding his feet*[3]. And next to him …' He glanced at a man with a high-domed forehead[4] and intense eyes who was sitting at the head of the table. Although he was not one of the most physically impressive men in the room, there was still something about him that suggested great inner strength[5]. Alec MacDonald. I believe him to have the best brain in the business and if anyone can steer[6] this enquiry in the right direction, it is he.'

A large, breathless[7] man lowered himself into the seat[8] on the other side of me. He was wearing a frogged jacket which was stretched tight across[9] his chest. 'Bradstreet,' he muttered.

'Frederick Chase.'

'Delighted.[10]' He took out an empty pipe and tapped it[11] on the table in front of him.

Inspector Lestrade began the meeting with a natural authority that seemed to outrank the[12] others in the room. 'Gentlemen,' he said. 'Before we get down to the[13] very serious business that brings us here today, it's fitting that we pay our respects to a[14] good friend and colleague whom we have recently lost. I refer, of course, to Mr Sherlock Holmes, who was known to many of us here and, by reputation, to the public at large[15]. He helped me in no small way[16] on one or two occasions, I will admit, starting with that business at[17] Lauriston Gardens[18] some years ago. It is true that he had a queer way about him[19], spinning those fine theories of his like gossamer[20] out of thin air[21] – and although some of it may have been no more than guesswork[22], none of us here would

1. Impossible d'être d'accord avec l'un
2. sans se mettre à dos l'autre.
3. cherche encore ses repères
4. front haut et bombé
5. force intérieure
6. orienter
7. essoufflé
8. se laissa choir sur le siège
9. une veste à brandebourgs qui lui compressai
10. Ravi.
11. la tapota
12. comme s'il était d'un rang supérieur aux
13. attelions au
14. il est juste que nous rendions hommage au
15. dans son ensemble
16. m'a été d'un grand secours
17. depuis l'affaire de
18. [voir « Une étude en rouge »]
19. s'y prenait d'une bien étrange façon
20. tissant comme une toile ses théories complexes,
21. sorties de nulle part
22. et bien que quelques-unes n'aient été que pures conjectures

deny that he was often successful and I'm sure we'll all miss him following his unfortunate demise[1] at the Reichenbach Falls.'

'Is there no chance that he could have survived?' The speaker was young and smartly dressed, about halfway down the table. 'After all, his body has never been found.'

'That much is true[2], Forrester,' Lestrade agreed. 'But we have all read the letter.'

'I was at that dreadful[3] place,' Jones said. 'If he fought Moriarty and fell, I am afraid there is very little chance that he could have been saved.'

Lestrade shook his head solemnly[4]. 'I'll admit that I've been wrong about one or two things in the past,' he said. 'Particularly where Sherlock Holmes was concerned[5]. But this time I have looked at the evidence and I can tell you without any doubt at all that he is dead. I would stake my reputation on it[6].'

'We should not pretend that the loss[7] of Sherlock Holmes is anything short of a[8] catastrophe,' the man sitting opposite me said. He was tall with fair hair[9] and as he spoke, Jones whispered to me[10], 'Gregson.' He continued: 'You mentioned the Lauriston Gardens affair, Lestrade. Without Holmes, it would have gone nowhere. Why, you were about to search the whole of London[11] for a girl called Rachel when in fact it was Rache, the German for revenge[12], that the victim had left as a final clue[13].' There were quite a few smiles around the table at that[14] and one or two of the detectives laughed out loud.

'There is one silver lining to the cloud[15],' Inspector Youghal said. 'At least we'll no longer find ourselves being caricatured[16] by his associ-

1. après sa mort tragique aux
2. C'est un fait
3. lugubre
4. avec gravité
5. à l'endroit de Sherlock Holmes
6. suis prêt à parier ma réputation.
7. perte
8. est rien de moins qu'une
9. cheveux blonds
10. me murmura son nom
11. Vous étiez quand même sur le point de ratisser tout Londres
12. l'équivalent allemand de « vengeance »,
13. indice
14. à ces mots
15. Il faut voir le bon côté des choses
16. Au moins, nous ne ferons plus l'objet de caricature

ate, Dr Watson. I was of the view that his scribblings did our reputations no good[1] at all.'

'Holmes was a damned odd fellow[2],' a fifth man exclaimed. As he spoke, he rubbed his eyeglass between finger and thumb[3] as if he were adjusting it to better see the others in the room. 'I worked with him, you know, on that business with the missing horse. Silver Blaze.[4] A very strange individual. Sherlock Holmes, not the horse. He had a habit of speaking in riddles[5]. Dogs that bark[6] in the night, indeed! I admired him. I liked him. But I'm not at all sure I will miss him.'

'I was always suspicious of his methods,' Forrester concurred[7]. 'He made it all sound easy enough and we took him at his word[8]. But is it really possible to tell a man's age from his handwriting[9]? Or his height from the length of his stride?[10] Much of what he said was unsound, unscientific[11] and occasionally preposterous[12]. We believed him because he got results, but it was not a sound platform[13] for modern detective work.'

'He made fools of all of us[14],' exclaimed yet another[15] inspector. It's true that I also benefited on one occasion from his expertise. But is it not the case, perhaps, that we were becoming too dependent on Mr Holmes? Did we ever solve anything without him?' He turned to the colleagues on his left and right. 'As hard as it is and as ungrateful[16] as it may sound, perhaps we should embrace his going as an opportunity[17] for us to achieve results on our own two feet[18].'

'Well said, Inspector Lanner.' It was MacDonald who had spoken and now all eyes were on him. 'I never met Mr Holmes myself,' he continued in his thick[19] Scottish accent. 'But I think we

1. ses scribouillages ne nous faisaient pas bonne presse
2. sacré numéro
3. lustrait son lorgnon entre le pouce et l'index
4. [voir « Flamme d'Argent »]
5. avait la fâcheuse habitude de parler par énigmes
6. aboient
7. abonda dans son sens
8. le croyions sur parole
9. de déduire l'âge d'un homme d'après son écriture
10. Ou bien sa taille d'après la longueur de ses pas ?
11. manquait de logique, d'étayage scientifique,
12. et était parfois complètement saugrenu
13. modèle fiable
14. nous tournait en ridicule, tous autant que nous étions
15. encore un autre
16. ingrat
17. saluer sa disparition et y voir l'occasion
18. d'obtenir des résultats en ne comptant que sur nous-mêmes
19. à couper au couteau

are agreed[1] that we owe him our thanks and our respect and it's now time to move on[2]. For better or for worse[3] he has left us on our own and, having acknowledged as much[4], let us consider the matter at hand[5]. He picked up a sheet of paper that had been lying in front of him and read from it. 'Mr Scott Lavelle, tortured and his throat cut. Henrietta Barlowe, smothered[6]. Peter Clayton, a petty criminal[7] who was known to us, stabbed[8]. Thomas Jerrold and Lucy Winters strangled. An entire household in a respectable suburb wiped out in the course of one night[9]. We cannot have it[10], gentlemen. It cannot be allowed.'

Everyone in the room murmured their agreement.

'And as I understand it, these are not the first atrocities that have taken place recently in Highgate. Lestrade?'

'You are right. There was a death not one month ago[11], a young man by the name of Jonathan Pilgrim. Hands tied, shot in the head.' Lestrade gazed at me as if I had been the one responsible and for a moment I felt the anger rise within me[12]. I had been close to Pilgrim. It was his death, more than anything, which drove me on in my[13] pursuit of Clarence Devereux. But I understood this was simply Lestrade's manner[14]. He meant nothing by it.[15] 'Pilgrim carried papers that showed him to be an American[16] only recently arrived in the country,' he continued. 'He must have had an interest in Lavelle as his body was found only a short distance from Bladeston House.'

I felt it was time for me to speak out and so I did.[17]

1. nous nous accordons tous à dire
2. passer à autre chose
3. Pour le meilleur ou pour le pire,
4. maintenant que c'est dit,
5. tournons-nous plutôt vers l'affaire qui nous intéresse
6. étouffée
7. petit délinquant
8. poignardé
9. décimée en l'espace d'une nuit
10. ne le tolèrerons pas
11. il y a de ça un mois à peine
12. sentis une colère monter en moi
13. qui m'avait lancé à la
14. la façon de faire de Lestrade
15. Il n'y avait aucun message caché.
16. indiquant qu'il était un citoyen américain
17. Mon tour était venu de prendre la parole.

'Pilgrim was investigating Clarence Devereux,' I said. 'I myself sent him[1] to this country for that purpose. Devereux and Lavelle were working in collaboration and must have somehow discovered my agent. It was they who killed him.'

'But in that case, who killed Lavelle?' Bradstreet asked.

MacDonald held up a hand[2]. 'Mr Chase,' he said, 'we have been given a full explanation of your presence in London by Inspector Jones and I must say that it is only due to the exceptional circumstances of this case[3] that you find yourself here today[4].'

'I'm grateful for it.'

'Well, you have him to thank. We will hear from you shortly. But it seems to me that if we are going to get to the bottom of these appalling murders[5], we need to go back to the very start ... even to the Reichenbach Falls.' He turned to an inspector who had not so far[6] spoken. This was a slight[7], grey-haired individual who had been nervously picking his nails[8] and who looked like someone who never wanted to be noticed[9]. 'Inspector Patterson,' he said, 'you were responsible for the apprehension[10] of Moriarty's gang. You helped to drive him abroad.[11] I think you should share with us exactly what occurred.'

'Certainly.' Patterson did not look up as he spoke, as if his report were engraved in the tabletop[12]. 'You are all aware that Mr Holmes approached me last February although it had been his intention, I think, to meet with Lestrade.'

'I was on another case,' Lestrade explained with a scowl[13].

1. l'ai envoyé personnellement

2. leva la main

3. c'est aux seules circonstances exceptionnelles de cette affaire

4. que vous devez d'être admis dans ce cercle

5. faire toute la lumière sur cette innommable tuerie

6. jusque-là

7. mince

8. se rongeait nerveusement les ongles

9. semblait toujours préférer passer inaperçu

10. arrestation

11. avez provoqué sa fuite à l'étranger.

12. comme si son rapport était gravé dans le bois de la table

13. d'un air renfrogné

1. à l'en croire, du moins
2. En personne.
3. je ne sais quelle théorie qu'il avait élaborée
4. qu'il occupait la chaire de mathématiques
5. on ne peut plus sérieux
6. en des termes les plus sombres
7. m'a fourni des preuves qui ne laissaient aucun doute
8. sur le bien-fondé de ce qu'il avançait
9. j'avais dessiné un schéma
10. révélant un impressionnant réseau criminel
11. en tirant sur sa pipe
12. avaient soudain décidé de se manifester
13. sentant Moriarty en position de faiblesse,
14. saisi l'occasion de se venger
15. qu'il régnait par l'intimidation et la menace
16. que nous étions loin de soupçonner
17. Le passage de Moriarty de l'anonymat
18. au devant de la scène

'In Woking, I believe. Well, yes, in your absence, Mr Holmes came to me and asked for my co-operation in the identification and arrest of a gang that had been operating in London for some time – or so he said[1] – and in particular, one man.'

'Professor Moriarty,' Jones muttered.

'The very same.[2] I have to say that at the time the name was unknown to me and when Holmes explained that he was famous throughout Europe for some theory he had devised[3] and, moreover, that he had held the Chair of Mathematics[4] at one of our most prestigious universities, I thought he was making fun of me. But he was of the utmost seriousness[5]. He referred to Moriarty in the very darkest terms[6] and went on to furnish me with evidence that could leave no doubt[7] of what he said[8].

'By the beginning of last month, assisted by Inspector Barton here, I had drawn together a schematic[9] – you might say a map – of London that showed an extraordinary, interlinking network of criminality[10].'

'With Moriarty at the centre,' Barton added, puffing on his pipe[11].

'Indeed. I might add that we were assisted by a great number of informers who suddenly chose to come forward[12]. It was as if, sensing Moriarty's weakness[13], they seized this moment to get their revenge[14], for there was no doubt that he had ruled by intimidation and threat[15]. We received anonymous letters. Evidence of his past crimes – about which we had no knowledge whatsoever[16] – suddenly came to light. Moriarty's journey from obscurity[17] to centre stage[18] was a very short one and, at a given signal from Holmes, for he was most particular about the timing, we pounced[1]. In the course of a single weekend[2], we made arrests in Holborn, Clerkenwell, Islington, Westminster and Piccadilly. We entered houses as far afield as[3] Ruislip and Norbury. Men of the utmost respectability[4] – teachers, stockbrokers, even an archdeacon[5] – were taken into custody[6]. On the Monday, I was able to telegraph Holmes who was by this time in Strasbourg and inform him that we had the entire gang.'

'All but[7] the leader himself,' Barton agreed and, around the table, the inspectors, who had been listening intently[8], nodded their heads in sombre silence[9].

'We now know that Moriarty had taken off after[10] Holmes,' Patterson concluded. 'I hold myself at least in part responsible for what ensued[11], but at the same time I cannot believe Holmes had not expected it. Why else[12] would he have left the country so abruptly? At any event, there you have it.[13] Barton and I are preparing the charges even now[14] and the cases will come to court soon enough[15].'

'Excellent work,' MacDonald said. He paused for a moment and frowned[16]. 'But am I alone in finding a disparity here?[17] In February of this year, you and Sherlock Holmes begin to close in on[18] Moriarty and at around about the same time an American criminal by the name of Clarence Devereux arrives in London, seeking an alliance with that same Moriarty[19]. How can it be?[20]'

'Devereux did not know that Moriarty was finished,' another inspector said. 'We've all seen the letter, sent in code. It was only in April that they agreed to meet.'

1. car il était très pointilleux sur le minutage, nous avons bondi
2. En un seul week-end,
3. avons perquisitionné des maisons aussi éloignées que
4. Des hommes tout ce qu'il y a de plus respectable
5. agents de change, et même un archidiacre
6. ont fait l'objet d'une interpellation
7. Tous sauf
8. attentivement
9. dans un silence grave
10. s'était lancé à la poursuite de
11. suis responsable, en partie du moins, de ce qui en a résulté
12. Pourquoi sinon
13. Mais enfin, ce qui est fait est fait.
14. préparons en ce moment-même les chefs d'inculpation
15. les membres arrêtés passeront bientôt devant le juge
16. fronça les sourcils
17. à y voir une incohérence ?
18. à resserrer le filet autour de
19. cherchant à s'allier avec ce même Moriarty
20. Comment cela peut-il être possible ?

1. Il arrivait à point nommé.
2. en cavale
3. tapa du poing
4. avec irritation
5. Tout ça n'est que foutaise !
6. avant que Sherlock Holmes n'attire notre attention sur lui
7. était bien réel, lui.
8. la moindre preuve qu'ils détiennent sur cet homme
9. Inutile
10. c'est volontiers que je les mets à votre disposition
11. vous êtes un jeune détective
12. agent subalterne
13. être mis au courant de tout
14. enquêteur en chef
15. ne veux pas vous contredire.
16. qu'il ne servait à rien de contrarier cet homme
17. m'a confié cette affaire
18. suit avec le plus vif intérêt à la façon dont elle évolue
19. griffonna

'Devereux could have been very useful to Moriarty,' Gregson suggested. 'His arrival couldn't have been better timed.[1] Moriarty was on the run[2]. Devereux could have helped him rebuild his empire.'

'I disagree!' Lestrade pounded his fist[3] on the table and looked around him peevishly[4]. 'Clarence Devereux! Clarence Devereux! This is all the merest moonshine.[5] We know *nothing* about Clarence Devereux. Who is he? Where does he live? Is he still in London? Does he even exist?'

'We knew nothing about Moriarty until Sherlock Holmes drew him to our attention[6].'

'Moriarty was real enough.[7] But I suggest we address ourselves to the Pinkerton Agency in New York. I would like to see every scrap of evidence that they have concerning this man[8].'

'There is no need[9],' I said. 'I brought copies of all the files with me and I will happily make them available to you[10].'

'You left America three weeks ago,' Lestrade responded. 'Much can have happened in that time. And with respect, Mr Chase, you are a junior agent in this business[11]. I wouldn't talk to a police constable[12] if I wished to be brought up to date[13]. I would prefer to deal with the people who sent you here.'

'I am, sir, a senior investigator[14]. But I will not argue with you.[15]' I could see there was no point antagonising the man[16]. 'You must address yourself to Mr Robert Pinkerton himself. It was he who assigned me to this case[17] and he takes the closest interest in every development[18].'

'We will do that.' MacDonald scribbled[19] a note in front of him.

'Clarence Devereux is here in London. I am certain of it. I have heard his name mentioned and I have felt his presence.'

The speaker was, by some margin[1], the youngest person in the room. I had noticed him sitting upright[2] in his chair throughout the lengthy speeches[3], as if he could barely prevent himself from breaking in[4]. He had fair hair, cut very short, and a keen, boyish[5] face. He could not have been more than twenty-five or twenty-six years old. 'My name is Stanley Hopkins,' he said, introducing himself to me[6]. 'And although I never had the honour of meeting Mr Sherlock Holmes, I very much wish he was still with us for I believe we face a challenge[7] such as none of us in this room has ever encountered[8]. I am in close contact with the criminal fraternity[9]. Being new to this profession and even newer to this rank[10], I make it my business[11] to maintain a presence in the streets of London – in Friars Mount, in Nichols Row, in Bluegate Fields …

'In the past few weeks, I have become aware[12] of a silence, an emptiness – a sense of fear. None of the auction gangs[13] are active. Nor are the pawners, nor the cardsharps.[14] The young women in the Haymarket and on Waterloo Bridge have been absent from their trade[15].' He blushed slightly[16]. 'I speak to them sometimes because they can be useful to me, but now even they have gone. Of course it may be the case that the superlative work[17] of Mr Barton and Mr Patterson has been rewarded with the state of affairs we have all wished for[18], if only in our dreams[19]: a London free of crime, that with Moriarty finished, his followers have become disheartened[20] and crept

1. de loin
2. droit comme un i
3. pendant les interminables palabres
4. comme s'il se retenait tout juste de ne pas intervenir
5. juvénile et avenant
6. à mon intention
7. car il me semble que nous sommes confrontés à un défi
8. comme aucun de nous n'en a connu jusque-là
9. la pègre
10. Débutant dans la profession, et encore plus cette fonction,
11. m'astreint
12. perçois
13. officines de paris
14. Ni les prêteurs sur gages, ni les escrocs au bonneteau.
15. ont déserté les trottoirs
16. rougit légèrement
17. il se peut que le travail inestimable
18. récompensé par l'état de choses que nous souhaitons tous,
19. dans nos rêves les plus fous
20. où, une fois Moriarty disparu, ses disciples, découragés

back into the sewer from which they came[1]. Sadly, I know that is not true. As the philosopher puts it, nature abhors a vacuum.[2] It may be that Devereux came here to ally himself with Moriarty. But finding Moriarty gone, he has simply taken his place.'

'I believe it too,' someone – I think Lanner – said. 'The evidence is there, in the streets.'

'Outbursts[3] of violence,' Bradstreet muttered. 'That business at the[4] White Swan.'

'And the fire on the Harrow Road. Six people died …'

'Pimlico …'

'What are you talking about?' Lestrade cut in[5], addressing himself to Hopkins. 'Why should we believe that anything has changed? Where's the proof?'

'I had one informer who was prepared to speak to me and I have to say that in a way I had a certain liking for him[6]. He had been in trouble from the day he climbed out of the cradle.[7] Petty stuff. Fare dodging, thimble-rigging[8] – but lately he had graduated in the school of crime.[9] He had fallen in with a bad lot[10] and I saw him less and less. Well, one week ago, I met him by arrangement in a rookery[11] near Dean Street. I could see at once[12] that he did not want to be there, that he had only come for old times' sake[13] for I had helped him once or twice in the past. "I can't see you, Mr Hopkins," he said to me. "It's all changed now. We can't meet any more." "What is it, Charlie?" I demanded. I could see that he was pale, his whole body shaking. "You don't understand …" he began.

1. regagnent les égouts dont ils sont sortis
2. Comme le dit le philosophe, la nature a horreur du vide.
3. Des pics
4. Cette histoire au
5. interjeta
6. d'une certaine manière, je m'étais attaché à lui
7. avait eu des ennuis depuis le berceau.
8. Petite délinquance, resquillage, escroquerie au bonneteau.
9. Mais dernièrement, il a pris du galon à l'école du crime.
10. fricotait avec des crapules
11. lui ai donné rendez-vous dans un taudis
12. tout de suite
13. en souvenir du bon vieux temps

'There was a movement in the alleyway[1]. A man was standing there, silhouetted against the gas lamp[2]. I could not see who he was and anyway he was already moving away. I cannot even be sure he had been observing us. But for Charlie, it was enough. He did not dare to speak the name but this is what he said. "The American," he said. "He's here now and that's the end of it[3]." "What do you mean? What American?" "I've told you all I can, Mr Hopkins. I shouldn't have come. They'll know!" And before I could stop him, he hurried away[4], disappearing into the shadows. That was the last I saw of him.[5]' Hopkins paused. 'Two days later, Charlie was pulled out of the Thames[6]. His hands were tied and death was due to drowning.[7] I will not describe his other injuries, but I will say only this: I have no doubt at all that what Mr Chase tells us is the truth. An evil tide[8] has come our way.[9] We must fight it before it overwhelms us all[10].'

There was a long silence after this. Then Inspector MacDonald once again turned to Athelney Jones. 'What did you find at Bladeston House?' he asked. 'Are there any lines of enquiry you can pursue?[11]'

'There are two,' Jones replied. 'Although I will be honest and say that there is a great deal about these murders that still remains unclear[12]. The evidence takes me in one direction.[13] Common sense takes me in quite another.[14] Still[15] … I found a name and a number in Lavelle's diary[16]: HORNER 13. It was written in capitals and circled[17]. There was nothing else on the page. It struck me at the time as very strange.[18]'

1. ruelle
2. sa silhouette se découpant dans la lumière du réverbère
3. rien ne sera plus jamais comme avant
4. sortit précipitamment
5. C'est la dernière fois que je l'ai vu.
6. on repêchait Charlie dans la Tamise
7. Mains attachées, mort par noyade.
8. vague diabolique
9. menace de s'abattre sur nous
10. qu'elle nous engloutisse tous
11. Y avez-vous trouvé une quelconque piste à suivre ?
12. que ces meurtres demeurent, en grande partie, une énigme
13. Les indices m'incitent à aller dans une direction.
14. Et le bon sens me dicte l'inverse.
15. Pour autant
16. agenda
17. entouré
18. Cela m'a intrigué au plus haut point.

'I arrested a man called Horner,' Bradstreet announced, rolling his pipe in his hands[1]. John Horner. He was a plumber[2] at the Hotel Cosmopolitan. Of course, I'd got completely the wrong man[3]. Holmes put me right.[4]'

'There is a tea shop in Crouch End,' Youghal added. It was run by a[5] Mrs Horner, I believe. But it closed long ago.'

'There was a block of shaving soap in the same drawer[6],' I recalled[7]. 'I wondered if that might be significant?' Nobody spoke so I continued. 'Could Horner perhaps be a druggist or a chemist's shop[8]?'

Again, this elicited no reply.[9]

'What else, Inspector Jones?' MacDonald asked.

'We met a man, an unpleasant character[10] by the name of Edgar Mortlake. Mr Chase knew him from New York and identified him as one of Devereux's associates. It seems that he is the proprietor of a club in Mayfair, a place called the Bostonian.'

That name caused a stir[11] around the table.

'I know it,' Inspector Gregson said. 'Expensive, trashy[12]. It opened only recently.'

'I visited the place,' Lestrade said. 'Pilgrim had a room there at the time of[13] his death. I looked through his things but I found nothing of any interest.'

'He wrote to me from there,' I concurred[14]. 'It was thanks to him that I knew about the letter that Devereux had sent to Moriarty.'

'The Bostonian is the home of almost every wealthy American[15] in London,' Gregson continued. 'It's owned by two brothers – Leland and Edgar Mortlake. They have their own chef[16]

1. faisant rouler sa pipe entre ses mains
2. plombier
3. je m'étais complètement trompé de type
4. m'a remis sur la bonne piste.
5. tenu par une certaine
6. aussi un savon à raser dans ce même tiroir
7. je me souvins
8. une droguerie ou une pharmacie
9. cela ne provoqua pas la moindre réponse.
10. personnage désagréable
11. des remous
12. tape-à-l'œil
13. y avait une chambre juste avant
14. renchéris-je
15. le refuge de la plupart des Américains fortunés
16. propre chef

and they create their own cocktails. There are two floors, the upper one of which is used for gaming[1].'

'Is it not obvious?' Bradstreet exclaimed. 'If Clarence Devereux is anywhere in London, surely that is where he is to be found[2]. An American club with an American name, run by a known felon[3].'

'I would have thought, in that case[4], it would be the last place he would present himself[5],' Hopkins said, quietly. 'Surely, the whole point is that he doesn't want to make himself known.[6]'

'We should raid the building[7],' Lestrade said, ignoring him. 'I myself will arrange it.[8] A surprise visit with a dozen or more officers this very day[9].'

'I would suggest the early evening,' Gregson said. 'For that is when it will be busiest[10].'

'Perhaps we will find this Clarence Devereux at the card table. If so, we will make short work of him.[11] We are not going to be colonized by criminals from foreign countries. This gangsterish violence must stop.[12]'

Soon afterwards, the meeting came to an end. Jones and I left together and as we made our way down the stairs, he turned to me.

'Well, it's agreed,' he said. 'We intend to mount a raid on a club which has but a tenuous link[13] with the man we are seeking and a man whose existence several of my colleagues are inclined to doubt[14]. Even if Clarence Devereux happens to be there[15], we will be unable to recognise him and going there will only tell him that we are on his tail[16]. What do you say, Chase? Would you not call it a complete waste of time?'

'I would not be so bold[17],' I replied.

1. l'étage est réservé au jeu
2. là qu'il se cache
3. aux mains d'un criminel notoire
4. serais plutôt d'avis
5. que c'est bien le dernier endroit où il se montrerait
6. C'est dans son intérêt de passer inaperçu.
7. Il faut faire une descente dans ce club
8. m'en charge personnellement.
9. aujourd'hui-même
10. il y aura le plus de monde
11. Dans ce cas, nous n'en ferons qu'une bouchée.
12. Il faut mettre fin à la violence des gangs organisés.
13. n'a qu'un lien ténu
14. et dont l'existence était plus que contestable au regard de certains de mes collègues
15. s'y trouve, par le plus grand des hasards
16. le préviendra juste que nous sommes à ses trousses
17. présomptueux

'Your reticence does you credit.[1] But I must return to my office. You can spend the afternoon seeing something of the city[2]. I will send a note to your hotel and the two of us will meet again tonight.'

1. est toute à votre honneur.
2. à visiter un peu la ville

NINE

The Bostonian

In fact, Jones was wrong. As things turned out[1], the raid on the Bostonian did prove useful in one small but significant respect[2].

It was already dark when I left my room at the hotel and as I stepped into the corridor I was aware of the door next to mine swinging shut[3]. Once again I did not see the occupant beyond a shadowy figure[4] who vanished[5] immediately as the door closed but it occurred to me that I had not heard him go past[6], which I should surely have done as the carpet was threadbare[7]. Had he been waiting outside as I made my preparations[8]? Had he left when he heard me approach? I was tempted to challenge him but decided against it[9]. Jones had been precise about the hour of our meeting. There might be a perfectly innocent explanation for the behaviour of my mysterious neighbour. At any event[10], he could wait.

And so we found ourselves, an hour later, standing beneath a gas lamp[11] on the corner of Trebeck Street, waiting for the signal – the scream of a whistle[12] and the tramp[13] of a dozen leather boots – which would announce that the adventure had begun. The club was in front of us: a

1. Finalement

2. dans une moindre mesure mais à un titre important

3. j'entendis qu'on refermait précipitamment la porte d'à côté

4. n'aperçus de son occupant qu'une silhouette indistincte

5. s'évanouit

6. je me rendis compte que je ne l'avais pas entendu passer,

7. ce qui était inévitable tant le tapis était usé

8. me préparais à sortir

9. me ravisai

10. Quoi qu'il en soit

11. sous un réverbère

12. coup de sifflet

13. suivi du piétinement

1. étroite bâtisse quelconque à la façade blanche
2. Mis à part
3. le piano qu'on entendait par intermittence dans la nuit
4. n'avait quasiment pas dit un mot
5. en pleine réflexion
6. Il faisait anormalement froid et humide pour la saison
7. si le temps accentuait sa douleur à la jambe
8. témoignage
9. avait sur lui la clé de la chambre
10. aurait pu avoir écrit l'adresse quelque part
11. négligent de nature
12. C'était une forte tête.
13. se montrer impulsif
14. très conscient du danger d'être découvert
15. C'est bien ce que je dis
16. se terra à nouveau dans le silence
17. fuyait mon regard
18. avait toujours une posture étrange

narrow, quite ordinary white-fronted building[1] on a corner. But for[2] the heavy curtains drawn across the windows and the occasional snatch of piano music jingling into the night[3], it could have been a bank. Jones was in a strange mood. He had been virtually silent[4] since I had joined him and appeared to be deep in thought[5]. It was unseasonably cold and damp[6] – it seemed as if the summer was never going to arrive – and we were both wearing heavy coats. I wondered if the weather was accentuating the pain in his leg[7]. But suddenly he turned to me and asked, 'Did you not find Lestrade's testimony[8] to be of particular interest?'

The question had taken me by surprise. 'Which part of it?'

'How did he know that your agent, Jonathan Pilgrim, had a room at the Bostonian?'

I thought for a moment. 'I have no idea. It could be that Pilgrim was carrying the key to his room[9]. Or I suppose he could have had the address written down[10].'

'Was he a careless man[11]?'

'He was headstrong.[12] He could be reckless[13]. But he was very aware of the danger of discovery[14].'

'My point exactly[15]: it's almost as if he wanted us to come here. I hope we are not making a grave mistake.'

He lapsed once again into silence[16] and I took out my watch. There were another five minutes until the raid began and I wished we hadn't arrived so early. It seemed to me that my companion was avoiding my eye[17]. He always stood awkwardly[18] and I knew that he was in fairly constant discomfort[1] and needed his walking stick. But as we waited there, he was more awkward than ever.

'Is there something the matter[2], Jones?' I asked at length[3].

'No. Not at all,' he replied. Then: 'As a matter of fact[4], there was something I wished to ask you.'

'Please![5]'

'I hope you will not find it presumptuous but my wife wondered if you might like to join us for dinner tomorrow night.' I was amazed that something so trivial should have caused him[6] so much difficulty but before I could answer, he continued quickly, 'I have of course described you to her and she is most keen to meet you and to hear something[7] of your life in America.'

'I would be delighted[8] to come,' I said.

'Elspeth does worry about me a great deal[9],' he went on. 'Between ourselves, she would be much happier if I were to find another occupation and she has often said as much[10]. Needless to say[11], she knows almost nothing of the events at Bladeston House. I have told her that I am engaged on a murder investigation but I have given her none of the details and would ask you to do the same. Fortunately, she does not often read the newspapers. Elspeth has a very delicate nature[12] and if she had any idea of the sort of people we were up against, she would be greatly troubled[13].'

'I am very glad to be invited,' I said. 'For what it's worth,[14] the food at Hexam's Hotel is atrocious. Please don't worry yourself, Inspector. I'll take my lead from you[15] and will answer any questions that Mrs Jones poses with the utmost discretion[16].' I looked up briefly into the gaslight.[17] 'My dearest mother never once discussed[18] my work

1. ressentait une gêne quasi constante
2. Quelque chose ne va pas
3. au bout d'un moment
4. À vrai dire
5. Je vous en prie !
6. stupéfait qu'un sujet aussi trivial puisse lui causer
7. elle a hâte de vous rencontrer et d'entendre le récit
8. ravi
9. se fait beaucoup de souci à mon sujet
10. changeais de profession, elle me l'a confié à plusieurs reprises
11. Cela va de soi
12. est de nature très fragile
13. auxquelles nous sommes confrontés, cela la perturberait fort
14. D'autant que
15. Je suivrai votre exemple
16. la plus grande discrétion
17. levai les yeux un instant vers le réverbère.
18. Pas une seule fois ma chère mère n'a abordé

with me. I know it caused her discomfort[1]. If only for that reason, I'll take the greatest care.[2]'

'Then it's agreed.' Jones looked relieved[3]. 'We can meet at Scotland Yard and travel together to Camberwell. You will also meet my daughter, Beatrice. She is six years old and as eager to know about my business[4] as my wife is to avoid it[5].'

I already knew that there was a child involved[6]. Beatrice was doubtless the recipient of the French puppet[7] that Jones had brought back from Paris. 'Dress?[8]' I asked.

'Come as you are. There is no need for formality.[9]'

Our discussion was interrupted by the shrill scream of a whistle[10] and at once the quiet street was filled with uniformed men running towards a single door. Jones and I were here as onlookers[11] – Lestrade had taken charge of the operation and he was the first to climb the steps and grab hold of the handle[12]. The door was locked. We watched him step back, search for the doorbell, and ring it impatiently[13]. Eventually, the door was opened. He and the police constables piled in[14]. We followed.

I had not expected the interior of the Bostonian to be quite so lavish[15], despite what Inspector Gregson had told us. Trebeck Street was narrow and poorly lit[16] but the front door took us into a glittering[17] world of mirrors and chandeliers, marble floors and ornate ceilings[18]. Paintings in gilt frames[19] covered every inch of the walls, many of them by well-known American artists[20] … Albert Pinkham Ryder, Thomas Cole. Anyone who had ever visited the Union Club in Park Avenue or the Metropolitan on 60th Street would have felt them-

1. que ce sujet lui causait de l'inquiétude
2. Ne serait-ce que pour cette raison, je ferai très attention.
3. apparut soulagé
4. aussi désireuse d'en savoir plus sur mon travail
5. que ma femme d'éviter le sujet
6. qu'il avait un enfant
7. la destinataire de la marionnette française
8. Tenue habillée ?
9. Laissons de côté les formalités.
10. cri strident d'un sifflet
11. en simples spectateurs
12. à saisir la poignée
13. chercher la sonnette et l'activer avec impatience
14. se bousculèrent à l'intérieur
15. si somptueux
16. étroite et mal éclairée
17. scintillant
18. de plafonds décorés
19. Des tableaux aux cadres dorés
20. signés, pour la plupart, de célèbres artistes américains

selves at home, and that was surely the point[1]. A rack of newspapers[2] by the entrance contained only American publications. The dozens of bottles set out on the brightly polished glass shelves[3] were largely American brands – Jim Beam and Old Fitzgerald bourbon, Fleischmann Extra Dry Gin. There were at least fifty people in the front room and I heard accents from the East Coast, from Texas, from Milwaukee. A young man in a tailcoat[4] had been playing a piano, the front panel removed[5] to show its inner workings[6]. He had stopped the moment we came in and sat there, his eyes fixed on the keys[7].

Police officers were already moving through the room and I could feel the indignation of the crowd as the men and women, all in their finest evening wear, separated to allow them to pass[8]. Lestrade had marched straight up to the bar as if demanding a drink[9] and the barman was staring at him, open-mouthed[10]. Jones and I hung back[11]. Neither of us had been sure of the wisdom of this enterprise[12] and we were both wondering where to begin. Two policemen were already climbing the stairs to the second floor. The rest of them were covering[13] the doors so that nobody could enter or leave the club without being challenged[14]. I will admit that I was greatly impressed by the Metropolitan Police[15]. They were well-organised and disciplined even if, as far as I could tell[16], they had no idea why they were here.

Lestrade was still haranguing[17] the barman when a door at the side opened and two men came out. I recognised them both at once. Edgar Mortlake we had already met. This time, his brother was with him. Just as the maid[18] at

1. se serait senti chez lui, ce qui était certainement le but
2. porte-revues
3. disposées sur les étagères de verre poli étincelantes
4. en queue de pie
5. dont on avait ôté le premier panneau
6. le mécanisme interne
7. touches
8. en tenue d'apparat, s'écartaient pour les laisser passer
9. comme pour exiger un verre
10. le fixait, bouche bée
11. restâmes en arrière
12. du bien-fondé de cette entreprise
13. bloquaient
14. sans être pris à partie
15. police de Londres
16. pour autant que je puisse en juger
17. houspillait toujours
18. bonne

Bladeston House had told us, the two of them were very much alike[1] (they were both dressed in black tie[2]) and yet they were nonetheless curiously different[3], as if some artist or sculptor had been at work[4] and deliberately created from one[5] a more brutal and hot-blooded representation in the other[6]. Leland Mortlake had the same black hair and small eyes as his brother but no moustache. He was a few years older and they weighed heavily on him:[7] his face was fleshier, his lips thicker,[8] his whole expression one of contempt[9]. He was several inches shorter[10] than Edgar but even before he spoke I could see that he was the more dominant of the two. Edgar was standing a few steps behind him. It was his natural position.

They had not seen Lestrade – or if they had, had chosen to ignore him. However, Edgar recognised both Jones and myself and, nudging his brother, led him over to us[11].

'What's this?' Leland demanded. His voice was hoarse[12] and he breathed heavily as if the act of speaking exhausted him.

'I know them,' Edgar explained. 'This one is a Pinkerton's man. Didn't trouble[13] to give me his name. The other is Alan Jones or something of the sort[14]. Scotland Yard. They were at Bladeston House.'

'What do you want?'

The question was aimed at[15] Jones and he replied. 'We are searching for a man named Clarence Devereux.'

'I don't know him. He's not here.'

'I told you I was unacquainted with him[16],' Edgar added. 'So why have you come here? If you wanted membership[17], you could have asked

1. ils se ressemblaient comme deux gouttes d'eau
2. ils portaient tous deux le même frac
3. mais ils présentaient néanmoins des différences intrigantes
4. en était à l'origine
5. avait cherché à faire de l'un
6. une version plus dure et plus tempétueuse de l'autre
7. Les quelques années qu'il avait de plus l'avaient fort marqué :
8. visage plus épais, lèvres plus charnues,
9. le mépris pour toute expression
10. faisait plusieurs centimètres de moins
11. d'un coup de coude, entraîna son frère dans notre direction
12. rauque
13. ne s'est pas donné la peine de me dire son nom.
14. ou quelque chose dans le genre
15. était destinée à
16. je n'ai jamais entendu parler de ce type
17. Si tout ce que vous vouliez c'est devenir membre

when we met in Highgate. Although I think you may find our annual fees a little beyond your means.[1]'

By now[2], Lestrade had noticed the exchange and came striding over[3]. 'You are Leland Mortlake?' he demanded.

'I am Edgar Mortlake. That's my brother, if you wish to speak to him.'

'We're looking for—'

'I know who you're looking for. I've already said. He's not here.'

'Nobody is leaving here tonight until they have given me proof of their identity,' Lestrade said. 'I wish to see the register of your guests – their names and addresses. I intend to search this club from the top floor to the basement.[4]'

'You cannot.'

'I very much think I can, Mr Mortlake. And I will.[5]'

'You had a man staying[6] here at the beginning of the year,' I said. 'He was here until the end of April. His name was Jonathan Pilgrim.'

'What of him?[7]'

'You remember him?'

Leland Mortlake stared vacantly,[8] his small eyes still filled with resentment[9]. But it was his brother who answered my question. 'Yes. I believe we did have[10] a guest with that name.'

'What room?'

'The Revere[11]. On the second floor.' The information was given reluctantly[12].

'Has it been occupied since?'

'No. It's empty.'

'I'd like to see it.'

1. cotisation annuelle un tantinet au-dessus de vos moyens

2. Entre-temps

3. fondit sur nous

4. la cave

5. Non seulement je le peux, M. Mortlake, mais je vais le faire.

6. Un homme a séjourné

7. Et alors ?

8. avait un regard absent,

9. ses petits yeux encore animés du même ressentiment

10. Je crois me souvenir que nous avons eu

11. [Paul Revere, figure de la guerre d'indépendance américaine]

12. n'était pas donnée de gaieté de cœur

Leland turned to his brother and for a moment I thought the two of them were going to protest. But before either of them could speak, Jones stepped forward[1]. 'Mr Chase is with me and he has the authorisation of Scotland Yard. Take us to the room.'

'Whatever you say.[2]' Edgar Mortlake looked at us with controlled fury and had we not been in London, surrounded by[3] the British police, I cannot say what might have ensued[4]. 'But this is the second time you have bossed me about[5] and I can tell you, Mr Jones, that I don't like it. There won't be a third time, of that I can assure you[6].'

'Are you threatening us[7]?' I demanded. 'Are you forgetting who we are?'

'I'm just saying that I won't stand for it[8].' Edgar lifted a finger[9]. 'And it is you, perhaps, who has forgotten who you're dealing with[10], Mr Pinkerton. You may rue the day that you chose to interfere.[11]'

'Dry up[12], Edgar!' Leland muttered.

'Whatever you say, Leland,' Edgar returned.

'This is an outrage[13],' the older brother continued. 'But you must do as you want. We have nothing to hide.'

We left Lestrade with them, the police already beginning the long process of[14] interviewing each and every one of the guests[15], painstakingly noting down their details[16]. Together, we climbed the stairs, arriving at a narrow corridor running left and right[17]. On one side, there was another large room lit by candelabra[18] and with several tables covered with green baize[19]. Evidently, this was where the gaming took place. We did not enter it, following the corridor in the other dir-

1. intervint
2. Si vous le dites.
3. si nous ne étions pas trouvés à Londres, encerclés par
4. je ne saurais dire ce qui se serait passé
5. que vous me donnez des ordres
6. je peux vous l'assurer
7. Seriez-vous en train de nous menacer ?
8. je ne le tolérerai plus
9. leva un doigt
10. à qui vous avez affaire
11. Vous pourriez regretter un jour de vous en être mêlé.
12. Tout doux
13. C'est scandaleux
14. le long processus consistant à
15. interroger chaque membre un à un
16. en consignant fastidieusement toutes les informations
17. étroit couloir courant sur la droite et sur la gauche
18. éclairée de candélabres
19. d'un tapis vert

ection past several bedrooms, each one named after a famous Bostonian[1]. Revere was about halfway down[2]. The door was unlocked.

'I cannot imagine what it is that you hope to find,' Jones muttered as we went in.

'I'm not sure I expect to find anything,' I replied. 'Inspector Lestrade said that he had already been here. And yet Pilgrim was a clever man. If he thought himself to be in danger,[3] there's a chance he might have tried to leave something behind.'

'One thing is certain. There is nothing to be discovered downstairs[4].'

'I quite agree.[5]'

At first glance, the room was unpromising[6]. There was a bed, freshly made[7], and a closet, empty. Another door led into a bathroom with both a water closet and a gas-heated bath[8]. The Bostonian certainly knew how to look after its guests[9] and I could not help feeling envious,[10] remembering my own shabby hotel[11]. The wallpaper, curtains and furnishings[12] were all of the highest quality. We began a search, opening the drawers, pulling up the mattress, even turning the pictures[13], but it was clear that once Jonathan Pilgrim had left, the room had been stripped and cleaned[14]. 'This is a waste of time,' I said.

'So it would seem.[15] And yet … what have we here?' As Jones spoke, he leafed through[16] a pile of magazines that stood on an occasional table at the foot of the bed[17].

'There is nothing,' I said. 'I've already looked.'

It was true. I had quickly thumbed through[18] the magazines – *The Century*, *The Atlantic Monthly*, *The North American Review*. But it was not the publications that interested Jones. He had pulled

1. chacune portant le nom d'un célèbre Bostonien
2. se trouvait à mi-parcours
3. S'il se savait en danger,
4. à chercher en bas
5. Je suis bien d'accord.
6. À première vue, la pièce ne promettait pas grand-chose.
7. qui venait d'être fait
8. un cabinet de toilette séparé et une baignoire avec chauffe-eau
9. prendre soin de ses pensionnaires
10. ne pouvais m'empêcher de les envier
11. en repensant au taudis qui me servait d'hôtel
12. Papier peint, rideaux et mobilier
13. retournant le matelas, et soulevant même les tableaux
14. la chambre avait été entièrement vidée et nettoyée
15. Il semblerait bien.
16. feuilletait
17. posée sur une table d'appoint au pied du lit
18. compulsé

1. avait extirpé un encart publicitaire
2. La meilleure lotion capillaire
3. Luxuriance
4. L'antidote universellement reconnue contre la calvitie,
5. les cheveux blancs et la moustache clairsemée.
6. Médecins et spécialistes certifient la lotion
7. garantie sans composants métalliques ou néfastes
8. chauve
9. une chevelure bien fournie
10. Vous regardez mais vous n'observez pas.
11. agenda
12. compétent
13. à dessein, dans l'espoir qu'on le retrouverait
14. Cela ne signifiait rien, bien entendu,
15. pour ceux qui ont fait le ménage.
16. Cela ne veut rien dire pour moi non plus !
17. peut bien avoir à faire
18. C'est ce que nous allons voir.
19. pour une fois, et malgré ses efforts contraires
20. Cela me change.

out a small advertising card[1] from one of them and showed it to me. I read:

POSITIVELY THE BEST
HAIR TONIC[2]
HORNER'S 'LUXURIANT[3]'

The world-renowned remedy for baldness,[4] grey hair and weak or thin moustaches.[5]

Physicians and Analysts pronounce it to be[6] perfectly safe and devoid of any Metallic or other injurious Ingredients[7].

Manufactured only by Albert Horner
13 Chancery Lane, London E1.

'Jonathan Pilgrim was not bald[8],' I said. 'He had a fine head of hair[9].'

Jones smiled. 'You see but you do not observe.[10] Look at the name – Horner. And the address: number thirteen!'

'Horner 13!' I exclaimed. They were the words we had found in the diary[11] in Scotchy Lavelle's desk.

'Exactly. And if your agent was as capable[12] as you suggest, it is quite possible that he left this here on purpose in the hope that it would be found[13]. It would, of course, mean nothing[14] to anyone cleaning the room.[15]'

'It means nothing to me either![16] What can a hair tonic possibly have to do[17] with Clarence Devereux or with the murders at Bladeston House?'

'We shall see.[18] It seems that for once, and despite his best efforts[19], Lestrade has actually helped our investigation. It makes a change.[20]'

Jones slipped the advertisement[1] into his pocket. 'We will say nothing of this[2], Chase. Agreed?'

'Of course.'

We left the room, closing the door behind us, and made our way back downstairs.

1. glissa la réclame

2. Ça reste entre nous

TEN

Horner's of Chancery Lane

It was just as well that[1] Horner's advertised itself[2] with a red and white barber's pole[3] for otherwise[4] we might not have found it. To begin with, it wasn't actually on Chancery Lane. There was a narrow, muddy thoroughfare that ran down to[5] Staples Inn Garden with a haberdasher's[6] – Reilly & Son – and the Chancery Lane Safe Deposit Company[7] on the corner and a little row of very shabby houses opposite[8]. The barber shop occupied the front parlour of one of these[9] with a sign[10] above the door and a further advertisement in the window: Shaving 1d; haircut 2d[11]. On one side was a tobacconist[12] that had closed down. The house on the other side looked fairly abandoned too.

A hurdy-gurdy man[13] was playing in the street, perched on a stool[14] and wearing a ragged top hat[15] and a worn-out, shapeless coat[16]. He was not very accomplished[17]. Indeed, had I been working in the vicinity[18], he would have driven me quite mad with the almost tuneless howling and tinkling[19] of his instrument. The moment he saw us, he stood and called out: 'Hair tonic in the ha'porths and pen'orths[20]. Try Horner's special

1. Heureusement,
2. signalait sa présence
3. par l'enseigne rouge et blanche des barbiers
4. car autrement
5. ruelle étroite et boueuse qui descendait jusqu'à
6. mercerie
7. [banque de dépôts de valeurs]
8. petite rangée de maisons en piteux état en face
9. rez-de-chaussée de l'une d'entre elles
10. pancarte
11. Barbe : 1 penny – Coupe : 2 pennies
12. bureau de tabac
13. joueur de vielle à roue
14. tabouret
15. vieux haut-de-forme
16. frac usé informe
17. doué
18. à proximité
19. braillements et tintements dissonants
20. pour un penny et un demi-penny

hair tonic! Get your cut or your shave here!' He was an odd[1] fellow, very thin and unsteady[2] on his feet. As we approached, he stopped playing and handed us a card from a satchel slung over his shoulder[3]. It was identical to the one we had found at the Bostonian.

We entered the building and found ourselves in a small, uncomfortable room with a single barber's chair facing a mirror[4] so cracked and dusty that it barely showed any reflection at all[5]. There were two shelves lined with[6] bottles of Horner's Luxuriant as well as other hair restorers and cantharides lotions[7]. The floor hadn't been swept and tufts of old hair were still strewn across it[8] – as unsavoury a sight as one could wish to see[9], though not as bad as the soap bowl,[10] a congealed mess which still carried the spiky fragments of men's beards[11]. I was already beginning to think that this was the last place in London I would wish to come for a haircut when the barber himself arrived.

He had climbed up a staircase in the back parlour[12] and tottered towards us,[13] wiping his hands on a handkerchief[14]. It was hard to determine his age – he was both old and young at the same time with a round, quite pleasant face, clean-shaven[15] and smiling. But he had a terrible haircut. Indeed, it was as if he had been attacked by a cat. His hair was long on one side, short on the other with patches missing altogether, exposing his skull[16]. Nor had it been washed for some time, leaving it with both[17] a colour and a texture that was disagreeable to say the least[18].

He was, however, amiable enough[19]. 'Good morning, gentlemen,' he exclaimed. 'Although

1. étrange
2. chancelant
3. nous tendit un bristol qu'il sortit de la sacoche à son épaule
4. un unique fauteuil faisant face à un miroir
5. si crasseux et fêlé qu'il ne reflétait plus grand-chose
6. étagères garnies de
7. , produits antichute et autres lotions à la cantharide
8. balayé et était jonché de mèches de cheveux des clients de la veille
9. un spectacle des moins ragoûtants
10. bol de savon à raser,
11. une soupe solidifiée parsemée de poils de barbe
12. au fond de la boutique
13. se dirigea vers nous en titubant
14. s'essuyant les mains dans un mouchoir
15. rasé de près
16. avec de véritables trous qui laissaient voir son crâne
17. ce qui leur conférait à la fois
18. pour le moins déplaisantes
19. tout à fait aimable

this cursed weather refuses to change![1] Have you ever known London so wet and so miserable and here we are in May! What can I do for you? One haircut? Two haircuts? You are fortunate in that I am very quiet today.[2]'

This was true in every sense[3]. Outside, the hurdy-gurdy player had at last chosen to take a rest[4].

'We are not here for a haircut,' Jones replied. He picked up one of the bottles and smelled the contents. 'Do I take it you are[5] Albert Horner?'

'No, sir. Bless you![6] Mr Horner died long ago. But this was his business and I took it over[7].'

'Quite recently, by the look of it[8],' Jones remarked. I glanced at him, wondering how he could have come to such a conclusion for, to my eye, both the man and the shop[9] could have been here for years. 'The barber's pole[10] is old,' Jones continued, for my benefit[11]. 'But I could not help noticing that the screws fastening it to the wall[12] are new. The shelves may be dusty,[13] but the bottles are not.[14] That tells the same tale.[15]'

'You're absolutely right!' the barber exclaimed. 'We've been here less than three months and we kept the old name. And why not? Old Mr Horner was well known and much admired. We're already popular among the lawyers and the judges[16] who work in this area – even if many of them insist on wearing wigs[17].'

'So what is your name?' I asked.

'Silas Beckett, sir, at your service.'

Jones produced the advertisement[18]. 'We found this in a club called the Bostonian. I take it that name means nothing to you[19], or the man who was staying there[20]. An American gentleman called Jonathan Pilgrim.'

1. Malgré ce maudit temps qui refuse de changer !
2. Vous tombez bien, c'est très calme aujourd'hui.
3. à bien des égards
4. s'était enfin décidé à faire une pause
5. Vous êtes bien
6. Dieu merci.
7. j'ai repris le flambeau
8. Assez récemment, de toute évidence
9. à mes yeux, l'homme comme la boutique
10. L'enseigne
11. à mon intention
12. Mais j'ai remarqué que les vis qui la fixent au mur
13. Il y a de la poussière sur les étagères,
14. mais pas sur les flacons.
15. Tout porte à croire la même chose.
16. parmi les avocats et les magistrats
17. tiennent à porter une perruque
18. sortit la réclame
19. J'imagine que ce nom ne vous dit rien
20. pas plus que celui de l'homme qui y résidait

'American, sir? I don't believe I've ever had an American in here.' He gestured at me. Apart from yourself.[1]'

Beckett was no detective. It was my accent that had given me away.

'And the name Scotchy Lavelle – have you heard it?'

'I speak to my customers, sir. But it's not often they tell me their name. Was he another American?'

'And Clarence Devereux?'

'You're running ahead of me[2], sir. So many names! Can I interest you in[3] a bottle of our hair tonic?' He asked this almost impertinently,[4] as if he were anxious to bring the interview to an end[5].

'Do you know him?'

'Clarence Devereux? No, sir. Perhaps you might try across the road, at the haberdasher's.[6] I am very sorry that I cannot be of assistance. In short,[7] it would seem we are wasting each other's time.[8]'

'That may be so, Mr Beckett, but there is just one thing you can tell me that would interest me.' I saw Jones examining the barber carefully. 'Are you a religious man?'

The question was so unexpected that I'm not sure who was more surprised – Beckett or I. 'I'm sorry?[9]' He blinked[10].

'Religious. Do you go to church?'

'Why do you ask?' Jones said nothing and Beckett sighed, clearly anxious to be rid of us[11]. 'No, sir, for my sins, I am not a regular churchgoer[12].'

'It is just as I thought[13],' Jones muttered. 'You have made it quite clear that you cannot help us, Mr Beckett. I will wish you a good day.'

1. À l'exception de vous.
2. Vous allez trop vite pour moi
3. Seriez-vous intéressé par
4. avec un air insolent,
5. comme s'il désirait écourter l'entretien
6. Vous aurez peut-être plus de chance en face, à la mercerie.
7. Au final,
8. il semblerait que nous ne puissions rien l'un pour l'autre.
9. Pardon ?
10. sourcilla
11. soupira, visiblement impatient de se débarrasser de nous
12. pour mon malheur, je ne compte pas parmi les fidèles
13. C'est bien ce que je pensais

We left the barber's shop and walked back up to Chancery Lane. Behind us, the hurdy-gurdy player struck up again[1]. As soon as we turned the corner, Jones stopped and laughed. 'We have stumbled onto[2] something quite remarkable here, my boy. Holmes himself would have been entertained by this[3]: a barber who cannot cut hair, a hurdy-gurdy player who cannot play, and a hair tonic that contains large quantities of benzoin[4]. Hardly a three-pipe problem[5], but not without interest.'

'But what is the meaning of it?' I exclaimed. 'And why did you ask Mr Beckett about his religious beliefs?'

'Is it not obvious to you?'

'Not at all.'

'Well, it will be made clear soon enough. We are having dinner together tonight. Why not come to Scotland Yard at three o'clock? We can meet outside, as we did before, and then everything will be explained.'

Three o'clock.

I was there exactly on time, stepping out of my hansom[6] on Whitehall with Big Ben chiming the hour[7]. We had stopped on the far side of the road[8], which is to say, the one opposite Scotland Yard. I paid the driver. It was a bright, cloudless afternoon, though still a little chilly[9].

I must set down[10] exactly what happened.

Ahead of me[11], crossing the road, I saw a boy whom I recognised instantly. It was Perry, who had sat next to me in the Café Royal and who had held a knife to my neck[12]. I stood there and it seemed to me that everything had become

1. reprit de plus belle
2. avons déniché
3. s'en serait délecté
4. une grande quantité de benjoin
5. Pas vraiment un problème à trois pipes
6. fiacre
7. au moment où Big Ben sonnait l'heure
8. de l'autre côté de la rue
9. quoique encore un peu fraîche
10. rapporter
11. À quelques mètres de moi
12. avait porté un couteau à mon cou

very still[1], as if an artist had taken the scene and captured it on a canvas[2]. Even at a distance, Perry was enveloped in what I can only describe as an aura of menace. This time, he was dressed as a naval cadet[3]. He had a cap, a dark blue double-fronted jacket with two lines of buttons[4], and a leather pouch hanging diagonally across his chest[5]. As before, he seemed to be squeezed into[6] the uniform he was wearing, his stomach pressing against the waistband[7], his neck too large for the collar. His hair looked even more yellow[8] in the afternoon sun.

Why was he here? What was he doing?

Athelney Jones appeared, walking out of Scotland Yard, looking for me, and I raised a hand in alarm[9]. Jones saw me and I pointed in the direction of the boy, who was walking briskly down the pavement,[10] his plump little legs carrying him ever further away[11].

Jones recognised him but he was too far away to do anything.

There was a brougham[12] waiting for Perry, barely fifty yards from where I was standing[13]. As he approached it, a door opened. There was a man inside, half hidden in the shadows[14]. He was tall, thin, dressed entirely in black. It was impossible to make out[15] his face but I thought I heard him cough[16]. Had Jones seen him? It was unlikely for he was quite a distance ahead[17] and on the wrong side of the road. The boy climbed into the brougham. The door closed behind him.

Without any further thought, I ran towards it.[18] I saw the driver whip up the horse and the carriage jolted forward[19] – but even so I might have been able to reach it[20]. Jones was on the edge

1. tout autour de moi s'était immobilisé
2. avait saisi la scène pour l'immortaliser sur une toile
3. en cadet de marine
4. veste à double boutonnière
5. sacoche cuir en travers de la poitrine
6. Comme la dernière fois, il était engoncé dans
7. ceinture
8. encore plus blonds
9. je levai la main pour l'alerter
10. cavalant sur le trottoir,
11. ses petites jambes dodues l'éloignant de plus en plus de moi
12. coupé de ville
13. à une cinquantaine de pas d'où je me trouvais
14. à demi tapi dans l'ombre
15. de distinguer
16. je crus l'entendre tousser
17. Il y avait peu de chances car il avait une longueur d'avance
18. Sans plus réfléchir, je me ruai dans sa direction.
19. fouetter son cheval et la voiture se mettre en branle
20. je pouvais encore le rattraper

1. Je voyais Jones du coin de l'œil.
2. s'aidant de sa canne pour aller plus vite
3. pas assez pour réduire la distance qui nous séparait
4. le trafic était dense
5. bifurquai
6. qui fonçait droit sur moi
7. obstruaient ma vue
8. perçants
9. Il semblait ne faire qu'un,
10. telle une créature bicéphale issue de la mythologie grecque
11. qu'ils tiraient
12. drame qui se déroulait sous leurs yeux
13. se débattait toujours avec
14. j'entendis des sabots battre le pavé, des roues grincer
15. cette même surface qui se rapprochait dangereusement
16. tandis que je plongeai en avant
17. chavira et le ciel passa devant mes yeux
18. m'avait évité de quelques centimètres
19. s'écartant brusquement avant de s'immobiliser
20. roulai sur le côté

of my vision.[1] He had begun to move too, using his walking stick to lever himself forward[2]. The brougham continued down Whitehall, picking up speed, heading for Parliament Square. I was running as fast as I could but I wasn't getting any nearer[3]. To reach it, I had to cross Whitehall but there was a great deal of traffic[4]. Already, the brougham was disappearing around the corner.

I veered[5] to one side. I had left the pavement and I was in the road.

Athelney Jones cried out a warning. I didn't hear him but I saw him calling to me, his hand raised.

Suddenly, there was an omnibus bearing down on me[6]. At first, I did not see it for two horses filled my vision[7]: huge, monstrous, with staring[8] eyes. They could have been joined together,[9] a single creature drawn from Greek mythology[10]. Then I became aware of the vehicle being hauled[11] behind them, the driver pulling at the reins, the half a dozen people crowded together on the roof, trapped there, horrified witnesses to the unfolding drama[12].

Somebody screamed. The driver was still struggling with[13] the reins and I was aware of hooves pounding down, the wheels grinding[14] against the hard surface, that same surface rushing up at me[15] as I threw myself forward[16]. The whole world tilted and the sky swept across my vision[17].

I might have been killed, but in fact the omnibus missed me by inches[18], veering away and then drawing to a halt[19] a short distance ahead. I had cracked my head and my knee but I was unaware of the pain. I twisted round[20], looking for the brougham, but it had already gone. The boy and his travelling companion had made their escape.

Jones reached me. To this day[1], I am not sure how he managed to cover the distance so quickly. 'Chase!' he exclaimed. 'My dear fellow![2] Are you all right? You were almost crushed …[3]'

'Did you see them?' I demanded. 'Perry! The boy from the Café Royal! He was here. And there was a man with him …'

'Yes.'

'Did you see his face?'

'No. A man in his forties or fifties[4], perhaps, tall and thin. But he was concealed, inside the carriage[5].'

'Help me …'

Jones was leaning down, helping me to my feet[6]. I was aware of a little blood trickling past my eye and wiped it away[7]. 'What was it all about[8], Jones?' I asked. 'Why were they here?'

My question was answered seconds later.

The explosion was so close that we felt it as well as heard it, a blast of wind and dust rushing to us where we stood[9]. All around us, horses whinnied and carriages veered out of control[10] as the drivers fought with the reins. I saw two hansoms collide with each other[11] and one tilted and crashed to the ground[12]. Men and women who had been walking past stopped, clutching onto each other, turning in alarm[13]. Pieces of brick and glass rained down on us[14] and a smell of burning pervaded[15] the air. I looked round. A huge plume of smoke was rising up from within[16] Scotland Yard. Of course! What else could have been the target[17]?

'The devils![18]' Jones exclaimed.

Together, we hurried across the road. By now the traffic had come to a standstill.[19] Without even

1. Encore aujourd'hui
2. Mon cher ami !
3. failli être écrasé…
4. d'une quarantaine ou d'une cinquantaine d'années
5. dissimulé par la voiture
6. se pencha pour m'aider à me relever
7. qui coulait près de mon œil et l'essuyai
8. Que se passe-t-il
9. un souffle d'air et de poussière s'abattant sur nous
10. hennissaient et des voitures échappaient à tout contrôle
11. fiacres entrer en collision
12. et l'un d'entre eux chanceler et se renverser
13. s'agrippant les uns aux autres, se retournant avec effroi
14. s'abattirent sur nous
15. de brûlé imprégnait
16. nuage de fumée s'échappait de
17. cible
18. Quels monstres !
19. Entre-temps, tout trafic était interrompu.

thinking that there might be a second device[1], we plunged into the building, fighting our way past the clerks, the constables[2] and the visitors who were desperately trying to find their way out. The lower floor at least seemed undamaged[3] but, as we stood there, a uniformed policeman appeared, coming down the stairs, his face blackened and blood streaming from a wound[4] in his head. Jones grabbed hold of him[5].

'What happened?' he demanded. 'What floor?'

'The third floor,' the man replied. 'I was there! It was so close …'

We wasted no time. We ran over to the stairs and began the long climb up, both of us aware that we had made the same journey together only the day before[6]. We passed many more police officers and assistants, making their way down, many of them hurt, clutching onto each other[7]. One or two of them urged us not to continue[8] but we ignored them. As we climbed higher, we smelled burning and there was so much smoke in the air it became hard to breathe. Finally, we reached the third floor and almost at once bumped into[9] a man whom I recognised from the conference. It was Inspector Gregson. His fair hair was awry[10] and he was in a state of shock but he did not seem to have been hurt.

'It was in the telegraph room,' he cried. 'A package brought by a messenger boy[11] was placed against the wall of your office, Jones. Had you been at your desk …[12]' Gregson broke off[13], his eyes filled with horror. 'I fear Stevens has been killed.'

Jones's face showed his dismay[14]. 'How many others?'

1. engin explosif
2. nous frayant un chemin parmi les employés, les policiers
3. rez-de-chaussée, au moins, paraissait intact
4. noirci et du sang s'écoulant d'une blessure
5. le saisit par le bras
6. pris ensemble le même escalier juste la veille
7. blessés pour beaucoup, prenant appui les uns sur les autres
8. nous mirent en garde de ne pas continuer
9. tombâmes aussitôt nez à nez avec
10. en pagaille
11. garçon de course
12. Si vous aviez été à votre bureau…
13. laissa sa phrase en suspens
14. bouleversement

'I can't say. We've been ordered[1] to evacuate the building.'

We had no intention of doing so.[2] We pressed forward, ignoring the casualties who were limping past,[3] some of them with their clothes torn, others streaming blood[4]. There was an uncanny silence[5] on the third floor. Nobody was screaming but I thought I could hear the crackle of flames[6]. I followed Jones, the two of us finally reaching the door of his office. Now it was open. I looked inside, into a scene of horror.

The office was not a large one. A single window looked out over the inner quadrangle[7], as Jones had told me. The room was filled with debris for the entire wall on the left had been shattered[8]. There was a wooden desk covered with dust and brickwork[9] and I could see at once that Gregson had been right. Had Jones been sitting there, he would have been killed. As it was, a young man lay on the floor with a police constable – dazed and helpless – crouching over him[10]. Jones hurried in and knelt beside the body[11]. It was obvious that he was dead. There was a dreadful wound[12] in the side of his head and his hand was outstretched, the fingers still[13].

'Stevens!' he exclaimed. 'He was my secretary … my assistant.'

Smoke was pouring in through the hole[14] in the wall and I saw that the damage[15] in the telegraph room had been even worse. The room was on fire, the flames licking at the ceiling, reaching up to the roof[16]. There were two more figures lying amongst the wreckage[17]. It was hard to be sure if they were men or boys as they had been horribly injured[18], both of them disfigured by the blast[19].

1. On a reçu l'ordre
2. Il n'était pas question pour nous de partir.
3. les blessés qui nous croisaient en boitant,
4. certains aux vêtements déchirés, d'autres blessés et saignant
5. silence qui faisait froid dans le dos
6. crépitement des flammes
7. donnait sur la cour intérieure
8. avait volé en éclats
9. bureau en bois couvert de gravats et de briques
10. penché sur lui, abasourdi et impuissant
11. s'agenouilla auprès du corps
12. plaie horrible
13. les doigts de sa main tendue étaient inertes
14. s'infiltrait par le trou béant
15. les dégâts
16. léchant le plafond, gagnant le toit
17. deux autres corps parmi les décombres
18. tant leurs blessures étaient graves,
19. défigurés par l'explosion

There was paper everywhere. Some of the pages seemed to be floating in the air. It must have been the heat.[1] The fire was rapidly spreading[2].

I went over to[3] Jones. 'There's nothing we can do!' I cried. 'We must do as we've been told[4] and leave the building. Go now!' I told the young constable.

He left and Jones turned to me; there were tears[5] in his eyes – though whether from grief or due to the smoke[6], I could not say. 'Was this meant for me?[7]' he asked.

I nodded[8]. 'I very much think so.'

I took hold of him and led him out of the office. It could not have been more than a few minutes since the detonation, but already we were alone on the third floor. I knew that if the fire spread, or if the smoke overwhelmed us[9], we might die here – and although Jones was unwilling[10], I forced him to accompany me to the staircase and back down. Behind us, I heard part of the ceiling collapse[11] in the telegraph office. We should perhaps have carried the dead secretary with us or at least covered the body as a mark of respect, but right then, it seemed to me, our own safety was paramount[12].

Several steam fire engines[13] had arrived by the time we burst out into the open air[14]. The firemen were already running forward, trailing their hoses across the pavement[15]. All the other traffic had disappeared. The road, which had been normal and busy just a short while ago[16], was eerily empty[17]. I helped Jones walk away from the building and, finding an unoccupied bench, set him down[18]. He was leaning heavily on his stick and there were still tears in his eyes.

1. C'était sans doute dû à la chaleur.
2. se propageait rapidement
3. rejoignis
4. suivre les ordres
5. des larmes
6. mais si elles étaient dues au chagrin ou à la fumée
7. Ça m'était destiné ?
8. hochai la tête
9. se répandait, ou si la fumée nous submergeait
10. résistait
11. une partie du plafond s'effondrer
12. notre propre sécurité prévalait
13. véhicules de secours à vapeur
14. débouchâmes à l'extérieur
15. étirant leurs longs tuyaux sur le trottoir
16. l'instant d'avant
17. sinistrement déserte
18. l'aidai à s'asseoir sur un banc inoccupé

'Stevens,' he muttered. 'He had been with me three years – and recently married! I was talking to him only half an hour ago.'

'I'm sorry.' I didn't know what else to say.

'This happened before. A bomb in Scotland Yard, six or seven years ago. It was the Fenians[1] and I wasn't in London. But this time ...' He seemed dazed[2]. 'You really believe I was the target?'

'I warned you,' I said. 'These people are ruthless[3] and it was only yesterday that[4] Edgar Mortlake threatened you.'

'Revenge for our raid on the Bostonian![5]'

'You cannot prove it, but I cannot see any other reason for this attack.' I broke off[6]. 'Had you not come out to greet me, you would have been sitting in your office. Do you not see that, Jones? You escaped by a matter of seconds.[7]'

He grabbed my arm[8]. 'You have been the saving of me.[9]'

'I am very glad of it.[10]'

We looked across the road, at the firemen operating the steam pumps[11] while others raised the ladders[12]. Smoke was still pouring out of the[13] building, thicker now, blanketing the sky[14].

'What now?' I asked.

Jones shook his head wearily[15]. There were black streaks on his cheekbones and across his forehead.[16] I guessed I must look the same[17]. 'I don't know,' he replied. 'But whatever you do, don't tell Elspeth![18]'

1. [mouvement nationaliste irlandais]
2. sonné
3. sans pitié
4. juste hier
5. Pour se venger de la descente au Bostonian !
6. m'interrompis
7. Vous vous en êtes tiré à quelques secondes près.
8. saisit mon bras
9. Vous avez été mon salut.
10. Vous m'en voyez ravi.
11. actionnaient les pompes
12. tandis que d'autres hissaient les échelles
13. s'échappait en continu du
14. s'épaississant et masquant le ciel
15. secoua la tête avec lassitude
16. Des traces noires lui barraient les joues et le front.
17. que je ne devais être guère plus présentable
18. Quoi qu'il en soit, pas un mot à Elspeth !

ELEVEN

Dinner in Camberwell

1. le train bien plus tard que prévu
2. la foule des passants semblait se fondre dans l'obscurité,
3. telle de l'encre se répandant sur une feuille
4. aucune décision ne serait prise
5. selon laquelle il avait échappé de justesse
6. à une tentative de meurtre semblait inévitable
7. une coincidence
8. qui avait appelé à la prudence
9. pas la moindre preuve sinon un bref échange
10. dont ils pourraient nier l'existence
11. élaboré
12. avaient tenu en échec

We took a much later train than we had intended[1], leaving Holborn Viaduct just as night fell and the crowds seemed to blend into the sudden darkness[2] like ink spattered on a page[3]. Jones was in a sombre mood. He had met Lestrade, Gregson and some of the other detective inspectors in the hours following the explosion but there were to be no decisions made[4] until the next day. The conclusion that he had narrowly escaped[5] an attempt on his life seemed inescapable[6]. We had the words spoken by Edgar Mortlake as the proof of it and surely the timing of the attack could not have been coincidental[7]. Lestrade was in favour of arresting both the brothers immediately but in the end it had been Jones himself who had urged caution[8]. He had no evidence beyond a brief conversation[9] that they might deny had ever taken place[10]. He had, he said, already devised[11] a better strategy – although he was not yet prepared to say what it was. I agreed. Clarence Devereux and his gang had run circles around[12] Pinkerton's for many years and would surely do the same with the British police. If we were going to reel them in, we would need to take the utmost care[1].

'It is unlikely[2] that Elspeth will have heard about the bomb,' Jones said, as our train drew into an area of[3] London known as Camberwell and we prepared to climb down, 'and I will have to tell her for it is inconceivable that I should withhold such information from her[4]. But the position of it![5] The possibility that I might have been the intended target ...'

'We will say nothing of that,' I said.

'She will somehow discern it[6]. She has a way of homing in on the truth.[7]' He sighed[8]. 'And yet still I do not understand these adversaries of ours[9]. What was it they hoped to achieve?[10] Had I been killed, there are any number[11] of inspectors who could have taken my place. You have met many of them yourself. And if they had really wanted me dead, there are many easier ways they could have achieved their aim[12]. Here we are now, on a station platform[13]. An assassin with a knife or a garrotte could do the job in the blink of an eye[14].'

'It is possible that their intention was never to kill you,' I said.

'That is not what you said before.'

'I said that you were the target and I still believe that to be the case. The truth is that it would not have mattered[15] to Clarence Devereux if you lived or died. It was no more than a demonstration of his power, his immunity from prosecution. He laughs in the face[16] of the British police and at the same time he warns them: do not come close, do not interfere with my business[17].'

'Then he misunderstands us.[18] After this, we will redouble our efforts.' He said no more until

1. les coincer, il nous faudrait prendre toutes les précautions
2. Il y a peu de chances
3. pénétrait un faubourg de
4. j'omette de lui dire une telle chose
5. Mais le lieu exact où l'engin a été placé !
6. le devinera toute seule
7. Elle a un don pour cerner la vérité.
8. soupira
9. nos adversaires
10. Quel était leur but ?
11. tout un tas
12. bien d'autres manières plus aisées d'arriver à leurs fins
13. sur le quai d'une gare
14. une garrotte pourrait s'en charger en un clin d'œil
15. il importait peu
16. Il rit au nez
17. ne vous mêlez pas de mes affaires
18. C'est mal nous connaître.

1. Que devons-nous conclure à propos du
2. les comprends
3. trouver un lien entre ces faits, ils défient tout sens commun
4. déroute sciemment son lecteur
5. si nous y parviendrons jamais
6. Un être immatériel.
7. qui m'est restée inconnue jusqu'à sa fin
8. à boiter
9. me ressaisir avant d'affronter ce qui m'attend
10. Vous préférez que
11. annuler
12. ont pris un tour encore pire
13. Le trajet était des plus courts
14. sembla nous avoir emmenés à une heure avancée de la nuit
15. s'insinuait dans les rues, pétrifiant l'air
16. transformant les derniers voyageurs en spectres

we had left the station. 'There is no logic, Chase, I tell you,' he continued. 'Who was the man in the brougham? What are we to make of the[1] meeting between Moriarty and Devereux, the role of this boy Perry, the murder of Lavelle, even Horner's of Chancery Lane? Separately, I have an understanding of them[2]. But when I try to bring them together, they defy common sense[3]. It is like reading a book in which the chapters have been published in the wrong order or where the writer has deliberately set out to confuse[4].'

'We will only find out the meaning of it when we find Clarence Devereux,' I said.

'I begin to wonder if we ever will[5]. Lestrade was right. He seems to be a phantom. He has no presence.[6]'

'Was not Moriarty the same?'

'That is true. Moriarty was a name, a presence – an entity unknown to me until the very end[7]. That was his power. It may well be that Devereux has learned from his example.' Jones was beginning to limp[8], resting heavily on his stick. 'I am tired. Forgive me if we talk no further. I must compose myself for whatever awaits me[9] at home.'

'Would you rather[10] I did not come?'

'No, no, my friend, to postpone[11] would only make Elspeth fear that events have taken a worse turn than they have[12]. We will dine together as planned.'

It had been but a short distance[13] from Holborn to Camberwell and yet the journey seemed to have taken us ever further into the night[14]. By the time we arrived, a thick fog was rolling through the streets, deadening the air[15] and turning the last commuters into ghosts[16]. A growler lumbered past.[1] I heard the clatter of the horse's hooves and the creak of the wheels[2] but the carriage itself was little more than[3] a dark shadow, vanishing around a corner[4].

Jones lived close to the station. I have to say that his property was very much as I had imagined it might be: a handsome terraced house with bay windows[5] and white stucco pillars[6] in front of a solid, black-painted door. The style was typically English, the effect one of calm and security. Three steps led up from the street and in climbing them[7] I had a strange sense that I was leaving all the perils of the day behind. Perhaps it was the warm glow[8] of light that I could discern, leaking through the edges of the curtained windows[9]. Or maybe it was the smell of meat and vegetables that wafted up from the kitchen[10] somewhere below. But I was already glad to be here. We entered a narrow hallway with a carpeted[11] staircase opposite and Jones led me through a doorway and into the front room. In fact the room ran the full length[12] of the house, with a folding screen pulled back to reveal[13] a dining table set for three[14] at the front, a library and a piano at the back. There was a fire burning in the hearth but it was hardly needed[15]. With the abundant furniture, the embroidered boxes and baskets[16], the dark red wallpaper and the heavy curtains, the room was already cosy enough[17].

Mrs Jones was sitting in a plush[18] armchair with a strikingly pretty six-year-old girl leaning against her,[19] the policeman puppet dangling over her arm[20]. Her mother had been reading to her but as we came in she closed the book and the little girl turned, delighted to see us. She had none of her

1. voiture de louage passa lourdement.
2. martèlement des sabots des chevaux et le couinement des roues
3. n'était qu'
4. qui s'évanouit au coin de la rue
5. une jolie maison mitoyenne avec des fenêtres en saillie
6. des colonnes en stuc blanc
7. en montant l'escalier
8. halo
9. qui filtrait à la lisière des rideaux tirés
10. qui s'échappait de la cuisine
11. recouvert d'un tapis
12. occupait toute la profondeur
13. un paravent replié dévoilant
14. dressée pour trois convives
15. dans la cheminée, mais ce n'était pas vraiment nécessaire
16. le mobilier fourni, les boîtes et autre paniers brodés
17. très chaleureuse
18. confortable
19. une ravissante petite fille de six ans louée contre elle,
20. la marionnette policier dans ses bras

father's looks[1]. With her light brown hair, tumbling in ringlets[2], her bright green eyes and smile, she was much more her mother's daughter, for Elspeth Jones clearly reflected her across the years[3].

'Not in bed yet, Beatrice?' Jones asked.

'No, Papa. Mama said I could stay up.'

'Well, this is the gentleman I imagine you wish to meet; my friend, Mr Frederick Chase.'

'Good evening, sir,' the girl said. She showed me the doll. 'This came from Paris. My papa gave him to me.'

'He seems a fine fellow[4],' I said. I always felt uncomfortable around children and tried not to show it.

'I have never met an American before.'

'I hope you will not find me very different from yourself. It was not so many years ago that my ancestors left this country. My great-grandfather[5] came from London. A place called Bow.'

'Is New York very loud?[6]'

'Loud?[7]' I smiled. It was such an odd choice of word.[8] 'Well, it's certainly very busy.[9] And the buildings are very tall. Some of them are so tall that we call them skyscrapers[10].'

'Because they scrape the sky[11]?'

'Because they seem to.[12]'

'That's enough now, Beatrice. Nanny[13] is waiting for you upstairs.' Mrs Jones turned to me. 'She is so inquisitive[14] that one day I'm sure she'll be a detective, just like her father.'

'I fear it will be some time before[15] the Metropolitan Police are prepared to admit women to their ranks[16],' Jones remarked.

'Then she can be a lady detective[17], like Mrs Gladden[18] in those excellent books of Mr

1. ne ressemblait pas du tout à son père
2. ses cheveux châtains qui tombaient en boucles
3. le portrait fidèle d'Elspeth Jones malgré les années
4. Il a l'air d'un gentil policier
5. arrière-grand-père
6. Est-ce qu'il y a beaucoup de bruit à New York ?
7. Du bruit ?
8. Le mot employé était étrange.
9. Une chose est sûre, il y a beaucoup de monde.
10. gratte-ciel
11. grattent le ciel
12. Parce qu'on dirait qu'ils grattent le ciel.
13. [la nurse]
14. curieuse
15. qu'il faille attendre quelque temps avant que
16. la police de Londres n'admette de femmes dans ses rangs
17. femme détective
18. [première femme détective de la littérature britannique]

Forrester's.' She smiled at her daughter. 'You may say good night to Mr Chase.'

'Good night, Mr Chase.' Obediently, the little girl hurried out of the room.[1]

I turned my attention to Elspeth Jones. She was, as I had at once perceived[2], very similar in looks to her daughter although her hair had been cut short over her forehead and gathered up in the Grecian style[3]. She struck me somehow as a very caring woman,[4] one who would bring a quiet intelligence to everything she did.[5] She was simply dressed in a shade of dusty pink[6] with a belt and a high collar and no jewellery that I could see. Now that Beatrice had gone, she gave me her full attention.

'Mr Chase,' she said. 'I am very pleased to meet you.'

'And you, ma'am,' I returned.

'Will you have some grog?' She gestured and I saw a jug[7] and three glasses had been set out on a brass table[8] beside the fire. 'It seems these wintery nights will never end[9] and I like to have something warm waiting when my husband returns home.'

She poured three glasses of the tincture[10] and we sat together in that slightly awkward silence that comes[11] when people meet each other for the first time and none of them is quite sure how to proceed[12]. But then the maid appeared to say that dinner was ready and once we had taken our places at the table, the company became more at ease[13].

The maid brought a pretty decent stew, boiled neck of mutton[14] with carrots and mashed turnips[15], certainly far superior to anything I had

1. Obéissante, la fillette quitta la pièce.

2. cela m'avait aussitôt frappé

3. étaient coupés court sur le front et relevés dans le style grec

4. Elle m'apparut comme une femme très attentionnée,

5. qui apportait une intelligence sereine à tout ce qu'elle faisait

6. vieux rose

7. pichet

8. guéridon en cuivre

9. que l'hiver ne finira jamais

10. nous en servit trois verres

11. dans ce silence un peu gêné qui s'installe

12. ne sait comment s'y prendre

13. tout le monde se détendit

14. ragoût plutôt bon de collier de mouton

15. de la purée de navets

been offered at[1] Hexam's, and while Athelney Jones poured the wine, his wife carefully steered[2] the conversation in the direction that she preferred. Indeed, her skill was that[3] she seemed natural and uncalculating[4] but I was aware that during the next hour we never once touched on anything to do[5] with the police. She asked me many questions about America: the food, the culture, the nature[6] of the people. She wanted to know if I had yet seen Thomas Edison's Kinetoscope[7], a device[8] that had been much discussed in the British press but which had yet to be exhibited[9]. Sadly, I had not.

'How do you find England?' she asked.

'I like London very much,' I replied. 'It reminds me more of Boston than New York, certainly in the number of art galleries and museums, the handsome[10] architecture, the shops. Of course, you have so much history here. I envy you that. Would that I had more time for leisure.[11] Every time I walk in the streets I find all manner of diversions[12].'

'Perhaps you might be tempted to remain[13] here longer.'

'It is not such a wild[14] supposition, Mrs Jones. It has long been my desire to[15] travel in Europe ... something that is true of many of my countrymen[16]. Most of us came from here, after all. If I am successful in this current[17] investigation with your husband, perhaps I might persuade my superiors to allow me a sabbatical[18].'

It was my first reference to the business[19] that had brought Athelney Jones and myself together and, as a steaming bread and butter pudding[20] was brought to the table by the little maid who

1. bien plus goûteux que tout ce proposait le restaurant du
2. dirigea
3. elle avait un don pour
4. agir avec naturel et sans préméditation
5. n'effleurâmes de près ou de loin aucun sujet en lien
6. caractère
7. [ancêtre du cinéma, inventé en 1889]
8. appareil
9. n'avait pas encore été exposé
10. superbe
11. Si seulement je disposais de plus de temps libre.
12. matière à me divertir
13. rester
14. folle
15. Cela fait bien longtemps que je souhaite
16. un désir partagé par nombre de mes compatriotes
17. actuelle
18. m'accorder un congé sabbatique
19. allusion à l'affaire
20. pudding fumant, fait de mie de pain et de beurre

seemed to pop up[1] from nowhere and disappear just as abruptly, our conversation turned to darker things[2].

'I must tell you something, my dear, that will concern you,' Jones began. 'But you will learn about it from the newspapers soon enough, rarely though you read them[3] ...' With that, he described the events of the afternoon, the attack on Scotland Yard and my own part in what had happened[4]. As agreed, he mentioned neither the position of the bomb nor the death of his secretary, Stevens.

Elspeth Jones listened in silence until he had finished. 'Were many people killed?' she asked.

'Three, but there were a great many injured[5],' Jones replied.

'It seems incredible that such an attack on the Metropolitan Police could be considered, let alone carried out[6],' she said. 'And this so soon after the unspeakable events in Highgate![7]' She turned to me, fixing me with her bright, inquisitive eyes[8]. 'You will forgive me, Mr Chase, if I say that some very dark forces have followed you from America.'

'I must disagree with you on one major[9] point, Mrs Jones. It was I who followed them.'

'And yet you have arrived at the same time.'

'Mr Chase is not to blame[10],' Jones muttered, reproachfully[11].

'I know that, Athelney. And if I suggested otherwise[12], I apologise. But I begin to wonder if this should even be a police matter[13]. Perhaps it is time for higher authorities to become involved[14].'

'It may well be that they already are.[15]'

1. surgir
2. prit un tour plus sombre
3. aussi rarement les feuillettes-tu
4. le rôle que j'y avais joué
5. beaucoup de blessés
6. puisse être envisagée, et encore moins perpétrée
7. les atrocités commises à Highgate !
8. regard vif et interrogateur
9. important
10. n'y est pour rien
11. sur un ton de reproche
12. le contraire
13. être laissé entre les seules mains de la police
14. s'y intéressent
15. Peut-être est-ce déjà le cas.

' "It may well be[1]" is not enough. Police officers have been killed!' She paused. 'Was the bomb very close to your office?'

Jones hesitated. 'It was on the same floor.'

'Were you the intended target[2]?'

I saw him consider[3] before he answered. 'It is too early to say. Several inspectors have offices close to where the bomb was placed. It could have been intended for any one of us. I implore you[4], my dear, let us speak no more of it.' Fortunately, the maid chose that moment to appear with the coffee. 'Shall we remove to the other room?[5]'

We left the table and returned to the back parlour where the fire was now burning low[6]. At the last moment, the maid had handed Mrs Jones a parcel wrapped in brown paper[7] and, as we sat down, she passed it to her husband. 'I am sorry to trouble you[8], Athelney, but I wonder if you would mind walking up the road to[9] Mrs Mills?'

'Now?'

'It is her laundry and some books for her to read[10].' She turned to me and continued in the same breath[11], 'Mrs Mills is a member of our congregation and recently widowed[12]. To add to her misfortunes[13], she has not been very well and we do what we can to be good neighbours.'

'Is it not rather late?[14]' Jones asked, still holding the parcel[15].

'Not at all. She does not sleep very much and I told her you would be looking in[16]. She was delighted to hear it. You know how fond she is of you[17]. Anyway, a stroll will do you good[18] before bed.'

'Very well. Perhaps Chase will accompany me ...?'

1. Peut-être
2. cible visée
3. réfléchir
4. Je t'en supplie
5. Passons au salon.
6. brûlait maintenant avec moins d'intensité
7. paquet enveloppé de papier brun
8. t'importuner
9. tu aurais la gentillesse d'aller jusque chez
10. son linge et quelques livres pour elle
11. poursuivit d'un seul trait
12. veuve depuis peu
13. malheur
14. N'est-il pas un peu tard ?
15. le paquet entre les mains
16. passerais la voir
17. combien elle t'apprécie
18. cela te fera du bien de te dégourdir les jambes

'Mr Chase has not finished his coffee. He will keep me company while you are gone.'

Her strategy was obvious[1]. She wanted to speak to me on my own[2] and had arranged things to that effect. Throughout[3] the evening, I had been amused to watch my friend, Athelney Jones, in the privacy[4] of his home. So forceful and single-minded when pursuing his investigation[5], he was altogether[6] quieter and less demonstrative in the company of his wife. Their closeness was indisputable.[7] They filled each other's silences and anticipated the other's demands. And yet I would have said that she was by far the stronger of the two. In her company, Jones lost much of his authority and it made me think that even Sherlock Holmes might have been a lesser detective[8] had he chosen to marry[9].

Her husband stood up. He took the parcel, kissed her gently on the forehead[10], and left the room. She waited until she had heard the front door open and close. Then she looked at me in a quite different way, no longer the hostess[11], and I realised that she was assessing me[12], deciding whether to draw me into some inner circle of confidence[13].

'My husband tells me that you have been a detective with Pinkerton's for some time,' she began.

'For longer than I care to remember[14], Mrs Jones,' I replied, 'although strictly speaking,[15] I am an investigator, not a detective. It is not quite the same thing.'

'In what way?[16]'

'We are more straightforward in our methods.[17] A crime is committed. We investigate it. But in most cases it is simply a matter[18] of procedure,

1. était évidente

2. en tête-à-tête

3. Pendant

4. intimité

5. Tout déterminé et énergique qu'il était pendant l'enquête

6. au contraire

7. Leur entente ne faisait aucun doute.

8. n'aurait sans doute pas été le détective qu'il était,

9. s'il avait choisi de se marier

10. front

11. plus tout à fait celui de l'hôtesse qui m'avait accueilli

12. me jaugeait

13. si j'étais digne de confiance

14. je m'en souvienne

15. à vrai dire,

16. En quoi est-ce différent ?

17. Nos méthodes sont plus directes.

18. question

which is to say that, unlike the British,[1] we do not go in so much for duplicity and deception[2].'

'Do you enjoy the work?'

I thought for a moment. 'Yes. There are people in this world who are very bad, who bring nothing but misery to others and I think it is right to bring them down[3].'

'You are not married?'

'No.'

'You have never been tempted?'

'You are very forthright.[4]'

'I hope I do not offend you. I only wish to know you a little better. It is important to me.'

'Then I will answer your question. Of course I have been tempted. But I have been of a solitary nature ever since I was a child and in recent years I have allowed my work to consume me[5]. I like the idea of matrimony[6] but I am not sure that for me it would be ideal.' I was uncomfortable with the way the conversation was turning[7] and tried to change the subject. 'You have a beautiful home, Mrs Jones, and a charming family.'

'My husband is very taken with you[8], Mr Chase.'

'For that I am grateful.[9]'

'And what, I wonder, do you make of him?[10]'

I put down my coffee cup. 'I'm not sure I know what you mean.'

'Do you like him?'

'Do you really want me to answer that?'

'I would not have asked you if I did not.'

'I like him very much. He has welcomed me as a stranger to this country and he has been singularly kind to me[11] when others, I am sure, would have been obstructive[12]. He is also, if I may say so, a brilliant man. In fact, I would go further and

1. ce qui revient à dire que, contrairement aux Britanniques,
2. nous versons peu dans la duplicité et les faux-semblants
3. les arrêter
4. Vous n'y allez pas par quatre chemins.
5. je me suis laissé accaparer par mon travail
6. mariage
7. Le tour que prenait la conversation me mettait mal à l'aise
8. vous apprécie beaucoup
9. Vous m'en voyez ravi.
10. La question que je me pose c'est : qu'en est-il pour vous ?
11. il s'est montré particulièrement bienveillant envers moi
12. m'aurait mis des bâtons dans les roues

add that I have never met a detective quite like him. His methods are extraordinary.'

'Does he remind you of anyone?'

I paused. 'He reminds me of Sherlock Holmes.'

'Yes.' Suddenly her voice was cold. 'Sherlock Holmes.'

'Mrs Jones – that you have deliberately arranged for your husband to leave is obvious[1]. But I don't know why, and I feel it is discourteous to discuss him[2] in his absence. So why don't you tell me. What is it that is on your mind?[3]'

She said nothing but examined me carefully and, sitting there with the firelight reflecting softly on her face, I suddenly thought her very beautiful. Eventually she spoke.[4] 'My husband keeps an office upstairs[5],' she said. 'He uses it sometimes as a retreat[6], when he is involved in a case[7]. Would you care to see it?[8]'

'Very much.'

'And I would very much like to show it to you. You need have no concern[9], by the way. I am permitted to enter when I wish and we will only be there for a minute or two.'

I followed her out of the room and up the stairs past watercolours[10] – mainly birds and butterflies – hanging in plain wooden frames on the striped paper[11]. We reached the first landing[12] and entered a small, uncarpeted room that looked out onto[13] the back garden. I knew at once[14] that this was where Jones worked. And yet it was not he who dominated[15] the room.

The first thing I saw, sitting on[16] a table, was a neat[17] pile of *Strand Magazines*, each one so well preserved as to appear brand new[18]. I did not need to open them to know what I would find

1. il est évident que vous avez fait en sorte que votre mari nous laisse seuls
2. inconvenant de parler de lui
3. Dites-moi plutôt ce que vous avez en tête ?
4. Elle finit par reprendre la parole.
5. a un bureau à l'étage
6. s'y retire parfois
7. enquête sur une affaire
8. Aimeriez-vous le voir ?
9. N'ayez crainte
10. orné d'aquarelles
11. avec des cadres en bois simple, accrochées sur le papier peint à rayures
12. étage
13. petite pièce au sol nu qui donnait sur
14. aussitôt
15. sa présence qui dominait
16. posée
17. impeccable
18. qu'on eût dit qu'ils avaient été achetés récemment

inside. They all carried accounts[1] of the adventures of Sherlock Holmes as narrated by Dr John H. Watson and the great detective was present all over the room in photographs, daguerreotypes[2] and newspaper headlines which had been tacked to the wall[3]: BLUE CARBUNCLE RECOVERED[4], COBURG SQUARE BANK ROBBERY FOILED[5]. On studying the books and monographs on the shelves, I saw that a great many of them had been written by Holmes. Among them was a sizeable[6] volume on the scientific analysis of bloodstains[7], another (*One Hundred and Sixty* Ciphers[8] *Examined*) on codes and a third, which reminded me of the train journey from Meiringen[9], on different types of tobacco ash[10]. There were other books by Winwood Reade, Wendell Holmes, Emile Gaboriau and Edgar Allen Poe, several encyclopedias and gazetteers[11] and a copy of the *Anthropological Journal* lying open at an article concerning the shape of the human ear[12]. Though austere in its general appearance – apart from the bookshelves[13], the only furniture was a desk, a chair and two small tables – the room was cluttered, with every inch of every surface holding one strange object or another[14]. I saw a magnifying glass, a Bunsen burner,[15] glass phials filled with chemicals,[16] a stuffed snake – a swamp adder[17], I think – a number of bones, a map of Upper Norwood, what might have been a mandrake root and a Turkish slipper[18].

I had been hovering in the doorway.[19] Elspeth Jones had gone in ahead of me and now twisted round[20]. 'This is where my husband works,' she said. 'He spends more time here than any other

1. Ils présentaient tous les récits
2. [daguerréotype : ancêtre de la photographie]
3. gros titres de journaux, punaisés au mur
4. escarboucle bleue retrouvée
5. braquage de banque déjoué à Coburg Square
6. épais
7. taches de sang
8. codes secrets
9. qui me rappela notre trajet en train depuis Meiringen
10. cendres
11. des revues
12. consacré à la forme de l'oreille humaine
13. étagères
14. étant occupé par un objet plus ou moins intrigant
15. une loupe, un bec Bunsen
16. des fioles contenant divers produits chimiques,
17. un serpent empaillé – une vipère des marais
18. racine de mandragore, une babouche turque
19. J'étais resté sur le pas de la porte.
20. se tourna à présent vers moi

room in the house. I am sure I do not need to tell you who has been his inspiration.'

'It is very evident.'

'We have already spoken his name.' She drew herself up. 'There are times when I wish I had never heard it!' She was angry and her anger made her quite different from the mother who had read to her child and the wife who had sat with me at the dinner table. 'This is what I want to tell you, Mr Chase. If you are to[1] work with my husband, it is vital that you understand. My husband first met Sherlock Holmes following the murder of one[2] Bartholomew Sholto, an investigation that concluded with the loss of the great treasure[3] of Agra. As it happens, he came out of it with some credit,[4] although he never saw it that way[5], and the account published by Dr Watson portrayed him in a particularly unflattering light[6].'

Jones had already alluded to it[7]. But I said nothing.

'The two of them met again on a rather less spectacular business[8], a break-in[9] in North London and the strange theft[10] of three porcelain figures'.

'The Abernettys.'

'He has told you?'

'He has alluded to it.[11] I know none of the details.'

'He doesn't speak of that affair very often – and with good reason[12].' She paused, composing herself[13]. 'Once again he failed.[14] Once again Dr Watson will have turned him into a laughing stock[15] although, fortunately, he has yet to publish this particular tale[16]. After it was all over, my husband spent weeks torturing himself. Why had he not

1. vous devez

2. suite au meurtre d'un certain

3. s'est conclue sur la disparition du somptueux trésor

4. Il s'en est vu attribuer quelque crédit,

5. quoiqu'il ne l'ait jamais vu sous cet angle

6. l'a dépeint sous un jour très peu flatteur

7. m'en avait déjà parlé

8. sur une affaire bien moins rocambolesque

9. cambriolage

10. l'intrigante disparition

11. Il l'a mentionnée.

12. à juste titre

13. pour reprendre son calme

14. Il a connu un nouvel échec.

15. Le Dr Watson le tournera, à nouveau, en ridicule

16. n'a pas encore publié ce récit-là

1. de l'étoupe
2. un indice qui parle de lui-même, quand on y songe
3. Comment avait-il pu passer à côté de la signification
4. manqué le moindre indice d'importance
5. traces de pas
6. pli
7. Comment pouvait-il seulement se prétendre inspecteur
8. alors qu'il s'était conduit en amateur empoté
9. avec lui
10. toute confiance
11. réellement l'ami que vous clamez être
12. d'un mal de dents, d'une sensation de faiblesse dans les os
13. Ses poignets et ses chevilles étaient enflés.
14. était surmené
15. du repos
16. souffrait de rachitisme
17. une maladie qui l'avait temporairement affecté
18. virulente
19. de congé
20. j'ai été à son chevet
21. Au début, je ne souhaitais que sa guérison
22. abandonner sa carrière dans la police
23. avait fini commissaire de police

realised that the dead man had been in prison? There was oakum[1] under his fingernails – a fairly obvious clue when you think about it[2]. Why had he been so blind to the significance[3] of the three identical figurines when it had been so immediately obvious to Mr Holmes? He had missed every single clue of any importance[4] … the footprints[5], the sleeping neighbour, even the fold[6] in the dead man's sock. How could he even call himself a detective[7] when he had been shown up as a bumbling amateur[8]?'

'You are too hard on him[9].'

'He was too hard on himself! I must speak to you in confidence[10], Mr Chase, hoping with all my heart that you are indeed the friend that you profess to be[11]. Following the Abernetty business, my husband became very ill. He complained of tiredness, toothache, a sense of weakness in his bones[12]. His wrists and his ankles swelled up.[13] At first, I thought he had overworked himself[14], that all he needed was rest[15] and a little sunshine. However, the doctor soon diagnosed something much more serious. He was afflicted with the rickets[16], a disease that had actually touched him briefly[17] when he was a child but which had returned in a much more serious and vengeful[18] form.

'He was forced to take a year off work[19] and during that time, I nursed him[20] day and night. To begin with, all I looked for was his recovery[21] but as the months passed and he became a little stronger, I began to hope that he might put his police career behind him[22]. His brother, Peter, is an inspector. His father had risen to become a superintendent[23]. There was, I knew, a sense of family tradition. But even so, with a young child and a wife who feared for him almost daily and with the knowledge that he would never recover his former strength[1], I allowed myself to believe that he might choose to begin a new life elsewhere[2].

'I was deceived.[3] My husband dedicated the year of his hiatus to the betterment[4] of his career as a detective. He had met Sherlock Holmes twice[5]. He had been beaten by him[6] twice. He was determined that, should they meet again, history would not repeat itself a third time. In short, Inspector Athelney Jones would make himself the equal of the world's most famous consulting detective and to that end he threw himself into his work with a vigour[7] that belied the disease that had crippled him[8]. You see some of the evidence around you but believe me when I say that this is but a small part of it[9]. He has read everything that Mr Holmes has ever written[10]. He has studied his methods and replicated his experiments[11]. He has consulted with every inspector who ever worked with him. He has, in short, made Sherlock Holmes the very paradigm of his own life.'

Everything she said made sense to me. From the moment I had met Athelney Jones I had been aware of his interest in the great detective. But I had not appreciated how much it went to the heart and soul of who he was[12].

'My husband returned to his office a few months ago,' Elspeth Jones concluded. 'He thinks he has fully recovered from the worst of his illness[13] – but what actually sustains him is his knowledge[14] of Holmes's work and his belief[15] that he is now Holmes's equal.' There was a terrible pause and then, faltering[16], she continued. 'I do not share

1. qu'il ne retrouverait jamais ses forces d'autrefois
2. ailleurs
3. Je me suis gravement trompée.
4. a consacré son année d'absence à faire avancer
5. à deux reprises
6. avait été battu à plates coutures
7. dans ce but, il s'est jeté à corps perdu dans son travail
8. niant le mal dont il avait souffert
9. ce n'en est qu'une infime partie
10. ait jamais écrit
11. reproduit ses expériences
12. perçu à quel point cela influençait jusqu'à son âme
13. s'est complètement remis de sa maladie
14. mais cela ne repose, en vérité, que sur sa connaissance
15. conviction
16. d'une voix vacillante

that belief. God forgive me for saying it.[1] I love my husband. I admire him. But more than anything, if he remains blinded by this cruel self-belief,[2] I fear for him[3].'

'You are wrong—' I began.

'Do not try to be kind to me[4]. Look around you. Here is the evidence. Heaven knows where this obsession will take him.[5]'

'What do you want me to do?'

'Protect him. I do not know these people he is up against[6], but I am terribly afraid for him. They would seem to be ruthless[7]. He, in his own way, is so lacking in guile[8]. Is it wrong of me to speak to you in this way?[9] I do not know how I would live without him and these dreadful murders, the attempt[10] today …'

She broke off[11]. The whole house was silent.

'Mrs Jones,' I said. You have my word that I will do everything I can to guide us both through to safety[12]. It is true that we find ourselves up against a formidable enemy[13] but I do not share your misgivings[14]. Your husband has already demonstrated to me, time and again[15], his extraordinary intelligence. I am perhaps a few years older than he, but even so I recognise the fact that I am the junior partner in this enterprise[16]. That said[17], I promise you with all my heart that I will look out for him[18]. I will stand by him.[19] And should we find ourselves in danger, I will do everything in my power to protect him.'

'You are very kind, Mr Chase. I can ask no more.[20]'

'He will be back very soon,' I said. 'We should go downstairs.'

1. Dieu me pardonne de le dire.
2. continue d'être aveuglé par cette cruelle confiance en lui,
3. j'ai peur pour lui
4. de m'épargner
5. Dieu seul sait jusqu'où son obsession le conduira.
6. à qui il se mesure
7. sans pitié
8. manque cruellement de duplicité.
9. Ai-je tort de vous parler en ces termes ?
10. et quand je pense à cette tuerie atroce, à l'attaque
11. s'interrompit
12. pour garantir notre sécurité à tous les deux
13. sommes confrontés à un ennemi redoutable
14. doutes
15. à maintes occasions
16. je ne fais que le seconder sur cette affaire
17. Cela étant dit
18. de veiller sur lui
19. Je resterai à ses côtés.
20. C'est tout ce que je vous demande.

She took my arm and we went back down together. Shortly afterwards[1], Jones returned and found us sitting before the fire, discussing the five boroughs[2] of New York. He did not see that anything was amiss[3] and I said nothing.

But as I returned to Camberwell station, I was deep in thought[4]. The night was still black, the fog rolling across the pavement[5]. Somewhere far away, a dog howled[6] in the darkness, warning me of things I did not want to know.

1. Peu de temps après

2. quartiers

3. qu'il se tramait quoi que ce soit

4. plongé dans mes pensées

5. se répandait sur le trottoir

6. hurlait

TWELVE

Foreign Soil[1]

1. En Terre étrangère
2. d'une humeur plus exubérante
3. faisant preuve d'un empressement
4. lui inspirait l'exemple donné
5. Vous serez soulagé d'apprendre
6. nous progressons
7. il faudra au moins une semaine
8. disparaissent
9. N'avez-vous pas remarqué
10. à quel endroit se trouvait
11. à huit pas
12. le salon du barbier
13. Vous quitterez
14. je démissionnerai

Jones was in a more ebullient mood[2] when we met the next day, exhibiting that strange alacrity of spirit[3] which, I now knew, had found its inspiration in the example set[4] by the greatest detective of all.

'You will be relieved to hear[5] that, finally, we make progress[6]!' he announced as we met outside my hotel.

'You have been back to Chancery Lane?' I asked.

'Silas Beckett and his associates can wait. I would say that it will be at least a week[7] before they slip away[8] into the night.'

'How can you be so sure if you have not returned?'

'I knew it before we left, my dear Chase. Did you not remark upon[9] the position of[10] the hurdy-gurdy player? He was standing precisely eight paces[11] from the front door of the barber's shop[12].'

'I'm afraid I do not follow you at all.'

'I begin to think that you and I might have a future together. You shall leave[13] Pinkerton's and I shall resign[14] from Scotland Yard. You will enjoy living in London. No! I am quite serious. The city has need[1] of a new consulting detective. We might even take rooms[2] on Baker Street! What do you say?'

'I am not sure what to say.'

'Well, we have more pressing matters at hand[3]. First, our friend Perry. We have now learned that he entered Scotland Yard at twenty minutes to three and claimed to be carrying a package for me[4], a large box wrapped[5] in brown paper. He was directed to my office[6] on the third floor.'

'Why didn't he leave it in your office?'

'He could not have done so. I was behind my desk and would have been sure to recognise him[7]. Instead, he placed it as near as he could, which was on the other side of the wall in the telegraph office. They are used to seeing messenger boys[8], apprentices and cadets coming in and going out and one more would have made no difference[9].'

'But you left.'

'I left to meet you, as we had arranged. Perry must have been just a minute or two ahead of me. That's how close it was![10] You saw him enter the carriage. Have you had any further thoughts as to the identity[11] of his companion?'

'I have no idea.'

'No matter.[12] Our adversaries may have made their first serious error, Chase. Had they chosen a hansom[13] for their adventure, it might have been impossible to find them. The streets of London are littered with hansoms, licensed and unlicensed[14], and the driver might never have come forward[15]. The brougham is an altogether rarer beast[16] and its driver is even now in our hands.'

'How did you find him?'

1. a grand besoin

2. nous installer

3. des questions plus urgentes à régler

4. a déclaré avoir un paquet pour moi

5. enveloppé

6. On lui a indiqué mon bureau

7. l'aurais reconnu à coup sûr

8. des garçons de course

9. un de plus ou de moins n'aurait rien changé

10. Cela s'est joué à peu de chose !

11. Avez-vous réfléchi quant à l'identité

12. Aucune importance.

13. fiacre

14. sont envahies de fiacres, avec ou sans licence

15. aurait pu ne jamais se faire connaître

16. Les coupés sont des engins autrement plus exotiques

'We have had three divisions on the streets[1], almost a hundred men. Did you really think that we would allow such an outrage as took place yesterday to go unpunished[2]? Not an inn, not an alley, not a coach house or stable[3] has been overlooked[4]. All night they have been out and now, finally, we have a man who remembers carrying a fare[5] to Whitehall, who picked up a second passenger moments before the explosion.'

'And where did they go?'

'I have yet to speak[6] to the driver. But if he can tell us where he took them, or where this man came from, then our task will have been accomplished and Devereux may yet fall into our hands[7].'

Jones had arrived in a cab, which was still waiting for us, and we travelled across[8] London, battling our way[9] through the interminable traffic, without speaking. I was grateful for[10] the silence. It allowed me to reflect on what Elspeth Jones had said to me the night before and to wonder if she had some intuition about what lay ahead[11]. For his part, Jones had not referred to[12] the dinner, although he must have been aware that his wife had arranged things so as to speak privately with me[13] for half an hour. Did he know that we had entered his study? In retrospect[14], I had found the encounter strangely disturbing[15]. I wished that she and I had spoken a little more … or perhaps less.

We finally drew in to a cabstand[16] near Piccadilly Circus, the very heart of the western end[17] of the city, the equivalent, if you like, of Times Square[18]. I saw at once a well-maintained, brightly polished brougham parked with a uniformed police constable[19] standing beside it. The driver, a

1. Trois divisions ont quadrillé les rues
2. nous laisserions un outrage comme celui d'hier rester impuni
3. Pas la moindre auberge, ruelle, remise à calèches ou étable
4. n'a été oubliée
5. avoir effectué une course
6. Je n'ai pas encore parlé
7. pourrait bien tomber entre nos mains
8. traversâmes
9. nous frayant un chemin
10. J'appréciai
11. elle avait pressenti ce qui nous attendait
12. n'avait fait aucune allusion
13. s'était arrangée pour me parler en privé
14. En y repensant
15. étrangement troublante
16. Nous nous arrêtâmes enfin à une station de taxis
17. en plein cœur des quartiers ouest
18. [quartier très animé de New York]
19. officier de police en uniforme

huge man in a topcoat that seemed to billow out[1] like a tent, was sitting in his place with the reins across his knees and a scowl on his face[2]. We climbed down.[3] 'Mr Guthrie?' Jones asked, striding forward[4].

'Aye[5], that's me,' the driver responded. 'And I bin 'ere an hour or more.[6] What's it to be[7] when a honest man is kept from 'is livelihood like this?[8]'

He had not moved, staring down at us as if he were as firmly tied into his seat[9] as the horse in its harness[10]. He really was a vast man, with rolling cheeks, side whiskers and crimson-coloured skin[11] that had come either from long exposure to the air in all weathers or, more likely, from sclerosis.

'I am sure we can recompense[12] you for your time,' Jones remarked.

'I don't want your recompents, guv'nor[13]. I want to be paid!'

'You will receive all the money that is due to you – but you must first tell me everything I wish to know. Yesterday you picked up[14] a man.'

'Yesterday I picked up several men.'

'But one of them you took to Whitehall, close to Scotland Yard. It was about three o'clock in the afternoon.'

'I know nothing of the hour.[15] What's an hour to me?[16]' He shook his huge head before Jones could interrupt and it seemed to me that the horse, in sympathy[17], did the same. 'All right, all right. I know what man you speak of. A tall gentleman. I can tell you that because 'e 'ad to fold 'imself over to get in[18]. Queer customer[19] – that's what I thought.'

'What age?'

1. pardessus qui semblait se gonfler au vent
2. rênes sur les genoux et un air renfrogné sur le visage
3. Nous descendîmes du fiacre.
4. s'avançant d'un pas rapide
5. [Forme ancienne ou régionale de « oui »]
6. Et j'suis là d'puis une heure ou plus.
7. C'est d'puis quand
8. qu'on empêche un honnête homme d'faire son travail ?
9. comme s'il était aussi solidement fixé à son siège
10. que le cheval à son harnais
11. des joues tombantes, des favoris et une peau cramoisie
12. dédommager
13. Patron [déformation de « governor »]
14. vous avez pris en charge
15. J'en sais fichtre rien, de l'heure.
16. Ça m'servirait à quoi, moi, d'savoir l'heure ?
17. par empathie
18. il a dû s'plier en quat' pour entrer là d'dans
19. Bizarre, ce client

1. Plus vieux qu' jeune
2. Le regard mauvais.
3. Un regard qu'on a pas envie d' croiser.
4. [Grande avenue de Londres]
5. Cela ne nous est d'aucun secours
6. c'est en dehors de la plupart des lignes d'omnibus
7. de n'importe où
8. aussi direct' que j'ai pu, avec la circulation
9. Y avait pas plus seul.
10. Y restait dans son coin
11. tout emmitouflé avec son chapeau sur les yeux
12. et le regard baissé vers son col
13. L'a toussé plusieurs fois mais pas un seul mot, qu'y m'a dit
14. ça fait deux mots
15. Pas même
16. renifla
17. Même mon ch'val est plus causant.
18. boum

'Thirty or forty.' He thought for a minute. 'Or maybe fifty. I can't say. Older than he was young[1] – that's all. Nasty eyes.[2] Not the sort of eyes you'd want to have looking your way.[3]'

'And where did you pick him up?'

'At the Strand[4].'

Jones turned to me. 'That is of no help to us[5],' he said, quietly. 'The Strand is one of the busiest cabstands in London. It is close to one of the main railway stations and all the drivers use it because it is clear of many of the omnibus routes[6].'

'So our mysterious passenger could have arrived from anywhere[7].'

'Precisely. Tell me, Mr Guthrie. You took him directly to Whitehall?'

'I took him as direct as the traffic would allow[8].'

'He was alone?'

'Alone as alone can be.[9] He kept 'imself to 'imself[10], wrapped up in the corner with 'is 'at over 'is eyes[11] and 'is eyes turned down to 'is collar[12]. He coughed a few times but not one word did he say to me[13].'

'He must have informed you of the destination.'

' "Whitehall," he said when he got in. And "Stop!" when he wanted to get out. Well, there's two words for you[14]. But nothing else. Not so much as[15] a please or a thank you.'

'You took him to Whitehall. What then?'

'He told me to wait.' The driver sniffed[16], realising his error. 'A third word, guv'nor. That was all it was. "Wait!" I've 'ad more communication from the 'orse.[17]'

'What happened?'

'You know what 'appened! All London knows what 'appened. There was a bang[18] as loud as a

Japanese mortar[1] in Vauxhall Gardens. What in 'eaven's name is that, thinks I.[2] But the cove, 'e don't give a jot.[3] 'Im and the boy just sit there[4] as we drive off. They don't want to stop. They don't even look round.[5] A toff[6] and a messenger boy and me and I'm just glad to be out of there[7], I can tell you.'

'Did they speak to each other, the man and the boy?'

'They spoke. But I didn't 'ear them. Not with me up front and[8] the doors and the windows closed.'

'Where did you take them?' I asked.

'Not so very far. Through Parliament Square and over to Victoria.'

'To a private house?'

'I don't know what it was. But I can tell you the number. I wouldn't normally remember. I've got no 'ead for numbers.[9] My 'ead is full of numbers so why should I remember one above another[10]? But this one was as easy as one two three. It *was*[11] one two three. One hundred and twenty-three Victoria Street and if there's nothing else, guv'nor,[12] I've got some more numbers for you. Sixpence the quarter hour waiting time[13] and I've been here two hours at the least. What do you say to that?[14]'

Jones gave the man some money and we hurried away together, striding along the pavement[15] past Fortnum & Mason[16] and up to Green Park. We hailed[17] another cab and Jones gave the driver the address. 'We have them![18]' he said to me. 'Even if they do not actually reside in Victoria Street, the house will lead us to them.'

'The man in the brougham,' I muttered. 'He could not have been Clarence Devereux. He

1. tir de mortier
2. Mais bon dieu, qu'est-ce donc qu' c'est, je me dis.
3. Mais le gonze, y bouge pas d'un iota.
4. Lui et le gamin, y restent assis là
5. Ils s're-tournent même pas.
6. Un rupin
7. j'suis juste content de partir de là
8. Impossible comme j'suis à l'avant avec
9. J' retiens pas les chiffres.
10. un plutôt qu'un autre
11. Justement, c'était
12. si y a rien d'autre, patron
13. Six pence le quart d'heure d'attente
14. Z'en dites quoi ?
15. nous nous éloignâmes rapidement, dévalant le trottoir
16. [grand magasin de produits de luxe]
17. hélâmes
18. Nous les tenons !

1. Il ne serait jamais monté dans une voiture à cheval
2. sans fermer préalablement les rideaux à l'intérieur
3. replié sur lui-même, le visage enfoncé dans son col
4. souffrant comme lui d'agoraphobie
5. m'est familière
6. Comment est-ce possible ?
7. m'interrompis
8. artère large et noire de monde
9. où la foule flânait entre les boutiques chic et les arcades
10. m'évoqua
11. elle ressemblait tout autant à une forteresse
12. avec des barreaux aux fenêtres
13. menant à
14. Je remarquai que Jones regardait vers le ciel
15. flottait
16. puis vers la rue jusqu'à une plaque
17. fixée à côté du portail
18. l'équipe de l'ambassadeur
19. éreintée
20. laissant ce mot prendre toute sa portée
21. aurait aussi bien pu déposer

would never have ventured out in a coach[1] without first covering the windows[2].'

'The driver said that he was withdrawn, his face buried in his collar[3].'

'Not enough, I think, for someone suffering as he does from agoraphobia[4]. There is something else, Jones. It is very strange but I feel that the address, 123 Victoria Street, is known to me[5].'

'How can that be?[6]'

'I cannot say. I have seen it somewhere, read it … I don't know.' I broke off[7] and once again we travelled in silence until we finally arrived in Victoria Street, a wide and well-populated thoroughfare[8] with the crowds drifting in and out of the elegant shops and arcades[9]. We found the house we were looking for, a solid, not very handsome building, recently constructed and clearly too large to be a private home. It immediately put me in mind[10] of Bladeston House and I saw that it had the same sense of impregnability[11], with barred windows[12], a gate, and a narrow path leading to[13] an imposing front door. I noticed Jones looking upwards[14] and followed his eyes to the American flag that fluttered[15] on the roof, then down to the plaque[16] set beside the main gate[17].

'It is the legation of the United States of America!' I exclaimed. 'Of course. We have had many communications with the envoy's staff[18] and Robert Pinkerton stayed here when he was in London. That's how I know the address.'

'The legation …'Jones repeated the word in a voice that was suddenly strained[19]. He paused for a moment, allowing its significance to sink in[20], and I understood that our coachman might as well have taken[21] his two passengers to the moon for all the good it would do us[1]. 'It is prohibited to us.[2] No officer of the law can enter a legation.'

'But this is where they came,' I exclaimed, 'Perry and his associate. Can it be possible?' I reached out and grabbed hold of the railing[3] as if I could prise it apart[4]. 'Has Clarence Devereux taken sanctuary within[5] his own country's legation? We must go in!'

'It is not possible, I tell you,' Jones insisted. 'We will have to address ourselves to the department of the Foreign Secretary[6]—'

'Then that is what we must do!'

'I do not believe we have enough evidence to support such a request[7]. We have only the word[8] of Mr Guthrie that he brought his passengers here and we cannot be sure that they even entered. It's exactly what happened at Highgate. I followed the boy to Bladeston House but we still cannot say with any certainty[9] that he ever went into the place[10].'

'Bladeston House! You may remember – Scotchy Lavelle boasted that he enjoyed the protection of the legation[11].'

'It was my first thought, Chase. At the time, it struck me as very singular.[12]'

'And there was an invitation in his desk. He and that woman had been summoned to this very place[13].'

'I have it in my office … or what remains of it[14].' Jones had removed anything of interest[15] from Bladeston House, including the diary and the block of soap that had led us to Horner's of Chancery Lane. 'A party to celebrate business enterprise[16].'

'Can you remember the date?'

1. que ça n'aurait pas été pire
2. Elle nous est interdite d'accès.
3. Je tendis les mains et agrippai la grille
4. comme si j'avais pu en écarter les barreaux
5. trouvé refuge au sein de
6. Ministère des Affaires étrangères
7. assez de preuves pour étayer une telle requête
8. le témoignage
9. affirmer avec certitude
10. qu'il y ait vraiment mis les pieds
11. s'était vanté d'être sous la protection de la légation
12. cela m'avait semblé très singulier
13. avaient été convoqués à cet endroit précis
14. ou ce qu'il en reste
15. prélevé tous les objets dignes d'intérêt
16. l'esprit d'entreprise

1. n'y assistera pas

2. Si l'un de nous deux y allait à sa place,

3. il prendrait de très gros risques

4. ainsi que Scotchy se voyait

5. que les affaires criminelles sont aussi des affaires

6. laisser passer une telle opportunité

7. nous nous adressons au

8. cela ne fera qu'avertir Clarence Devereux de nos intentions

9. Vous partez du principe qu'il est ici.

10. deux invités parmi tant d'autres

11. les yeux fixés sur

12. close

13. s'était arrêté

14. comme s'il avait honte de montrer ses couleurs

Jones glanced at me. He could see at once what I had in mind. 'I believe it was for tomorrow night,' he replied.

'Well, of one thing we can be certain,' I said. 'Scotchy Lavelle won't be attending[1].'

'For either of us to go in his place[2] would be an extremely serious matter[3].'

'For you, perhaps, but not for me. I am, after all, an American citizen.'

'I will not let you enter on your own.'

'There can be no possible danger. It is a reception for English and American businessmen ...'I smiled. 'Is that really how Scotchy thought of himself[4]? I suppose criminal enterprise passes as business of a sort[5].' I turned to Athelney Jones and he could surely see I was determined. 'We cannot let this opportunity pass us by[6]. If we apply to the[7] Foreign Secretary, it will only warn Clarence Devereux of our intentions[8].'

'You assume he is here.[9]'

'Does not the evidence suggest it? We can at least take a look inside,' I continued, quickly. 'And surely the risk is small. We will be two guests among many[10].'

Jones stood, supporting himself on his stick, gazing at[11] the gate and the door that remained fastened[12] in front of him. The wind had dropped[13] and the flag had fallen, as if ashamed to show its colours[14].

'Very well,' he said. 'We'll go.'

THIRTEEN

The Third Secretary[1]

The American legation had been transformed for the minister's reception. The gate stood open[2] and torches had been arranged in two lines, blazing the way to[3] the front door. There were half a dozen footmen[4], equally brilliant[5] in their bright red coats and old-fashioned wigs[6], bowing to the guests as they climbed down[7] from the phaetons and landaus which had assembled outside[8]. With the lights glowing[9] behind the windows, the piano music playing on the other side of the front door and the flames throwing dark orange shadows[10] across the brickwork[11], it really was easy to forget that this was a rather drab[12] building and that we were in London, not New York. Even the flag was flying.

Athelney Jones and I had arrived together, both of us in tailcoats and white tie[13]. I noticed that he had exchanged his usual walking stick for another with an ivory handle[14] and wondered if he had one for every occasion. He looked nervous, for once unsure of himself– and I had to remind myself how much of a risk he was taking[15], coming here[16]. For a British police officer to enter a foreign legation under false pretences[17] and in

1. Le secrétaire adjoint
2. Le portail était grand ouvert
3. éclairant l'allée qui menait à la porte d'entrée
4. valets de pied
5. tout aussi resplendissants
6. perruques à l'ancienne
7. et qui s'inclinaient devant les invités descendant
8. des phaétons et des landaus rassemblés à l'extérieur
9. qui brillaient
10. qui projetaient des ombres orange foncé
11. sur la façade en briques
12. plutôt terne
13. en queue de pie et nœud papillon blanc
14. poignée d'ivoire
15. je me rappelai le risque considérable qu'il prenait
16. en venant ici
17. sous une fausse identité

pursuit of a criminal investigation[1] could be the end of his career. I saw him hesitate, contemplating the open doorway. Our eyes met.[2] He nodded[3] and we moved forward.

He had retrieved[4] the invitation that he had taken from Bladeston House. Fortunately it had survived both the explosion and the fire although, on close inspection, it was slightly singed[5]. 'The Envoy Extraordinary and Minister Plenipotentiary[6], Mr Robert T. Lincoln, requests the pleasure of the company of ...' The words were written in perfect copperplate[7] and to this had been added: '... Mr Scotland Lavelle and guest.' We were fortunate that the woman whom we had known, all too briefly[8], as Hen[9] had not been named. We had decided that if we were questioned, I would claim[10] to be Scott, Scotchy or Mr Scotland, as he now seemed to be[11]. Jones would be the anonymous guest and if asked[12] would give his own name.

But in fact, neither of us was examined in any way[13]. A footman glanced at our invitation and waved us through to a wide entrance hall[14], lined with books that were obviously artificial – they did not pretend to be otherwise[15] – as well as two plaster replicas[16] of classical Greek goddesses, one at each end. The party was taking place on the second floor. It was from here that the piano music was coming. A thickly carpeted staircase led up[17], but in order to begin the climb[18], the guests had to pass a line of four men and a woman who had positioned themselves purposefully so as to be able to greet[19] each and every one of them.

1. dans le cadre d'une enquête criminelle
2. Nos regards se croisèrent.
3. Il hocha la tête
4. récupéré
5. en y regardant de plus près, elle avait légèrement roussie
6. L'ambassadeur extraordinaire et Ministre plénipotentiaire
7. calligraphiés en belle ronde
8. que nous avons connue, quoique brièvement
9. sous le nom de Hen
10. prétendrais
11. comme il semblait se faire appeler ici
12. si on lui posait la question
13. ne fut l'objet de la moindre interrogation
14. nous invita à traverser un large vestibule
15. ne s'embarrassaient pas de vraisemblance
16. reproductions en plâtre
17. escalier recouvert d'un épais tapis menait à l'étage
18. avant de pouvoir entamer l'ascension
19. à dessein de manière à pouvoir accueillir

The first man I barely[1] noticed for he was standing with his back to the door[2]. He had grey hair and drooping eyelids[3] and there was something so dull and self-effacing[4] about him that he seemed completely unsuited to be part of a welcoming committee[5]. He was also the shortest of the four of them – even the woman towered over him[6].

It was clear that this lady was the wife of the envoy. Though in no way beautiful[7], with a prominent nose[8], pale skin and hair packed too tightly into curls[9], she was still undeniably regal[10], greeting all those who approached her as if she alone were the reason they had come[11]. She was severely dressed in brown wool twill with puffed out gigot sleeves[12] and a ribbon around her neck. As I took her hand and bowed, I smelled lavender water.

'Scotland Lavelle,' I murmured.

'You are very welcome, Mr Lavelle.' The monarch herself could not have said it with less enthusiasm.[13]

Her husband, standing next to her, was more genial[14], a large, square-shouldered[15] man with deep black hair which swept across his head in two contradictory waves[16]. The smile on his face was fighting a losing battle[17] with the seriousness in his eyes and his every movement seemed formal to the point of being stilted[18]. His cheeks and indeed his mouth were obliterated by a huge beard and moustache which stretched all the way to his ears and which I might almost have described as lopsided and even unkempt[19]. I had seen him addressing the people at the front of the line and it occurred to me that both he and

1. à peine
2. car il se tenait le dos à la porte
3. des paupières tombantes
4. si terne et effacé
5. inadapté au rôle de comité d'accueil
6. le dominait
7. Elle n'était absolument pas belle
8. grand nez
9. coiffés en boucles trop serrées
10. mais possédait une indéniable majesté
11. comme s'ils ne s'étaient déplacés que pour elle
12. en sergé de laine brune avec de larges manches gigot
13. La Reine elle-même n'aurait pu y mettre moins d'enthousiasme
14. avenant
15. aux épaules carrées
16. balayaient son crâne en deux vagues opposées
17. menait une bataille perdue d'avance
18. ses gestes étaient si formels qu'ils en devenaient guindés
19. asymétrique voire hirsute

his wife were concealing something, with greater or lesser success[1]. They had been touched quite recently by some sort of sadness and it was still with them, here in the room.

I found myself standing in front of him and once again repeated my false name. By now I was getting used to it.[2] He seized my hand in a powerful grip.[3] 'I am Robert Lincoln,' he said.

'Mr Lincoln ...' The name was of course well known to me.

'It is a great pleasure to welcome you to my London home, Mr Lavelle. May I present to you my councillor[4], Mr White?' This was the third man in the line, also bearded[5], about ten years younger than the envoy. That gentleman bowed. 'I hope the evening is both enjoyable and useful to you.[6]'

I waited until Athelney Jones had made his introductions[7] and together the two of us climbed the stairs.

'Lincoln ...?' he asked.

'The son of Abraham Lincoln,' I replied. How could I have forgotten that this descendant of one of America's most famous families had been sent to the court of King James? A seat had actually been reserved for Robert Lincoln at the Ford Theatre on the night his father had been assassinated and the sympathy[8] that many people felt for him had been translated into enthusiastic support[9]. It was said that Lincoln might himself run for president at the time of[10] the next election.

'This imposture will be the undoing of me[11],' Jones muttered, half seriously.

'We are in[12],' I replied. 'And, so far, without any difficulty.[13]'

1. dissimulaient quelque chose, avec plus ou moins de succès
2. Je commençais à m'y faire.
3. Il serra ma main d'une poigne puissante.
4. conseiller
5. également barbu
6. vous permettra de joindre l'utile à l'agréable
7. ait fini de se présenter
8. compassion
9. s'est traduite par un puissant soutien populaire
10. pourrait bien être candidat à la présidence lors de
11. Cette imposture me mènera à ma perte
12. Nous y sommes
13. Et jusqu'ici, pas le moindre problème.

'I cannot find it in my heart to believe[1] that a criminal organisation could be hiding itself in the sanctuary of an international legation. Such an idea does not bear thinking about.[2]'

'They invited Scotchy,' I reminded him. 'Let's see if we can find the fat boy and the man from the brougham.'

We passed through an archway[3] and into a room that stretched the entire length of the building with floor-to-ceiling windows that might have provided[4] views over the gardens at the back had they not been heavily curtained[5]. There was a crowd of some hundred people already gathered together[6] with a young man at the piano playing the syncopated[7] rhythms which, I imagined, would have been unfamiliar to Athelney Jones but which I recognised as originating from the streets of New Orleans. A long table stood with glasses[8] and what looked like bowls of fruit punch, and waiters were already circulating with plates of food … raw oysters with cucumbers and radishes[9], fishballs[10], vol-au-vents and so on. It amused me to see that many of the dishes carried labels[11] advertising the ingredients ; among them were E. C. Hazard's tomato ketchup, Baltimore vinegar and Colburn's Philadelphia Mustard. Later on, one of the tables would be displaying[12] Chase and Sanborn's finest coffee. But then this was a business gathering[13] and so perhaps the legation staff considered these notices to be part of the etiquette[14].

There was not a great deal we could do.[15] This was the room in which the reception was to take place and there was no question of our creeping around the legation[16] in search of Clarence De-

1. Au fond de moi, je me refuse à croire
2. Une telle chose est inimaginable.
3. sous un porche voûté
4. des baies vitrées qui auraient offert
5. si elles n'avaient pas été cachées par d'épais rideaux
6. déjà rassemblées
7. syncopés
8. Sur une longue table étaient posés des verres
9. des huitres crues accompagnées de concombres et de radis
10. des boulettes de poisson
11. de nombreux plats étaient affublés d'étiquettes
12. proposerait fièrement
13. réception à vocation commerciale
14. jugeait que ces étiquettes faisaient partie du savoir-vivre
15. Nous ne pouvions pas faire grand-chose.
16. il était hors de question d'aller fouiner dans la légation

vereux. If he was here, there was a chance we might stumble across him[1] – or at least across somebody who knew him. If not, we had wasted our time.

We drank some mint julep (*Bourbon from Four Roses, Kentucky*, the label read[2]) and mingled with[3] the other guests. There were soon a couple of hundred people present, all of them in their finest evening dress[4], and I noticed the little man from the door among them. He was angrily dismissing a waiter[5] who had approached him with a plate of curried sausages[6]. 'I do not eat meat!' The words, expressed in a high-pitched[7] voice, seemed somehow ungracious[8] and out of keeping with the affair[9]. Then, finally, the envoy, his wife and his councillor came up from the entrance hall, signalling that the assembly was complete[10]. From that moment on, wherever Robert Lincoln placed himself, a small crowd gathered round him[11], and such was his command of the room[12] that Jones and I were unable to escape being drawn into one such circle[13].

'What is to be done with this business of seal hunting[14]?' someone asked him. With his whiskers and beady eyes[15], it struck me that there was something seal-like about the interlocutor himself[16]. 'Will we go to war over the Bering Sea?'

'I think not, sir,' Lincoln replied in his quiet way[17]. 'I am quite confident[18] that we will be able to negotiate a settlement[19].'

'But they are American seals!'

'I am not convinced the seals think of themselves as American, Canadian or anything else. Particularly when they end up as somebody's handbag[20].' The envoy's eyes twinkled for

1. tomber sur lui par hasard
2. disait l'étiquette
3. nous mêlâmes aux
4. parés de leurs plus beaux atours
5. Il chassait avec rage un serveur
6. saucisses au curry
7. aiguë
8. quelque peu désobligeants
9. ne cadraient pas avec l'ambiance policée de la soirée
10. était au complet
11. où que se trouvât Robert Lincoln, un attroupement se formait
12. son pouvoir d'attraction était tel
13. nous retrouvâmes pris dans un tel attroupement
14. cette histoire de chasse aux phoques
15. sa moustache tombante et ses yeux perçants
16. l'interlocuteur lui-même n'était pas sans évoquer un phoque
17. avec le calme qui le caractérisait
18. absolument certain
19. accord
20. finissent transformés en sacs à main

a moment[1]. Then he turned and suddenly he and I were face to face. 'And what brings you to London[2], Mr Lavelle?' he asked.

I was so impressed that he had remembered my name – or, at least, the name I had given him – that I faltered[3] and Jones had to answer for me. 'We are in business together, sir. Company promoters.[4]'

'And you are?'

'My name is Jones.'

'I am delighted to see you here.' He nodded at the younger man standing next to him. 'My friend, Mr White, believes that we should look to[5] Central and South America as our natural trading partners[6]. But it is my belief that Europe is the future. If I or my staff can be of any assistance in your enterprise[7] …'

He was about to move on[8] but before he could so do, I suddenly blurted out[9]: 'You could indeed help us in one respect[10], sir.'

He swayed on his foot.[11] 'And how is that?[12]'

'We are seeking an introduction to[13] Clarence Devereux.'

I had spoken the words deliberately loudly[14] and was it my imagination or did a certain hush descend on the room[15]?

The envoy looked at me, puzzled[16]. 'Clarence Devereux? I cannot say I know the name.[17] Who is he?'

'He is a businessman from New York,' I replied.

'In what sort of business?'

But before I could answer, the councillor stepped in[18]. 'If this gentleman has registered his address with the legation[19], I am sure one of the secretaries will be able to assist you,' he said.

1. pétillèrent l'espace d'une seconde
2. qu'est-ce qui vous amène à Londres
3. j'eus un moment d'hésitation
4. Nous sommes promoteurs commerciaux.
5. considérer
6. partenaires commerciaux les plus proches
7. pouvons vous être d'une aide quelconque
8. passer à autre chose
9. je m'exclamai soudainement
10. Nous aurions en effet besoin de votre aide sur un sujet
11. se balança sur un pied.
12. Et de quelle façon ?
13. cherchons à rencontrer
14. J'avais sciemment élevé la voix
15. un étrange silence s'abattit-il sur la pièce
16. perplexe
17. Ce nom ne me dit rien.
18. intervint
19. a fait inscrire son adresse au registre de la légation

'You can call at any time.' Gently, without seeming to do so, he led the envoy away.[1]

Jones and I were left alone.

'Mr Jones! Mr Pinkerton!'

My heart sank, hearing myself addressed in this way.[2] I turned and found myself facing Edgar and Leland Mortlake. Although dressed more formally in white tie, as the occasion demanded[3], the two men presented exactly the same appearance that they had at the Bostonian and it was as if no time had passed between then and now[4].

'Perhaps I am mistaken,' Edgar Mortlake began, 'but I am sure I just heard the envoy addressing you as[5] Scotland Lavelle. I knew it couldn't be right[6] when I heard the name as poor Scotchy is in no state to attend[7].'

'An outrage![8]' Leland Mortlake rasped, his thick lips curling in a scowl.[9]

'It seems to me that you have no right to be here. You were not invited. And if you are present it is only by theft[10] – you stole the invitation, did you not? – and by lying[11] to the envoy of the United States of America.'

'We came in pursuit of our enquiries[12] and following an attack on my office that led to the death of two police officers,' Jones replied. 'You will, of course, pretend you know nothing of that. But we can discuss this at another time. We will leave.[13]'

'I don't think so.' Edgar raised a hand and a younger, rather pompous-looking[14] man, one I had not seen downstairs, came hurrying over, as if he sensed trouble[15]. 'These two gentlemen are detectives. One is a Pinkerton's agent. The other is from Scotland Yard. They have entered the le-

1. Délicatement, l'air de rien, il éloigna l'ambassadeur.

2. En entendant mon nom, mon cœur se serra dans ma poitrine.

3. l'exigeait

4. comme si notre entrevue venait juste d'avoir lieu

5. vous appeler

6. qu'il y avait anguille sous roche

7. n'est pas en état d'assister

8. Scandaleux !

9. grinça Leland Mortlake, sa bouche lippue formant un rictus

10. à la faveur d'un vol

11. à la faveur d'un mensonge proféré

12. dans le cadre de notre enquête

13. Nous allions partir.

14. à l'allure plutôt pompeuse

15. comme s'il avait senti qu'il y avait un problème

gation under false pretences[1] and have interrogated the envoy himself.'

The official stared at us. 'Is this true?' he asked.

'It is true that I am a police officer,' Jones replied. 'And I did speak just now with Mr Lincoln. But it was not my intention to meet him and I certainly did not interrogate him.'

'You must have them removed,' Edgar snapped.[2]

'Arrested,' Leland added. As always, one word seemed to be all he could manage[3].

The official was clearly uncomfortable, aware that this conversation was taking place in a crowded room with the envoy and his wife no more than a few feet away[4]. Jones had maintained his equanimity[5] but I could see that he was deeply troubled. Meanwhile, the two brothers were gloating[6], enjoying our predicament[7]. 'Gentlemen, you had better come with me[8],' the official said, at length[9].

'Gladly.[10]' Jones and I followed him out of the room, leaving the party behind. Neither of us spoke until we had reached the corridor and the doors had been closed. But finding ourselves alone, Jones turned to our escort. 'I do not deny[11] that we should not be here and that, at the very least[12], this is a most serious breach of protocol[13]. For that I can only apologise[14]. But I can assure you that you will find redress with my superiors[15] and now, with your permission, my friend and I will leave.'

'I am very sorry,' the official replied. 'I do not have the authority[16] to make that decision. I must speak to my own superiors before I can permit you to depart.' He gestured.[17] 'There is a room

1. sous de faux semblants
2. Faites-les sortir, déclara Edgar d'un ton cassant.
3. il ne semblait capable de prononcer qu'un seul mot à la fois
4. à quelques mètres de là
5. Jones avait gardé son sang-froid
6. souriaient d'un air satisfait
7. ravis de nous voir dans cette situation délicate
8. vous feriez mieux de me suivre
9. finalement
10. Volontiers.
11. Je ne démens pas
12. c'est pour le moins
13. une très sérieuse violation du protocole
14. je ne peux que vous présenter mes excuses
15. vous obtiendrez réparation auprès de mes supérieurs
16. pouvoir
17. Il fit un geste de la main.

just down here. If you will wait a few minutes, you will not be detained for long[1].'

We could not argue.[2] The official showed us into[3] an office where, I presumed, visiting members of the public might find themselves, for it was sparsely furnished[4] with a table and three chairs. A picture of Benjamin Harrison, the twenty-third President of the United States, hung on one wall and a large window looked out onto Victoria Street with the beacons still alight below[5]. The door closed and we were left on our own[6].

Jones sat down heavily[7]. 'This is a bad business[8],' he remarked.

'And one that is entirely my fault,' I said, adding quickly, 'I cannot tell you how much I regret the impulse that brought us here tonight[9].'

'All in all it was probably futile.[10] But I will not blame you, Chase. It was my own decision and there is some significance in the fact that the brothers Mortlake were both here.[11]' He shook his head. 'That said, I do not care to think what may ensue.[12]'

'They will not fire[13] you.'

'They may have no choice.'

'Well, what does it matter?' I exclaimed. 'You have the most remarkable mind I have ever encountered[14]. From the moment we met in Meiringen, I saw that you stood apart from[15] Lestrade and the rest of them. In all my years with the Pinkertons, I have never met an agent like you. Scotland Yard may choose to dispense with you[16], but let me assure you, my dear Jones, that they will come searching for you, wherever you are[17]. London needs a new consulting detective. You were saying the same only yesterday.[18]'

1. nous ne vous retiendrons pas longtemps
2. Nous ne pouvions pas refuser.
3. nous conduisit dans
4. sommairement meublé
5. et sur les réverbères qui brûlaient encore
6. nous nous retrouvâmes seuls
7. se laissa tomber sur une chaise
8. La situation est grave
9. ce coup de tête qui nous a conduit ici
10. Tout compte fait, cela n'aura probablement servi à rien.
11. la présence des frères Mortlake est significative
12. Cela dit, je préfère ne pas penser à ce qui va suivre.
13. démettre de vos fonctions
14. que j'ai jamais connu
15. vous étiez à mille lieux de
16. pourrait choisir de se passer de vous
17. ils viendront vous recruter, où que vous soyez
18. Hier encore, vous disiez la même chose.

'It was in my mind[1], it is true.'

'Then you should make it an actuality[2]. And maybe I will stay here a little longer myself, just as your wife suggested. Yes – why not? I can become your very own Watson, but I can promise you I will cast you in a more flattering light[3]!' He smiled at that. I went over to the window, looking out at the footmen and the waiting coaches[4]. 'Why must we wait here?' I asked. 'The devil with it[5], Jones, let us be on our way[6]. We can face the consequences tomorrow.'

But before Jones could reply, the door opened and the official returned. He walked towards me and drew the curtain[7], deliberately blocking the view.

'Are we to be allowed to leave?[8]' I demanded.

'No, sir. The third secretary[9] wishes to meet with you in private.'

'Where is he?'

'He will be here presently[10].'

No sooner had he spoken than there was a movement at the door and the secretary walked in. I recognised at once the short, grey-haired[11] man I had seen in the entrance hall. Now that we were in close proximity, he seemed even smaller than I had first thought, putting me in mind of the puppet[12] that Jones had purchased[13] for his daughter. He had a very round face with the eyes, nose and mouth grouped tightly – almost too tightly – together[14]. His hair was thin and wispy, showing through to[15] a skull that was peppered with liver spots[16]. Most peculiar of all were[17] his fingers, which, though perfectly formed, were too small for his hands, perhaps half the length they should have been[18].

1. Je l'envisageais
2. le mettre en pratique
3. je vous dépeindrais sous un jour plus flatteur
4. les calèches garées
5. Au diable tout cela
6. partons d'ici
7. tira le rideau
8. Allons-nous être autorisés à partir ?
9. Le secrétaire adjoint
10. tout de suite
11. aux cheveux gris
12. me rappelant la marionnette
13. achetée
14. très rapprochés, presque trop, les uns des autres
15. clairsemés, laissant apparaître
16. un crâne constellé de taches de vieillesse
17. Mais le plus étrange, c'était
18. peut-être même de la moitié de la taille normale

'Thank you, Mr Isham,' he said, dismissing the official in the queer, high-pitched voice[1] I had noted earlier. 'Shall we sit down, gentlemen? This is an unfortunate business[2] and we need to be brief[3].'

We sat down.

'Let me introduce myself. My name is Coleman De Vriess and I hold the position of third secretary[4] here at the legation. You are Inspector Athelney Jones of Scotland Yard?' Jones nodded and he turned to me. 'And you …?'

'My name is Frederick Chase. I am an American citizen[5], an agent with[6] the Pinkerton Agency in New York.'

'Why are you here?'

It was Jones who replied. 'You will be aware of the outrage that took place[7] two days ago at Scotland Yard. I believe that I was the target of an attack that left three men dead and many more wounded[8].'

'And your enquiries brought you here?'

'We believe that the man responsible may be hiding behind the protection of the legation, yes.'

'And who might that man be?'

'His name is Clarence Devereux.'

De Vriess shook his head. 'Apart from[9] the envoy and his wife, this legation has only twelve permanent members of staff[10],' he said. 'I can assure you I have never met the man of whom you speak[11]. And of course we are aware of what happened at Scotland Yard. How could you think otherwise?[12] Mr Lincoln himself sent a message of condolence to your Commissioner[13] and I can understand your desire to apprehend the perpetrator[14] by any means at your disposal[15]. At the

1. congédiant l'officiel d'une voix curieusement aiguë
2. Cette affaire est regrettable
3. nous devons être brefs
4. occupe le poste de secrétaire adjoint
5. citoyen
6. détective de
7. Vous êtes sûrement au courant du drame qui s'est produit
8. a fait trois victimes et de nombreux blessés
9. En dehors de
10. employés permanents
11. dont vous parlez
12. Comment pouvez-vous croire le contraire ?
13. Préfet de Police
14. coupable
15. par tous les moyens dont vous disposez

same time, however[1], I cannot stress too highly the impropriety[2] of what you have done, coming here tonight. You are aware, sir, of the principle of extraterritoriality, that the residence of the envoy is protected from British law and that for a police officer to come here in this manner is a flagrant abuse[3] of international protocol.'

'Wait a minute!' I cried. 'We have seen two men in this building tonight, Edgar and Leland Mortlake, and we know them to be gangsters of the very worst kind[4]. I have seen their files[5] at Pinkerton's. I know them for what they are.[6] Yes, Inspector Jones and I may have stepped outside the niceties of the law[7], but are you going to sit there protecting them and obstructing us[8], particularly in light of what has occurred[9]?'

'It is the responsibility of this legation to protect American citizens,' De Vriess returned. His voice had not changed but there was anger in his eyes. 'To the best of my knowledge[10], the two gentlemen of whom you speak are businessmen, nothing more. Do you have evidence of any crime they have committed in this country? Is there any good reason to request their extradition? No. I thought not.[11] And if I may say so, there is nothing to be gained by adding slander[12] to the list of charges which will be brought against you[13].'

'What is it you plan to do?' Jones asked.

'You have my sympathy, Inspector Jones.' From the look on the third secretary's face[14], he had anything but[15]. He folded his hands on his lap[16], lacing his fingers together. The tips barely reached his knuckles[17]. 'It is my intention to lodge a formal complaint with[18] your superiors first thing tomorrow[19] and I will accept nothing less than

1. Ceci étant dit
2. je ne saurais trop insister sur l'inconvenance
3. est une violation flagrante
4. de la pire espèce
5. dossiers
6. Je connais leur vraie nature
7. avons peut-être empiété sur les subtilités du droit
8. rester assis là, à les protéger en entravant la justice
9. à la lumière de ce qui s'est produit
10. À ma connaissance
11. C'est bien ce que je pensais.
12. il n'y a rien à gagner à ajouter la diffamation
13. à la liste des accusations dont vous ferez l'objet
14. À en juger par l'expression du secrétaire adjoint
15. c'était bien la dernière chose qu'il avait à notre égard
16. ses genoux
17. L'articulation
18. J'ai l'intention de porter plainte auprès de
19. à la première heure demain matin

your dismissal from the force[1]. As to your friend, there is little we can do to rein in[2] Mr Pinkerton's agents. They are well known for their excesses and for their irresponsible behaviour. I will have you removed[3] from this country, Mr Chase, and you may well find yourself being prosecuted in an American court[4]. And that, gentlemen, is all. I have a party to return to. You will be shown to the door.[5]'

Jones stood up. 'I have one question,' he said.

'And what is that?'

'When you came into this room, you addressed me, correctly, as[6] Athelney Jones. I wonder how you came by[7] that information as neither of the Mortlake brothers were fully acquainted with my first name[8]?'

'I do not see the relevance[9]—'

'But I do![10]' To my astonishment, Jones strode across the room[11] and, using his walking stick, hooked the edge of the curtain and threw it back[12], revealing the scene outside. For a moment I thought there was something he wanted us to see but then I realised he had quite another aim in mind[13]. The effect on the third secretary was extraordinary. It was as if he had been struck in the face[14]. For a moment, he sat in the chair, staring wildly, gasping for breath[15]. Then he twisted round[16], unable to look outside for one minute longer[17].

'I would advise you against reporting me to anyone[18], Clarence Devereux!' exclaimed Jones.

'Devereux …?' I got to my feet, staring at the cowering figure[19].

'Now everything is explained,' Jones went on. 'The connections between Lavelle, the Mortlakes

1. je compte bien exiger votre renvoi des forces de police
2. contrôler
3. Je vais vous faire expulser
4. pourriez bien vous retrouver devant un tribunal américain
5. On va vous raccompagner à la sortie.
6. m'avez appelé, à juste titre,
7. avez obtenu
8. aucun des frères Mortlake n'avait connaissance de mon prénom
9. en quoi cela est pertinent
10. Mais moi si !
11. Jones traversa la pièce à grandes enjambées
12. saisit le bord du rideau et le tira violemment
13. que son but était tout autre
14. frappé au visage
15. les yeux écarquillés, le souffle coupé
16. il se détourna
17. une minute de plus
18. Je vous déconseille de me dénoncer à qui que ce soit
19. fixant la silhouette recroquevillée devant moi

and the legation; the reasons why the carriage came to this place and why you can never be found. Is Mr Lincoln aware, I wonder, of the sort of man he employs as his third secretary?'

'The drapes![1]' the man who had called himself Coleman De Vriess muttered in a high-pitched whisper[2]. 'Close them, damn you[3]!'

'I will do no such thing. Admit who you are![4]'

'You have no right to be here. Get out!'

'We are leaving, of our own volition[5]. But let me tell you, Devereux. We know who you are now. We know where you are. And although you may hide in the legation for a while to come[6], you can no longer rely on[7] its protection. We have found you and we will not let you go[8]!'

'You will die before you come close.'

'I think not!'

'You cannot touch me. And I swear to you –[9] you will regret this day!'

Jones was ready to leave but I was not. 'You are Devereux?' I exclaimed, looming over[10] this small, trembling man. 'You are the criminal mastermind we have so long feared[11]? It was you who came to London believing that you could yoke the entire underworld to your desires[12]? I would not believe it but for the evidence of my own eyes[13] and what I see is beneath contempt[14].'

With an animal snarl[15], Devereux lunged at me[16] and might have grabbed hold of me had Jones not pulled me back[17].

'Can we not arrest him?' I cried. 'I have travelled halfway around the world to find this man. We can't just leave him.'

'There is nothing we can do. We have no authority here.'

1. Les rideaux !
2. dans un chuchotement suraigu
3. que diable
4. Il n'en est pas question. Avouez d'abord qui vous êtes !
5. de notre propre chef
6. pendant un certain temps
7. dépendre de
8. vous ne nous échapperez pas
9. Vous ne pouvez pas m'atteindre. Et je peux vous assurer que
10. me dressant devant
11. génie du crime que nous avons si longtemps redouté
12. pouviez façonner la pègre toute entière selon vos désirs
13. si je ne le voyais pas de mes propres yeux
14. absolument méprisable
15. grondement bestial
16. se jeta sur moi
17. m'aurait empoigné si Jones ne m'avait pas tiré en arrière

1. Je sais ce que vous ressentez.
2. Il ne faut pas qu'on nous trouve ici.
3. fondre sur
4. quel que soit le nom qu'il utilise
5. à la traînée de sang
6. au sort tragique
7. mis à mort si impitoyablement
8. si je n'avais pas laissé mon canif
9. l'aurais poignardé sans la moindre hésitation
10. m'avait saisi
11. trouble psychologique
12. l'a plongé dans un tel état
13. siffla
14. était pris de convulsions
15. Et ce sera une mort lente.
16. me traîna hors de la pièce
17. Ce n'est qu'une fois revenus à l'air libre
18. que je me libérai de l'emprise de mon ami
19. que je me retournai, aspirant l'air du soir à pleins poumons
20. En personne.

'Jones ...'

'Forgive me, Chase. I know your feelings.[1] But we have no choice. We must leave now. We cannot be found here.[2]'

Still I wanted to fall upon[3] Devereux, De Vriess, whatever he called himself[4]. The man was trembling, his eyes half-closed. I thought of the trail of blood[5] that had brought us here, the fate[6] of Jonathan Pilgrim, who had been so mercilessly put to death[7] by this creature or his cohorts. I remembered all the suffering he had caused. I believe, had I not left my jackknife[8] at the hotel when I changed, I would have plunged it into him with no second thought[9] but Jones had seized hold of me[10]. 'Come!'

'We can't!'

'We must! We have no evidence against him, nothing but the strange psychological condition[11] that has reduced him to this state[12].'

'You will die for this,' Devereux hissed[13]. He was half-covering his eyes, his whole body contorted[14]. 'And it will be slow.[15] I will make you pay.'

I wanted to reply but Jones dragged me out of the room[16]. The corridor was empty and nobody tried to apprehend us as we continued down the stairs and back out into the street. Only once we were in the open[17], away from the legation gates, did I free myself from my friend's grip[18] and spin round, sucking in[19] the evening air. 'That was Devereux! Clarence Devereux!'

'None other.[20] Was it not obvious? When we first entered the hall, he had his back to the door. It was his agoraphobia. He did not dare look out! And before he came into the room, he sent his lackey in to draw the curtains[1] for the same reason.' Jones laughed. 'And his name! There's vanity for you.[2] Coleman De Vriess. CD. He chooses to hide behind the same initials.'

'But did we really have to leave him? For Heaven's sake[3], Jones, we have just discovered the greatest criminal of his generation and we walk out without apprehending him, without saying another word!'

'If we had tried to apprehend him, all would have been lost[4]. Our own position was tenuous[5] for we were there under false pretences. I have no doubt that Mr Lincoln and his friends are unaware of[6] the sort of man they are protecting but even so[7] their natural instinct would have been to come to his defence, to support one of their own[8].' Jones smiled grimly[9]. 'Well, the game has changed. Now we are at liberty[10], we can regroup and plan our next move[11].'

'To arrest him!'

'Of course.'

I looked back at the legation – at the coaches, the footmen, the flickering[12] lights. It was true. We had found Clarence Devereux. There was only one problem. How in Heaven's name were we going to draw him out?[13]

1. a envoyé son laquais fermer les rideaux

2. Un bel exemple de vanité.

3. Nom de Dieu

4. tout aurait été perdu

5. Nous étions nous-mêmes dans une position des plus précaires

6. Je suis sûr que M. Lincoln et ses amis ignorent

7. néanmoins

8. de soutenir l'un des leurs

9. d'un air grave

10. en liberté

11. prochain coup

12. vascillantes

13. allions nous bien pouvoir le faire sortir de là ?

FOURTEEN

Setting the Trap[1]

1. Tendre le piège

2. d'un sommeil agité

3. pénible voisin

4. n'avait pas quitté sa chambre une seule fois

5. hanter

6. en tout cas c'est ce que m'avait dit la femme de chambre

7. renonçai à le faire

8. Pour autant que je sache

9. menace

10. si je ne l'avais pas entendu tousser et vu une fois apparaître à la fenêtre

11. Plus troublants encore furent

12. malveillants

13. les pieds dans une mare de sang

I slept fitfully[2] that night. My rest was once again disturbed by my troublesome neighbour[3] who had never once left his room[4] but who seemed to haunt[5] the hotel with his presence. He seemed to eat neither breakfast nor dinner. He had arrived at the same time as me – or so the maid told me[6] – but he never went out. I thought of confronting him but decided against it[7]. For all I knew[8], he might be a perfectly innocent traveller, transformed into a threat[9] only by my imagination. Indeed, had it not been for the noise of his coughing and that one, brief glimpse at the window[10], I would not even be aware of his existence.

Far more disturbing were[11] my weird, distorted dreams of Clarence Devereux. I saw his face, his malevolent[12] eyes, those ridiculous fingers of his, too small for any man. 'I do not eat meat!' I heard him cry, but then I found myself lying on an oversized plate with a knife on one side, a fork on the other, and I was certain he was about to eat me. I was back at the legation with Robert Lincoln and his wife. I was at Bladeston House with blood pooling around my feet[13]. Finally, I was at the Reichenbach Falls, plunging down for an eternity with the water crashing around me[1] only to open my eyes[2] and find myself in bed, the sheets crumpled and a rainstorm[3] lashing against[4] the windows.

I had no appetite and ate little breakfast for I was anxious to hear from Jones as to what, if anything, had ensued as a result of our evening's adventure[5]. The news, when we met, was not good. Contrary to my expectations[6], an official complaint[7] had already been made by the American legation, naming Jones and addressed to the Commissioner.

'Our friend Coleman De Vriess had the temerity to sign it himself,' Jones said as we sat together in another cab, splashing through the puddles that the brief storm had left behind[8]. 'It was delivered[9] at nine o'clock this morning. Fast work, would you not say?[10]'

'What will happen?' I asked.

'I will almost certainly lose my position[11].'

'This is my doing ...[12]'

'Tut, man[13], it is of no importance. My beloved Elspeth will be delighted for one[14] and anyway we have several days before any action will be taken[15]. First there will have to be an interrogation, then a committee, then a report, a review[16] and finally a recommendation. This is how the British police force works. A great deal can happen in that time.[17]'

'But what can we do?'

'We have a dilemma, it is true. We cannot arrest Clarence Devereux. It will be difficult even to interview him without the permission of his envoy and I suspect that will not be forthcoming[18], particularly in the light[19] of last night's events.

1. plongeant pour l'éternité dans une eau rugissante
2. ouvrant finalement les yeux
3. les draps froissés et une pluie torrentielle
4. abattant contre
5. les éventuelles conséquences de nos aventures de la veille
6. Contrairement à ce que j'espérais
7. plainte
8. roulant dans les flaques laissées par le bref orage
9. Elle a été déposée
10. Ils sont efficaces, vous ne trouvez pas ?
11. perdre ma place
12. C'est de mon fait...
13. Tss, voyons
14. Ma chère Elspeth sera ravie, quant à elle,
15. avant que des démarches soient entreprises
16. réexamen
17. Il pourrait se produire beaucoup de choses pendant ce temps.
18. j'imagine qu'on ne l'obtiendra pas de si tôt
19. à la lumière de

What proof do we have that he is involved in any nefarious activity[1]?'

'You have seen the files that I brought from New York. And you heard what your colleague Stanley Hopkins had to say. Devereux's name is known all over London'

'But the name of Coleman De Vriess is not. I have to say, it is an ingenious idea for a criminal to hide behind the curtain of[2] diplomatic immunity.' Jones chuckled[3]. He did not appear remotely put out.[4] 'No. There is only one way we can lay our hands[5] on Mr Devereux and that is to capture him red-handed[6]. We must set a trap[7]. The moment he makes an appearance outside[8] the legation, we will have him.'

'Where will we begin?'

'The answer is perfectly obvious. Indeed ...[9] Slow down[10], driver! I believe we have arrived.'

We had driven but a[11] short distance and, looking around me, I saw that we had returned to the top of Chancery Lane. I had almost forgotten Silas Beckett and his unpleasant barber's shop[12], such had been the pace of events[13]. But as we climbed down, I saw that a group of police constables were waiting for us, out of sight of[14] both the shop and the hurdy-gurdy man whose lamentable playing[15] could be heard around the corner. 'Stay close to me,' Jones commanded. Then, to the nearest of the officers[16]: 'You know what to do?'

'Yes, sir.'

'Do not on any account show yourselves until we are[17] in the shop.'

This was something else that Jones had inherited[18] from Sherlock Holmes; the maddening

1. soit impliqué dans quelque activité sordide
2. se réfugier derrière son
3. eut un petit rire
4. ne semblait pas énervé le moins du monde.
5. mettre la main
6. de le prendre la main dans le sac
7. lui tendre un piège
8. À la seconde où il mettra un pied hors de
9. D'ailleurs...
10. Ralentissez
11. n'avions parcouru qu'une
12. son désagréable salon de coiffure pour homme
13. tant les événements s'étaient précipités
14. hors de la vue du
15. dont les notes discordantes
16. à l'agent le plus proche
17. Ne vous montrez sous aucun prétexte avant que nous soyons
18. hérité

habit[1] of not explaining himself until the last minute – and not even then, it would seem[2], for he did not say a word as we turned the corner and began to walk down the rutted track[3] that led to Staples Inn Gardens. The moment we appeared, the hurdy-gurdy man stopped playing and I recalled[4] that he had behaved in exactly the same way the last time we had come here. It would have been natural for Jones to make straight for[5] the barber's shop – was that not why we were here?[6] – but instead he walked up to[7] the silent musician.

'Hair tonic, sir?' the man asked. 'Cut or shave?[8]'

'Not today, thank you,' Jones replied. 'But since you mention it, I would be interested to see the style of your own hair[9].' And before the man could stop him, he had reached out and plucked the top hat off his head[10], revealing a shock of bright red hair[11]. 'It is just as I thought.[12]'

'What do you mean?' I asked.

'Red hair!'

'What can the colour of his hair possibly have to do with the matter?'

'It has everything to do with it.' He turned to the indignant[13] musician. 'I believe I am addressing[14] Mr Duncan Ross – at least, that is the name you were using two years ago. Your true name, however, is Archie Cooke and this is not the first time you have been engaged on an enterprise such as this[15]!' The other man started and would have fled[16] but for the weight of the musical instrument which held him down[17]. Jones grabbed his arm. 'You and I are going to enter the barber's shop together. Let me advise you against making any trouble.[18] It may go easier for you in the end.[19]'

1. cette exaspérante manie
2. ou de ne pas le faire du tout, semblait-il aujourd'hui,
3. ruelle pleine d'ornières
4. me souvins
5. de se diriger directement vers
6. n'était-ce pas la raison de notre venue ici ?
7. s'approcha du
8. Une coupe ou un rasage ?
9. j'aimerais admirer votre coupe de cheveux.
10. tendu le bras et lui avait arraché son haut-de-forme
11. tignasse d'un roux vif
12. C'est exactement ce que je pensais.
13. indigné
14. Je crois bien que je m'adresse à
15. pour ce genre de travail
16. sursauta et se serait enfui
17. si le poids de son instrument ne l'avait pas cloué au sol
18. Je vous déconseille de tenter quoi que ce soit.
19. Cela se finira mieux pour vous.

'I am an honest man!' Cooke protested. 'I play music. I'm paid to advertise the shop. I know nothing more.'

'That's enough of that[1], Archie. I know everything. Disown your partner if you must[2], but waste no more of my time.'

The three of us crossed the road and re-entered the dingy parlour[3] where we had first met Silas Beckett. I noticed that Archie was limping[4] heavily. As the door closed behind us, the barber appeared, once again climbing up from the basement. He was astonished to see the hurdy-gurdy player and one look at Jones told him that his game – whatever it was – was up[5]. I thought he would turn and run. There might be another way out of the building.[6] But Jones had anticipated him.

'Stay where you are, John Clay!' he commanded, releasing the other man and propelling him[7] into the well-worn leather chair[8]. 'Yes! I know your true name. I know exactly what you are doing here. Do not attempt to run. I have officers at both ends of the street. But if you will trust me and play fair with me[9], there is still a chance that this may not end too badly for you[10].'

The barber considered. Then I saw him slump and it was as if he had allowed a coat to slip from his shoulders[11]. He had visibly changed into an older, wiser[12] man and when he spoke his voice had altered too[13]. 'I prefer *Mr* Clay,' he said.

'I am surprised to see you out of jail so soon.'

'The judge, a very civilised gentleman, recognised the damage that a lengthy sentence would have on a delicate constitution such as mine[14].' It was hard to believe that it was the same man

1. Ça ira comme ça

2. Vous pouvez désavouer votre partenaire si vous y tenez

3. le petit salon miteux

4. boitait

5. sa combine, quelle qu'elle fût, était finie

6. Le bâtiment avait peut-être une autre issue.

7. relâchant l'autre homme et le poussant

8. dans le vieux fauteuil en cuir tout usé

9. jouez franc feu

10. vous ne vous en sortiez pas trop mal

11. s'affaisser comme s'il avait retiré un manteau trop lourd

12. plus sage

13. avait changé elle aussi

14. une longue peine causerait à ma constitution fragile

speaking. 'It may also have helped that we had, by coincidence, both gone to the same school.'

'What …?' I began.

'Let me introduce you to Mr John Clay, the well-known murderer, thief, smasher and forger[1] – or so Sherlock Holmes described him. He is a criminal of the utmost ingenuity[2], Chase, the inventor of the so-called Red-Headed League[3].'

'The robbery at Coburg Square!' I exclaimed. Had I not seen a newspaper article about the very same, pinned to the wall[4] in Jones's study?

'The failed[5] robbery. When I first came here, I found it hard to believe that I was encountering the very same[6] John Clay and that he had once again returned to his favourite *modus operandi*[7]. And yet I quickly perceived it had to be the case. You will permit me to explain, Mr Clay?'

'You can do what you like, sir. It is a matter of indifference to me.[8]'

'Very well. What we were presented with here[9] was a barber's shop that had been expressly designed to put off customers[10]. Not only was the room filthy[11], but the barber's own hair has been quite hideously cut[12]. It would be a foolish soul who would allow the razor to come anywhere near their head[13] in such a place or, for that matter[14], to purchase a hair tonic whose principal ingredient would appear to be glue. Why[15], I would be more comfortable at Sweeney Todd[16]'s! But that, of course, was the idea.[17] For Mr Clay had more pressing matters to attend to[18]. Just across the road is the Chancery Lane Safe Deposit Company. For five years or more it has provided strongrooms[19] for London's wealthiest[20] families.'

'Six thousand safes[21],' Clay muttered, sadly.

1. passeur de fausse monnaie et faussaire
2. d'une ingéniosité exceptionnelle
3. prétendue Ligue des rouquins
4. épinglé au mur
5. manqué
6. j'étais tombé nez à nez avec le même
7. il avait repris ses bonnes vieilles habitudes
8. Ça m'est bien égal.
9. Ce que nous avions devant nous
10. sciemment conçu pour décourager les clients
11. très sale
12. le coiffeur lui-même arborait une coupe hideuse
13. Seul un idiot laisserait le rasoir du coiffeur s'approcher de sa tête
14. d'ailleurs
15. Voyons
16. [barbier célèbre pour avoir assassiné nombre de ses clients]
17. Mais tout cela était fait exprès, bien sûr.
18. avait d'autres chats à fouetter
19. elle prête ses salles des coffres
20. les plus fortunées
21. coffres-forts

'Mr Clay has been tunnelling beneath the road[1], intending to break into the vault[2]. His associate, Archie Cooke, was a necessary part of the operation, providing two services. First, the appalling noise of his playing[3] would cover the sound of the digging taking place[4] beneath his feet. I was able to work out how far the tunnel extended[5] by his position in the street. You are, I believe, almost there.'

'Another few days and we will be done[6].'

'He also provided a warning should anyone approach the shop.'

'He stopped playing!' I said.

'Precisely. The silence would alert Mr Clay and give him time to climb back up to the surface. He could not, however, change his trousers. I saw at once that the knees were very creased[7] – the very same clue[8] that Holmes noticed last time, by the way.'

'You asked if he was religious.'

'He had clearly been kneeling.[9] Had he been at prayer[10], the result might have been the same. As soon as he told me that he did not attend church[11], I knew that my conclusion was correct. On the last occasion[12], Mr Clay used an ingenious fabrication[13] to persuade a London pawnbroker to absent himself from his premises[14]. This present ruse shows that he has lost none of his inventiveness[15].'

John Clay bowed. There was something close to a smile on that strange, boyish[16] face. 'I have to say, sir, that it gives me some consolation to be arrested by the best. Sherlock Holmes last time and now you! Permit me to say, though,[17] that I have never actually murdered anyone. There was

1. a creusé un tunnel sous la route
2. afin de s'introduire dans la chambre forte
3. l'effroyable son de son instrument
4. travaux d'excavation
5. J'ai pu calculer jusqu'où s'étendait le tunnel
6. nous aurons fini
7. tout froissés
8. exactement le même indice
9. Il était clair qu'il s'était agenouillé.
10. en train de prier
11. qu'il n'allait pas à la messe
12. La fois précédente
13. un mensonge élaboré
14. un prêteur sur gage londonien de s'absenter de sa boutique
15. rien perdu de son inventivité
16. enfantin
17. Permettez-moi d'ajouter, cela dit,

a death, it is true, but we had both been drinking[1] and the person in question fell. He was not pushed.'

'I have no interest in your past, Mr Clay. It may be that you can escape arrest[2] – or at least ameliorate your situation by assisting me. Can I trust you to be honest?'

'You are speaking, sir, to a distant relative[3] of Her Majesty the Queen – albeit one who has long been ignored[4]. If it is possible to come to some sort of arrangement[5] that will help me in my current difficulties, I will be true to my word[6].'

'It is as I hoped.[7] Let me tell you then how I found my way to Chancery Lane in the first place. My friend and I visited the scene of a number of vicious murders, Bladeston House in Highgate. The owner, one[8] Scott or Scotchy Lavelle, had written the name of this establishment, and part of its address, in his diary.'

'I knew Lavelle. I didn't kill him. But I can't say I was too sorry to hear of his demise[9].'

'Is the name Jonathan Pilgrim familiar to you?'

'No.'

'He was an agent of Pinkerton's, the American law-enforcement agency, and he also knew of your scheme[10]. He was himself murdered but he left behind one of your advertising cards which also brought us here.'

There was a brief silence. Then Clay drew himself up[11]. 'Archie, old pal, make some tea. Gentlemen, can I invite you into my back parlour[12]? I never thought I would be glad to meet two officers of the law, nor to have the bracelets snapped on my wrists[13], but I am glad to see you. Have tea with me and I will tell you my story. You have

1. nous étions tous les deux ivres
2. Il se pourrait que vous échappiez à l'arrestation
3. un parent éloigné
4. quoi que j'aie été ignoré depuis longtemps
5. trouver un arrangement quelconque
6. tiendrai parole
7. C'est ce que j'espérais.
8. un certain
9. j'étais fâché d'apprendre sa mort
10. il était au courant de votre combine
11. se redressa
12. salle du fond
13. ni de me faire passer les menottes

my word, on my royal blood,[1] that it is my overwhelming desire to help![2]'

We repaired[3] to the back room and sat on rickety chairs at a bare wooden table[4] while Archie poked among the coals[5]. Following Jones's revelations, Clay seemed to have regained so much of his composure[6] that the three of us could have been three old friends, discussing something that we had been planning from the start.

'I came out of Holloway[7],' Clay began. 'Not a pleasant place. To a gentleman of breeding, something like a pigsty[8] and I couldn't even pay chummage[9] to get a room of my own. Never mind[10]. The judge, a charming man as I may have mentioned, had at least been lenient[11] – and I cast about me[12], wondering what I might do next. The failure of my red-headed scheme[13] had been something of a shock to me. What do you say, Archie? It had required a great deal of preparation. It was a shame that Holmes got involved.[14] Another few days and we'd have got away with it.[15]

'This was in February and the moment I stepped outside, I knew that something was wrong. All my old chums were lying low[16] and the pubs of Shoreditch could have been funeral parlours for all the fun that was to be had[17]. It was as if the Ripper himself[18] had come back to haunt the streets of London ... that or something worse.

'It was worse, as I found out soon enough. A new mob[19] had arrived. Americans, it was said. I have never been very partial to Americans myself, present company excepted.[20] In my view, it was a great shame that my ancestor, King George the Third, allowed the colonies to slip through his fingers[21]. But I digress ... These people had

1. Je vous promets, au nom de mon sang bleu,
2. que je ne désire rien de plus que de vous aider !
3. Nous nous retirâmes
4. des chaises bancales autour d'une table en bois nu
5. tandis qu'Archie ranimait les braises
6. tellement retrouvé son aplomb
7. [prison de Londres]
8. bien élevé, c'est une vraie porcherie
9. je ne pouvais même pas me payer
10. Mais peu importe.
11. clément
12. pensait à l'avenir
13. L'échec du coup des rouquins
14. s'en soit mêlé.
15. À quelques jours près, on s'en serait tiré.
16. vieux amis faisaient profil bas
17. étaient tellement calmes qu'on se serait cru au funérarium
18. Jack l'éventreur
19. pègre
20. mais je ne dis pas ça pour vous
21. ait laissé les colonies lui glisser entre les doigts

come over from New York and, having planted themselves in the city, they had spread[1] like syphilis. I have lost many friends, many colleagues. They didn't play by our rules[2] and for six weeks the streets and alleyways had been running with[3] blood and I can assure you that I'm not employing a metaphor in this particular instance. I mean it.[4] These people were vicious.'

The kettle[5] had boiled. Archie filled the teapot and brought it to the table. He was still moving with difficulty and I saw that he was in pain.

'Where was Moriarty?' I asked.

'Moriarty? I never met him myself, although I knew of him, of course.[6] We all did. There was a man to be feared if ever there was one.[7] And he took his cut too![8] There was no crime committed in London that he didn't take his share of and we all used to complain about it – in whispers[9] – although to be fair he[10] was always there when you needed him. I'll say that for him.[11] But he'd gone, disappeared. This fellow, Clarence Devereux, had taken his place. And Devereux made Moriarty look like a fairy godmother[12] though he too never showed himself, sending his lieutenants to do his dirty work[13].

'Archie and I were sitting in our little lodging house owned by a Jew[14] in Petticoat Lane when they came calling[15], Scotchy Lavelle, a nasty, pig-eyed man[16], surrounded by a bunch of hooligan boys. They were English, to their eternal shame and damnation[17], for that was how these newcomers worked. They recruited straight from the gutter.[18] That gave them the muscle for an army drawn from the rookeries and the opium dens[19] who would do anything for half a crown[20]. No

1. s'étant implantés dans la ville, ils se sont répandus
2. ne respectaient pas nos règles du jeu
3. ruelles ruisselaient de
4. Je ne plaisante pas.
5. bouilloire
6. mais je le connaissais de réputation.
7. S'il y avait un homme à craindre, c'était bien lui.
8. Et il n'oubliait pas non plus de prélever sa part !
9. à mi-voix
10. cela dit, il faut bien avouer qu'il
11. On ne peut pas lui enlever ça.
12. aurait fait passer Moriarty pour un agneau
13. sale boulot
14. pension tenue par un Juif
15. sont venus nous voir
16. homme cruel aux yeux porcins
17. maudits soient-ils
18. leur main-d'œuvre dans le caniveau
19. venue des quartiers pauvres et des fumeries d'opium
20. une petite pièce

loyalty. No patriotism. And they were well informed. They knew everything about the city and the professionals who worked it[1] – the busters and the screwmen, the skittle-sharps[2] and the rest of them. And they knew about me.[3]

'They bust in[4] while we were having breakfast and tied Archie to a chair. Scotchy did nothing himself. He stood there, strutting[5], while his boys did the dirty work for him. Then, finally, he laid out[6] his proposition. Why do I call it that? It was a demand and it would be death[7] if I refused, no doubt of that.

'There was an empty shop just off[8] Chancery Lane, opposite the Safe Deposit Company. They reckoned[9] it would take me a few weeks to tunnel underneath the road and break in[10]. The place was filled with gold and silver, jewellery[11] and cash. They would pay the rent for the premises[12] but Archie and me, we would do all the filthy work, squatting underground[13]. We'd take all the risk. And what did they want in return for their kindness[14]? Mr Devereux would take half of everything, they told me. Half! Even Moriarty never demanded more than twenty per cent.'

'And you agreed?' Jones asked.

'When you're surrounded by five cutthroats and the bacon's gone cold[15], it's best not to argue[16]. Even so, I have my dignity. I protested in no uncertain terms[17]. And that was when that devil turned to poor Archie. "Hurt him!" he said. The words were spoken. There was nothing I could do.'

'You could have stopped them,' Archie mumbled.

1. qui en profitaient
2. les cambrioleurs, arnaqueurs, surineurs
3. Et ils avaient entendu parler de moi.
4. ont fait irruption
5. en se pavanant
6. a présenté
7. un ordre et je le paierais de ma vie
8. tout près de
9. estimaient
10. entrer par effraction
11. de bijoux
12. boutique
13. le sale boulot, accroupis sous terre
14. en échange de cette faveur
15. coupe-gorges et que vous ne pouvez plus gagner votre croûte
16. il vaut mieux ne pas discuter
17. en des termes clairs

'It all happened too quickly. It was horrible. They pulled his shoe off and right in front of me …' Clay stopped. 'Show them, Archie.'

The red-haired boy leaned down[1] and took his shoe off. And now I understood why he had been limping when we brought him into the barber's shop. He had lost the nail[2] from his big toe, which was still swollen and bloody[3].

'They did this to me!' he whispered, and there were tears in his eyes.

'They used a pair of pliers[4],' Clay continued. 'There was a lot of screaming and it quite put me off my breakfast[5], I can tell you. And I knew it could be worse. If I refused, they might start on me[6]! I had never seen such wanton savagery[7] and of course I knew at that point I had no choice.

'We moved in here.[8] It was my idea to reopen the barber's shop and – you've got it in one[9] – to do everything in my power to prevent customers from entering[10]. In the entire time we've been here, I've only had to give half a dozen haircuts[11] – and didn't do too bad a job, though I say so myself[12]. I've been underground with Archie as my lookout[13] and it's been the devils own work[14], I can tell you. Mudstone, limestone, chalk![15] Whatever happened to good old-fashioned London clay?[16]'

'After the murder of Scott Lavelle, did you hear from Clarence Devereux?' Jones asked.

Clay shook his head. 'Not from Devereux. I read about the death in the newspapers and Archie and I went out and celebrated with a bottle of gin. I thought it was too good to be true. The next day we had a visit from an even nastier piece of work[17]. I've never been a nark, but I'll make an

1. se pencha
2. l'ongle
3. enflé et ensanglanté.
4. des tenailles
5. ça m'a plutôt coupé l'appétit
6. aurait pu s'en prendre à moi
7. barbarie
8. On a emménagé ici.
9. vous l'avez deviné
10. tout pour décourager les clients d'entrer
11. je n'ai eu que quelques coupes de cheveux à faire
12. et je ne m'en suis pas trop mal tiré, à mon avis
13. qui faisait le guet
14. un boulot infernal
15. Des roches argileuses, calcaires, de la craie !
16. Où était passée la bonne vieille argile de Londres ?
17. un type encore pire

exception for these fine fellows.[1] His name was Edgar Mortlake. He was tall, well-dressed with oily[2] black hair.'

'We know him.'

'You don't want to know him![3] He gave us another two weeks to get into the vault. After that, he said, we'd lose another toenail.'

'*You* didn't lose a toenail![4]'

'You know what I mean, Archie. That was what he said and we've been working night and day ever since.'

'And what was the arrangement to be[5], once you had broken into the vault?'

'Mr Mortlake said he would communicate with us personally.'

'You are to hand over the proceeds to him?[6]'

'Oh yes. He wants to see it all for himself. They trust no one, these Americans. You can forget your honour among thieves.[7] Archie and I even wondered if they would be content with half[8]. They might draw us into a trap and cut both our throats.'

'There will be a trap,' Jones muttered. 'But it will not be you who falls into it. And now, I would very much like to see this tunnel of yours[9]. It must be quite a feat of engineering[10]. And I would be interested to know how you intended to break through the walls[11] of the vault itself.'

'It is only London brick.[12] There is steel plating[13] on the first floor but the safes are less well protected below. Mr Devereux had made the necessary enquiries, I'll at least give him that.[14]'

We got up from the table, leaving the tea unpoured[15], and made our way down a steep and narrow staircase that brought us into a cellar[16]

1. un mouchard mais je ferais une exception pour ces phénomènes
2. gras
3. Ce n'est pas un homme qu'on a envie de fréquenter !
4. C'est pas toi à qui on a arraché un ongle à un orteil !
5. devait être votre arrangement
6. Vous devez lui remettre le butin ?
7. Le code d'honneur entre voleurs, on oublie.
8. s'ils se contenteraient de la moitié
9. votre tunnel
10. une vraie prouesse technique
11. comment vous comptiez percer les murs
12. Ce n'est que de la brique.
13. un blindage en acier
14. sait comment obtenir des informations, je dois bien l'avouer
15. sans avoir bu le thé
16. cave

beneath the shop. There was barely enough room for the four of us as most of the floor was taken up[1] by mounds of soil and broken brickwork[2]. One of the walls had been battered through[3] and, crouching down[4], I saw a circular tunnel disappearing into the distance, lit by oil lamps and held up by rough planks[5] of wood. It amazed me that John Clay would have been able to breathe in there.[6] Even in the cellar, the air was warm and dank[7]. He would only have been able to progress on his knees, with his body bent forward,[8] passing the loose soil behind him as he went.

'You have been more than forthright with me[9], Mr Clay,' Jones remarked, the oil lamps casting dark shadows across his face[10]. 'And whatever crimes you may have committed in the past, they are not, for the time being, under consideration[11]. A great evil has come to this country, just as I was warned[12], and here is the opportunity to be rid of it once and for all[13]. Come, Chase. Let us return to the surface. We have been in the dark for far too long and little time remains[14].'

We climbed the stairs and left the barber's shop. I had never seen Jones more determined nor more confident[15], leaving me in no doubt whatsoever that[16] although he seemed to hold all London in his grip[17], Devereux's time would soon be done[18].

1. car presque tout l'espace était occupé
2. par des tas de terre et de briques cassées
3. défoncé
4. en m'accroupissant
5. soutenu par des planches
6. ait pu respirer là-dedans
7. humide
8. d'avancer à genoux, en rampant
9. très honnête avec moi
10. projetant des ombres noires sur son visage
11. ils n'entrent pas, pour l'instant, en ligne de compte
12. comme on m'en avait averti
13. de s'en débarrasser une fois pour toutes
14. le temps presse
15. ni plus sûr de lui
16. et j'étais persuadé que,
17. même s'il tenait tout Londres sous son emprise
18. le règne de Devereux touchait à sa fin

1. [bassin reliant la Tamise aux docks à l'est de Londres]

2. audacieux

3. au petit matin

4. se sont introduits

5. qui abrite des fortunes familiales et commerciales

6. Forte de six milles coffres et chambres fortes

7. et gardée en continu par des veilleurs de nuit armés

8. tenue en haute estime

9. imprenable

10. tenacité

11. avaient creusé

12. Ils ont ensuite entrepris de piller

13. s'emparant de biens évalués à

14. aurait été récompensée plus grassement encore

15. sans la vivacité d'esprit

16. avait remarqué un étrange courant d'air

17. ont assiégé le bâtiment

FIFTEEN

Blackwall Basin[1]

From *The Times* of London
20th May 1891

A DARING[2] ROBBERY IN LONDON

The whole of London has been outraged by a crime that took place in the small hours of the morning[3] when thieves broke into[4] the Chancery Lane Safe Deposit, which has been a place of security for businesses and families[5] for the past six years. Boasting six thousand safes and strongrooms[6] with armed night watchmen on constant patrol[7], this highly regarded[8] institution might have seemed impregnable[9]. However, the thieves, with extraordinary fortitude[10], had burrowed[11] underneath the street and broke in through the walls of one of the lower vestibules. They then proceeded to ransack[12] many of the strongboxes, seizing goods valued at[13] several hundred pounds. Their audacity might have been rewarded with even greater returns[14] but for the quick-wittedness[15] of Mr Fitzroy Smith, the night supervisor, who became aware of a strange draught[16] in the corridor and went downstairs to investigate. However, clients of the Chancery Lane Safe Deposit have besieged the building[17] since the break-in was discovered,

> clamouring to know[1] if their own valuables have been removed[2]. The case is being investigated by Inspector A. MacDonald of Scotland Yard, but so far no arrests have been made.

I have no idea how Jones had persuaded *The Times* to fall in with his plans[3] but this was the story that appeared[4] twenty-four hours after our meeting with John Clay. It led, inevitably, to a panic,[5] a mob of the well-to-do besieging[6] Chancery Lane, and I cannot say for sure how he managed them, either[7]. I would imagine that officials at the Safe Deposit were suitably emollient[8]: 'No, sir, *your* strongbox was not interfered with[9]. Sadly[10], we cannot let you inside today. The police are still pursuing their enquiries.'

To close a major business for forty-eight hours as a result of a robbery that had never taken place was certainly quite an achievement[11], but then the stakes were high[12] and, the fact was, Jones was running out of time[13]. The Commissioner had read the letter from Coleman De Vriess and had called an enquiry to take place[14] at the first opportunity and, as Jones had made clear to me, a Scotland Yard enquiry was akin to a formal dismissal[15].

It was a Wednesday when the newspaper story broke[16]. I did not see Jones then but he sent a note to the hotel and we met the following day at an address in Chiltern Street, just south of Baker Street Station. The building in question turned out to be very small and narrow, though well lit[17], with a sitting room on the first floor and a bedroom above. It had been empty for some time although it had been dusted and kept clean[18]. Jones was as self-assured as I had ever seen him[19],

1. exigeant à grands cris de savoir
2. si leurs objets de valeur avaient ou non été volés
3. de se plier à ses plans
4. l'article était paru
5. Inévitablement, il avait causé un accès de panique,
6. une foule de nantis ayant envahi
7. je ne sais pas non plus comment il a géré cette situation
8. ont dû faire preuve d'une infinie patience
9. n'a pas été touchée
10. Malheureusement
11. un exploit remarquable
12. l'enjeu était de taille
13. et le fait est que Jones manquait de temps
14. ordonné une enquête
15. revenait à un licenciement pur et simple
16. l'article est sorti faisant sensation
17. mais bien éclairé
18. bien qu'il ait été épousseté et entretenu régulièrement
19. aussi sûr de lui que d'habitude

standing in front of the fireplace with his walking stick in front of him.

At first, I was puzzled[1]. What part could this address possibly play[2] in our investigation? Was it in some way connected with John Clay? Jones soon enlightened me[3]. 'Mr Clay is safe at his lodgings[4] in Petticoat Lane. I have two men keeping watch on him[5] and his associate, Archie Cooke. But I do not think they will attempt to fly the coop[6]. The truth is that they are both as fond of Mr Devereux as we are and will be happy to see him brought to justice[7], particularly if, by helping us, they are able to escape it themselves.'

'They have made contact with him?'

'He understands that they are holding several hundred pounds' worth of articles stolen[8] from the Chancery Lane Safe Deposit, of which he believes himself to be entitled to half[9]. The article in *The Times* was particularly well phrased[10], I thought – but will it be enough to entice him out of[11] the legation? Who knows? Perhaps he will decide to send his agents, but even that may be enough to provide us with the evidence we need to make an arrest. We must just hope that he moves quickly. Mr Clay has made it clear to them that he needs to leave London urgently. That was of course my doing.[12] Let us see what unfolds[13].'

'And what of this place? Why are we here?'

'Is it not obvious, my dear Chase?' Jones smiled and it occurred to me that I was seeing him as he might once have been, before his illness had struck him down. 'Whatever may happen in the next few days, it is clear to me that my career with Scotland Yard is finished. This is a conversation we have already begun[14]. But we have spo-

1. perplexe
2. Quel rôle cette adresse pouvait-elle avoir
3. m'éclaira
4. en sécurité dans sa pension
5. qui veillent sur lui
6. essayeront de quitter le nid
7. traîné en justice
8. détiennent plusieurs centaines de livres d'objets volés
9. dont il croit pouvoir s'octroyer la moitié
10. bien tourné
11. l'attirer hors de
12. Cela est bien entendu de mon fait.
13. ce qui se passe maintenant
14. que nous avons déjà entamée

ken before, you and I, of working together. Why should we not make it a reality? Do you not think it might work?'

'And these rooms ...?'

'... are for rent on very reasonable terms[1]. There is one bedroom – for you. I will, of course, continue to live with my dear Elspeth and Beatrice. But would not this be an ideal consulting room[2]? Twelve steps from the street and just round the corner from[3] ... well, it's of no matter[4]. Would you consider it[5], my dear fellow? You have already told me that you are unmarried and have no family ties[6]. Does America hold so very much for you[7] that you would wish to return?'

'And how would I live?'

'It would be an equal partnership. The money we would make as consulting detectives would, I am sure, be more than enough.'

For a moment, I was unsure how to reply[8]. Inspector Jones,' I said at length, 'you never cease to surprise me and meeting you has certainly been one of the most remarkable experiences of my life. Will you forgive me[9] if I ask for a little more time to consider your proposal?'

'Of course.' If he was disappointed[10] by my reticence, he tried not to show it[11].

'What you say is true,' I continued. 'I have led a somewhat[12] solitary life in New York and I have allowed my work to consume me[13]. I know that my time with the Pinkerton Agency is coming to an end[14] and it might be good for me to consider new horizons. Even so, I must give the matter more thought[15]. What say we leave any decision until[16] our work is done and Clarence Devereux is

1. sont à louer à un prix très raisonnable
2. cabinet de consultation
3. au coin de
4. cela importe peu
5. Voulez-vous bien y réfléchir
6. pas de liens familiaux
7. est-elle si importante pour vous
8. je ne savais que répondre
9. Vous ne m'en tiendrez pas rigueur
10. déçu
11. il essaya de n'en rien laisser paraître
12. quelque peu
13. je me suis laissé dévoré par mon travail
14. touche à sa fin
15. je dois y réfléchir plus sérieusement
16. Et si nous ne prenions pas de décision avant que

brought to justice? From the way things are proceeding, that cannot be too long.[1]'

'I utterly concur.[2] But shall I tell the landlord[3] that we are interested? I am sure he can be persuaded to keep the rooms for a week or two. And after that, if you are in agreement, we will have to set about finding a[4] Mrs Hudson[5] to look after us. That is of the foremost importance[6]. As to the future and our ability to sustain ourselves[7], I have many friends within Scotland Yard. Business will be forthcoming[8], I assure you.'

'Your Holmes to my Watson?[9] Maybe it's not such a bad idea. They have, after all, left a gap that must be filled.'

He stepped forward and held out a hand. I took it.[10] And in that moment, I think we were as close as we would ever be[11]. I was still quite dazed[12] by the suggestion but I could tell that my friend Jones was fired with enthusiasm, as if he were about to achieve something that he had been searching for his entire life.

That same evening, John Clay received a message from Clarence Devereux, delivered by a street urchin who had been paid sixpence for his pains[13]. He was to present himself – along with the entire proceeds[14] of the Chancery Lane Safe Deposit robbery – at Warehouse[15] 17, Blackwall Basin. The meeting would take place at five o'clock in the afternoon, the following day. There was no signature on the note. The words, written in capital letters, were short and simple. Jones examined both the ink and the paper with his usual forensic eye[16] but there was nothing that connected it with America or with the legation.

1. Au rythme où vont les choses, cela ne devrait pas tarder.
2. Je suis tout à fait de votre avis.
3. propriétaire
4. si vous en êtes d'accord, nous nous mettrons en quête d'une
5. [nom de la logeuse de Sherlock Holmes]
6. de la plus grande importance
7. à notre capacité de vivre de ce travail
8. Nous aurons des clients
9. Vous seriez mon Holmes et moi votre Watson ?
10. me tendit la main. Je la serrai.
11. plus proches que jamais
12. un peu hébété
13. gamin des rues qu'on avait payé six pennies pour sa peine
14. Il devait se présenter, avec tout le butin
15. entrepôt
16. avec son expertise habituelle

Even so[1], neither of us had any doubt as to[2] the identity of the sender.

The trap was set.[3]

And so to the Friday.[4] I had barely finished breakfast when the Boots informed me that I had a visitor. 'Show him in[5],' I said. There was still tea in the pot for two.

'He's outside,' Boots returned, with a scowl[6]. 'He's not the sort to be seen[7] in a respectable establishment. He's in the hall.'

Intrigued, I set down my napkin and left the room to find the most reprehensible-looking fellow[8] waiting for me by the front door. I saw at once that he was dressed as a sailor, though one who would have disgraced any ship[9] that would choose to have him as part of its crew[10]. His red flannel shirt hung out of his canvas trousers[11] and he had an ill-fitting[12] pilot's coat whose sleeves barely reached halfway down his arms[13]. He was unshaven[14], his face stained with indigo[15], and there was a filthy bandage wrapped around his ankle. He had a crutch tucked[16] under his arm and if it were not for the absence of a parrot[17], the picture of piracy and dissolution could not have been more complete[18].

'Who are you?' I demanded. 'What is it you want?'

'Beg pardon[19], sir.' The man touched a dirty finger to his forelock.[20] 'I come from Blackwall Basin.'

'And what is your business with me?'

'To bring you to Mr Clay.'

'I'll be damned if I'll go anywhere with you.[21] Are you telling me that Clay sent you here? How did he know this address?'

1. Néanmoins
2. quant à
3. Le piège était en place.
4. Et le vendredi arriva.
5. Faites-le entrer
6. grimace
7. L'est pas du genre à avoir sa place
8. un type à l'allure des plus répréhensibles
9. mais sa dégaine aurait déshonoré n'importe quel navire
10. équipage
11. chemise de flanelle pendait hors de son pantalon en toile
12. mal ajusté
13. lui arrivaient à peine aux coudes
14. n'était pas rasé
15. portait des marques bleues
16. béquille coincée
17. il ne lui manquait qu'un perroquet
18. pour incarner la piraterie et la débauche
19. j'm'excuse
20. leva un doigt sale à son front en guise de salut
21. Plutôt mourir que de vous accompagner où que ce soit.

'It was given to him by that policeman. What's his name? Jones! He's waiting for you even now[1].'

'Waiting for me where?'

'I'm right in front of you Chase. And the two of us should be on our way!'

'Jones!' I stared at him and as I did so, the detective moved forward, leaving the chimera of the sailor behind[2]. 'Is it really you?' I exclaimed. 'Well, I'll be damned! You had me completely fooled.[3] But why are you dressed like this? Why are you here?'

'We must set out at once[4],' Jones replied, and his voice was completely serious. 'Our friend Mr Clay will be at the warehouse later but we must be there ahead of him[5]. Devereux will not suspect that anything is amiss[6]. He will have read the newspaper and he knows that Clay lives in fear of him[7]. Even so, we can take no chances.[8] Everything must be prepared.'

'And the disguise[9]?'

'A necessary addition – and not just for me.' He leaned down and picked up a cloth bag which he threw at me[10]. 'A sailor's jacket and trousers – they came from the slop-house[11] but they are less filthy than they appear. How quickly can you get changed? I have a cab waiting outside.'

Jones had suggested to me that I might one day recount[12] our adventures – in the new *Strand*, perhaps – and it was as if, in taking me to the London docks, he had set me my first, impossible task. For how can I begin to describe the extraordinary panorama, the sprawling metropolis on the edge of the city[13], that now presented itself to me? My first impression was of a darkening sky but it was only smoke, vomiting out of

1. en ce moment même
2. laissant derrière lui ce faux marin
3. Et bien, ça alors ! Vous m'avez bien eu.
4. nous mettre en route immédiatement
5. arriver là-bas avant lui
6. qu'il se trame quoi que ce soit
7. en a une peur bleue
8. Toutefois, nous ne devons prendre aucun risque.
9. déguisement
10. se pencha et ramassa un sac de toile qu'il me lança
11. [gargote répugnante]
12. raconter
13. métropole tentaculaire qui s'étendait aux alentours de Londres

the chimneys and reflecting drearily[1] in the water below. Against this were silhouetted a hundred cranes[2] and a thousand masts, a fleet of sailing ships, steamboats, barges, coasters and lighters[3], few of them moving, the majority of them frozen together in a grey tableau. I had never seen so many different flags. It seemed that the whole world had gathered here and as I drew nearer I saw negroes, lascars, Poles and Germans[4] all shouting in different languages as if the tower of Babel had just fallen and they were fighting their way out of the debris.

The river itself ran black and indifferent to the chaos it had propagated. A network of canals had been cut inland, giving berth[5] to Russian brigs, to hoys laden with straw[6], to luggers and sloops[7], while the cranes swung round[8] with sacks of grain and great lengths of timber still smelling of turpentine[9], and the scene was as much an assault on the nose as on the eyes with[10] spices, tea, cigars and, above all, rum, making their presence known long before they were seen[11]. After a while, it became impossible to progress any faster than walking pace[12]. Our way was blocked by a tangle[13] of sailors and stevedores[14], horses, vans and wagons and even the widest passageways proved unequal to the task of processing[15] this great mass of humanity.

Eventually, we climbed down. We were surrounded by shops – a carpenter's, a wheelwright's, a blacksmith's, a plumber's[16] – vague figures going about their business behind dirty windows. A butcher in a blue apron strode past[17] carrying a fat, squealing pig[18] in a tiny cage, the whole thing balanced on his shoulder. A crowd of

1. tristement
2. grues
3. caboteurs et péniches
4. des Indiens, des Polonais et des Allemands
5. avait été creusé dans les terres pour permettre le mouillage
6. des bricks russes, des voiliers chargés de paille
7. des lougres et des sloops
8. se balançaient
9. de longues poutres sentant encore la térébenthine
10. assaillait aussi bien le nez que les yeux à coups d'
11. rhum, qui annonçait leur présence bien avant qu'on les voie
12. d'avancer plus vite qu'au pas
13. enchevêtrement
14. de dockers
15. les allées les plus larges ne suffisaient pas à charrier
16. menuisier, charron, forgeron, plombier
17. boucher en tablier bleu passa d'un pas rapide
18. transportant un cochon gras et couinant

ragamuffin[1] children – chasing each other or being chased – scattered on each side. There was a cry of warning and something foul and odorous[2] splashed down from an open doorway above.[3] Jones grabbed hold of me and we continued past a chandler[4] and the inevitable pawnbroker[5], an old Jew sitting in the doorway, examining a pocket watch with an oversized magnifying glass[6]. Ahead of us, I saw the first of the warehouses, a construction of woodwork, iron and brick, mouldering[7] in the damp and half-sinking into the ground, which seemed unable to bear its weight. There were derricks jutting out[8] in every direction and barrels of wine, boxes of hardware[9] and all manner of sacks and hogsheads being lifted[10] on ropes and pulleys, unloaded onto platforms[11] and then swallowed up[12] inside.

We continued, leaving some of the crowds behind us. The warehouses appeared to be numbered without rhyme or reason[13] and we quickly came upon number seventeen which was square and solid, four storeys high[14], located on the corner where a canal met the river with large doorways open front and back[15]. Jones led us to a pile of old nets strewn on the towpath and threw himself down[16], inviting me to do the same. A couple of crates[17] and a rusting cannon completed our *fête champêtre*. Jones took out a bottle of gin and I opened it and took a cautious sip[18]. It contained only water. I understood his purpose[19]. We had several hours to wait until the rendezvous. Dressed as we were – for I was now in the attire of[20] an itinerant dockworker – we would give no cause for suspicion, easily blending in[21] with the scenery. We might be two dissolute labourers[22],

1. loqueteux
2. cri d'avertissement et une substance malodorante
3. jaillit d'une fenêtre au-dessus de nous
4. fournisseur d'équipement maritime
5. prêteur sur gages
6. montre à gousset avec une énorme loupe
7. pourrissant
8. des mâts de charge qui se dressaient
9. des boîtes pleines d'outils
10. et toutes sortes de sacs et de fûts qui étaient soulevés
11. par des cordes et des poulies, chargés sur des quais
12. engloutis
13. numérotés sans rime ni raison
14. haut de quatre étages
15. portes ouvertes à l'avant et à l'arrière
16. vieux filets jonchant le chemin de halage et s'y installa
17. caisses
18. j'en bus une gorgée avec précaution
19. son but
20. vêtu comme
21. nous fondant
22. journaliers aux mœurs dissolues

waiting for the foreman to take pity on us[1] and give us a day's work.

Fortunately, it was a warm day and I must confess I quite enjoyed lying there in silent companionship[2] with the constant activity going on all around us, I did not dare take out my watch – there was always the possibility that we were being observed – but from the movement of the clouds I could tell how the afternoon was passing and I was confident that Athelney Jones would be aware of any movement or anything that might suggest that Clarence Devereux was on his way[3].

In fact it was John Clay and Archie Cooke who arrived first, the two of them sitting next to each other on a light cart[4] with a great pile of merchandise covered by a tarpaulin[5] behind them. Clay, in his vanity[6], had cut his hair short, ridding himself[7] of the strange appearance he had adopted when he was pretending to be a barber. I expected the two of them to stop but they drove straight into the warehouse without noticing us.

'Now it begins,' Jones muttered, barely glancing at me[8].

Another hour passed. There were still crowds of people in the dock, for labour would continue until night fell and perhaps even beyond. Behind us, a barge laden with corn and oil-cake was slowly pulling out[9], churning through the sluggish water, on its way to who knew where[10]. Clay had disappeared inside the building. I could just make out[11] the back of the vehicle that had brought him here but the rest of it was lost in the shadows. The sun must surely be setting but the sky remained the same miserable shade of grey[12].

1. attendant que le contremaître nous prenne en pitié

2. d'être allongé là en compagnie silencieuse,

3. approchait

4. charrette

5. marchandises recouvertes d'une bâche

6. par vanité

7. se débarrassant

8. en me jetant à peine un coup d'œil

9. chargée de maïs et de tourteaux se retirait lentement

10. agitant l'eau stagnante, en route pour on ne sait où

11. distinguer

12. restait triste et gardait la même nuance de gris

1. avec des rideaux aux fenêtres

2. et deux domestiques à l'air sombre

3. des croque-morts en route vers le cimetière

4. atteint notre but et attiré

5. évaluer lui-même les biens volés

6. me donna un coup de coude

7. nous nous avançâmes d'un pas traînant

8. s'arrêta

9. Tous nos espoirs reposaient sur

10. immobile et concentré

11. qui était en jeu

12. Nous fûmes tous deux déçus.

13. et examina le décor avec un air de dégoût

14. ou tout du moins je l'espérais

15. avec quatre étages de gradins entourant une scène centrale

16. fournissant un excellent point de vue à un public absent

17. vitrail

Another carriage approached, this one a brougham with the windows curtained[1] and two grim-faced attendants[2] behind the horse. They could have been undertakers on their way to[3] the cemetery and the sight of the window, covered by a heavy black curtain, made me wonder if we might have achieved our aim and drawn[4] Clarence Devereux out of the legation. Could he have come to assess the stolen property for himself[5]? Jones nudged me[6] and we shuffled forward[7], watching as the carriage came to a halt[8] just in the shadow of the entrance. All our hopes rested on[9] the opening of the door. Next to me, Jones was still, watchful[10], and I remembered that, for him, it was his entire career that was at stake[11].

We were both to be disappointed.[12] It was Edgar Mortlake, the younger of the two brothers, who stepped out and surveyed his surroundings with distaste[13]. Two hooligan boys had travelled with him – these people never went anywhere alone – and they stood either side of him, providing the same protection that had been in evidence when we first met him at Bladeston House. Jones and I moved closer still keeping to the shadows and remaining out of sight. It was quite possible that Mortlake had agents outside the building but the two of us posed no obvious threat – or so I hoped[14]. At least we now had a better view of what was happening inside.

The setting reminded me of a theatre of Shakespeare's time with the four tiers surrounding a central stage[15] and providing an excellent vantage point for an audience that had failed to appear[16]. The building was as tall as it was wide, dominated by a circular stained-glass window[17] which might have been stolen from a chapel. There were wooden beams criss-crossing each other[1], dangling ropes[2] – some of them connected to hooks and counterweights[3] to lift goods to the upper floor – slanting platforms and, hidden away here and there,[4] tiny offices. The ground floor, where the drama was to take place[5], was open and almost empty with a light scattering of sawdust[6]. It seemed that I had watched the entire cast[7] arrive.

The cart was parked to one side, the horse snorting and shifting its head[8] impatiently. A pair of trestle tables had been set up[9] and John Clay and Archie Cooke were standing in front of them, rather in the manner of two shopkeepers with a difficult customer[10]. There were about fifty different objects on display: silver cutlery and candlesticks[11], jewellery, several oil paintings, glassware and china, banknotes[12] and coins. I had no idea where they had all come from – Chancery Lane Safe Deposit had, of course, not been touched – but supposed Jones must have supplied them, perhaps from the evidence room[13] in Scotland Yard.

From where we were standing, we were able to hear the conversation that ensued. Mortlake strode the full length of the tables[14], his hands clasped behind his back. He was wearing the dark frock coat that he seemed to favour[15] but he had left his walking stick behind. He stopped opposite John Clay, his eyes glinting with hostility[16]. 'A poor haul[17], Mr Clay,' he muttered, 'quite miserable. Not at all what we had expected.'

'We were unlucky, Mr Mortlake,' Clay replied. 'The tunnel worked well enough[18] – although it was the devil's own work, you have no idea!

1. des poutres en bois qui s'entrecroisaient
2. des cordes qui pendaient
3. des crochets et des contre-poids
4. plates-formes inclinées et cachés ici et là
5. où la pièce allait se jouer
6. et recouvert d'une légère couche de sciure
7. tous les acteurs
8. s'ébrouant et remuant la tête
9. Deux tables à tréteaux avaient été installées
10. rappelant deux commerçants en prise avec un client tatillon
11. des couverts et des bougeoirs en argent
12. des verres et de la porcelaine, des billets de banque
13. dans la salle des pièces à conviction
14. longea les tables à grands pas
15. redingote noire qui semblait être sa préférée
16. brillants d'animosité
17. piètre butin
18. a fonctionné plutôt bien

But we were disturbed before we could open too many of the boxes.'

'This is all of it?' Mortlake stepped closer so that he towered over[1] the smaller man. 'You haven't thought to hold something back[2]?'

'This is all of it, sir. You have my word as a gentleman.[3]'

'Upon our lives![4]' Archie croaked[5].

'It is indeed your lives that will be forfeit[6] if I find you are lying to me.'

'There's a thousand pounds here,' Clay insisted.

'That's not what I read in the newspapers.'

'The newspapers lied. The Safe Deposit Company would not want to alarm their customers. A thousand pounds, Mr Mortlake! Five hundred each. Not so bad for a few weeks' labour, the labour in question being Archie's and mine[7]. You and your friends come out of it handsomely[8].'

'My friends are of a different opinion. In fact, I must inform you that Mr Devereux is far from satisfied. He had expected more and feels that you have disappointed him; that you are, in effect, in breach of contract[9]. He has therefore instructed me to take all of it[10].'

'All of it?'

'You may keep this.' Mortlake leaned forward and plucked out a silver eggcup[11]. 'A souvenir of your work.'

'An eggcup?'

'An eggcup and your life. And the next time Mr Devereux has need of your services, you will perhaps come up with a strategy that leads to a decent return[12]. There is a bank in Russell Square that has come to our attention and I would advise

1. afin de dominer par sa taille
2. Vous n'auriez pas plutôt gardé une partie pour vous ?
3. Je vous donne ma parole de gentleman.
4. On le jure sur nos vies !
5. ajouta Archie d'une voix rauque
6. que vous perdrez
7. surtout que c'est Archie et moi qu'avons fait tout le boulot
8. vous en tirez à bon compte
9. n'avez, dans les faits, pas rempli votre part du contrat
10. donné l'ordre de tout saisir
11. attrapa un coquetier en argent
12. veillerez à élaborer un plan plus profitable

you against leaving[1] – or trying to leave – London. We will see you in due course[2].'

Mortlake nodded at[3] the hooligan boys who produced sacks that they proceeded to fill[4], sweeping the goods off the tables[5]. Athelney Jones had seen enough. I saw him stride into full view[6], at the same time producing a whistle from his pocket[7]. He blew a single, long blast[8] and suddenly a dozen policemen in full uniform appeared at both ends of the warehouse, blocking the exits. To this day I am not sure where they had been concealed[9]. Could they have come off one of the boats that had been moored[10] nearby? Had they been tucked away[11] in one of the offices? Wherever they had come from, they had been well drilled and closed in around us[12] as Jones and I walked purposefully[13] towards the little group.

'Stand where you are, Mr Mortlake,' Jones announced. 'I have witnessed everything that has taken place here and I have heard you name your accomplice. I am arresting you for conspiracy to commit burglary[14] and for receiving stolen goods. You are exposed as part of a criminal network that has brought terror and bloodshed[15] to the streets of London but this is the end of it. You, your brother and Clarence Devereux will answer to the courts[16].'

Throughout this lengthy speech[17], Edgar Mortlake had stood there, showing no expression at all. When Jones had finished he turned not to the detective but to the thief, John Clay, who was blinking uncomfortably[18]. 'You knew of this[19],' he said, simply.

'They gave me no choice. But I will tell you that, in actual fact, I don't give a jot[20]. I've had enough

1. déconseille de quitter
2. en temps voulu
3. fit un signe de tête aux
4. sortirent des sacs qu'ils se mirent à remplir
5. raflant tout ce qui se trouvait sur les tables
6. avancer à découvert
7. sortant de sa poche un sifflet
8. sifflement strident
9. où ils s'étaient cachés
10. Avaient-ils pu sortir d'un des bateaux amarrés
11. entassés
12. bien entraînés et formèrent un cercle autour de nous
13. d'un pas résolu
14. association de malfaiteurs en vue de commettre un cambriolage
15. carnage
16. en répondrez devant les tribunaux
17. long discours
18. plissait les yeux, l'air mal à l'aise
19. Vous étiez au courant
20. en vérité, je m'en contrefiche

1. votre cupidité
2. pardonner
3. Vous salissez notre réputation de criminels.
4. se portera mieux sans vous
5. trahis
6. fendre l'air
7. donné une gifle au voleur
8. largement pire
9. dissimulé
10. lame tranchante montée sur une sorte de mécanisme
11. qui avait surgi comme la langue d'un serpent
12. je nourris l'espoir qu'il avait raté sa cible
13. suffoquant, nous interrogeant du regard
14. Je regardais impuissant le cauchemar qui
15. dégainé leurs pistolets
16. se déployèrent et se mirent à tirer sur
17. d'une seule salve
18. Tandis que les corps tombaient
19. prit une machette qui traînait sur une caisse
20. tranchant
21. attrapé

of your threats, your violence, your greed[1] and I cannot forgive[2] you for what you did to my friend Archie. You give crime a bad name.[3] London will be better off once it's seen the back of you[4].'

'You have betrayed[5] us.'

'Wait …' Clay began.

I saw Mortlake's hand swing through the air[6] and thought he had slapped the other man across the face[7] although it was strange, for there was no sound of any contact. Clay looked puzzled too. Then I realised it was far, far worse[8]. Mortlake had something concealed[9] in his sleeve, a viciously sharp blade on some sort of mechanism[10] which had sprung out like a snake's tongue[11]. He had used it to cut Clay's throat. For just one moment, I entertained the hope that he had missed[12], that Clay had not been harmed, but then a thin line of red appeared above the thief's collar. Clay stood there, gasping for air, looking to us for explanation[13]. Then the wound opened and a torrent of blood poured out. Clay fell to his knees and Archie screamed and covered his eyes. I could only watch as the nightmare[14] continued before me.

The hooligan boys had dropped the sacks that they had been carrying and produced guns[15]. Moving almost mechanically, they spread out and began to blast at[16] the policemen, killing two or three of them in the first volley[17]. Even as the bodies fell to the ground[18], one of them picked up a machete – it was lying on a crate[19] – and swung it through the air, severing[20] a rope just a few feet away. Mortlake had reached out and taken hold of[21] a second rope: the two of them were connected and there must have been a counterweight for he was suddenly lifted high into the air like a magician performing a trick or perhaps an acrobat at the circus. In seconds, even as the noise of the gunfire[1] and the smoke from the revolvers billowed out[2], he had become a tiny figure four storeys up[3], swinging himself[4] onto a platform and disappearing from sight.

'Get after him![5]' Jones shouted.

Most of the policemen were armed and returned fire. Hopelessly outnumbered[6], Mortlake's protectors continued to empty their pistols but were quickly shot down[7], one of them spinning onto a trestle table[8], which collapsed beneath him. I could only wonder at[9] the sense of loyalty or fear that had persuaded them to sacrifice their lives for their master who had to their fate[10].

I had not stayed to watch any more of the shootout[11]. Ducking down[12], afraid for my own safety, I had obeyed Jones's command and had already reached a wooden staircase that zigzagged from floor to floor. There was a second, similar set of stairs at the far end and, as I watched, three policemen peeled off to cover them[13]. Mortlake might have made a dramatic escape from the area of combat[14] but he must still be trapped within the building.

I climbed the stairs, which creaked and bent beneath my weight[15]. Dust and the smell of gunpowder filled my nostrils.[16] Finally, I reached the top and – breathless, my heart pounding[17] – I found myself in a narrow passageway with a wooden wall on one side of me and an unprotected drop[18] on the other. Glancing back down, I saw Athelney Jones had taken charge of the situation. He was not physically able to follow me. Clay lay spreadeagled in a widening

1. coups de feu
2. s'élevait en volutes
3. quatre étages au-dessus de nos têtes
4. se hissant
5. Rattrapez-le !
6. Désespérément moins nombreux
7. furent rapidement abattus
8. atterrissant sur une table à tréteaux qui s'effondra
9. J'étais impressionné par
10. à leur sort
11. le reste de la fusillade
12. Baissant la tête
13. se détachèrent du groupe pour y grimper
14. avait beau s'être échappé avec éclat du champ de bataille
15. grincèrent et ployèrent sous mon poids
16. La poussière et l'odeur de poudre emplissaient mes narines.
17. à bout de souffle et le cœur battant
18. un vide sans protection

1. les bras en croix dans une mare de sang de plus en plus grande
2. tache d'encre rouge
3. des barriques, des caisses, des fûts et des sacs ventrus
4. arme terrible
5. surgir
6. cachettes
7. me rattrapant lentement
8. J'arrivai à une ouverture.
9. était replié sur lui-même
10. entre les deux
11. la ruée des nuages
12. quelques remorqueurs se dirigeaient vers l'est
13. chaines rouillées montées sur un espèce de treuil complexe
14. battant au vent
15. sans plus oser avancer
16. maculé de sang
17. dépassait toujours
18. [célèbres producteurs de théâtre, fin du XIXe siècle]
19. vindicatif

pool of blood[1] which seemed even more shocking from this height, like a vast red ink blot[2]. There were casks, crates, hogsheads and bulging sacks[3] scattered all around me and I proceeded slowly, suddenly remembering that although I was unarmed, Mortlake carried a dreadful weapon[4] and could leap out[5] from any of a hundred hiding places[6]. The three police officers had also reached the top but were some distance away, silhouetted against the round window, proceeding slowly towards me[7].

I came to an opening.[8] It was as if part of the wall had been folded back[9] – not exactly a door nor a window but something in between[10]. I saw the grey of the evening and the rushing clouds[11]. The Thames was before me, a couple of tugs making their way east[12] but otherwise still and silent. In front of me was a long platform connected to the warehouse by two rusting chains with a complicated winch system constructed beside it[13]. Perhaps Mortlake had hoped to use it to lower himself back down, but either it wasn't working or I had arrived too quickly for there suddenly he was, in front of me, his coat flapping in the breeze[14] and his dead eyes fixed on mine.

I remained where I was, not daring to move forward[15]. The knife, now stained with blood[16], was still jutting[17] from his sleeve. Standing there on the platform, with his oily black hair and moustache, he reminded me more than ever of an actor on the stage. I'm sure the Kiralfy brothers of New York[18] never presented a character more vengeful[19] nor more dangerous.

'Well, well, well,' he exclaimed. 'Pinkerton, you surprise me. I have come upon your sort before, Bob Pinkerton's boys[1], and they are not usually so astute[2]. You seem to have outplayed me.[3]'

'You have nowhere to go, Mortlake!' I returned. I did not dare move any closer forward. I was still afraid that he would rush at me[4] and use that hideous weapon. He stood where he was.[5] The sluggish water of the river was below him but if he tried to jump he would surely drown[6], if the fall did not kill him first. 'Put down your weapon. Give yourself up.[7]'

His reply was a profanity of the worst sort[8]. I felt the presence of the police officers nearby and saw them out of the corner of my eye[9], gathering uncertainly[10] in the doorway behind me. Not exactly the cavalry, but I was relieved that I was no longer on my own[11].

'Give us[12] Devereux!' I said. 'He is the one we want. Turn him in[13] and it will go easier for you.'

'I will give you nothing but this: the promise[14] that you will regret this until the end of your days. But trust me, Pinkerton, there won't be many of them[15]. You and I will have our reckoning[16].'

In a single movement, without hesitating, Mortlake turned and jumped. I saw him fall through the air, his coat flapping up behind him, and watched as he plunged feet first into the river, disappearing beneath the surface. I ran forward, the wood tilting[17] beneath me and suddenly I was dizzy[18] and might have fallen myself had not one of the constables grabbed hold of me[19].

'It's too late, sir!' I heard a voice shouting. 'He's finished.'

1. J'en ai déjà croisé, des types de Bob Pinkerton

2. si malins que ça

3. On dirait bien que t'as gagné cette partie.

4. il se jette sur moi

5. Il ne bougeait pas.

6. s'y noierait à coup sûr

7. Rends-toi.

8. un juron de la pire espèce

9. du coin de l'oeil

10. se rassemblant avec hésitation

11. de ne plus être livré à moi-même

12. Livre-nous

13. Dénonce-le

14. Tout ce que je vais vous livrer, c'est la promesse

15. tes jours sont comptés

16. on règlera nos comptes.

17. s'inclina

18. j'eus un vertige

19. si l'un des policiers ne m'avait rattrapé

I was being held and I was grateful for it.[1] I stared down[2] at the water but there was nothing more to see, not even a ripple[3].

Edgar Mortlake had gone[4].

1. Quelqu'un me retenait et je lui en étais reconnaissant.
2. Je regardai en bas
3. pas même un remous
4. avait disparu

SIXTEEN

We Make an Arrest

That evening, we raided the[1] Bostonian for a second time.

Inspector Jones had instructed me to meet him at eight o'clock and, accompanied by an impressive entourage of uniformed constables, we marched in at exactly that hour, once again silencing the pianist as we made our way past the gilded[2] mirrors and marble panels[3], in front of the bar with all its glittering[4] crystal and glass, ignoring the muttered protests[5] of the largely American assembly, many of whom were having their evening interrupted for a second time. This time we knew exactly where we were going. We had seen the Mortlakes emerge from a door on the other side of the bar. This must be where their private office was to be found.

We entered without knocking. Leland Mortlake was sitting behind a desk, framed by[6] two windows with red velvet[7] curtains. There was a glass of whisky in front of him and a fat cigar, smouldering in an ashtray[8]. At first, we thought he was alone but then a youth[9] of about eighteen with oily hair and a pinched[10], narrow face got to his feet, rising up from the place where he had been

1. avons fait une descente au
2. dorés
3. panneaux en marbre
4. scintillants
5. murmures désapprobateurs
6. encadré par
7. velours
8. qui se consumait dans un cendrier
9. jeune garçon
10. étroit

kneeling[1] next to Mortlake. I had seen his type[2] many times before and felt revolted[3]. For a moment neither of us spoke. The boy stood there, sullen[4], unsure what to do.

'Get out of here, Robbie,' Mortlake said.

'Whatever you say[5], sir.' The boy hurried past us, anxious to be on his way[6].

Leland Mortlake waited until the door had closed, then turned to us, coldly furious. 'What is it?' he snarled[7]. 'Don't you ever knock?[8]' tongue, moist and grey, flickered[9] briefly between his bulbous lips[10]. He was wearing evening clothes and his hands, curled into fists, rested[11] on the desk.

'Where is your brother?' Jones demanded.

'Edgar? I haven't seen him.'

'Do you know where he was this afternoon?'

'No.'

'You are lying. Your brother was at a warehouse in the Blackwall Basin. He was taking receipt of[12] a collection of items[13], stolen from the Chancery Lane Safe Deposit. We surprised him there and would have seized[14] him had he not committed murder in front of our eyes. He is now a wanted man[15]. We know that you and he organised the theft in collaboration with a third man, Clarence Devereux. Do not deny it![16] You were with him only the other night at the American legation.'

'I do deny it. I told you the last time you came. I know no Clarence Devereux.'

'He also calls himself Coleman De Vriess.'

'I don't know that name either.'

'Your brother may have slipped[17] through our fingers but you have not[18]. You will come with me now for questioning[19] at Scotland Yard and you

1. agenouillé
2. ce genre de personnes
3. dégoûté
4. renfrogné
5. Comme vous voulez
6. impatient de partir
7. grogna
8. On ne vous a jamais appris à frapper ?
9. langue humide passa
10. grosses lèvres
11. poings serrés, reposaient
12. On lui livrait
13. objets
14. capturé
15. recherché par la police
16. Ne le niez pas !
17. filé
18. pas vous
19. pour être interrogé

will not leave until you have informed us of his whereabouts[1].'

'I will do no such thing.[2]'

'If you will not come of your own volition[3], I will have no choice but to place you under arrest[4].'

'On what charge?[5]'

'Obstruction and as an accessory to murder[6].'

'Ridiculous!'

'I do not think so.'

There was a long silence. Mortlake was sitting there, fighting for breath[7], his shoulders rising and falling while the rest of his body remained still[8]. I had never thought it possible for the human face to display such intense hatred[9] but the very blood was swelling in his cheeks[10] and I was worried that if he had some weapon – a gun – close at hand[11], perhaps in one of the drawers[12] of his bureau, he would not hesitate to use it and to hell with[13] the consequences.

Finally he spoke. 'I am an American citizen, a visitor to your country. Your accusations are false and scandalous. I wish to telephone my legation.'

'You can telephone them from my office,' Jones replied.

'You have no right—'

'I have every right. Enough of this![14] Will you accompany us or must I call my men into the room?'

Scowling horribly[15], Mortlake rose from his seat. His shirt was hanging out[16] of his trousers and, with a slow, deliberate movement, he tucked it back in[17]. 'You are wasting your time,' he murmured. 'I have nothing to tell you. I have not seen my brother. I know nothing of his affairs.'

'We shall see.[18]'

1. avant de nous avoir révélé où il se cache
2. Il n'en est pas question.
3. de votre plein gré
4. que de vous placer en état d'arrestation
5. Pour quel motif ?
6. complicité de meurtre
7. respirant difficilement
8. restait immobile
9. d'afficher une haine si profonde
10. le sang lui montait au visage
11. à portée de main
12. tiroirs
13. au diable
14. Ça suffit !
15. Nous fusillant du regard
16. pendait hors
17. la rentra à l'intérieur
18. C'est ce qu'on va voir.

We stood there, the three of us, each waiting for the other to make a move[1]. Finally, Leland Mortlake smashed out[2] the cigar, then walked to the door, his bulky frame[3] passing between us. I was glad that there were two policemen waiting outside for, with every moment that[4] we stood in the Bostonian, I felt myself to be in enemy territory. As we made our way back past the bar, Mortlake turned to the barman and called out[5]: 'Inform Mr White at the legation.'

'Yes, sir.'

Henry White had been the councillor, introduced to us by Robert Lincoln himself. I had a suspicion that Mortlake was bluffing, attempting to intimidate us. Jones ignored him anyway.

We continued through the silent, indignant[6] crowd, some of them jostling against us as if they were unwilling[7] to let us leave. A waiter reached out as if to take hold of[8] Mortlake and, imposing myself between them, I pushed them apart[9]. I was quite relieved[10] when we passed through the door and found ourselves in Trebeck Street. There were two growlers[11] waiting for us. I had already noticed that Jones had decided to spare his prisoner the indignity of a[12] Black Maria[13], the famous coach used by Scotland Yard. A lackey at the door handed Mortlake a cape and a walking stick but Jones took hold of the latter[14]. 'I will keep this, if you don't mind. You never know what you might find in such a device[15].'

'It is a walking stick, nothing more. But you must do as you must[16].' Mortlake's eyes blazed[17]. 'You will pay for this. I promise you.'

We stepped onto the pavement. It seemed to me that the street was darker than ever, the gas lamps

1. fasse un geste
2. écrasa
3. large carrure
4. car, pendant tout le temps où
5. lui lança
6. indignée
7. nous bousculant comme s'ils refusaient
8. tendit le bras comme pour saisir
9. je les éloignai l'un de l'autre
10. soulagé
11. fiacres
12. épargner à son prisonnier l'affront d'être emmené en
13. [surnom des fourgons de police au Royaume-Uni]
14. s'empara de cette dernière
15. dans un tel objet
16. faites comme bon vous semble
17. lançaient des éclairs

unequal to their struggle against[1] the night sky and the thin drizzle[2] that was falling constantly. The cobblestones with their oily reflections[3] provided more illumination. One of the horses snorted[4] and Mortlake stumbled[5]. I was close by and reached out to steady him, for it appeared that he had lost his footing[6]. But one glance in his direction showed[7] that something much worse had occurred. All the colour had left his face.[8] His eyes were wide[9] and he was gasping for breath, grinding his jaw[10] as if he were trying to say something but could no longer speak. He seemed to be terrified … frightened to death[11] was the thought that crossed my mind.

'Jones …'I began.

Inspector Jones had already seen what was happening and had taken hold of[12] his prisoner, one arm stretched across his back[13]. Mortlake was making the most horrible sound and I saw some sort of foam[14] appear on his lower lip. His body began to convulse.

'A doctor!' Jones shouted.

There was no doctor to be found[15]; certainly not in the empty street and nor[16], it would seem, in the club itself. Mortlake fell to his knees, his shoulders heaving[17], his face distorted[18].

'What is happening?' I cried. 'Is it his heart?'

'I don't know. Lay him down.[19] Surely a doctor can be found, for Heaven's sake?'

It was already too late. Mortlake pitched forward[20] onto the pavement and lay still. It was only then that we saw it, illuminated by the street lamp; a slender reed protruding[21] from the side of his neck. 'Do not touch it!' Jones commanded.

'What is it? It looks like a thorn[22].'

1. les réverbères à gaz incapables de rivaliser avec
2. crachin
3. Les pavés et leurs reflets huileux
4. s'ébroua
5. trébucha
6. le retenir, car il semblait avoir perdu l'équilibre
7. m'apprit
8. Il était livide.
9. écarquillés
10. suffoquait en grinçant des dents
11. mort de peur
12. saisi
13. placé dans son dos
14. écume
15. à l'horizon
16. pas non plus
17. crispées
18. déformé
19. Allongez-le.
20. tomba en avant
21. fin roseau dépassait
22. épine

'It is a thorn! It is poisoned. I have seen this before but I cannot believe … I *will not* believe … that it has happened a second time.'

'What are you talking about?'

'Pondicherry Lodge!' Jones knelt beside the prostrate form[1] of Leland Mortlake. He had stopped breathing and his face was utterly white[2]. 'He is dead.'

'How? I don't understand! What has happened?'

'He has been the victim of a blowpipe[3]. Someone has fired a dart[4] into his neck as we attempted to get him out of the club and we allowed it to happen even while he was in our hands[5]. It is strychnine or some such poison[6]. It has taken immediate effect.'

'But why?'

'To silence him[7].' Jones looked up at me with anguish[8] in his eyes. 'And yet it cannot be[9]. Once again, Chase, I tell you, nothing is as it seems. Who could have known we were coming tonight?'

'Nobody could have known. I swear[10] that I told no one!'

'Then this attack must have been planned whether we were here or not[11]. The blowpipe, the dart, they were already prepared. It had been decided that Leland Mortlake must die long before we arrived.'

'Who would want to kill him?' I stood there, all sorts of thoughts rushing through[12] my mind. 'It must have been Clarence Devereux! He is playing some devilish[13] game. He killed Lavelle. He tried to kill you … for who else could it have been in the brougham that was parked nearby[14]? Now he has killed Mortlake.'

1. s'agenouilla à côté du corps étendu
2. complètement livide
3. sarbacane
4. décoché une fléchette
5. bien qu'il soit entre nos mains
6. un poison de ce genre
7. le réduire au silence
8. de l'angoisse
9. pourtant c'est impossible
10. jure
11. indépendamment de notre venue
12. se bousculant dans
13. diabolique
14. stationné à proximité

'It could not have been Devereux at Scotland Yard.'

'Why not?'

'Because the driver dropped him[1] in the street – had it been Devereux, he would surely have been unable to step out into the open[2].'

'Then if it was not him, who was it?' I gazed helplessly. 'Was it Moriarty?'

'No! That cannot be possible.'

We were both of us attenuated[3], drenched through[4] by the drizzle, close to exhaustion[5]. It seemed that an eternity had passed since we had ridden out[6] together to the London docks and that expedition too had not worked out[7] as we had planned. We stood facing each other, helpless, while around us the police officers crept forward, staring at the corpse with dismay[8]. The door of the club suddenly slammed shut[9], cutting off the light. It was as if the people who worked there wanted nothing more to do with us.

'Deal with this[10], Sergeant!' Jones called to one of the policemen, although I could not tell which. All the life seemed to have gone out of him. His face was drawn[11] and there was nothing in his eyes. 'Have the body removed[12] and then take down the details of everyone in the club. I know we have done it once before but we must do it again! Allow no one to leave until you have their statements.[13]' He turned to me and spoke more quietly. 'They will find nothing. The killer will have already left. Come with me, Chase. Let us get out of this damned[14] place.'

We walked down the street and into Shepherd's Market[15]. There we found a public house[16] on a corner – the Grapes. We went inside, into the

1. l'avait déposé

2. s'aventurer à découvert

3. affaiblis

4. trempés jusqu'aux os

5. au bord de l'épuisement

6. pris un fiacre

7. ne s'était pas déroulée

8. s'avançaient sans bruit, observant le corps avec désarroi

9. se referma d'un grand coup

10. Occupez-vous de lui

11. Ses traits étaient tirés

12. Faites emmener le corps

13. Veillez à ce que personne ne parte sans avoir donné de déposition.

14. maudit

15. [quartier populaire du centre de Londres]

16. taverne

warmth, and Jones ordered half a pint of red wine which we shared between us. He had also produced[1] a cigarette, which he lit. It was only the second time I had seen him smoke. At length[2], he began to talk, choosing his words carefully[3].

'Moriarty cannot be alive. I will not believe it![4] You must remember the letter … the coded letter that began all this. It was addressed to Moriarty and it was found in the pocket of the dead man. It follows, therefore,[5] that the dead man must in all probability have been Moriarty. As always, the logic is inescapable[6]. It was only because he was killed that Devereux and his cohorts were able to take his place, fully establishing themselves[7] in London. And it is only because of the letter that we have been able to proceed thus far[8].'

'Then if it is not Moriarty taking revenge[9], it must be his former[10] associates. Even before he set out[11] for Meiringen, he could have left them instructions …'

'There you may be right. Inspector Patterson said that he had arrested them all but he may have been mistaken[12]. Certainly, we seem to have stumbled onto two opposing factions[13]. On the one side, Lavelle, the Mortlakes, Clarence Devereux. And on the other …'

'… the fair-haired boy[14] and the man in the brougham.'

'Perhaps.'

'I am wasting my time!' I said. I could feel my clothes, damp[15] against my skin. I drank the wine but it tasted of nothing and barely warmed me at all. 'I have come all the way from America in pursuit of Clarence Devereux and I have found him but you say I cannot touch him. I have Edgar

1. sorti de sa poche
2. Enfin
3. avec soin
4. Je refuse de le croire !
5. Il s'ensuit, par conséquent,
6. incontestable
7. et de s'installer
8. que nous avons pu parvenir jusqu'ici
9. une vengeance de Moriarty
10. anciens
11. de partir
12. il a pu se tromper
13. nous avons dû tomber sur deux factions rivales
14. blondinet
15. humides

Mortlake in front of me but he escapes. Scotchy Lavelle, John Clay, Leland Mortlake … all of them dead. And my young agent, Jonathan Pilgrim … I sent him here and that cost him his life. I feel the shadow of Moriarty hanging over us at every turn[1] and frankly, Jones, I have had enough[2]. Without you, I would have got nowhere[3] but even with your help I have failed. I should return home, hand in my notice[4] and find some other way to spend my days[5].'

'I will not hear of it[6],' Jones returned. 'You say we are making no progress but that is far from true. We have found Devereux and know his true identity. At the same time his own forces have been decimated, his latest scheme[7] – the robbery at Chancery Lane – undone[8]. He cannot escape. I will have men[9] at every port in the country …'

'Three days from now[10], you may no longer have the authority.[11]'

'And much can happen[12] in three days.' Jones laid a hand on my shoulder. 'Do not be dispirited[13]. The picture is a murky one, I grant you.[14] But still it begins to take shape[15]. Devereux is a rat in a hole but even now he must be fearful[16]. He will have to strike out.[17] It may be that he will finally make the mistake that allows us to capture him. But believe me, he will act soon.'

'You think so?'

'I am sure of it.'

Athelney Jones was right. Our enemy did indeed act[18] – but not in a way that either of us could have foreseen[19].

1. planer au-dessus de nous en permanence
2. j'en ai assez
3. mes efforts n'auraient abouti à rien
4. donner ma démission
5. d'occuper mes journées
6. Ne dites pas ça
7. intrigue
8. est tombée à l'eau
9. Je vais poster des hommes
10. D'ici trois jours
11. vous n'aurez peut-être plus le pouvoir de faire cela
12. il peut se passer beaucoup de choses
13. découragé
14. Le tableau est sombre, je vous l'accorde.
15. à prendre forme
16. en ce moment-même il doit être inquiet
17. Il va être obligé d'attaquer.
18. est effectivement passé à l'action
19. n'aurait pu l'anticiper

SEVENTEEN

Dead Man's Walk

1. d'inattendu
2. dès que j'ai vu
3. Ses traits
4. sur lesquels sa longue maladie avait laissé des traces,
5. le faire asseoir
6. sur le point de s'évanouir
7. perdu son emploi
8. comme désormais je le connaissais bien
9. me souvenant de
10. ne l'aurait pas affecté
11. me donnèrent raison
12. enlevé
13. la retiennent en otage
14. car il faudra plusieurs semaines pour que

I knew that something terrible and unexpected[1] had happened the moment I set eyes[2] on Athelney Jones at Hexam's Hotel the next day. His features[3], in which the long history of his illness was always written,[4] were more drawn and haggard than ever and he was so pale that I felt obliged to lead him to a chair[5], for I was certain he was about to faint[6]. I did not let him speak but ordered hot tea and lemon and sat with him until it arrived. My first thought was that his meeting with the Commissioner had already taken place and that he had lost his position[7] with the Metropolitan Police, but knowing him as I now did[8] and recalling[9] our conversation in the rooms in Chiltern Street, I knew that such an event would hardly matter to him[10] and that whatever had happened was much, much worse.

His first words proved me right[11]. 'They have taken[12] Beatrice.'

'What?'

'My daughter – they are holding her ransom[13].'

'How do you know? How can it be possible?'

'My wife sent me a telegram. It was brought by a messenger for it will be weeks before[14] our own telegraph room has been repaired. I received it in my office, this morning; an urgent summons[1] telling me to come home at once. Of course I did as I was instructed[2]. When I arrived, Elspeth was in such distress that she could barely make herself understood[3] and I was obliged to give her a few drops of sal volatile[4] to calm her down. Poor woman! What must have been going through her thoughts as she waited for me to return – alone and with no one to console her?

'Beatrice disappeared this morning. She had gone out with her nanny, Miss Jackson, a good reliable[5] woman who has been with us these past five years. It was their custom always to stroll[6] together on Myatt's Fields, quite close to the house. This morning, Miss Jackson's attention was briefly diverted by an elderly woman[7], asking her for directions[8]. I have interviewed her and I have no doubt that this old woman, whose face was hidden by a veil[9], was part of the conspiracy and served as a distraction. When Miss Jackson next turned round[10], Beatrice had gone[11].'

'Could she not have simply strayed[12]?'

'It would not have been in her character[13], but even so the nanny tried to persuade herself of exactly that. It is human nature to cling onto one's hopes, no matter how far-fetched they may be[14]. She made a thorough search of the park and the surrounding area[15] before she called for assistance. Nobody had seen our daughter. It was as if she had vanished from the face of the earth[16] and, not wishing to delay any further[17], Miss Jackson hurried home in considerable distress. Elspeth was waiting for her. She did not need to be told

1. message
2. je me suis exécuté
3. à peine à parler
4. des sels
5. de confiance
6. Elles avaient pour habitude de se promener
7. a été brièvement détournée par une vieille femme
8. qui lui a demandé son chemin
9. dissimulé par un voile
10. s'est retournée
11. avait disparu
12. s'égarer
13. dans sa nature
14. de s'accrocher à un espoir, si illusoire soit-il
15. a ratissé le parc et les alentours
16. disparu de la surface de la terre
17. afin de ne pas perdre plus de temps

what had happened for a note had already been slipped through the door[1]. I have it here.'

Jones unfolded[2] a sheet of paper and handed it to me[3]. There were but[4] a few words, written in block capitals[5], all the more menacing for their stark simplicity[6].

WE HAVE YOUR DAUHTER. REMAIN AT HOME. TELL NO ONE. WE WILL CONTACT YOU BEFORE DAY'S END.

'This tells us almost nothing,' I said.

'It tells us a great deal[7],' Jones replied, irritably. 'It is from an educated man pretending to be an uneducated one. He is left-handed[8]. He works in, or has access to, a library[9], though one that is seldom visited[10]. He is single-minded and ruthless[11] but at the same time he is acting under stress, which makes him impetuous. The letter was written in the heat of the moment[12]. Almost certainly, I am describing Clarence Devereux for I believe him to be the author of this letter.'

'How can you know so much?'

'Is it not obvious? He pretends to misspell[13] "daughter" but his spelling is correct in every other respect, even to the extent of including[14] the apostrophe in "day's". Searching for a piece of paper, he has reached for a book on a shelf and torn out[15] one of the flyleaves[16]. You can see that two sides of the page are machine-cut while the outer edge is deckled[17]. The book has not been read. Observe the dust and the discolouration – caused by sunlight – along the top. He used his left hand to tear it from the binding[18]. His thumb, slanting outwards, has left a clear impression[19]. It was an

1. glissée sous la porte
2. déplia
3. me la tendit
4. Elle ne contenait que
5. capitales d'imprimerie
6. et rendus d'autant plus menaçants par leur austère simplicité
7. beaucoup de choses
8. gaucher
9. bibliothèque
10. peu fréquentée
11. déterminé et sans pitié
12. dans le feu de l'action
13. mal orthographier
14. il met même
15. attrapé un livre sur une étagère et en a arraché
16. l'une des pages de garde
17. découpés à la machine alors que le bord extérieur est ébarbé
18. l'arracher de la reliure
19. pouce, en glissant vers l'extérieur, a laissé une marque nette

act of vandalism, the mark of a man in a hurry[1], and it would have been noticed[2] if the book had been frequently used.' Jones buried[3] his head in his hands. 'Why is it that my skills[4] can tell me all this but could not forewarn me[5] that my own child might be in danger?'

'Do not distress yourself[6],' I said. 'Nobody could have foreseen this. In all my years as an agent I never encountered anything like it[7]. For Devereux to have targeted[8] you in this way … it's an outrage! Have you informed your colleagues at Scotland Yard?'

'I dare not.[9]'

'I think you should.'

'No. I cannot put her at risk[10].'

I thought for a moment. 'You should not be here. The note commands you to remain[11] at home.'

'Elspeth is there now. But I had to come. If they have set upon me[12] in this manner, it is almost certain that they will try something similar with you. She agreed with me. We had to warn you[13].'

'I have seen nobody.'

'Have you been out of the hotel?'

'Not yet. No. I spent the morning in my room, writing my report for Robert Pinkerton.'

'Then I found you in time[14]. You must return with me to Camberwell. Is it too much to ask of you?[15] Whatever occurs[16], we must face it together.'

'All that matters[17] is the return of your daughter.'

'Thank you.'

I reached out and briefly laid[18] a hand on his arm. 'They will not harm her[19], Jones. It is you and me that they want.'

1. pressé
2. remarqué
3. enfouit
4. mon talent
5. m'avertir
6. Ne vous tourmentez pas ainsi
7. rien vu de tel
8. pris pour cible
9. Je n'ose pas
10. la mettre en danger
11. rester
12. s'en sont pris à moi
13. vous mettre sur vos gardes
14. à temps
15. Est-ce que je vous peux vous demander ça ?
16. Quoi qu'il arrive
17. compte
18. posai
19. ne lui feront aucun mal

'But why?'

'I cannot say, but we must prepare for the worst.' I stood up. 'I will return to my room and fetch[1] my coat. I wish I had brought my gun with me from New York. Finish the tea and rest a little[2]. You may have need of your strength.'

We travelled together on the train back to Camberwell, neither of us speaking as we made our way through the outer reaches[3] of London. Jones sat with his eyes half-closed, deep in thought[4]. For my part, I could not help but[5] reflect on the much larger journey that we had undertaken[6] together, the one that had started in Meiringen. Were we about to reach its end?[7] Right now it might seem that Clarence Devereux had the upper hand[8] but I consoled myself with the thought that he might finally have outreached himself[9] and that, by striking at[10] the detective's family, he had made his first false move[11]. It was the action of a desperate man and perhaps one that we might be able to turn against him[12].

The train seemed almost deliberately slow, but at last we reached our destination and hurried back to the house where I had been a guest, at dinner, only a week before. Elspeth Jones was waiting for us in the room where she and I had first met. She was standing with one hand resting[13] on a chair. It was the same chair where I had found her sitting, reading to her daughter. She saw me and made no effort to conceal the anger[14] in her eyes. Perhaps I deserved[15] it. She had asked me for my protection and I had promised her that all would be well[16]. How vain those words now seemed.[17]

'You have heard nothing?[18]'

1. aller chercher
2. reposez-vous un peu
3. confins
4. perdu dans ses pensées
5. je ne pouvais m'empêcher de
6. entrepris
7. Allait-il bientôt prendre fin ?
8. le dessus
9. être allé trop loin
10. attaquant
11. faux pas
12. pourrait se retourner contre lui
13. posée
14. ne tenta même pas de dissimuler la colère
15. méritais
16. tout irait bien
17. Comme ces mots semblaient vains à présent.
18. Vous n'avez pas eu de nouvelles ?

'No. And there is nothing here?'

'Not a word. Maria is upstairs. She is inconsolable although I have told her she cannot be blamed[1].' Maria, I assumed, was Miss Jackson, the nanny. 'Did you see Lestrade?'

'No.' Jones lowered[2] his head. 'God forgive me[3] if I am making the wrong decision, but I cannot disobey their instructions.'

'I will not allow you to face them alone.'

'I am not alone. Mr Chase is with me.'

'I do not trust[4] Mr Chase.'

'Elspeth!' Jones was offended[5].

'You are unkind[6], Mrs Jones,' I began. 'Throughout this business[7], I have done everything I can—'

'You will forgive me if I speak openly[8].' The woman turned to her husband. 'In the circumstances, I cannot be expected to do otherwise.[9] From the very start, when you left for Switzerland, I was afraid of something like this. I have had a sense of approaching evil[10], Athelney. No – do not shake your head at me like that. Do we not learn in the church that evil has a physical presence, that we may feel it like a cold winter or a coming storm[11]? "Deliver us from evil!" We say it every night. And now it is here. Maybe you invited it. Maybe it was coming anyway[12]. I do not care who I offend. I will not lose you to it.[13]'

'I have no choice but to do as they ask.'

'And if they kill you?'

'I don't believe they want to kill us,' I said. 'It would do them no good[14]. To begin with[15], other officers would take our place soon enough. And although the murder of a Pinkerton's man might be received[16] with a certain indifference, the death of a Scotland Yard inspector would be

1. être tenue pour responsable
2. baissa
3. Que Dieu me pardonne
4. n'ai pas confiance en
5. outré
6. cruelle
7. Depuis le début de cette affaire
8. franchement
9. vous ne pouvez attendre de moi que j'agisse autrement
10. le sentiment que le mal s'approchait de nous
11. orage qui menace
12. il nous aurait frappé de toute façon
13. Je refuse de te perdre à cause de lui.
14. ne les avancerait à rien
15. Pour commencer
16. perçu

quite another matter[1]. There is no way our enemy would wish to bring such trouble upon himself[2].'

'Then what is his intention?'

'I have no idea. To warn us, to frighten us – perhaps to show us the extent of his power.'

'He will kill Beatrice.'

'Again, I don't think so. He is using her to reach[3] us. You have the letter as proof of that. I know these people. I know the way they work. These are New York methods. Extortion. Intimidation. But I swear to God[4], they will not harm[5] your child – simply because they have nothing to gain.'

Elspeth nodded very slightly[6] but did not look at me again. The three of us sat at the table and so began what I can honestly describe as the longest afternoon of my life with the clock on the mantelpiece[7] sonorously marking[8] every second that passed. We could do nothing but wait. Conversation between us was impossible and although the little maid[9] came up with tea and sandwiches, none of us ate. I was aware of the traffic moving outside and the sky already darkening[10] but I must have slipped[11] into a reverie because I was suddenly aware of a loud knock on the door, jerking me awake[12].

'It is she!' Elspeth exclaimed.

'Let us pray[13] ...'Jones was already on his feet although the long time spent sitting had locked[14] his muscles together and he moved awkwardly[15].

We all followed him to the front door but when he threw it open[16] there was no sign of his daughter. A man in a cap[17] stood there, holding out[18] a second message. Jones snatched it from him[19]. 'Where did you receive this?' he demanded.

1. une toute autre affaire
2. ne veuille s'attirer de tels ennuis
3. atteindre
4. je jure devant Dieu
5. ne feront aucun mal à
6. hocha très légèrement la tête
7. au-dessus de la cheminée
8. égrenant bruyamment
9. bonne
10. qui s'assombrissait déjà
11. dû sombrer
12. me tirant brutalement de ma stupeur
13. Espérons-le
14. engourdi
15. avec maladresse
16. l'ouvrit précipitamment
17. coiffé d'une casquette
18. et lui tendait
19. le lui arracha des mains

The messenger looked indignant. 'I was in the pub. The Camberwell Arms. A man gave me a bob[1] to deliver this.'

'Describe him to me! I am a police officer and if you hold anything back it will go the worse[2] for you.'

'I've done nothing wrong. I'm a carpenter by trade[3] and I hardly[4] saw him. He was a dark fellow[5] with a hat and a scarf drawn over his chin[6]. He asked me if I wanted to earn a shilling and he gave me this. He said there was two men in the house and I was to give it to either of them. That's all I know.'

Jones took the letter and we returned to the sitting room where he opened it. It was written in the same hand[7] as the first but this time the language was even terser[8].

DEAD MAN'S WALK. BOTH OF YOU. NO POLICE.

'Dead Man's Walk!' Elspeth said, with a shudder[9]. 'What a horrible name. What is it?' Jones did not answer her question. 'Tell me!'

'I do not know. But I can look it up in my index. Give me but a minute …'

Elspeth Jones and I stood there together as Jones clumped upstairs[10] to his study. We waited while he searched through the various paragraphs he had brought together over the years[11] – Holmes, of course, had done the same. And I am sure we both counted every one of his steps as he made his way back down.

'It is in Southwark[12],' he explained, as he entered the room.

'Do you know what it is?'

1. [shilling, en argot]
2. me cachez des choses, cela ira d'autant plus mal
3. menuisier de profession
4. à peine
5. un type à la peau mate
6. foulard devant le menton
7. de la même écriture
8. succinct
9. frisson
10. monta péniblement l'escalier
11. rassemblé au fil des ans
12. [quartier situé au Sud du London Bridge]

1. vous inquiétez
2. est laissé à l'abandon
3. reculé
4. C'est un endroit comme un autre.
5. d'autres indices
6. il me paraît très improbable
7. rusés
8. tout indique
9. en ce moment même
10. est adressée à nous deux
11. mon chéri
12. à votre place
13. vils
14. complainte

'I do, my dear, and you must not concern yourself[1]. It is a cemetery – one that has fallen into disuse[2]. It was closed down years ago.'

'Why a cemetery? Are they telling you that our daughter …'

'No. They have chosen somewhere quiet and out of the way[3] for whatever business it is that they wish to conduct. This is as good a place as any.[4]'

'You must not leave!' Elspeth seized the note as if she could find further clues[5] in its brief message. 'If they have Beatrice there, you can now go to the police. You *must* go to the police. I will not allow you to put yourself in danger.'

'If we do not obey their instructions, I think it very unlikely[6] that we will find our girl there, my love. These people are cunning[7] and give every indication[8] that they know what they are doing. It may be that they are watching us even as we speak[9].'

'How is that possible? Why do you think that?'

'The first note was addressed to me alone. This one refers to both of us[10]. The messenger was told there are two men in this house. They know that Chase is here.'

'I will not let you do this!' Elspeth Jones spoke quietly but her voice was filled with passion. 'Please listen to me, my dearest one[11]. Let me go instead of you[12]. Surely these people cannot be so wicked[13] that they will ignore a mother's pleas[14]. I will exchange myself for her—'

'That is not their desire. It is Chase and I who have to go. We are the ones they wish to speak with. But you do not have to be afraid. What Chase said was right. They have nothing to gain from harming us. It is my belief that Clarence Devereux wishes to strike some sort of deal[1] with us. That is all. At any event[2], there is no point in this speculation[3] when Beatrice's life is at stake[4]. If we refuse to obey their instructions, they will do their worst[5]. Of that[6] there can be no doubt.'

'They do not say what time they want you.'

'Then we must leave immediately.'

Elspeth did not argue[7]. Instead[8], she took her husband in her arms, embracing him[9] as if for the last time. I will confess that I had my doubts about what Jones had just said. If Clarence Devereux had merely[10] wished to speak to us, he would not have kidnapped a six-year-old girl and used her to drag us to a disused cemetery[11]. He might have nothing to gain by harming us but that wouldn't stop him doing so[12]. I knew him. I knew how he operated. We might as well have argued with the scarlet fever as with him[13] and once we were in his hands he would destroy us simply because it was in his nature.

We left the house. It seemed to me that the night was unseasonably cold[14] although there was not the slightest breeze[15]. Jones held his wife at the door, the two of them gazing into each other's eyes, and then, suddenly, we were alone in the seemingly empty[16] street. And yet I knew that we were being watched.

'We are leaving, damn you!' I cried. We are alone. We will come to Dead Man's Walk and you can do with us as you please[17]!'

'They cannot hear us,' Jones said.

'They are nearby,' I replied. 'You said as much yourself.[18] They know we are on our way[19].'

1. conclure un marché

2. De toute façon

3. il est inutile de faire des suppositions

4. en jeu

5. opteront pour le pire

6. Sur ce point

7. ne discuta pas

8. À la place

9. le serrant

10. simplement

11. nous attirer dans un cimetière abandonné

12. de le faire

13. C'était comme tenter d'amadouer la scarlatine

14. anormalement froide pour la saison

15. le moindre souffle de vent

16. qui semblait déserte

17. faire de nous ce que vous voulez

18. Vous l'avez dit vous-même.

19. en route

1. pardessus
2. poignée sculptée en forme de tête de corbeau
3. approprié
4. à venir
5. Très vite, il avait atteint sa capacité maximale
6. enterrés les uns tout près des autres
7. pierres tombales et les stèles
8. réconfort
9. inclinés de manière étrange, penchés
10. pris dans une éternelle lutte de territoire
11. infâme odeur de décomposition
12. les plus récentes
13. peu profondes, échouant à remplir leur mission
14. rare
15. des morceaux de cercueils putréfiés
16. fragments d'ossements humains sortant
17. oublié
18. ligne de chemin de fer
19. [hospice où les pauvres étaient contraints au travail]
20. un portail rouillé
21. pourris

We were not a great distance from Southwark and made our way there by cab. Jones wore a greatcoat[1] and I noticed that he had brought with him a new walking stick, this one with a handle carved in the shape of a raven's head[2]. It was a suitable[3] accessory for a cemetery. He was unusually tense and silent and it struck me that he hadn't believed a word of what he had said to his wife either. We were heading into mortal peril and he knew it. He had known it when he invited me along[4].

Dead Man's Walk has long since disappeared. It was one of those cemeteries built in the first part of the century when nobody understood how many people would live in London and therefore, inevitably, die there. All too quickly it had become oversubscribed[5] with so many bodies crammed in next to one another[6] that the tombstones and memorials[7], rather than providing the solace[8] and remembrance that had been intended, had become a hideous spectacle, slanting at strange angles, leaning[9] on each other, locked in an eternal struggle for space[10]. For many years, a foul and putrid smell[11] had hung over the place. The later[12] graves were desperately shallow, unequal to the task[13], and it would not be uncommon[14] to find rotting pieces of coffin wood[15] or even shards of human bone poking through[16] the soil. Inevitably, the cemetery had been abandoned. Other cemeteries had been sold off and some had become parks. But Dead Man's Walk had been left behind[17], a long irregular space between a railway line[18] and an old workhouse[19], with rusting gates[20] at each end, a few mouldy[21] trees and a sense that it belonged neither to this world nor to the next but existed in a dark, dismal province of its own[1].

The cab dropped us as the church bells were striking eight o'clock, the hollow chimes[2] echoing in the dark. I saw at once that we were expected and my spirits sank[3]. There were a dozen roughs[4] waiting for us, so dirty and ragged[5] that they could themselves have been summoned[6] from the graves that surrounded them. They were dressed, for the most part, in close-fitting coatees[7], greasy corduroys[8] and boots. Some of them were bareheaded[9], others wore billycocks and carried cudgels[10] which they balanced[11] on their shoulders or on the crooks[12] of their arms. Torches had been lit, throwing red light across the gravestones[13] as if they were determined to make the scene even more hellish[14]. How long they had been there, I could not say, but it seemed incredible to me that we were simply going to deliver ourselves to them[15]. I had to remind myself that there was no alternative, that we had made our choice.

Still, we lingered[16] at the gate.

'Where is my daughter?' Jones called out.

'You came alone?' The speaker was a bearded man with long, tangled hair[17] and a broken nose that threw uneven shadows[18] across his face.

'Yes. Where is she?'

There was a pause. A sudden breeze whispered through[19] the cemetery and the flames bowed in recognition[20]. Then a figure appeared, stepping out[21] from behind a monument with a stone angel perched above. For a moment, I thought it might be Clarence Devereux but then I remembered that his condition[22] would not allow him to show himself in this open space. It was Edgar

1. dans sa propre contrée sombre et lugubre
2. carillon grave
3. étions attendus et mon moral sombra
4. voyous
5. dépenaillés
6. être sortis
7. vestes d'uniforme ajustées
8. de pantalons en velours côtelé pleins de taches de graisse
9. tête nue
10. des chapeaux melons et tenaient des gourdins
11. posés en équilibre
12. dans le creux
13. pierres tombales
14. infernale
15. nous livrer à eux
16. nous attardâmes
17. un barbu avec de longs cheveux emmêlés
18. projetait une ombre irrégulière
19. traversa
20. s'inclinèrent en conséquence
21. sortant
22. mal dont il souffrait

1. en larmes
2. en bataille
3. des traces de suie
4. déchirée et tachée
5. indemne
6. On s'en contrefiche
7. préféreriez éviter de voir
8. couteau à longue lame
9. étincelait
10. , suspendu au-dessus de
11. Par bonheur
12. lui trancherait la gorge sans hésiter
13. regard
14. rendant toute fuite impossible
15. sans relâcher
16. fripouille aux cheveux frisés
17. orgelet
18. s'éloignèrent
19. un homme de parole

Mortlake. I had last seen him plunging into the river and to my eyes he now seemed more dead than alive, moving slowly, as if the impact of the water had broken several of his bones. He was not alone. Beatrice Jones, pale and tearful[1], was holding his hand. Her hair was unbrushed[2] and there were smuts[3] on her face. Her dress was torn and soiled[4]. But she looked unharmed[5].

'We don't give a damn[6] about your dear little daughter!' Mortlake shouted. 'It's you we want. You and your infernal friend.'

'We're here.'

'Come closer. Come and join us! We have nothing to gain by keeping her. We have a carriage waiting to send her home. But if you do not do as I say, you will see something you might rather not[7].' He had lifted his other hand, revealing a long-bladed knife[8], which glinted[9] in the flames as it hung over[10] the little girl. Mercifully[11], she could not see it. I had no doubt at all that he would use it if we did not obey his instructions. He would cut the girl's throat where she stood[12]. Jones and I exchanged a glance[13]. Together, we moved forward.

At once we were surrounded, the hooligan boys moving behind us, cutting off any means of escape[14]. Mortlake stepped towards us, still holding onto[15] Beatrice. She had recognised her father but was too terrified to speak. 'Take the girl back home.' He handed her to one of the younger men, a curly-haired rogue[16] with a smile and a stye[17] in one eye. The two of them walked off[18] together. 'You see, Inspector Jones? I am true to my word[19].'

Jones waited until his daughter had left the cemetery. 'You are a coward[1] – a man who steals a child and uses her for his own evil ends[2]. You are beneath contempt[3].'

'And you are the cripple[4] who killed my brother.' Mortlake was very close to Jones now, his face inches away[5], staring at him with eyes on the edge of madness[6]. 'You will suffer for that, I assure you. But first there are some questions you must answer. And answer them you will![7]'

Mortlake nodded[8] and I saw one of the roughs step forward with a shillelagh[9], which he swung viciously through the air, hammering it into the back of Jones's head[10]. Jones fell without another word and I realised that I was now alone with the enemy, that they were all around me, and that Mortlake had already turned to me. I knew what was coming. I expected it. But I was still unprepared for the explosion of pain that sent me hurtling forward[11] into a tunnel of darkness and certain death.

1. lâche
2. pour parvenir à ses fins
3. absolument méprisable
4. éclopé
5. à quelques centimètres de lui
6. avec un regard presque dément
7. Et je vous garantis que vous allez me répondre !
8. hocha la tête
9. [gourdin d'origine irlandaise]
10. leva sauvagement avant de frapper Jones sur la tête
11. me précipita

1. Le frigo à viande

2. Sinon comment aurais-je pu avoir si froid ?

3. En reprenant conscience

4. à proximité d'une lumière vacillante

5. ou la gravité de mes blessures

6. le coup que j'avais reçu résonnait encore dans ma tête

7. froid glacial

8. frissonnait

9. J'avais perdu toute sensation

10. même mes dents me faisaient mal

11. laissé pour mort sur la banquise

12. à l'intérieur

13. du béton

14. sous

15. serrai mes bras

16. un semblant de chaleur corporelle

17. m'efforcer de garder mon calme

18. affalé

EIGHTEEN

The Meat Rack[1]

I was almost afraid to open my eyes for I was quite convinced that I must be dying. How else could I be so cold?[2]

As consciousness returned[3], I found myself lying on a stone floor with a light flickering somewhere close by[4]. I had no idea how long I had been here nor how badly I had been hurt[5], although my head was still pounding from the blow I had received[6]. I wondered if I had been removed from London. The chill[7] had penetrated right through to my bones and my body was shuddering[8] involuntarily. There was no feeling whatsoever[9] in my hands and my very teeth were aching[10]. It was as if I had been transported to the frozen north and left to perish on an ice floe[11]. But no. I was indoors[12]. It was concrete[13], not ice, beneath[14] me. I pulled myself into a sitting position and wrapped my hands[15] around me, partly to conserve what little bodily warmth remained[16], partly to hold myself together[17]. I saw Athelney Jones. He had already regained consciousness but he looked quite close to death. He was sitting slumped[18] against a brick wall with his walking stick next to him. There were sparkles[1] of ice on his shoulders, his collar and his lips.

'Jones ...?'

'Chase! Thank God you are awake.'

'Where are we?' A cloud of white vapour emerged from my mouth as I spoke.

'Smithfield, I think. Or somewhere similar.'

'Smithfield? What is that?'

My question answered itself. We were in a meat market[2]. There were a hundred carcasses in the room. I had seen them but, with my senses returning to me only slowly, I had been unable to grasp[3] what they were. Now I examined them; whole[4] sheep, stripped bare[5], missing their heads, their fleeces[6] or anything that would have identified them as God's creatures, lying with their limbs stretched out[7], stacked up[8] in piles that reached almost to the ceiling. Small pools of blood had trickled out[9] and then frozen solid, the colour more mauve than red. I looked around me. The chamber was square with two ladders[10] attached to rails so that they could slide from one end to the other[11]. It reminded me of the cargo hold[12] of a ship. A steel[13] door provided the only possible way out, but I was certain it was locked and to touch it would have torn the skin from my fingertips[14]. Two tallow candles[15] had been placed on the floor. Otherwise, we would have been left in the pitch dark[16].

'How long have we been here?' I asked. It was as much as I could do to enunciate the words.[17] My teeth were locked together.[18]

'Not long. It cannot be long.'

'Are you hurt?'

'No. No more than you.'

1. paillettes
2. marché à viande
3. comprendre
4. entiers
5. complètement dépouillés
6. toisons
7. les pattes tendues
8. entassés
9. avaient dégouliné
10. échelles
11. glisser d'un bout à l'autre de la pièce
12. cale à marchandises
13. en acier
14. arraché la peau de mes doigts
15. bougies de suif
16. l'obscurité totale
17. J'arrivai à peine à articuler
18. Ma mâchoire était engourdie par le froid.

1. nous en réjouir
2. la tirant vers lui
3. Tout ça est de ma faute.
4. injuste
5. haletants, saccadés, aussi dénués de chaleur
6. que les carcasses de moutons
7. en être autrement
8. pour être énoncé
9. mordant
10. C'est dans l'ordre des choses.
11. nous retranchâmes
12. nous échappaient peu à peu
13. sort
14. grand
15. chambres froides
16. devaient être remplis de charbon
17. devait œuvrer sans relâche
18. un air glacé, et mortel
19. une invention récente
20. mais cette idée n'était pas d'une grande consolation
21. en tout cas
22. ne pas perdre à nouveau connaissance

'Your daughter …?'

'Safe … or so I believe. We can at least give thanks for that[1].' Jones reached out and took hold of his stick, dragging it towards him[2]. 'Chase, I am sorry.'

'Why?'

'It was I who brought you here. This is my doing.[3] I would have done anything – anything – to get Beatrice back. But it was not fair[4] to bring you into this.' His words were breathless, staccato, as stripped of warmth[5] as the butchered sheep[6] that surrounded us. It could not be otherwise[7]. Every word, even as it was uttered[8], had to fight against the biting[9] cold.

And yet I replied: 'Do not blame yourself. We began together and together we will end. It is as it should be.[10]'

We retreated[11] into silence, conserving our strength, both of us aware that our lives were slipping away from us[12]. Was this to be our fate[13], to be left here until the blood had frozen in our veins? Jones was almost certainly correct. This had to be a major[14] meat market – and one that was surrounded by cold rooms[15]. The walls that contained us would be packed with charcoal[16] and somewhere nearby a compression refrigerating machine would be grinding away[17], pumping glaciated – and lethal – air[18] into the chamber. The mechanism was fairly new[19] and we might be the first to be killed by it – not that I could find a great deal of consolation in the thought[20].

I still refused to believe that they intended to kill us – not immediately, at any rate[21] – and it was this thought that made me determined not to slip back into unconsciousness[22]. Edgar Mortlake had said that there were questions for us to answer. Our suffering[1] now must surely be no more than a prelude to that interrogation. It would end soon enough.[2] With fingers that could barely move, I fumbled[3] in my pockets only to discover that my trusty jackknife[4], the one weapon that I always carried with me, had gone. It barely mattered.[5] I would have been in no state[6] to use it.

I cannot say how many minutes passed. I was aware that I was falling into a deep sleep, which had stretched out like a chasm beneath me[7]. I knew that if I closed my eyes I would never open them again but still I could not stop myself. I had stopped shivering[8]. I had reached some strange condition beyond[9] cold and hypothermia. But even as I felt myself drifting away[10], the door opened and a man appeared, barely more than a silhouette in the flickering light. It was Mortlake. He looked down at us with contempt[11].

'Still with us?[12]' he asked. 'You'll have cooled down a little[13], I suppose. Well, come this way, gentlemen. Everything has been made ready[14] for you. On your feet, I say![15] There is someone I believe you wish to see.'

We could not stand.[16] Three men came into the room and pulled us to our feet, handling us[17] with as much care as if we had become carcasses ourselves. It was strange to have their hands on me but to feel nothing. However, even opening the door had raised the temperature a little and the movement seemed to restore[18] my almost frozen blood. I found that I could walk. I watched Jones stand with all his weight resting on his walking stick, attempting to regain at least something of his[19] dignity before he was propelled[20] towards

1. supplice
2. Il prendrait bientôt fin.
3. fouillai
4. fidèle canif
5. Cela n'avait que peu d'importance.
6. Je n'aurais pas été en état
7. s'était ouvert comme un gouffre sous mes pieds
8. de frissonner
9. un état étrange, au-delà du
10. alors que je me sentais partir
11. mépris
12. Vous êtes encore vivants ?
13. Ça vous aura rafraîchi un petit peu les idées
14. préparé
15. Levez-vous, je vous dis !
16. Nous ne tenions pas debout.
17. nous remirent sur pieds, nous traitant
18. rétablir la circulation de
19. un semblant de
20. poussé violemment

the door. Neither of us spoke to Edgar Mortlake. Why waste our words? He had already made it clear that he intended to enjoy[1] our pain and humiliation. He had us completely in his power[2] and anything we said would only give him the excuse to torment us more. Helped by the ruffians[3] who had surely accompanied us from the cemetery, we made our way out of the storage room[4] and into a vaulted[5] corridor, the rough stonework like that of a tomb. Walking was difficult on feet that had no sensation and we stumbled forward[6] until we came to a flight of stairs, leading down, the way now lit by gas lamps. We had to be half-carried or otherwise[7] we would have fallen. But the air was warmer. My breath no longer frosted.[8] I could feel the movement returning to my limbs[9].

A second corridor stretched out at the bottom[10] of the stairs. I had the impression we were some distance underground. I could feel it in the heaviness of the air and the strange silence that pressed upon my ears[11]. I was already walking unaided but Jones made tortuous progress, relying[12] on his stick. Mortlake was somewhere behind us, doubtless relishing what was to come[13]. We turned a corner and stumbled to a halt[14] in a remarkable place, a long subterranean chamber whose existence might never be suspected by those who walked above.

It was formed of brick walls and vaulted ceilings with arches, dozens of them, arranged opposite each other in two lines. Steel girders[15] had been fixed in place above our heads with hooks[16] suspended on the ends of rustingchains. The floor consisted of cobblestones[17], centuries old and heavily worn[18], with tramlines swerving

1. comptait bien savourer
2. à sa merci
3. crapules
4. chambre froide
5. voûté
6. avançâmes en trébuchant
7. Il leur fallait nous porter quasiment, sans quoi
8. Mon souffle ne se condensait plus.
9. mes membres
10. s'étirait en bas
11. pesait sur mes tympans
12. s'appuyant
13. salivant d'avance à l'idée de ce qui nous attendait
14. nous nous arrêtâmes d'un seul coup
15. poutres
16. crochets
17. pavés
18. usés

and criss-crossing each other[1] on their way into the bowels[2] of the earth. Everything was gaslit, the lamps throwing a luminescent haze that hung suspended in mid-air, like a winter's fog. The air was damp and putrid. A pair of trestle[3] tables had been set up in front of us with a number of implements[4] which I could not bring myself[5] to examine and there were two rickety[6] wooden chairs; one for Jones, one for myself. Another three men, making six in total, awaited us. They presented an even grimmer spectacle than they had at Dead Man's Walk for we were their prisoners, entirely in their hands[7]. It was we who were the dead men now.

None of them was speaking and yet I heard echoes … voices, far away and out of sight. There was the clang of steel striking steel[8]. The complex must be vast and we were in but one secluded corner of it[9]. I thought of shouting out[10], calling for help but knew it would be pointless[11]. It would be impossible for any rescuer to tell where the sound had come from and I would surely be struck down before I could utter[12] two words.

'Sit down!' Mortlake had given the order and we had no choice. We sat on the chairs and, even as we did so, I heard an extraordinary sound: the crack of a whip[13], the rattle of wheels turning on the cobbles[14], the clatter of horses' hooves[15]. I turned my head and saw a sight I will never forget: a glistening black carriage, pulled by two black horses, hurtling towards us with a black-clad coachman[16] at the reins. It seemed to form itself out of the darkness[17], like something from a tale by the[18] Brothers Grimm. Finally, it drew to

1. rails qui s'incurvaient et s'entrecroisaient
2. entrailles
3. à tréteaux
4. d'instruments
5. que je ne pouvais pas me résoudre
6. branlantes
7. à leur merci
8. claquement de l'acier frappant contre l'acier
9. n'en occupions qu'un recoin isolé
10. me mettre à crier
11. inutile
12. assommé avant d'avoir pu prononcer
13. claquement d'un fouet
14. grincement des roues sur des pavés
15. fracas des sabots de chevaux
16. et déboulant vers nous avec un cocher vêtu de noir
17. se matérialiser à partir des ténèbres elles-mêmes
18. conte des

a halt[1]. The door opened and Clarence Devereux stepped out.

Such an elaborate entrance for so small a man[2]! And all for an audience of just two[3]! Slowly, deliberately he walked towards us, dressed in a top hat and cape with a brightly coloured silk waistcoat[4] visible beneath and what could have been a child's gloves on his tiny hands. He stopped a few feet away, his face pale, examining us through heavy-lidded[5] eyes. It was only here, of course, that he could feel at ease. For a man with his strange condition, to be buried underground might come as a relief[6].

'Are you cold?' he asked, his thin voice filled with mock concern[7]. He blinked[8] twice. 'Warm them up![9]'

I felt my arms and shoulders seized[10] and saw the same thing happening to Jones. All six men closed in on us[11] and while Devereux and Mortlake watched, they began to beat us, taking it in turns to pound us with their fists[12]. There was nothing I could do but sit there and take it[13], brilliant lights exploding in my eyes each time my face was struck[14]. When they had finished I could feel blood streaming from my nose. I tasted it in my mouth. Jones was bowed over[15], one eye closed, his cheek swollen[16]. He had not uttered a sound while the punishment was administered but then nor, for that matter, had I[17].

'That's better,' Devereux muttered once the men had finished and stepped back[18] and we were sitting panting[19] in our chairs. 'I want to make it quite clear to you that I dislike this. I will add that I abhor the methods that brought you here. The kidnap of a little girl is not something

1. s'arrêta
2. pour un si petit homme
3. deux malheureuses personnes
4. gilet en soie de couleur vive
5. aux paupières tombantes
6. être enfermé sous terre est sans doute un soulagement
7. sa voix grêle feignant l'inquiétude
8. cligna des yeux
9. Réchauffez-les !
10. sentis qu'on m'attrapait les bras et les épaules
11. se refermaient sur nous
12. nous martelant de leurs poings à tour de rôle
13. encaisser les coups
14. qu'on me frappait au visage
15. courbé
16. enflée
17. moi non plus, au demeurant
18. se reculèrent
19. haletants

I would normally have suggested and if it is any consolation to you, Inspector Jones, I can assure you that she is now back with her mother. I could have used her more. I could have tortured her in front of you. But whatever you may think of me, I am not that sort of man. I am sorry that she will never set eyes on her father again[1] and that her last memories of you will not have been pleasant ones. But I dare say she will forget you in time[2]. Children are very resilient[3]. We can, I think, dismiss her from our thoughts[4].

'Nor do I usually make it my business[5] to kill police officers and lawmen. It creates too many aggravations[6]. Pinkerton's is one thing but Scotland Yard quite another and it may well be that one day I will regret this. But for too long now the two of you have been causing me difficulties. What really bothers me[7] is that I do not quite understand how you have managed to achieve so much[8]. That is why you are here and the pain you have just suffered is only a foretaste[9] of what is to come. I see that you are both shivering, by the way. I will do you the favour of supposing that it is through exhaustion and cold rather than fear. Give them a little wine!'

He gave the order with exactly the same tone that he had used to initiate the beating[10]. At once a cup of red wine was pressed into my hand. Jones was given the same. He did not drink but I did, the dark red liquid wiping away[11] the taste of my own blood.

'In just a few weeks you have reached the very heart[12] of my organisation and you have left a trail of destruction in your wake[13]. My friend Scotchy Lavelle was tortured and killed and, quite

1. reverra jamais son père

2. elle finira probablement par vous oublier

3. se remettent facilement

4. la chasser de notre esprit

5. Je n'ai pas non plus pour habitude

6. complications

7. me chiffonne

8. en arriver là

9. avant-goût

10. ordonner notre passage à tabac

11. éclipsant

12. atteint le cœur

13. en détruisant tout sur votre passage

inexplicably, his entire household was murdered with him. Now, Scotchy was a very careful man. He had plenty of enemies in New York and he knew how to keep his head down[1]. He had rented a quiet house in a quiet neighbourhood[2] and it makes me wonder[3]: how did you ever find him? Who told you where he lived? He was, I admit, known to Pinkerton's and I have no doubt that you, Mr Chase, would have recognised him. But you had been in England less than forty-eight hours and yet[4] you went directly to Highgate, and for the life of me[5], I cannot work out[6] how you did it.'

I thought that Jones would explain that we had followed the messenger boy Perry from the Café Royal but he remained silent. Devereux, however, wanted a reply and it struck me that our situation, already bad, might become considerably worse if he didn't get one.

'It was Pilgrim,' I said.

'Pilgrim?'

'He was an agent. He worked for me.'

'Jonathan Pilgrim,' Mortlake growled. 'My brother's secretary.'

Devereux looked puzzled[7]. 'He was a Pinkerton? We knew that he was an informer – we discovered he was telling tales[8] and we made him pay for it. But I was of the understanding[9] that he worked for Professor Moriarty.'

'Then you were mistaken[10],' I said. 'He was working for me.'

'He was English.'

'He was American.'

'And he gave you Scotchy's address? It is possible he was working for you, I suppose, although

1. rester discret
2. dans un quartier sans histoire
3. je m'interroge
4. pourtant
5. en toute bonne foi
6. je ne parviens pas à comprendre
7. étonné
8. mouchardait
9. j'avais cru comprendre
10. faisiez erreur

it's a shame we never thought to ask him ourselves. I did tell Leland that he had been in too much haste to be rid of him[1]. Still, I wonder if you are trying to deceive me[2], Mr Chase, and would warn you most sincerely not to do so[3]. It may be that you have underestimated[4] me for you have seen me at my weakest[5]. But if you lie to me, I will know and you will pay. You have nothing to add[6]? Well, let us move on[7]. Pilgrim told you the address. You came to Bladeston House. And that very same night[8] Scotchy and his entire household were killed in their sleep. How did that happen? *Why* did it happen?'

'That is not for us to answer.[9]'

'We shall see. Scotchy said nothing to you. Of that I am sure. He would have said nothing to the police and I am equally certain that he would have left no incriminating[10] papers, no letters, no clues. He was, as I say, a careful man. And yet, the very next day you turned up[11] at my club.'

'Jonathan Pilgrim had written to me from that address. And the police knew that he had a room there.'

'How could they have known? How did they even discover Pilgrim's identity? Do you take us for amateurs, Mr Chase? Do you really think we would have abandoned the body without emptying its pockets first? There was no way the police could have connected Pilgrim with us but they did – and that in itself tells me[12] that something is wrong.'

'Perhaps you should invite Inspector Lestrade to this little gathering of yours[13]. I'm sure he'll be glad to give his side of the tale[14].'

1. s'était débarrassé de lui avec bien trop d'empressement
2. me duper
3. vous mets sincèrement en garde de ne pas le faire
4. sous-estimé
5. en position de faiblesse
6. ajouter
7. continuons
8. le soir même
9. Ce n'est pas à nous de le dire.
10. compromettant
11. avez débarqué
12. ce simple fait me laisse à penser
13. votre petite réunion
14. ravi de vous donner sa version des événements

'We do not need Lestrade. We have you.' Devereux thought for a moment, then continued. 'And then, just twenty-four hours later, we find you in Chancery Lane at the scene of a robbery that has been weeks in preparation and which I expect[1] to return many thousands of pounds in profit[2] – not just the property of London's wealthier classes, but their secrets too. Once again, I am trying to place myself in your shoes[3]. How did you know? Who told you? Was it John Clay? I do not think so. He wouldn't have had the nerve[4]. Was it Scotchy? Unthinkable![5] How did you find your way there?'

'Your friend Lavelle had left a note in his diary.' This time it was Jones who had replied, speaking through broken teeth and lips that were stained with blood. He still had not touched his wine.

'No! I will not accept that, Inspector Jones. Scotchy would never have been so stupid.'

'And yet I assure you it is the case.'

'Will you still assure me in half an hour's time? We shall see.[6] You were responsible for the failure of that particular enterprise[7] and at the time I was prepared to accept it. It was, after all, just one of many[8]. But what I cannot accept, what must be answered tonight[9], is your intrusion into the legation. How did you come to be there? What led you to me[10]? For the sake of my future safety[11] in this country, I must know. Do you hear what I am telling you, Inspector Jones? This is why I have taken such pains[12] to bring you here. You came face to face with me in my own home. Taking advantage[13] of my affliction, you humiliated me. I am not saying that I intend to punish

1. dont j'attends
2. un retour sur investissement de plusieurs milliers de livres
3. me mettre à votre place
4. cran
5. Ce serait inconcevable !
6. C'est ce que nous verrons.
7. l'échec de ce projet
8. qu'un projet parmi tant d'autres
9. ce dont vous devez répondre ce soir
10. vous a conduit jusqu'à moi
11. Dans l'intérêt de ma sécurité future
12. me suis donné tant de mal
13. Tirant parti

you for this, but I must take steps to ensure[1] that it never happens again.'

'You have too great a belief in your own abilities[2],' Jones said. 'Finding you was simple. The trail[3] from Meiringen to Highgate to Mayfair and to the legation was obvious. Anyone could have followed it.'

'And if you think we're going to tell you our methods, you can go to the devil!' I added. Why should we talk to you, Devereux? You plan to kill us anyway. Why not just get it over with and be done with it[4]?'

There was a lengthy silence. Throughout all this[5], Edgar Mortlake had been staring at us with a silent, smouldering hatred[6], while the other men stood around[7], barely interested in what was being discussed.

'All right. So be it.[8]' Devereux had been twisting the middle finger of his glove[9]. Now his hands fell to his sides[10]. He seemed almost saddened[11] by what he had to say.

'Do you know where you are? You are underneath Smithfield, one of the greatest meat markets in the world. This city is a ravenous beast that feeds on more flesh[12] than you can begin to imagine. Every day, it arrives from all over the world – oxen, pigs, lambs, rabbits, cocks, hens[13], pigeons, turkeys, geese[14]. They travel thousands of miles from Spain and Holland and much further afield[15], from America, Australia and New Zealand. We are on the very edge of the market here. We cannot be heard and we will not be disturbed. But not so far from where you are sitting, the butchers in their half-sleeves and aprons[16] have arrived. Their carts and wicker baskets[17]

1. prendre des mesures pour m'assurer
2. Vous vous accordez trop de crédit
3. piste allant
4. s'y mettre tout de suite ? Finissons-en !
5. Durant toute la conversation
6. nous avait fixé en silence avec un regard plein de haine
7. se tenaient autour de nous
8. Allons-y.
9. était occupé à tortiller le majeur de son gant
10. retombèrent le long de son corps
11. attristé
12. bête vorace qui consomme plus de chair
13. bœufs, porcs, agneaux, lapins, coqs, poules
14. dindes, oies
15. bien plus loin encore
16. avec leurs tabliers et leurs manches relevées,
17. Leurs charriots et paniers d'osier

are waiting to be filled. Snow Hill is around the next corner[1]. Yes. The market has its own underground station and soon the first train will draw in[2], direct from Deptford docks. It will be unloaded[3] here … five hundred tons a day. All that life reduced to tongues and tails, kidneys[4], hearts, hindquarters, flanks and endless casks of tripe[5].

'Why am I telling you this? I have a personal interest[6] which I will share with you, before I leave you to your fate[7]. My parents came originally from Europe but, as a child, I was brought up in the Packinghouse District[8] of Chicago and remember it well. My house was on Madison Street, close to the Bull's Head Market and stockyards[9]. I see it all even now …[10] the steam hoists and the refrigerator cars[11], the great herds[12] being driven in, their eyes wide with fear. How could I forget? The meat market pervaded[13] my life. The smoke and the smells were everywhere. In the summer heat, the flies came in their tens of thousands[14] and the local river ran red[15] with blood – the butchers were not too delicate when it came to the disposal of offal[16]. Enough meat to feed an army! I say it quite literally for much of the produce was sent to feed the Union[17] troops who were still fighting the Civil War.

'Will it surprise you to learn that I grew up with the strongest disinclination ever[18] to eat meat myself? From the moment I was able to make my own decisions, I became what has come to be called a vegetarian – a word that originated here in England, you might like to know. The lifelong condition from which I have suffered[19] I also blame on my childhood[20]. I used to have nightmares about the animals trapped in their pens[21],

1. au coin de la rue
2. entrera en gare
3. déchargé
4. réduite à un étalage de langues, queues, rognons
5. cuissots, flancs et à des fûts de tripes à perte de vue
6. anecdote
7. de vous abandonner à votre sort
8. été élevé dans le quartier des abattoirs
9. des parcs à bestiaux
10. Je les revoie encore aujourd'hui…
11. monte-charges à vapeur et les wagons réfrigérants
12. grands troupeaux
13. a imprégné
14. par dizaines de milliers
15. ruisselait
16. s'agissait de se débarrasser des abats
17. [armée des états du Nord pendant la guerre de Sécession]
18. la plus grande réticence qui soit
19. La maladie dont je souffre depuis toujours
20. je l'attribue également à mon enfance
21. piégés dans leur enclos

awaiting the horrors of the slaughterhouse[1]. I saw their eyes staring at me through the bars. And somehow their fear transmitted itself to me. In my young mind, it occurred to me that the animals were safe only while they remained locked up[2], that once they were removed[3] from their cages they would be butchered[4]. And so I in turn became afraid of[5] open spaces, the outside world. As a child, I drew the covers over[6] my head before I could sleep. In a way, those covers have remained in place ever since[7].

'I ask you both for a moment to consider the suffering and cruelty inflicted on animals simply to sate[8] our appetite. I mean this quite seriously, for it has a bearing[9] on your immediate future. Let me show you …' He walked over to the tables and gestured at the objects on display[10].

I could not help myself. For the first time, I examined the saws[11], the knives, the hooks, the steel rods and the branding irons[12] that had been laid out for our benefit[13].

'Animals are beaten. They are whipped[14]. They are branded[15]. They are castrated. They are skinned[16] and thrown into boiling water and I do not believe that they are always dead when this is done. They are blinded[17] and they are brutalised and at the very end, they are hung upside down[18] and their throats are cut. All of this will happen to you if you do not tell me what I wish to know. How did you find me? How do you know so much about my business? Who do you actually[19] work for?' He held up[20] a hand. 'You, Inspector Jones, are with Scotland Yard. And you, Mr Chase, are with Pinkerton's. But I have dealt with[21] both these organisations in the past and I know their

1. abattoir
2. enfermés
3. sortis
4. massacrés
5. à mon tour, je me mis à redouter
6. tirais les couvertures par-dessus
7. depuis lors
8. assouvir
9. incidence
10. désigna les objets placés en évidence
11. scies
12. crochets, les tiges en acier et le fer à marquer
13. disposés à notre intention
14. fouettés
15. marqué au fer rouge
16. dépecés
17. aveuglés
18. suspendus la tête en bas
19. en réalité
20. leva
21. eu affaire à

methods. The two of you are different. You break international conventions by entering the sanctity[1] of a legation and I begin to wonder which side of the law you are actually on. You interview Scotchy Lavelle and the next day he is murdered. You arrest Leland Mortlake and seconds later he dies with a poisoned dart in his neck.

'I take a great deal of risk in dealing[2] with you in this manner and, believe me, I wish it could be otherwise[3]. I am above all[4] a pragmatist and I know that the forces of the law – both in England and America – will redouble their efforts after your deaths. But I have no alternative. I must know. The one thing I can offer you, if you will co-operate and tell me the truth – is a fast and painless end[5]. The smallest blade, inserted into the spine of a bull[6], will kill it instantly. The same can be done for you. There is no need for violence. Tell me what I want to know and it will be much easier for you.'

There was a lengthy silence. Far away, I heard the sound of metal striking metal but it could have been a mile away, above or beneath the surface of the road. We were utterly[7] alone, surrounded by the six men who were preparing to do unspeakable[8] things to us. And our screams would do us no good[9]. If anyone did chance to hear us[10], we would simply be mistaken for animals being slaughtered[11].

'We cannot tell you what you want to know,' Jones replied, 'because your assertions are based on a false premise[12]. I am a British police officer. Chase has spent the last twenty years working with the Pinkertons. We followed a trail, albeit a strange one,[13] that led us to the legation and to

1. violant le sanctuaire
2. traitant
3. que l'on puisse procéder autrement
4. par-dessus tout
5. mort rapide et indolore
6. lame, introduite dans la colonne vertébrale d'un bœuf
7. complètement
8. atroces
9. nos cris seraient en pure perte
10. nous entendait par hasard
11. en train d'être abattus
12. postulat erroné
13. piste, certes fort étrange,

Chancery Lane. It is possible that you have enemies of whom you are ignorant[1]. Those enemies led us to you. And you yourself were careless[2]. Had you not communicated with Professor Moriarty in the first place, our investigation would never have begun.'

'I did not communicate with him.'

'I read the letter with my own eyes.'

'You are lying.[3]'

'Why would I lie? You have made my situation perfectly clear to me. What do I have to gain by deceit[4]?'

'The letter may have been written by Edgar or Leland Mortlake,' I cut in. 'Perhaps it came from Scotchy Lavelle. But it was just one of many mistakes that you made. You have the upper hand[5], but do what you will with us[6], others will come after us. Your time is over[7]. Why do you pretend otherwise[8]?'

Devereux looked at me curiously, then turned back to Jones. 'You are protecting someone, Inspector Jones. I do not know who they are, nor why you are prepared to suffer so much on their account[9], but I am telling you that I know it. How do you think I have survived so long, untouched by the law and unhindered[10] by those rivals who would gladly see my downfall[11]? I have an instinct. You are playing me false.[12]'

'You are wrong!' I shouted, and at the same time I launched myself out[13] of my chair. I had taken Mortlake and the other men unawares[14]. They had been lulled[15] by Devereux's long speech and our own seeming lethargy[16]. Now, before anyone could stop me, I threw myself onto[17] Devereux, one hand grabbing[18] his silk waistcoat,

1. dont vous ignorez l'existence
2. négligent
3. Vous mentez.
4. en vous trompant
5. le dessus
6. quoi que vous nous infligiez
7. touche à sa fin
8. le contraire
9. à cause de cette personne
10. sans être entravé
11. assisterait avec joie à ma chute
12. Vous vous jouez de moi.
13. m'élançai
14. par surprise
15. endormis
16. léthargie apparente
17. me jetai sur
18. saisissant

the other around his throat. Would that[1] I could have reached one of the knives set out on the table! Still, I brought him crashing to the ground and was half-strangling him[2] when several hands seized hold of me and I was pulled free[3]. I felt a cosh strike[4] against the side of my head, not hard enough to knock me unconscious, and a moment later someone's fist crashed into[5] the side of my face. Dazed[6], and with fresh blood streaming from my nose, I was thrown back into my chair.

Clarence Devereux stood up, his face pale with anger. I knew that he had never been attacked in this way – certainly not in front of his own men. 'We are finished,' he rasped[7]. 'I had hoped we might conduct ourselves as gentlemen but the business between us is over and I will not stay to watch you being torn apart[8]. Mortlake! You know what to do. Do not let them die until you have heard the truth – then report back to me[9].'

'Wait ...!' Jones cried.

But Devereux ignored him. He climbed back into the coach. The driver pulled hard on the reins, turning the horses round. Then he whipped them on and the whole contraption[10] disappeared down the tunnel, the way they had come[11].

Mortlake walked over to the table. He took his time, running his hand over the implements[12]. Finally he chose what looked like a barber's razor[13]. He flicked it open[14] to reveal a curious notched blade[15] which he held up to the light[16]. The six men from the cemetery closed in on us[17].

'All right,' Mortlake said. 'Let's begin.'

1. Si seulement
2. Je le projetai au sol et je l'étranglai à moitié
3. on me fit lâcher prise
4. matraque s'abattre
5. un poing s'écrasa sur
6. Hébété
7. dit-il d'une voix rauque
8. pour vous regarder être mis en pièces
9. venez me rejoindre
10. l'équipage
11. par où il était arrivé
12. laissant courir sa main sur les instruments
13. rasoir à barbe
14. l'ouvrit d'une pichenette
15. curieuse lame marquée d'entailles
16. leva à la lumière
17. se rapprochèrent de nous

NINETEEN

A Return to Light

After the beating I had received, I was too weak[1] to move. I could only sit there watching as Mortlake balanced the razor at his fingertips[2], holding it out before him[3] as if to admire its beauty. Never before had I felt so helpless[4]. At that moment, I accepted that I had set too much store by[5] my own capabilities and that all my plans and aspirations were about to come to this bloody end[6]. Clarence Devereux had beaten me. Small consolation that he had briefly felt my fingers around his throat. Their impression would have faded[7] long before he reached the safety of the legation and by then[8] I would be lost in a vortex of pain. I felt hands fall, heavy, on my shoulders. Two of Mortlake's men had approached and stood either side of me, one of them holding a length of rope[9]. The other grabbed hold of my wrist, preparing to tie me down[10].

But then Inspector Jones spoke. 'Hold off![11]' he said, and I was astonished to hear him sound so calm. 'You are wasting your time, Mortlake.'

'You believe so?'

'We will tell you everything your master wishes to know. There is no need for this squalid

1. faible

2. avait posé le rasoir en équilibre au bout de ses doigts

3. le tenant devant lui

4. impuissant

5. surévalué

6. allaient bientôt connaître une fin sanglante

7. allait s'estomper

8. au même moment

9. morceau de corde

10. attrapa mes poignets et se prépara à me ligoter

11. Attendez !

1. Ces méthodes sordides et inhumaines sont inutiles.
2. devons mourir
3. investigation
4. sans grand intérêt
5. posé sa canne sur ses genoux
6. vous avilissez
7. vous soit d'une quelconque utilité
8. là n'est plus la question
9. alors qu'il était sous votre garde
10. par vous arracher la langue
11. C'est vous dire à quel point
12. pivota la canne pour en pointer l'extrémité
13. dévissé
14. que l'intérieur était creux
15. le tourna
16. assourdissante
17. gouffre
18. estomac
19. tandis que des lambeaux
20. jaillissaient de son dos
21. L'explosion l'avait presque déchiré en deux.
22. tendus vers l'avant, les épaules voûtées
23. fine volute de fumée sortait en s'enroulant

and inhuman behaviour.[1] It has been made clear to us that are to die[2] in this place so what is to be gained by remaining silent? I will describe to you, step by step, the journey[3] that brought us here and my friend, Mr Chase, will corroborate every word I say. But you will find it of little value[4]. Let me assure you of that now.' Jones had drawn up his walking stick across his lap[5] as if it might provide a barrier between himself and his tormentors. 'We have no secrets and no matter how much you debase yourself[6] in God's eyes, you will discover nothing that will be of any use[7].'

Mortlake considered, but only briefly. 'You don't seem to understand, Inspector Jones,' he replied. 'You have information and I am sure you will provide it. But that is no longer the point[8]. My brother Leland died in your custody[9] and even if his killer was completely unknown to you, I hold you responsible and will make you pay. I might start by removing your tongue[10]. That is how[11] indifferent I am about what you have to say.'

'In that case, I'm afraid you leave me no choice.' Jones swung the stick round so that the tip faced[12] towards Mortlake and at the same moment I saw that he had unscrewed[13] the raven's head to reveal a hollow interior[14]. Holding the stick with one hand, he inserted the index finger of the other and twisted[15]. At once there was an explosion, deafening[16] in the confined space, and a great red chasm[17] appeared in Mortlake's stomach[18] even as gobbets[19] of blood and bone erupted out of his back[20]. The blast had almost torn him in half.[21] He stood there, the knife falling away, his arms thrown forward, his shoulders hunched[22]. A wisp of smoke curled up[23] from the bottom of the walking stick which, I now understood, had concealed an ingenious gun. Mortlake groaned. Fresh blood poured over[1] his lip. He fell to the ground and lay still.

The gun had one bullet[2] only.

'Now!' Jones shouted and the two of us rose up from our chairs together, even as the six remaining hoodlums stared in wonderment[3] at what had occurred. With remarkable speed – I would never have expected him to be so vigorous[4] – Jones lashed out with the stick[5] and although it was now useless as a firearm, it struck[6] the man nearest to him in the face, sending him reeling back[7] with blood spouting from his nose. For my part, I seized hold of the rope which would have been used to bind me[8] and pulled it towards me, then swung my elbow[9] into the throat of my assailant who, losing his balance[10], was unable to defend himself and fell, gurgling[11], to his knees.

For just one brief instant, I thought that we had succeeded and that against all the odds we were going to make good our escape[12]. But I had allowed my imagination[13] and the sudden reversal of fortune to get the better of me[14]. There were still four thugs[15] who had not been harmed and two of them had produced revolvers. The man whose face Jones had struck[16] was also armed and I could see that he was in no mood for reasoned debate[17]. They had formed a semi-circle around us and were about to fire[18]. We could not reach them. There was nothing to prevent them gunning us down.

And then the lights went out[19].

The gas lamps, long lines of them stretching in every direction, simply flickered and died[20] as if

1. s'épanchait de
2. balle
3. crapules observaient l'air ébahi
4. cru capable d'une telle vigueur
5. passa à l'attaque avec sa canne
6. une arme à feu bien inutile, elle atteignit
7. le faisant basculer en arrière et tomber à la renverse
8. me ligoter
9. balançai mon coude
10. perdant l'équilibre
11. s'étouffant
12. contre toute attente nous allions parvenir à nous échapper
13. m'étais laissé emporter par mon imagination
14. et ce soudain renversement de situation
15. voyous
16. que Jones avait frappé au visage
17. pas d'humeur à discuter
18. sur le point de tirer
19. s'éteignit
20. vacillèrent et s'évanouirent

extinguished by a sudden rush of air[1]. One moment we were trapped, about to die. The next we were plunged into a darkness that was all-encompassing[2], absolute. I think there might have been a part of me that wondered if I had not indeed been killed, for surely death would not be so very different from this. But I was alive and breathing and my heart was most certainly pounding[3]. At the same time, I was utterly[4] disconnected from everything around me, unable to see even[5] my own hands.

'Chase!'

I heard Jones call out my name and felt his hand on my sleeve, pulling me down. The truth is that by doing so he saved my life. Even as I dropped to the ground[6], Mortlake's gang opened fire. I saw the blaze of the muzzles[7] and felt the bullets as they fanned out[8] over my head and shoulders, smashing[9] into the wall behind me. Had I remained standing, I would have been torn apart.[10] As it was, I was fortunate[11] to avoid any ricochets.

'This way![12]' Jones whispered. He was crouching[13] beside me and, still holding onto my arm, he pulled me with him, away from the men, away from the torture implements spread[14] over the tables, further into the great nothingness[15] that our world had become. There was a second blast of guns[16] but this time I felt that the bullets came less close and I knew that with every inch that we shuffled away, the chances of our being hit[17] were diminishing. My hand felt something. It was the wall of the passageway[18] that had been behind us when Devereux was making his speech and through which we had first entered.

1. comme soufflées par un courant d'air
2. la plus totale
3. tambourinait bel et bien dans ma poitrine
4. totalement
5. ne serait-ce que
6. Alors que je me laissai tomber par terre
7. les canons de leurs pistolets s'embraser
8. passaient
9. et venaient s'encastrer
10. Si j'étais resté debout que j'aurais été mis en pièces.
11. En l'occurrence, je fus déjà chanceux
12. Par ici !
13. accroupi
14. étalés
15. au plus profond du néant
16. série de détonations
17. avec chaque centimètre parcouru, nos chances d'être touchés
18. tunnel

Following Jones's lead[1] I stood up, pressing my hands against the brickwork[2]. I was still blind.[3] But if I stayed close to the wall, it would surely lead me out[4].

Or so I thought.[5] Before we could take another step, a yellow light glimmered[6], spreading over the floor and illuminating the whole area around us. With a sense of dread[7], I turned and saw Mortlake spread out[8] on the ground and, next to him, the man with the beard and the broken nose who had first addressed us at the cemetery. He was holding up an oil lamp that he had somehow managed to light[9]. Despite all our efforts, we had moved only a short distance from the group. Not far enough. Once again, we were in plain sight[10].

'There they are!' he shouted. 'Kill them!'

I saw the guns turned on me once more and with a sense of resignation, I waited for the end. But we were not the ones who died.

Something invisible punched[11] the man in the head. The side of his skull exploded and a spurt[12] of red liquid burst out over his shoulder. As he tumbled sideways, still clutching[13] the oil lamp, distorted shadows fell over the other five men. They had not yet had a chance to shoot[14] and by the time their companion crashed to the floor, it was too late. The light had gone out again. He had been shot – but by whom[15]? And why? We could not answer these questions now. In the dark or in the light, we were still in mortal danger and would be[16] until we reached the surface and the safety of the street[17].

Taking advantage of the confusion behind us – our assailants were still not certain what had occurred – we broke into a stumbling run[18]. I was

1. Je suivis l'exemple de Jones et

2. maçonnerie

3. J'avançais toujours à l'aveugle.

4. il me conduirait sûrement dehors

5. Enfin c'est ce que je croyais.

6. se mit à s'éclairer faiblement

7. Avec appréhension

8. étendu

9. réussi à allumer on ne sait comment

10. livrés à la vue de tous

11. cogna

12. giclée

13. tombait à la renverse, agrippant toujours

14. pas encore eu le temps de tirer

15. par qui

16. le resterions

17. le lieu sûr qu'était la rue

18. nous mîmes à courir d'un pas mal assuré

aware of two contradictory impulses warring[1] in my mind. I wanted to be away[2] as quickly as I could but, being quite blind in the pitch dark[3], I was also afraid of crashing into some obstacle. I could hear Jones somewhere beside me but I was no longer sure if he was near or far. Was it my imagination or was the ground rising slightly[4] beneath my feet? That was the crucial test. The higher we climbed, the more likely we were[5] to reach street level where we might be safe.

And then I saw a light flickering about fifty yards away, a candle lit by a match. How could it be? Who had lit it? I staggered to a halt and called out to Jones, a single word.[6] 'There!' It was directly in front of us, a tiny beacon surely designed to[7] draw us out of danger. I had no sense of distance, not knowing even where I stood. I was certain that the candle had been placed there deliberately to help us, but even if it had been lit by the devil himself, what choice did we have? Moving faster, hearing the footsteps of our pursuers close behind, we pressed forward[8]. Another gunshot. Again the bullet rebounded off the wall and I felt brick dust stinging[9] my eyes. A shouted profanity.[10] And then something else, still far away, but coming rapidly closer – a huge sound, a heavy panting, the grinding of metal[11], and I smelled burning. The air around me became warm and moist.

There was an underground steam train heading towards us, making for[12] Snow Hill, the station that Devereux had mentioned. I could not see it but the sound of it was becoming more thunderous with every second that passed. The darkness had become a curtain in front of my

1. Je sentais deux réflexes contradictoires s'opposer en moi
2. m'éloigner
3. noir complet
4. le sol était-il légèrement incliné en pente
5. Plus nous grimpions, plus nous avions de chances
6. m'arrêtai en chancelant et interpellai Jones d'un seul mot
7. lueur sûrement destinée à
8. avançâmes de plus belle
9. de la poussière de briques me piquer
10. Quelqu'un hurla un juron.
11. un fort halètement, un grincement métallique
12. qui fonçait vers nous, en direction de

eyes and I was desperate to tear it free[1]. I had a sudden terror that I might have strayed onto the railway tracks[2], that I would set eyes on the locomotive only when it bore me down[3]. But then it turned a corner and although I still could not see it – I was aware only of its immense bulk[4] – a beam of light suddenly engulfed me[5], illuminating the arches and the vaulted ceiling in such a way as to make them fantastical, not part of a London meat market but some sort of supernatural kingdom inhabited by[6] ghosts and monsters.

Jones stood beside me and we both knew that the train would have revealed us to our pursuers. It was on a track[7] parallel to the passage where we stood, separated by a series of archways[8], and as it moved forward the light cut in and out[9], creating a strange effect in which any movement was reduced to a series of still[10] images such as one might see in a Coney Island[11] entertainment machine. At the same time, smoke was belching out of its chimney and steam billowing out of its cylinders[12], the two swirling together[13] and embracing each other like two phantom lovers. The train itself was a fantastic thing: the closer it came, the more dreadful it seemed and if this were a kingdom then here, surely, was the dragon.

I looked round; I could not help myself. Four men stood behind me and they were very close, having made faster progress than either Jones or I could manage. They were making use of the sudden illumination that had been given to them. The train would pass by in less than half a minute and it was only while its light was pinning us down[14] that they could finish[15] us. I saw them running forward, there one second, invisible the

1. voulais à tout prix le déchirer
2. de m'être aventuré sur les rails par erreur
3. n'apercevrais le train que lorsqu'il me foncerait dessus
4. masse
5. faisceau de lumière m'enveloppa soudain
6. peuplé de
7. voie
8. arcades
9. s'entrecoupait
10. fixes
11. [où se trouve un parc d'attractions]
12. de la vapeur s'élevait en volutes de ses cylindres
13. se mêlaient
14. pendant que nous étions pris dans la lumière des phares
15. achever

next, in this terrible black and white world with the beam finding its way intermittently through the gaps in the brickwork and the fumes threatening to smother us all[1].

Jones shouted something at me but I no longer heard the words. Four men suddenly became three. Another had thrown himself forward, impossibly[2], a fountain of blood erupting from his shoulders. The train was almost upon us[3]. And then a figure stepped out from behind a mouldering brick column[4]. It was the boy Perry, his face lit up in a demonic smile and his eyes ablaze[5]. He ran towards me, lifting a huge butcher's knife in his right hand. I fell back.[6] But I was not his target. One of Mortlake's men had crept up on me[7], had been inches away from me. The boy plunged the blade into his throat, jerked it out[8] and thrust it in again. Blood curtained down, splashing onto[9] his arms. He was close enough for me to hear his high-pitched[10] laughter. His mouth was stretched open[11], showing bright white teeth. The roar[12] of the locomotive filled my ears and I was no longer breathing air, only carbon and steam. My throat was on fire.

Darkness. The train had rushed by[13], leaving only the carriages clanking past[14], one after another.

'Chase!' It was Jones calling my name. 'Where are you?'

'Here!'

'We must get out of this charnel house[15].'

The candle was still flickering. We made for it[16], unsure what we were leaving in our wake[17]. I thought I heard the soft thud[18] of a bullet finding its target, not a revolver but some sort of

1. tous nous étouffer
2. s'était invraisemblablement jeté en avant
3. tout proche
4. silhouette surgit de derrière une colonne en décomposition
5. le regard brûlant
6. battis en retraite
7. s'était approché de moi en silence
8. la retira d'un coup sec
9. Un flot de sang s'écoula, éclaboussant
10. aigu
11. grande ouverte
12. rugissement
13. passait à toute vitesse
14. qui défilaient en cliquetant
15. charnier
16. nous dirigeâmes vers elle
17. sans trop savoir ce que nous laissions derrière nous
18. bruit sourd

airgun[1]. And the boy was there too. I heard a scream followed by a terrible gurgle[2] as his blade cut through flesh[3]. Somehow, Jones and I linked arms and, choking[4], with tears streaming from our eyes, we ran forward, aware that the ground was indeed sloping upwards[5], and more steeply with every step[6]. We reached the candle and saw that it had been deliberately placed at a corner. Looking round it, we saw the moonlit sky[7]. A flight of metal stairs led to an opening[8]. With the last of our strength, we staggered forward[9] and climbed into the faint light of dawn[10].

Nobody followed us. We had left the horrors of that subterranean[11] world behind. It was quite possible that Devereux's men had all perished, but even if some of them had appeared there would have been little they could do for we were now surrounded by other people: butchers and delivery boys, market clerks and inspectors, buyers and sellers, creeping in silence to their work[12]. We saw a policeman and rushed towards him.

'I am Detective Inspector Athelney Jones of Scotland Yard,' Jones gasped[13]. 'I have been the victim of a murderous attack. Call for reinforcements[14]. I must have your protection.'

God knows what we must have looked like, drawn[15] and desperate, bruised[16] and covered in blood, our clothes dishevelled, our skin streaked with dirt and soot[17]. The policeman looked at us with equanimity[18]. 'Now, now[19], sir,' he said. What's all this about?'

The sky was already turning pink when we made our way back to Camberwell. I had travelled with Jones – I could not return to my hotel until we

1. pistolet à air comprimé
2. gargouillis
3. entaillait la chair
4. nous prîmes par le bras et, en suffoquant,
5. remontait
6. et qu'elle devenait plus raide à chaque pas
7. clair de lune
8. une ouverture
9. Puisant dans nos dernières forces, nous avançâmes en titubant
10. faible lumière de l'aube
11. souterrain
12. se rendant au travail en silence
13. haleta
14. des renforts
15. épuisés
16. pleins de bleus
17. dépenaillés, la peau striée de crasse et de suie
18. sereinement
19. Allons, allons

had seen the conclusion of the night's work together. We had spoken little but as we reached Denmark Hill, seated together in the carriage that the policeman had eventually been persuaded to provide[1], he turned to me.

'You saw him.'

'You mean Perry, the child who led us to Bladeston House?'

'Yes. He was there.'

'He was.'

'I still do not understand it, Chase ...'

'Nor I[2], Jones. First he tries to murder you at Scotland Yard. Now it is as if he wished to save you.'

'He and the man who was with him. But who were they and how did they find us?' Jones closed his eyes, deep in thought. He was close to exhaustion[3] and would have slept but for the uncertainty[4] of what lay ahead[5]. We only had Devereux's word[6] that Beatrice had been returned and we had no reason to trust anything he said. 'You did not tell them about Perry,' he continued. 'When Devereux asked you how we found our way to Highgate, you did not say that we had followed the child from the Café Royal.'

'Why should I have told him the truth?' I said. 'It seemed better to leave him uncertain[7]. And it was more important for me to hear him freely admit to the murder of Jonathan Pilgrim. He did so.[8] Of course, we always knew he was responsible, but now we have heard it with our own ears and can testify to it in a court of law[9].'

'If we can ever drag him before it[10].' 'We will[11], Jones. After tonight, he cannot be safe anywhere[12].'

1. nous avions finalement obtenu du policier
2. Moi non plus
3. épuisement
4. s'il n'avait pas été dans l'incertitude
5. quant à la suite des événements
6. promesse
7. le laisser dans l'incertitude
8. Ce qu'il fit.
9. en témoigner devant un tribunal
10. l'y traîner un jour
11. y arriverons
12. nulle part

We reached the front door of Jones's house but we had no need to open it. Seeing our carriage pull up[1], Elspeth came flying out, her hair loose and a shawl[2] around her shoulders. She fell into her husband's arms.

'Where is Beatrice?' Jones asked.

'She is upstairs, asleep. I have been worrying myself to death[3] about you.'

'I am here. We are safe.'

'But you are hurt. Your poor face! What has happened to you?'

'It is nothing. We are alive. That is all that matters.'

The three of us went into the house. The fire was blazing and breakfast was already being cooked but I was asleep, in an armchair, long before it was served.

1. s'arrêter devant

2. en sortit précipitamment, les cheveux défaits et un châle

3. morte d'inquiétude

TWENTY

Diplomatic Immunity

It seemed strange that, in the end, the entire affair – my long and painful search for the greatest criminal who ever came out of America – should come down to[1] the formality of a meeting with three men in a room. We went back to the legation in Victoria Street, this time using our own names and with the full knowledge of the Chief Commissioner[2]. Indeed, permission had been sought as far up as the[3] office of the Foreign Secretary, Lord Salisbury himself. And so we found ourselves sitting in front of the envoy[4], Robert T. Lincoln, and his councillor, Henry White, both of whom had greeted us[5] on the night of the party. The third man was Charles Isham, Lincoln's secretary, a rather wayward[6] young man now wearing a mauve jacket and a floppy cravat[7]. It was he who had arrested us at the behest[8] of Edgar and Leland Mortlake.

We were in a room that must surely be used as a library; two entire walls being lined with[9] books, hefty legal tomes[10] which had surely never been read. The walls opposite were painted an anaemic shade of grey[11], covered with portraits of former[12] envoys, the earliest of them

1. se résume à
2. avec le soutien du préfet de police
3. la requête était montée jusqu'au
4. ambassadeur
5. ceux-là même qui nous avaient accueillis
6. assez imprévisible
7. cache-col tombant
8. sur l'ordre
9. étaient garnis de
10. de gros ouvrages juridiques
11. gris triste et pâle
12. anciens

in high collars and stocks[1]. Wire screens had been drawn over[2] the windows, blocking the view into Victoria Street, and I wondered if this might presage a visit from Devereux himself. He had not been there when we arrived, nor had his name yet been mentioned[3]. We were at least certain that he must be somewhere in the building, assuming, that is,[4] that he had returned there after his appearance at Smithfield market. Inspector Jones had positioned police constables around the building, all of them out of uniform[5]. They had been discreetly watching everyone who came and went during the day.

Robert Lincoln I have already described. Large and ungainly though he was[6], I had found him an impressive person when he had been the host at his reception, graciously acknowledging[7] the many guests who wished to speak to him while ensuring that any conversation took place on his own terms[8]. He was the same now, sitting in a high-backed[9] chair with an antique table beside him. Even in this quieter and more confidential setting[10], he commanded the room. He did not need to speak. He thought long and hard before he made any pronouncement and his sentences were brief and to the point[11]. White seemed to be the more worried[12] of the three, sitting to one side and examining us with ever watchful eyes[13]. It was he who had begun the conversation.

'I must ask you, Inspector Jones, quite what you had in mind[14] when you came here a few days ago, masquerading under a false name[15] and carrying an invitation which you had purloined[16]. Were you unaware of the seriousness[17] of your conduct?'

1. les premiers de la lignée en faux-col et jabot

2. Des panneaux en treillis métalliques recouvraient

3. et son nom n'avait pas encore été mentionné

4. si l'on partait du principe

5. en civil

6. Tout costaud et inélégant qu'il était

7. saluant avec courtoisie

8. tout en gardant l'ascendant sur la moindre conversation

9. à haut dossier

10. cadre plus calme et plus intime

11. ciblées

12. inquiet

13. d'un œil attentif

14. ce qui a bien pu vous passer par la tête

15. vous présentant sous une fausse identité

16. usurpée

17. gravité

'It has been made very clear to me and I can only extend[1] my apologies to you and to the envoy. Let me say, though, that the situation was a desperate one. I was in pursuit of a dangerous gang of criminals. There had been much bloodshed[2]. They attempted to kill me … an explosion that claimed more than one life[3].'

'How can you be sure that they were responsible?' Lincoln asked.

'I cannot, sir. All I can say is that Chase and I pursued them to[4] this address. A brougham driver brought them here directly from Scotland Yard immediately following the outrage[5].'

'He could have been mistaken.[6]'

'It is possible, but I do not believe it. Mr Guthrie seemed quite certain of himself. Otherwise, I would not have entered in the manner that I did.'

'That was my suggestion,' I said. I was not feeling well and knew that I presented a disagreeable sight[7]. The ill treatment[8] that I had received at the hands of Mortlake's thugs had been more serious than I had thought: the whole side of my face was swollen, my eye blackened, my lip cracked so that I spoke with difficulty. Jones looked little better[9]. Smartly presented though we both were[10], I was aware that we must resemble the victims of a train wreck[11]. 'I was responsible,' I continued. 'I persuaded Inspector Jones to come.'

'We are well aware[12] of the methods of the Pinkerton Agency,' Isham muttered. He had been unsympathetic from the start. 'Inciting riots.[13] Attempting to incriminate hard-working men[14] because they had chosen, quite legitimately, to go on strike[15]—'

1. présenter
2. de sang versé
3. qui a fait plusieurs victimes
4. les avons suivis jusqu'à
5. méfait
6. Il a pu se tromper.
7. allure déplaisante
8. mauvais traitements
9. n'était guère mieux
10. Tout élégants que nous étions
11. accident de train
12. familiers
13. Attiser les émeutes.
14. Incriminer de respectables travailleurs
15. faire grève

'As far as I am aware[1], we have been guilty of none of those things. Certainly, I was not involved in the[2] Chicago railway strikes[3] or any others.'

'That's not in question now[4], Charlie,' Lincoln said, quietly.

'We acted unlawfully[5],' Jones continued. 'I admit it. But as things turned out, we were[6] ... I will not say justified, but at least we were proven right[7]. The criminal known as Clarence Devereux was indeed seeking refuge within[8] these walls, using the assumed[9] name of Coleman De Vriess. Or perhaps that is his real name and Devereux is his alias. Either way[10], we discovered him here. And that was what led him to strike back at us in a way that was unparalleled[11] in all my years as an officer of the law.'

'He kidnapped your daughter.'

'Yes, Minister,' Jones said, addressing the envoy formally. 'His men took my six-year-old child and used her as bait[12] to capture Chase and myself.'

'I have two daughters,' Lincoln muttered. 'And only recently I lost a son to sickness[13]. I understand your anguish[14].'

'Last night, in the catacombs beneath Smithfield meat market[15], Clarence Devereux threatened us with torture and death. We are only here thanks to a miraculous escape, which we are still hard-pressed to explain[16]. Well, that is for another time[17]. But right now, sir, I can swear that the man who assaulted us and who is responsible for a catalogue[18] of crimes in both your country and mine is the same man whom you call your third secretary. I am here to request – even to demand[19] – that we be allowed[20] to question him

1. Pour autant que je sache
2. n'ai pas pris part aux
3. [célèbre épisode de grève dans les chemins de fer en 1888]
4. Ce n'est pas la question
5. en toute illégalité
6. il s'est avéré que c'était
7. nos soupçons étaient fondés
8. avait bel et bien trouvé refuge entre
9. d'emprunt
10. Quoi qu'il en soit
11. à répliquer avec une férocité que je n'avais jamais connue
12. appât
13. mon fils a été emporté par une maladie
14. détresse
15. dissimulées sous le marché à la viande de Smithfield
16. que nous peinons encore à nous expliquer
17. le temps des éclaircissements viendra
18. liste
19. exiger
20. que nous soyons habilités

and, in due course[1], bring him to face justice in a court of law.'

There was a lengthy silence after this. Everyone was waiting for Lincoln to speak but instead he nodded at his councillor who stroked his beard[2] pensively and then addressed us thus[3]: 'I regret that it is not quite as simple and as straightforward[4] as you would like, Inspector Jones. Let us set aside[5], for a moment, your personal testimony and whether or not it is to be believed[6].'

'Wait!' I began, already outraged[7] by the position he had chosen to take. But Jones raised a hand, cautioning me to[8] stay silent.

'I am not saying that I doubt your word even though I will admit that your methods, your intrusion here, leave much to be desired[9]. I can also see for myself the injuries sustained by you[10] and by your associate, Mr Chase. No. What is of the essence[11] here is the principal of extraterritoriality. An envoy is the representative of those who sent him and almost a century ago, Thomas McKean, the Chief Justice[12] of Pennsylvania, set down[13] that the person of the public minister serving abroad[14] is both sacred and inviolable and that to suggest otherwise[15] would be a direct attack on the sanctity of the nation state[16]. I must add that this protection extends to all who serve under the[17] envoy. How could it be otherwise[18]? To deny his servants[19] the same privilege of diplomatic immunity would cause all manner of difficulties and would eventually undermine[20] the independence of the envoy himself.'

'Forgive me, sir. But surely the envoy has the right to waive that immunity if he deems it appropriate[21]?'

1. le moment venu
2. caressait sa barbe
3. en ces termes
4. direct
5. Mettons de côté
6. la question de sa véracité
7. indigné
8. m'invitant à
9. laissent pour le moins à désirer
10. blessures que l'on vous a infligées, à vous
11. Ce qui importe
12. président de la Haute Cour de justice
13. a établi
14. ministre en poste à l'étranger
15. remettre ce principe en cause
16. portée à l'intégrité de la nation
17. sous les ordres du
18. pourrait-il en être autrement
19. Refuser à ses subalternes
20. toutes sortes de problèmes et pourrait même menacer
21. lever cette immunité s'il le juge nécessaire

'That has never been the practice of the United States. Our view is that the legation remains outside the civil law[1] of the country in which it finds itself. It is, you might say, an island. I am afraid that these premises[2] are protected from criminal process[3]. Mr De Vriess, like Mr Isham and myself, can refuse to testify in both civil and criminal proceedings[4]. Indeed, even were he to choose otherwise[5], he would still require authorisation from the envoy himself.'

'You are saying, then, that we cannot prosecute him?'

'That is exactly what I am saying.'

'But you would surely agree that natural law, basic humanity, demands[6] that all crimes must be punished.'

'You have given us no evidence[7],' Isham cut in[8]. 'Mr Chase has been injured[9]. You have been forced to endure the temporary loss[10] of your daughter. But nothing that you say fits[11] the character of Mr De Vriess as we know him.'

'And what if[12] I am telling the truth? What if I tell you that, unbeknownst to you[13], Coleman De Vriess has taken advantage of[14] the system that you describe? Will you gentlemen sit here and protect a man who has come to London only to inflict terror[15] on its population?'

'It is not we who protect him!'

'But still[16] he is protected. His associate, Edgar Mortlake, was sipping cocktails within these very walls[17]. With my own eyes I saw Mortlake cut the throat of a man who had crossed him[18]. It was he who took my girl, and his brother, Leland, the coldblooded partner in his schemes[19], was responsible for the murder of the Pinkerton agent,

1. se soustrait à la loi civile
2. lieux
3. toute poursuite judiciaire
4. témoigner dans une cour civile comme pénale
5. En fait, même s'il en décidait autrement
6. l'humanité élémentaire, exige
7. preuve
8. lança
9. est blessé
10. affronter la disparition temporaire
11. ne coïncide avec
12. Et si malgré tout
13. à votre insu
14. exploite à dessein
15. infliger un état de terreur
16. Et pourtant
17. sirotait des cocktails ici même
18. qui l'avait défié
19. son impitoyable complice

Jonathan Pilgrim. Would you stand up for them[1] if they were still alive? When my friend Chase came to England, he brought with him files that were filled with the vile activities of this gang, carried out[2] all over America. I have seen them. I can show them to you. Murders, thefts, blackmail[3], extortion … Clarence Devereux was the chief architect of all this misery[4], the same Clarence Devereux who only last night threatened to torture us to death, like cattle[5]. I know that you are honourable men; I refuse to believe that you will stand in the way of due process[6] and continue to live with this viper among you.'

'The evidence!' Isham insisted. 'It is all very well for you to speak of process.[7] I myself have studied the law. Probatio vincit praesumptionem.[8] There! What do you say to that?'

'You speak in Latin, sir. I speak of a daughter stolen from my arms.'

'If we cannot prosecute him, can we at least not question him?' I asked. 'Surely we have the right to interview him, inside Scotland Yard and with any counsel that you wish to provide[9]. We will prove to you the truth of our allegations and then, if we cannot prosecute him here, at least we can see him sent home to face justice in America[10]. Inspector Jones is right. He should be anathema to you.[11] Do you really doubt us? You see the injuries we have both suffered. From where do you think they came?'

Charles Isham still looked doubtful but Henry White glanced at Lincoln who came to a decision. 'Where is Mr De Vriess?' he asked.

'He is waiting in the next room.'

'Then perhaps you might ask him to step in[12].'

1. Est-ce que vous prendriez leur défense
2. perpétrées
3. chantage
4. le maître architecte de toutes ces atrocités
5. du bétail
6. entraverez l'exercice légitime de la justice
7. C'est bien joli de parler de procédure.
8. [en latin : La preuve l'emporte sur la présomption.]
9. tous les avocats que vous voulez
10. il sera expulsé et répondra de ses crimes aux États-Unis
11. Il ne mérite que l'anathème.
12. entrer

It was progress of sorts[1]. Isham, the secretary, stood up and went to a pair of adjoining doors[2] and opened them – and a second later, after a brief, murmured exchange, Clarence Devereux stepped into the room. I cannot quite express the strange thrill that I felt to see him[3], to know that he further[4] harm. Certainly, he was meek enough, affecting that same self-deprecation[5] that he had displayed[6] when we first set eyes on him, barely noticing him[7], that night at the legation. He pretended to be startled[8] to be in such grand company, blinking[9] nervously in front of the envoy and his advisors. Nor did he seem to recognise Jones and myself, looking at us as if we were complete strangers[10]. He was wearing the same coloured silk waistcoat that he had worn[11] the night before but in every other respect he could have been a quite different man[12].

'Minister?' he queried[13], as Isham closed the door.

'Please take a seat, Mr De Vriess.'

Another chair was made available[14] and Devereux sat down, keeping a distance between himself and us. 'May I ask why I have been summoned[15] here, sir?' He looked at us a second time. 'I know these gentlemen! They were here on the night of the Anglo-American trade[16] celebration. One of the guests recognised them as imposters[17] and I was forced to eject them. Why are they here?'

'They have made some very serious allegations about you[18],' White explained.

'Allegations? About me?'

'May I ask where you were last night, Mr De Vriess?'

1. déjà un progrès
2. une double porte
3. fébrilité que m'inspira sa vue
4. plus de
5. doux comme un agneau, avec la même modestie feinte
6. dont il avait fait preuve
7. lui accordant peu d'importance
8. surpris
9. clignant des yeux
10. de parfaits inconnus
11. gilet de soie coloré dont il était vêtu
12. à tout autre égard, il n'était plus le même homme
13. s'enquit-il
14. On apporta une autre chaise
15. convoqué
16. commerce
17. les a démasqués
18. de graves allégations à votre sujet

1. m'aventurer hors de ces murs à moins qu'il y ait une urgence
2. prétendent
3. cherchent à se venger
4. mal venu de faire de telles déclarations
5. une terrible méprise
6. mauvaise identification
7. me confondent
8. s'éclairèrent
9. Voilà l'explication.
10. quiproquo
11. nous ont violentés et nous auraient tués
12. dégoût pour la
13. à l'origine de
14. n'est qu'affabulation
15. défaites donc votre col pour voir
16. Comment justifiez-vous leur présence ?

'I was here, Mr White. Where else could I have been? You know that I am unable to venture out unless it is a matter of urgency[1] and even then I can only do so with the most careful preparation.'

'They claim[2] they met you at Smithfield market.'

'I will not call it a lie, sir. I will not say that they are seeking revenge[3] for what took place here a week ago. It would be quite wrong to make such assertions[4] in front of His Excellency. I will say only that it is the most dreadful error[5]. That this is a case of mistaken identity[6]. They have confused me[7] with someone else.'

'You do not know the name Clarence Devereux?'

'Clarence Devereux? Clarence Devereux?' His eyes brightened[8]. 'CD! There you have it.[9] We share the same initials! Is this the cause of the misunderstanding[10]? But no, I have never heard the name.'

Lincoln turned to Jones, inviting him to speak.

'You deny that you imprisoned us last night, that you and your men abused us and would have put us to death[11] if we had not managed to get away? Did you not tell us of your childhood in Chicago, your hatred of[12] meat, the fear that led to[13] your agoraphobia?

'I was born in Chicago. That is true. But the rest of it is fantasy[14]. Minister, I assure you …!'

'If you were not there, then undo your collar[15],' I exclaimed. 'Explain to us the marks around your neck. I placed them there with my own hands and I'm glad I did it. Will you tell us how you came by them?[16]'

'It is true that you attacked me,' Devereux replied. 'You seized me by the neck. But it was not in any meat market. It was here, in this legation.

You came here under false pretences[1] and became violent when it fell upon me[2] to eject you.'

'Perhaps that is the motive for all this,' Isham remarked. He was so fervent[3] in his defence of Devereux that I began to wonder if he had not been in some way bribed or coerced[4]. 'There is clearly enmity[5] between these three gentlemen. I will not impugn[6] their motives but it seems very likely[7] to me that a mistake has been made. And I would point out[8], Minister[9], that Mr De Vriess has been a good and loyal servant[10] of the American government both in Washington for the past six or seven years and here. Certainly, there can be no doubt about his affliction[11]. Is it likely, given his illness, that he could be the mastermind[12] of an international criminal network? Looking at him now, is that what you see?'

Lincoln sat in gloomy[13] silence, then slowly shook his head. 'Gentlemen,' he said. 'It grieves me to say that you have not made your case.[14] I will not doubt your word, for you are both honourable men, I am sure. But Isham is right. Without physical evidence, it is impossible for me to proceed[15] and although I can promise you we will investigate this matter further[16], it must be done within the grounds of this legation and in keeping with its rules[17].'

The meeting was over[18]. But suddenly Jones got to his feet[19] and I recognised at once the energy and the determination that I knew so well. 'You want evidence?' he asked. 'Then perhaps I can give it to you.' He took out of his pocket a piece of paper with a jagged edge[20] and a few words written in block capitals. He laid it on the table beside Lincoln. I saw the words: WE HAVE

1. faux-semblants
2. il m'a incombé
3. virulent
4. si on ne l'avait pas soudoyé, ou même contraint à le faire
5. animosité
6. ne contestera pas
7. probable
8. ajouterais
9. Excellence
10. employé
11. maladie
12. à la tête
13. maussade
14. J'ai le regret de vous dire que vous ne m'avez pas convaincu.
15. donner suite
16. davantage
17. dans les murs de la légation et en accord avec ses règles
18. touchait à sa fin
19. bondit de sa chaise
20. au bord déchiré

YOUR DAUHTER. 'This was the note that was sent to me to entice me[1] into the cemetery known as Dead Man's Walk,' Jones explained. 'It was the means by which Devereux was able[2] to capture both Chase and myself.'

'What of it?[3]' Isham asked.

'It has been torn[4] from a book and the moment[5] I saw it I knew it had been taken from a library just such as this[6].' Jones turned to the bookshelves. 'The sun hits[7] these windows at a strange angle,' he continued. 'As a result, it falls onto very few[8] of your books but I remarked, the moment I came in here, that a few volumes at the very end have been allowed to fade[9]. The top of this page, as you can see, has also been damaged.' Without asking permission, he went over to the shelves and examined them. 'These books have not been read for some time,' he continued. 'They are all perfectly aligned … all except one which has been recently removed and which has not been replaced in its exact position.' He took out the offending volume[10] and brought it over to Lincoln. 'Let us see …' He opened it.

The frontispiece[11] had been torn out. The jagged edge[12] was there for all to see and it was obvious – indeed, it was unarguable[13] – that it matched the edge[14] of the page on which the kidnapper had written his note.

The open book was greeted[15] by a silence that was profound and it occurred to me then that great trials have turned on less[16]. Though Lincoln and his advisors gave nothing away[17], they stared at it as if they read in it all the mysteries of life, and even Devereux visibly shrank into[18] himself, recognising that the game might, after all, be lost.

1. m'attirer
2. moyen qui a permis à Devereux
3. Mais encore ?
4. déchirée
5. dès que
6. exactement comme celle-ci
7. tape sur
8. Il en résulte que les rayons de soleil n'atteignent que quelques-uns
9. à l'extrémité, ont été décolorés
10. sortit le volume incriminé
11. [illustration en face d'un titre de livre]
12. bord déchiré
13. indiscutable
14. correspondait à celui
15. accueilli
16. se sont tenus pour moins que cela
17. ne laissaient rien paraître
18. se ratatinait sur

'There can be no doubt that this page was taken from this library,' Lincoln said at last. 'How do you explain this, Mr De Vriess?'

'I cannot. It is a trick[1]!'

'It would seem to me that you might, after all, have a case to answer[2].'

'Anyone could have removed that book. They could have done so themselves when they were here!'

'They did not come to the library,' Isham muttered. These were the first words he had spoken on our side[3].

Devereux was becoming desperate. 'Minister, you yourself argued just moments ago that I am protected from the criminal process.'

'So you are and so you must be.[4] And yet I cannot stand by[5] and do nothing. Two officers of the law have identified you. It cannot be denied[6] that grave events have taken place. And now they have evidence …'

Another long silence was interrupted by the councillor of the legation. 'It would not be without precedent for[7] a member of the diplomatic corps to be questioned by the police,' White said. Even I was surprised by the speed with which these gentlemen were shifting ground[8] – but then, of course[9], they were politicians. 'If there is a case to be made against you, it is only reasonable[10] that you should, at the very least[11], co-operate, for how else will we clear your name[12]?'

'Even outside the legation, you will still enjoy[13] its full protection,' Isham added. 'We can extend to you the right of innocent passage[14] – *ius transitus innoxii*. It will allow our friends in the British

1. ruse
2. qu'il vous faudra, au final répondre à ces accusations
3. pour notre défense
4. Vous l'êtes, et il ne saurait en être autrement.
5. rester simple spectateur
6. Il est indéniable
7. Ce ne serait pas la première fois qu'
8. ils changaient leur fusil d'épaule
9. après tout
10. vous êtes mis en accusation, il va de soi
11. au minimum
12. sinon, comment espérer laver votre réputation
13. continuerez à bénéficier de
14. droit de passage inoffensif

police the right to interview you whilst still placing you outside[1] their jurisdiction.'

'And then?'

'You will be returned[2] here. If you have been unable to explain yourself satisfactorily, it will be for the minister to decide what will be done next.'

'But I cannot leave! You know I cannot venture[3] outside.'

'I have a closed wagon[4] waiting for you,' Jones said. 'A Black Maria might strike fear into the heart of[5] ordinary criminals but for you it will be a place of refuge. It has no windows and a door that will remain securely fastened[6] – I can assure you of that. It will transport you directly to Scotland Yard.'

'No! I will not go!' Devereux turned to Lincoln and for the first time I saw real fear in his eyes. 'This is a trick, sir. These men do not intend[7] to interview me. They mean to kill me. The two of them are not what they seem[8].' The words tripped out[9], faster and faster. 'First there was Lavelle. They saw him and the very next day[10] he was murdered in his own home, along with his entire household[11]. Then Leland Mortlake, a respected businessman! Your Excellency will remember meeting him. He was no sooner arrested than[12] he was poisoned. And now they have come for me. If you force me to leave with them, I will never reach Scotland Yard – or if I do I will die there. They will kill me before I step into this Black Maria of theirs[13]! I have nothing to answer for.[14] I am an innocent man. I am not well.[15] You know that. I will answer any questions you put to me[16] and allow you a complete examination of

1. bien que vous demeuriez en dehors de
2. On vous reconduira
3. m'aventurer
4. fourgon fermé
5. inspire plutôt de la crainte aux
6. verrouillée
7. n'ont pas l'intention
8. ce qu'ils prétendent
9. se bousculaient
10. en l'espace d'une journée
11. lui et toute sa maisonnée
12. À peine fut-il arrêté qu'
13. ne mette un pied dans leur maudite Black Maria
14. Je n'ai rien à me reprocher.
15. Je n'ai pas la santé.
16. me soumettrez

my life but I swear to you, you are sending me to my death[1]. Do not make me go!'

He sounded so pathetic and so frightened that I would have been inclined to believe him myself had I not known that it was all an act[2]. I wondered if Lincoln might not take pity on him[3] but the envoy cast his eyes down[4] and said nothing.

'We mean him no harm[5],' Jones said. 'You have my word on it[6]. We will speak with him. There are many, many questions that remain unanswered. Once we have satisfied ourselves on these[7] – and have a full confession – we will return him to you according to diplomatic law. Lord Salisbury[8] himself has agreed. It is indifferent to us whether this man faces justice in Britain or in the United States. Our only concern is[9] that he should not escape the consequences of what he has done.'

'Then it is agreed,' Lincoln said. He got to his feet, suddenly tired. 'Henry – I want you to send an envoy to Scotland Yard. He is to be present throughout the cross-examination[10] – which will not begin until he arrives. I wish to see Mr De Vriess back[11] at the legation before nightfall[12].'

'It may take more than one day to arrive at the truth.'

'I am aware of that, Inspector Jones. In that event, he will be returned to you tomorrow. But he is not to spend[13] even one night behind bars.'

'Very well, sir …'

Without another word, and without even glancing at Devereux, Lincoln left the room.

'I must not go![14] I will not leave!' Devereux grabbed hold of the arms[15] of the chair like a child, tears welling in his[16] eyes, and the next few minutes were as strange and as undignified[17] as

1. vous en conjure, vous m'envoyez à la mort

2. si je ne savais pas pertinemment que c'était une comédie

3. n'allait pas le prendre en pitié

4. baissa les yeux

5. ne lui voulons aucun mal

6. parole

7. Quand nous aurons obtenu satisfaction

8. [Ministre des Affaires Étrangères]

9. Seul nous importe

10. à tous les interrogatoires

11. que M. De Vriess soit de retour

12. la tombée de la nuit

13. il est hors de question qu'il passe

14. Je ne veux pas y aller !

15. agrippa les accoudoirs

16. lui montèrent aux

17. les plus étranges et les plus indignes

any I can remember[1]. We had to call more officials into the room and prise him away[2] by force. While White and Isham watched in dismay, he was dragged[3] downstairs, a whimpering wretch who began to screech[4] the moment he saw the open door. Only the night before, this same man had stood, surrounded by his cronies, sentencing us to a painful death[5]. It was almost impossible to compare that man with the creature he had become.

A cover was found and thrown over[6] his head and we were able to escort him out to the gate where the Black Maria was waiting. White had come with us. 'You are not to begin your questioning until my representative arrives.'

'I understand.'

'And you will accord Mr De Vriess the respect due to the[7] third secretary of this legation.'

'You have my word on it.'

'I will see you again this evening. Is it too much to hope that this business will be concluded by then?[8]'

'We will do what we can.'

These were[9] the arrangements that Jones had made for the transfer of Clarence Devereux from the legation. Five police constables had come from Scotland Yard, all of them hand-picked[10] by Jones himself. Nobody else was to be allowed to come close. There was to be no chance of a[11] second poison dart being fired from somewhere in the crowd. Nor was the mysterious sniper who had come[12] to our rescue at Smithfield market going to be presented with a target.[13] Devereux himself was blind[14] and unable to resist and we made sure that he was surrounded, protected by

1. que j'aie jamais vécues
2. l'arracher
3. avec désarroi tandis qu'on le traînait
4. chiffe molle qui se mit à piailler
5. hommes de main, nous condamnant à une mort douloureuse
6. On trouva une couverture pour lui couvrir
7. qui lui est dû en tant que
8. Pouvons-nous espérer que l'affaire soit résolue d'ici là ?
9. Voici
10. triés sur le volet
11. Il ne fallait pas risquer qu'une autre
12. Ni qu'on offre au mystérieux sniper, qui avait volé
13. à notre secours au marché de Smithfield, une cible de choix.
14. avançait à l'aveugle

a human shield[1] until he reached the Black Maria, which had been parked directly beside the gate. The vehicle – in fact it was dark blue – was a solid box on four wheels and it had been thoroughly searched before it set out[2]: once Devereux was inside, Jones was fairly certain that he would be safe. The doors were already open and, with utmost care, we bundled him in[3]. The interior was dark, with two benches facing each other, one on either side. To any[4] ordinary criminal, it might have seemed a dreadful[5] mode of transport but the irony was that, given his condition, Devereux would find it almost homely[6]. We closed and locked the doors. One of the constables climbed onto the footplate[7] at the back and would remain standing there for the entire journey. So far[8], everything had gone according to plan.

We prepared to leave. Two more police officers took their places next to each other, sitting behind the horses at the front of the Black Maria. Meanwhile, Jones and I climbed into a curricle[9] that had been parked behind, Jones taking hold[10] of the reins. The other two constables would walk ahead in the road[11] ensuring that the way was clear[12]. Our progress would be slow but the distance was not great. More policemen, the same men who had been watching the legation, would be waiting for us at every corner[13]. It struck me that we resembled nothing so much as[14] a funeral procession. There were no mourners[15] standing in respectful silence, but we set off[16] with almost as much solemnity.

The legation disappeared behind us. Henry White was standing on the pavement, watching us go, his countenance grave[17]. Then he turned

1. bouclier
2. méthodiquement fouillé avant de partir
3. l'embarquâmes tout emmailloté
4. Aux yeux de tout autre
5. terrible
6. presque douillet
7. marchepied
8. Jusque-là
9. cabriolet
10. s'emparant
11. marcheraient à l'avant
12. pour s'assurer que la voie était dégagée
13. virage
14. Je songeai que le tout devait rappeler
15. proches endeuillés
16. nous mîmes en route
17. de son regard grave

and went back the way he had come. 'We've done it!' I said. I could not disguise my sense of relief[1]. 'The bloodiest[2] criminal who ever came to this country is in our custody and it is all thanks to[3] you and your genius with that book! Finally, it is over[4].'

'I am not so sure.'

'My dear Athelney – can you not rest[5] for one moment? I tell you, we have succeeded. *You* have succeeded! See – we are already well on our way[6].'

'And yet, I wonder—'

'What? You have your doubts even now?'

'They are more than doubts. It does not work. None of it works. Unless …[7]'

He stopped. Ahead of[8] us, the police constable was pulling at the reins. A boy pushing a barrow laden with[9] vegetables had turned across the street, blocking our path[10] because one of the wheels seemed to have got stuck in a rut[11]. Another policeman walked ahead to help clear the path.

The boy looked up[12]. It was Perry, dressed now in a ragged tunic and belt[13]. A moment before, his hands had been empty but suddenly he lifted them[14] and the surgeon's knife with which he had once threatened me was already there, glinting[15] in the sun. Without a word he brought it swinging round[16]. The second policeman fell in a welter[17] of blood. At the same moment, there was a shot – it sounded like a piece of paper being torn – and the officer who had been holding the reins of the Black Maria was hurled sideways, crashing down into[18] the road. A second shot and his companion followed. One of the horses reared up, knocking into[19] the other. A woman emerging from a shop

1. dissimuler mon soulagement
2. plus sanguinaire
3. entre nos mains et c'est entièrement grâce à
4. fini
5. souffler
6. sommes déjà bien avancés
7. Cela n'a pas de sens. À moins que…
8. Devant
9. charrette à bras chargée de
10. la voie
11. roues semblaient coincée dans une ornière
12. redressa la tête
13. d'une tunique en lambeaux avec une ceinture
14. se dressèrent soudain
15. m'avait déjà menacé, apparut aussitôt, scintillant
16. le fit tournoyer
17. marre
18. projeté sur le côté, s'écrasant sur
19. se cabra, heurtant

began to scream and scream. A carriage coming the other way veered onto[1] the pavement, almost hitting her, and crashed into a fence[2].

Athelney Jones had produced a gun. Against all the rules, he must have carried it into the legation and it had been in his pocket all along. He brought it up and aimed at the child[3].

I took out my own gun. Jones looked at me and I think I saw shock, dismay and finally resignation[4] pass through his eyes[5].

'I'm sorry,' I said, and shot him in the head.

1. vira de bord

2. alla finir sa course dans une barrière

3. mit l'enfant en joue

4. la stupeur, l'amertume, et finalement la résignation

5. se succéder dans ses yeux

TWENTY-ONE

The Truth of the Matter

1. que je me sois joué de vous

2. ne m'êtes pas particulièrement cher

3. me suis donné le plus grand mal pour éviter toute imposture

4. avoir tapé

5. dalle

6. Je n'ai fait que signaler, à juste titre d'ailleurs

7. étiquette

8. poignet

9. à présent

10. couverture

11. Pendant tout ce temps, j'ai veillé à être au plus juste

12. vous les ai dévoilés

13. qu'il se noyait

It would appear, my dear reader, that I have deceived you[1] – although, in truth, you are not very dear to me[2] and anyway, I have taken the greatest pains to avoid any deception at all[3]. That is to say, I have not lied. At least, I have not lied to *you*. It is perhaps a matter of interpretation but there is all the difference in the world, for example, between 'I am Frederick Chase' and 'Let me tell you that my name is Frederick Chase' which I remember typing[4] on the very first page. Did I say that the body on the slab[5] in Meiringen was James Moriarty? No. I merely stated, quite accurately[6], that it was the name written on the label[7] attached to the dead man's wrist[8] It should not have escaped your attention, by now[9], that I, your narrator, am Professor James Moriarty. Frederick Chase existed only in my imagination … and perhaps in yours. You should not be surprised. Which of the two names appeared on the front cover[10]?

All along, I have been scrupulously fair[11], if only for my own amusement. I have never described an emotion that I did not feel. Even my dreams I have made available to you[12]. (Would Frederick Chase have dreamed of drowning[13] in the Reichenbach Falls? I don't think so.) I have presented my thoughts and opinions exactly as they were. I did like[1] Athelney Jones and even tried to prevent him pursuing the case[2] when I learned he was married. I did think him a capable man – though obviously with limitations[3]. His attempts at disguise[4], for example, were ridiculous. When he presented himself dressed as a pirate or a fisherman on the day we set out for Blackball Basin, I not only recognised him, I had to work hard to prevent myself laughing out loud[5]. I have faithfully recorded[6] every spoken word, mine and others. I may have been forced to withhold[7] certain details from time to time, but I have added nothing extraneous[8]. An elaborate game, you might think, but I have found the business of writing a curiously tedious one[9] – all those hours spent pummelling away at a machine[10] that has proved unequal to the task of[11] eighty thousand two hundred and forty-six words (a peculiarity of mine,[12] the ability to count and to recall[13] the number of every word as I go[14]). Several of the keys have jammed[15] and the letter e is so faded as to be indecipherable[16]. One day, someone will have to type the whole thing again. My old adversary, Sherlock Holmes, was fortunate indeed to[17] have his Watson, the faithful chronicler of his adventures, but I could afford no such luxury[18]. I know that this will not be published in my lifetime, if at all[19]. Such is the nature of my profession.

I must explain myself. We have travelled thus far[20] together and we must come to an understanding before we go our separate ways[21]. I am tired. I feel I have written enough already but

1. éprouvais un attachement sincère pour
2. le dissuader de poursuivre l'enquête
3. quoiqu'il ait eu, de toute évidence, ses limites
4. tentatives de travestissement
5. prendre sur moi pour ne pas éclater de rire
6. fidèlement retranscrit
7. omettre
8. qui ne soit superflu
9. l'acte d'écriture étrangement laborieux
10. occupées à taper sur une machine
11. qui s'est révélée incapable de taper
12. c'est l'une de mes particularités
13. de mémoriser
14. au fur et à mesure
15. touches se sont coincées
16. effacée au point d'être indéchiffrable
17. pouvait s'estimer heureux d'
18. pas me permettre ce luxe
19. de mon vivant, voire jamais
20. jusque-ici
21. réussir à s'entendre avant que nos chemins se séparent

even so it is necessary to go back to the start – indeed, even further than that – to put everything into perspective. I am reminded of the Gestalt theory[1] proposed by Christian von Ehrenfels in his fascinating volume, *Über Gestaltqualitäten* – I was reading it, as it happens, on the train to Meiringen – which questions the relationship between the brain and the eye. There is an optical illusion that has become popular. You think you are seeing a candlestick[2]. Then, on closer examination, you perceive that it is in fact two people facing each other. This has, in some ways, been a similar exercise[3] though hardly quite so trivial[4].

Why was I in Meiringen? Why was it necessary to fake[5] my own death? Why did I meet with Inspector Athelney Jones and become his travelling companion and friend? Well, let me turn on the electric light and pour another brandy[6]. Now. I am ready.

I was the Napoleon of crime. It was Sherlock Holmes who first called me that and I will be immodest enough to[7] admit that I was rather pleased[8] by the description. Unfortunately, as the year of 1890 drew to its close[9] I had no idea that my exile on St Helena was about to begin. The few scant[10] details that he relates about my life are essentially correct and it is not my intention to expand on them[11] very much here. I was indeed one of two boys – twins – born to a respectable family in the town of Ballinasloe, County Galway. My father was a barrister[12] but when I was eleven or twelve years old he became involved with the Irish Republican Brotherhood[13] and, knowing the danger into which this might place him, determined[14] that my brother and I should be sent to

1. [gestaltisme : vision globale des perceptions en psychologie]
2. chandelier
3. Ce fut un exercice similaire à celui-ci, en quelque sorte,
4. quoiqu'un peu moins vain.
5. mettre en scène
6. me servir un autre Cognac
7. serai immodeste au point d'
8. ravi
9. touchait à sa fin
10. quelques rares
11. de m'y attarder
12. avocat
13. [mouvement révolutionnaire irlandais fondé en 1858]
14. décida

England to complete our education. I found myself[1] at Hall's Academy in Waddington where I excelled at astronomy and mathematics. From there I went to Queen's College, Cork, where I studied under the great George Boole[2] and it was with his guidance[3] that, at the age of twenty-one, I published the treatise on Binomial Theorem[4] which, I am proud to say, caused quite a stir across[5] Europe. As a result, I was offered[6] the Mathematical Chair of a university, which was the scene of a great scandal that was to change the course of my life. I do not intend to elucidate[7] on the precise nature of that scandal, but I will admit that I am not proud of what took place. Although my brother stood by me[8], neither of my parents ever spoke to me again.

But the man had hereditary tendencies of the most diabolical kind[9]. A criminal strain ran in his blood ...[10]

That was what Holmes – or Watson – wrote but they were quite wrong and my parents would have been mortified had they read it[11]. They were, as I have said, respectable people, and there was never a hint of misconduct in my long family tree[12]. My readers may find it hard to accept that an ordinary teacher might decide, quite deliberately, to break out into[13] a criminal career, but such I assure you was the case. At the time, I was working as a private tutor[14] in Woolwich, and although it is true that a number of my students were cadets from the Royal Military Academy which was close by, I was not quite the 'army coach' that has been stated[15]. One of these, a pleasant, hard-working man by the name of Roger Pilgrim, had first accrued gambling debts[16] and had thence fallen

1. me retrouvai
2. [mathématicien et logicien anglais du XIXe siècle]
3. sous son égide
4. traité sur le Binôme de Newton
5. fit grand bruit dans toute
6. on me proposa
7. ne compte pas en dire plus
8. m'ait soutenu
9. des plus diaboliques
10. instinct criminel coulait dans ses veines...
11. s'en seraient trouvés mortifiés s'ils l'avaient lu
12. moindre écart de conduite aussi loin que remonte ma lignée
13. de son propre chef, de se lancer dans
14. précepteur
15. en rien le « répétiteur de l'armée » que l'on a prétendu
16. accumulé les dettes de jeu

in with a group of swells[1]. He came to me one evening in great distress. It was not the police that he feared – his own gang had turned on him over[2] a small sum of money which they believed he owed[3] and Pilgrim quite seriously believed he would be torn limb from limb[4]. I agreed, somewhat reluctantly, to intercede on his behalf[5].

It was then that I made the discovery that was to change my life a second time, viz., that the criminal underclass[6] – the thieves, burglars, counterfeiters and conmen who were the plague of[7] London – were all unremittingly[8] stupid. I thought I would be afraid of them. As things turned out,[9] I would have felt more anxiety walking through a field of sheep. I saw at once that what they lacked, crucially, was[10] organisation and that as a mathematician I was ideally suited to the task[11]. If I could bring the same discipline to their nefarious activities that I could to[12] binomial coefficients I would create a force that could take on[13] the world. I will confess that although it was the intellectual challenge that first interested me, I was already thinking of personal profit for I was growing tired of living hand to mouth[14].

It took me a little over three years to achieve my goals and perhaps one day I will describe that process, although it is, frankly, unlikely. Apart from any other considerations, I have never been one to blow my own trumpet[15]. Anonymity has always been my watchword[16] – after all, how could the police pursue a man whose very existence was unknown to them[17]? I will merely[18] say that Roger Pilgrim stayed with me and provided the physical support – which is to say, the persuasion[19] – that was occasionally required although we very

1. s'était ainsi acoquiné avec une bande d'escrocs
2. s'était ligué contre lui au sujet d'
3. qu'il leur devait selon eux
4. découpé en morceaux
5. à contrecœur, d'intervenir pour son compte
6. à savoir, que le sous-prolétariat criminel
7. autres escrocs qui infestaient
8. irrémédiablement
9. Il s'avéra, en fait,
10. aussitôt qu'il manquait cruellement d'
11. fait pour cette tâche
12. agissements délétères qu'aux
13. dominer
14. car j'en avais assez de tirer le diable par la queue
15. du genre à chanter mes propres louanges
16. crédo
17. dont ils ignoraient jusqu'à l'existence
18. simplement
19. les moyens physiques, autrement dit la force de persuasion

seldom resorted to[1] violence. Not for us the heavy-handed[2] methods of Clarence Devereux and his gang. We became close friends. I was the best man[3] at his wedding and still remember the day his wife gave birth to their first child, Jonathan. And so, we arrive at the beginning.

As the year 1890 drew to a close[4], I was very comfortable and confident that my career would continue to thrive[5]. There was not a felon[6] in London who did not work for me. There had, inevitably, been bloodshed along the way[7] but things had settled down[8] and all that was behind me. Even the meanest and most feeble-minded criminals had come to appreciate that they were better off[9] working under my protection. Yes, I took a goodly share of their profits but I was always there when circumstances turned against them, readily paying for their bail or defence[10]. I could also be very useful. A cracksman searching for a fence?[11] A swindler desirous of a false referee?[12] I brought them together, opening doors in more than one sense.

There was, of course, Sherlock Holmes. The world's greatest consultant detective could not fail to come to[13] my attention but curiously I never gave him much thought[14]. Did I have anything to do with the absurd Musgrave ritual[15] or the equally unlikely Sign of Four[16]? What did I care about the marriage of Lord St Simon[17] or that trivial scandal in Bohemia[18]? I know Watson would have you think[19] that we were great adversaries. Well, it helped his sales. But the fact was that we were operating in quite separate fields of activity and, but for a single occurrence, we might never have met.

1. nous ne recourions qu'en de rares occasions à la
2. brutales
3. témoin
4. touchait à sa fin
5. prospérer
6. criminel
7. Au gré de mon ascension, le sang avait inévitablement coulé
8. s'étaient tassées
9. qu'il était dans leur intérêt de
10. payant aussitôt leur caution ou leur avocat
11. Un cambrioleur cherchait un receleur ?
12. Un escroc désirait une référence inventée de toutes pièces ?
13. était destiné à attirer
14. ne lui ai jamais accordé beaucoup d'importance
15. [« Le Rituel des Musgrave », Arthur Conan Doyle]
16. [« Le Signe des quatre »]
17. [« Un Aristocrate célibataire »]
18. [« Un Scandale en Bohême »]
19. aimait vous laisser croire

That occurrence was the arrival of Clarence Devereux and his entourage – Edgar and Leland Mortlake and Scotchy Lavelle. Everything that I told Athelney Jones about them was true. They were vicious criminals who had enjoyed spectacular success in America. What was not true, however, was my assertion that they intended to[1] join forces with me. Quite the contrary, they came to England to stamp me out, to take over[2] my criminal empire, and in the months that followed, they acted with a speed and violence that took me quite by surprise. Using the foulest[3] methods, they turned my followers against me. Anyone who protested, they killed – always bloodily[4], as a warning to everyone else. They also used police informers against me, feeding[5] information both to Scotland Yard and to Holmes so that I found myself fighting a war on three fronts. So much for honour among thieves![6] Perhaps I had become over-confident.[7] Certainly I was unprepared. But I will say this much in my own defence: they were not gentlemen. They were Americans. They paid not the slightest attention to the rules of sportsmanship and civility[8] to which I had always deferred[9].

Well, I have already said that criminals are stupid. To that I should have added that they are also self-serving[10]. Very quickly, my associates realised which way the wind was blowing and 'fell in line'[11], as I believe the saying goes[12]. One by one, my closest advisors abandoned me. I cannot blame them[13]. I think, had I been in their shoes[14], I would have done the same. At any event[15], by the start of April I found myself, unbelievably[16], a fugitive. My one advantage was that Devereux

1. l'affirmation selon laquelle ils comptaient
2. me rayer de la carte, prendre le contrôle de
3. les plus viles
4. avec de grandes effusions de sang
5. fournissant des
6. Oublié, le code des voleurs !
7. Sans doute étais-je devenu présomptueux.
8. n'avaient que faire du fair-play ou même du civisme
9. auxquels je me suis toujours astreint
10. ne servent que leurs propres intérêts
11. que le vent tournait, et se sont mis au garde-à-vous
12. comme on dit
13. leur en vouloir
14. si j'avais été à leur place
15. Quoiqu'il en soit
16. contre toute attente

had no idea what I looked like[1] and could not find me. He would have killed me if he had.

At this point[2], I had just three close allies[3]. All of them have already appeared in this narrative.

Peregrine, Percy or Perry was perhaps the most remarkable of the three. Although almost impossible to believe, he had begun life as the youngest son of the Duke of Lomond and would have been entitled to a comfortable, even a cosseted, life[4] had he not taken violent exception to[5] the private school in Edinburgh where he had been sent at the age of seven. The place was run[6] by Jesuits who gave their students the Bible and the birch in equal measure[7] and, after one week, Perry ran away and came south to London. His despairing parents began a nationwide search[8] and offered a huge reward for information as to his whereabouts[9], but a boy who is determined not to be found will not be, and Perry disappeared cheerfully[10] into the metropolis, sleeping under arches[11] and in doorways in the company of the thousands of other children who somehow managed to scratch a living[12] in the capital. For a short while – and there is a certain irony in this – he was a member of the Baker Street Irregulars[13], the gang of street urchins who attended upon[14] Sherlock Holmes, but the wages were derisory[15] and anyway, Perry had quickly discovered that he preferred crime. I am deeply fond of him[16] but I will admit that there is something quite disturbing[17] about him, perhaps a result of cross-breeding[18] within the Lomond family. By the time I met him, he was eleven years old and had already, to my knowledge, killed at least twice. He killed more frequently after I had taken him into my

1. à quoi je ressemblais
2. À ce moment-là
3. alliés
4. hérité d'une vie d'aise et de gâteries
5. s'il n'avait pas violemment rejeté
6. Elle était dirigée
7. dispensaient des cours de religion tout autant que des punitions physiques à leurs élèves
8. lancèrent des recherches dans tout le pays
9. récompense contre toute information sur sa situation
10. gaiement
11. arcades
12. gagner leur croûte
13. Irréguliers de Baker Street
14. gamins des rues qui assistaient
15. gages étaient dérisoires
16. ai beaucoup d'affection pour lui
17. troublant
18. consanguinité

1. chose inévitable
2. soif de sang
3. potelé
4. goût des déguisements
5. s'immiscer
6. voie
7. vouait une haine à toutes
8. Nul besoin de s'attarder sur le
9. joueur, chasseur de gros gibiers
10. Cela ne cadrait simplement pas avec le personnage.
11. Bourru et sujet à des accès de rage incontrôlables ou presque, il est surprenant
12. grassement
13. à vrai dire
14. l'éliminait de la course
15. arme de prédilection
16. fusil à air comprimé avec silencieux
17. ingénieur
18. d'imaginer le rôle qu'il occupe dans ce récit
19. avions pris des chemins différents
20. lui avait choisi une retraite prématurée
21. riche

service – there was no preventing it[1] – and I must add, somewhat regretfully, that his bizarre blood-lust[2] could occasionally be useful to me. Nobody ever noticed Perry. He seemed to be nothing more than a blond, rather plump[3] child, and with his fondness for disguises[4] and theatricality he could inveigle himself[5] into any room, any situation. He found his métier[6] with me. I will not say that I became a second father to him – it would have been far too dangerous as Perry had a loathing of[7] authority figures and would gladly have murdered the first. But we were, in our own way, close.

I need write less about[8] Colonel Sebastian Moran. I have described him already and Dr Watson will provide any further information you may require. Educated at Eton and Oxford, a soldier, gambler, big-game hunter[9] and, above all, sniper, Moran was my first lieutenant for many years. We were never friends. That simply was not his way.[10] Gruff in manner and prone to almost uncontrollable fits of rage, the wonder is[11] that he stayed with me for as long as he did and, in truth, he only did so because I paid him handsomely[12]. He would never have joined Devereux for he had a strong antipathy towards Americans – indeed[13], to many foreigners — and that marked him out[14] from the start. If I remind you that his weapon of choice[15] was a silenced airgun[16], invented by the German mechanic[17] Leopold Von Herder, you will perhaps be able to work out his role in this tale[18].

Finally, I come to Jonathan Pilgrim, the son of my old student, Roger. His father and I had gone our separate ways[19] – he to an early retirement[20] in Brighton. He had become a wealthy[21] man during his time with me and his wife had been afraid for him from the start, so I was hardly surprised and only a little saddened[1] when he begged leave to part from me[2]. There are all too few[3] friends in the life of a master criminal, too few people one can trust, and he was both[4]. However, we corresponded occasionally[5] and sixteen years later he sent me his son who had grown up as wayward[6] as his father had once been. Quite what his mother made of this strange apprenticeship[7] I will never know but Roger had recognised that Jonathan would turn to crime with or without me and had decided that with me was the better option[8]. He was an extraordinarily good-looking[9] boy with a freshness and an openness that one could not help but like[10], and to this day[11] I regret the fact that, in my desperation[12], I allowed him to infiltrate Devereux's inner circle[13]. Everything that you have read in this narrative, everything I have done, began with his murder.

Never has a man felt more alone than I, when I came across Jonathan's body in Highgate, where we had arranged to meet so that he could provide me with whatever fresh information he had gathered[14]. The manner of his death, the way he had been bound[15] and then executed, disgusted me. As I knelt beside him, with tears streaming[16] from my eyes, I knew that Clarence Devereux had outmanoeuvred me and that this was as low as my fortunes could fall[17]. I was finished. I could flee the country. I could do away with myself.[18] I could not endure any more.

I gave way to this foolishness[19] for perhaps five seconds. It was replaced by a fury and a thirst for revenge[20] that entirely consumed me– and it was at that exact moment that a plan formed in

1. attristé
2. me pria de le congédier
3. Rares sont les
4. or il était les deux pour moi
5. nous écrivions de temps en temps
6. était devenu, en grandissant, aussi indocile
7. Ce que sa mère pensa de ce curieux apprentissage
8. qu'à mes côtés, l'option lui paraissait plus sûre
9. beau
10. auxquelles on ne pouvait que s'attacher
11. aujourd'hui encore
12. en désespoir de cause
13. le cercle proche
14. recueillies
15. Sa mise à mort, le fait qu'on l'avait attaché
16. m'agenouillai devant son cadavre, des larmes déferlant
17. déjoué mes plans, et que je ne pourrais pas tomber plus bas
18. Il ne me restait plus qu'à fuir le pays. Qu'à en finir.
19. me suis laissé aller à ces niaiseries
20. soif de vengeance

my head so daring and unexpected[1] that I was certain it must succeed[2]. You must remember my circumstances. I had Colonel Moran and I had the boy, but apart from them there was nobody I could call upon for help[3] and the three of us were hopelessly outnumbered[4]. All my former associates had been turned against me. Worse still[5], I had no way of finding Clarence Devereux for, like me, he had never revealed himself. Thanks to[6] Pilgrim, I had learned about the Mortlakes and their club, the Bostonian. I knew, however, that none of the gang would ever betray[7] their leader to me. Pilgrim had also directed me to Scotchy Lavelle who lived close to where the body had been found but he was an extremely cautious[8] man. His house was like a fortress. It might be possible to kill him but I needed to reach him, to get from him the information that would allow me to bring down[9] the rest of the gang.

Suppose, then, that I were to draw[10] Scotland Yard and all its resources to my cause? Was it possible that I could somehow use them to defeat my enemy, working as it were from inside with neither party aware of[11] who I was? The greatest mathematical insights – the diagonal argument[12], for example, or the theory of ordinary points[13] – have always come in a flash[14]. So it was with my idea.[15] I would have to die in a way that was memorable and unarguable but then I would return, in another guise[16]. I would both use the Metropolitan Police to do my work for me and conceal myself within them[17], seizing any opportunity that came my way. Clearly I could not pretend to be a detective myself. It would be too easy to check my credentials[18]. But suppose I had

1. si audacieux et inattendu
2. de son succès
3. dont je pouvais attendre de l'aide
4. désespérément en sous-nombre
5. Pire encore
6. Grâce à
7. ne trahirait
8. prudent
9. d'anéantir
10. que je parvienne à rallier
11. infiltré comme je l'étais sans qu'aucun des partis ne sache
12. découvertes mathématiques – l'argument de la diagonale
13. théorie des équations différentielles ordinaires
14. ont toujours surgi comme des éclairs
15. Il en fut de même pour ce plan.
16. incontestable, pour mieux revenir sous une fausse identité
17. me fondrais dans ses rangs, guettant la moindre opportunité
18. références

come from far away? Almost at once my thoughts turned to[1] the Pinkerton Agency in New York. It made complete sense[2] that they would have followed Devereux and the others to England. At the same time, the well-known lack[3] of co-operation between the two agencies would play into my hands[4]. If I presented myself with the right documents and files, surely no one would suspect me or question my right to be there[5]?

First, I placed certain papers – including the address of the Bostonian – in Jonathan Pilgrim's pockets. They were there for the police to find. Next, I prepared to die. It almost amused me to rope Sherlock Holmes into my scheme[6] but who better to help me take my last bow on the stage[7]? Holmes was almost certainly unaware that he had been helped in his investigations by Clarence Devereux. Three times – in January, February and March – he had crossed my path and had, I knew, prepared extensive notes on my affairs which he would eventually deliver[8] to the police. At the end of April, I called on him at his rooms in[9] Baker Street. My one fear was that he would have learned how desperate things had become for me[10] and how little power I really had, but fortunately this was not the case. He accepted me for what I pretended to be, a vengeful and dangerous foe[11], determined to have him removed from the scene[12].

I should also mention that I had taken some elementary precautions before I risked meeting[13] Holmes face to face and I am surprised that he did not perceive this for he knew how important to me my anonymity had always been[14]. A wig, a little whitening, hunched shoulders[15] and shoes designed to give me extra height[16] … Holmes was

1. immédiatement me vint en tête
2. serait tout à fait logique
3. légendaire absence
4. en ma faveur
5. se demanderait si j'étais dans mon bon droit
6. d'entraîner Sherlock Holmes dans mon intrigue
7. qui mieux que lui pouvait m'aider à tirer ma révérence
8. qu'il livrerait ensuite
9. lui rendis visite dans son appartement de
10. la précarité de ma situation
11. redoutable adversaire assoiffé de vengeance
12. à l'éliminer
13. de me risquer à rencontrer
14. car il ne pouvait ignorer quel cas je faisais de mon anonymat
15. perruque, le visage poudré, le dos voûté
16. me grandir de quelques centimètres

not the only master of disguise and it delights me[1] that the description of me which he gave to Watson – 'extremely tall and thin, his forehead domes out in a white curve[2]' – was entirely inaccurate[3]. I could not know then how things would play out[4] and it has always been my habit to prepare for every eventuality.

I do not need to repeat our words. Dr Watson has got there first.[5] I will simply say that, by the end of our conversation, Holmes was in fear of his life and that I followed it up[6] with several attacks upon him– all of them designed to frighten, not to kill.

Holmes did exactly as I hoped. He sent Inspector Patterson a list of my former[7] colleagues, not knowing that they were all, by now, employed by Devereux, then fled to the Continent[8]. Along with[9] Perry and Colonel Moran, I followed, waiting for the opportunity to put the first climax of my scheme into action[10]. It came at Meiringen, at the Reichenbach Falls.

I guessed that Holmes would have to visit that dreadful place[11]. It was in his nature. No tourist, not even a man in fear of his life, could pass by without gazing down at the rushing waters[12]. I made my way there ahead of him, walked the narrow path[13] and knew at once that I had the setting I required[14]. It would be perilous. Of that there could be no doubt. But I like to think that only a mathematician could survive what might seem to be a suicidal plunge[15] into the rapids. Who else could so carefully calculate all the necessary angles, the volume of the water plunging down[16], the exact speed of descent and the odds of not drowning or being smashed to pieces[17]?

1. je me délecte
2. le front bombé formant une courbe pâle
3. erronée
4. tourneraient
5. ce qui s'y est dit. Le Dr. Watson l'a fait le premier.
6. craignait pour sa vie, et que j'ai confirmé ses craintes
7. anciens
8. puis se réfugia sur le continent
9. Escorté de
10. d'exécuter le premier temps fort de mon intrigue
11. visiterait forcément cet horrible endroit
12. ne passerait par là sans admirer la cascade rugissante
13. le devançai sur l'étroit sentier
14. su immédiatement que j'avais là le décor idéal
15. à ce qui aurait tout l'air d'un plongeon suicidaire
16. qui s'y jette
17. la probabilité de ne pas se noyer ou s'écraser sur les rochers

The next day, when Holmes and Watson set out[1] from the Englischer Hof, everything was in place. Colonel Moran was concealed, high above the falls[2], a necessary safeguard should anything go amiss[3]. Perry, who had perhaps thrown himself too strenuously into the part[4], was disguised as a Swiss lad[5]. I myself was waiting on the shoulder[6] of the hill nearby. Holmes and Watson arrived and Perry produced the letter, supposedly written by the landlord, summoning Watson back[7] to the hotel. Holmes was left alone. It was at this point that I presented myself and the rest, one might say, is history[8].

The two of us exchanged words. We prepared for the end. Do not think for a minute that I was entirely sanguine about the[9] chances of my success. The water was pouring down ferociously and there were jagged[10] rocks all around. Had there been any alternative[11], I would gladly have considered it. But I must seem dead, and with that in mind I naturally permitted Holmes to write his letter of farewell[12]. I was a little surprised that he felt a need to record what was going to happen[13] but then I had no idea that we were both, in fact, preparing to fake our own deaths[14], a situation which in retrospect strikes me as slightly[15] bizarre. However, it was his testimony that I most needed and I watched him leave the note close to his alpenstock[16] before we squared off and began to grapple like a pair of wrestlers[17] at the London Athletic. This was, for me, the most disagreeable part of the experience for I have never been fond of human contact and Holmes reeked of[18] tobacco. I was really quite grateful when he

1. se mirent en route
2. caché, en amont des chutes
3. indispensable garde-fou si quelque chose tournait mal
4. s'était sans doute un peu trop investi dans son rôle
5. jeune garçon
6. contrefort
7. exhortant Watson à rentrer
8. si l'on peut dire, est entré dans l'Histoire
9. confiant quant à
10. à vif éparpillés
11. Si une autre alternative s'était offerte à moi
12. d'adieu
13. consigner ce qui était sur le point d'arriver
14. mettre en scène notre propre mort
15. m'apparaît pour le moins
16. [bâton d'escalade]
17. de nous mettre en garde et nous empoigner tels deux lutteurs
18. Holmes empestait le

brought his bartitsu skills to the fore[1] and threw me over the edge[2].

It nearly killed me. Such a strange and horrible experience to be plummeting endlessly as if out of the sky and yet to be[3] surrounded by water, barely able to breathe. I was blind. The howl[4] of the water was in my ears. Although I had worked out[5] exactly how many seconds it would take me to reach the bottom, I seemed to hang there for an eternity. I was vaguely aware of the rocks rushing towards me and actually touched them with one leg, although very lightly, for otherwise I would have shattered the bone[6]. Finally, I plunged into the freezing water, all the air was punched out of me and I was swirling, turning[7], almost being reborn in a sort of life after death. Somewhere within me I realised that I had survived but could not break[8] surface in case Holmes was watching. I had instructed Colonel Moran to keep him busy, to distract his attention by hurling small boulders[9] in his direction, and it was while this was happening that I swam to the shore and crawled out[10], shivering and exhausted, into a place of concealment[11].

How strange – indeed, how almost laughable[12] – it is that both Holmes and I used the same incident to make our disappearance from the world; I, for the reasons I have described, and he[13] …? Well, there is no satisfactory answer to that. It is clear though that Holmes had an agenda of his own[14], that he wished to hide away for the three years that came to be known as 'the great hiatus', and it was a constant worry to me that he would turn up again[15] for I, almost alone in the world, knew[16] that he had survived. I even sus-

1. reconnaissant quand il déploya sa maîtrise du bartitsu [art martial mixte né en Angleterre à la fin du XIXe siècle]
2. me poussa dans le vide
3. chuter sans fin comme si vous tombiez du ciel, tout en étant
4. grondement
5. calculé
6. mais à peine, sinon l'os se serait brisé
7. expulsé de mes poumons et je tourbillonnais, tournoyais
8. remonter à la
9. faisant rouler des petits rochers
10. rive, où je me hissai à bout de bras, frissonnant et éreinté
11. avant de trouver une cachette
12. risible
13. quant à lui
14. une raison bien à lui
15. je craignais sans répit qu'il ne refasse surface
16. car j'étais le seul au monde, ou presque, à savoir

pected for a while that he might have taken the room next to mine at Hexam's Hotel and that it was he whom I heard coughing[1] in the darkness. Where did he go during this time and what did he do when he got there? I neither know nor care.[2] The important thing was that he did not interfere with my plans and I was very relieved not to see him again.

All that was required[3] now was a body to take my place, the final proof of what had occurred. I had already prepared one. That very morning I had come across a local man[4] returning from the village of Rosenlaui. I had taken him for a labourer or a shepherd but in fact he turned out to be[5] Franz Hirzel, the chef[6] of the Englischer Hof. He vaguely resembled me in age and in his general physical appearance and it was with some regret that I murdered him. I have never enjoyed taking a life, particularly when the person concerned is an innocent bystander[7], as Hirzel undoubtedly was. My needs, however, were too great for any scruples.[8] Perry and I dressed him in clothes similar to the ones I was wearing, complete with a silver pocket watch[9]. I had myself sewn[10] the secret pocket containing the coded letter which I had written in London. Now I dumped him in the water and hurried away[11].

If Athelney Jones had thought about it for one moment, it would have been extremely unlikely[12] that Clarence Devereux would write a formal letter inviting Professor James Moriarty to a meeting. Word of mouth[13] would have been safer – and why go to the trouble of[14] inventing such a peculiar code? He might also have asked why Moriarty should have felt compelled[15] to carry the

1. tousser
2. Je l'ignore et ne m'en porte pas plus mal.
3. ce qui me manquait
4. j'avais justement croisé un homme du coin
5. ouvrier ou un berger, mais il n'était autre que
6. cuisinier
7. simple spectateur qui n'a rien à se reprocher
8. pour me permettre d'avoir des scrupules
9. jusqu'à la montre gousset en argent
10. cousu
11. le jetai à l'eau avant de décamper
12. il aurait jugé extrêmement peu probable
13. Faire passer le message à l'oral
14. s'astreindre à
15. s'était senti obligé

1. s'était embêté à la coudre

2. que je semais

3. pour les attirer dans mon stratagème

4. m'avait jusqu'ici boudé, s'était enfin ralliée à ma cause

5. et en même temps si obtus, si confiant

6. qui a causé sa perte

7. fut entre mes mains une simple marionnette, semblable au

8. que j'avais disséminés à dessein

9. prêteur sur gages

10. gilet

11. laissé en évidence, les étiquettes sur mon bagage

12. Sur le reste, il s'est grossièrement mépris.

13. traversée de l'Atlantique

14. les besoins du rôle

15. manches usées ne révélaient rien du tout

16. comme il le fallait

letter with him all the way to Switzerland, why he had bothered sewing it[1] into his jacket. It was all extremely unlikely, but it was the first of a series of clues that I was laying[2] for the British police, to draw them into my scheme[3].

From the moment I met Inspector Jones, I knew that providence, which had for so long turned against me, was finally on my side[4]. It would have been impossible for Scotland Yard to have chosen a better representative for the task I had in mind. Jones was so brilliant in so many ways, so obtuse in others, so trusting[5], so naïve. When his wife told me his story, his strange obsession with Sherlock Holmes, I could hardly believe my luck. To the very end he was completely malleable – and that was his misfortune[6]. He was as much a puppet in my hands as the[7] toy policeman he had purchased for his daughter on the way home.

Take that first meeting in the police station at Meiringen. He picked up every clue that I had deliberately laid out[8] for whatever detective might arrive: the Pinkerton's watch (purchased, in fact, from a pawnbroker[9] in Shoreditch), the false American accent, the waistcoat[10], the newspaper brought from Southampton and prominently displayed, the labels on my case[11]. As to the rest of it, he was hopelessly wrong.[12] I had cut myself shaving in the poor light of a Paris hotel, not on a transatlantic crossing[13]. The clothes I was wearing had been purchased deliberately for the masquerade[14] and did not in fact belong to me, so the smell of cigarettes and the worn-out sleeve were completely irrelevant[15]. But he made his deductions and I was suitably[16] impressed. For him to believe in me[1], I had to make him think that I believed in him.

I told him about the letter and urged him on[2] until he examined the chef's body for a second time and found it. Using an extract from A Study in Scarlet[3] was perhaps over-theatrical but at the time it amused me and I thought it might distract from[4] the other improbabilities I have already described. I was impressed by the speed with which Jones deciphered[5] the letter – of course I would have been ready to help had he not been up to the task[6] – but in fact the code had been constructed in a way that made it fairly simple to crack[7]: the quite unnecessary insertion of the word MORIARTY made the process straightforward[8].

And so to the Café Royal. It was as if I had set out a series of stepping stones[9] – the letter, the meeting, Bladeston House – each one leading to the next, and it was my task only to make the necessary connections. Perry arrived, dressed as a telegraph boy and pretending to be an emissary of Clarence Devereux. We acted out a scene that we had already rehearsed[10] and he hurried out, but not too quickly, allowing Jones to follow. The bright blue jacket was quite deliberate[11], by the way. It ensured that Perry did not get lost in the crowd[12]. For the same reason, he sat on the roof[13] of the omnibus to Highgate rather than inside it. He did not enter Bladeston House. At the last moment, he hurried round the back, stripped off his blue jacket and lay on it,[14] concealed behind a nearby shrub[15]. Having lost sight of him, Jones assumed[16] he must have gone in through the garden gate. Why would he have done otherwise?[17]

1. Pour qu'il croit à mon histoire
2. le tannais
3. Une Étude en rouge
4. cela détournerait son attention
5. décrypta
6. s'il ne s'était pas montré à la hauteur
7. qui le rendait assez simple à déchiffrer
8. évident
9. disposé des pierres de gué
10. avons joué une scène que nous avions répétée ensemble
11. veste bleu vif n'avait pas été choisie au hasard
12. foule
13. plate-forme
14. en fit le tour, retira sa veste bleue pour s'allonger dessus,
15. dissimulé par un arbuste à proximité
16. Comme il l'avait perdu de vue, Jones se dit
17. Comment aurait-il pu soupçonner autre chose ?

1. en prise avec
2. domestique
3. d'en évaluer les
4. Ça vous démange de fouiner partout, hein ?
5. Et comment !
6. loquet
7. verrou afin de savoir précisément où percer
8. me suis montré honnête envers vous
9. Ce que j'ai omis
10. verser un puissant opiacé
11. crochetâmes le verrou et perçâmes le portail
12. me laissa entrer
13. nous mîmes au travail

Scotchy Lavelle would never have invited me into his home but the following day, confronted by[1] a detective from Scotland Yard, he had no choice. We got past the manservant[2], Clayton, and met with Lavelle himself and though the two of us, Jones and I, seemed to have a common purpose, in fact we were diametrically opposed. He was enquiring about crimes of the recent past. I was preparing a crime that would take place in the immediate future. For, being inside Bladeston House, I was able to take stock of its[3] defences.

'Want to nosey around, do you?[4]' Lavelle asked.

I most certainly did.[5] It was I who insisted on visiting the kitchen and continued from there down to the garden gate. I needed to see the metal hasp[6]. Again, how fortunate to be a mathematician with a precise eye for measurements. I made a mental image of the position of the second lock so I would know where to drill[7] when I returned. And once again, I played fair with you[8], my reader. I stated that I was the first to re-enter the kitchen and that I was briefly alone. What I failed[9] to mention was that it gave me time to slip a strong opiate[10] into the curry that would be served for dinner. Everything was now set for the next stage of my plan.

I returned just after eleven o'clock with Perry, who loved this sort of adventure. We picked the lock and drilled through[11] the gate, then Perry climbed up to the second floor. Jones was right about that. We made no noise but we were reasonably confident that we would not be disturbed. Perry let me in[12] through the kitchen door – I had told him where he would find the key – and then we set to work[13].

I am not proud of what took place that night. I am not a monster, but circumstances had compelled me[1] to do monstrous things. First we silenced[2] Clayton, the kitchen boy, the cook and the American mistress of Scotchy Lavelle. Why did they have to die? Simply because, had they been interrogated the following day, they would all have sworn[3] that the telegraph boy never entered the house and, with nothing to lose, they might have been believed. If so, the entire scheme would have unravelled[4] and I could not afford to take the chance. Perry committed[5] three of the murders and I rather fear that he enjoyed them. I myself smothered[6] Henrietta and then carried Lavelle downstairs, still deeply asleep. I tied him[7] to a chair and woke him with cold water. Then I inflicted a great deal of pain on him[8]. It was a disagreeable business but at that stage I did not know where Clarence Devereux could be found. Nor did I know[9] what he was planning. To give him his due[10], Lavelle was courageous and resisted for quite some time, but no man can withstand the torment of a smashed knee[11] when it is manipulated[12] and from him I learned of the robbery that was about to take place in Chancery Lane. Lavelle also told me that Devereux was to be found in the American legation, but he did so with a certain bravado[13], for in his mind his master was out of my reach[14]. I could not break into the legation and Devereux never emerged. I saw at once that, with his agoraphobia, my enemy was a true snail within a shell[15]. How could I possibly winkle him out[16]?

I let Perry cut Lavelle's throat – give the boy a treat[17] – and we left together. But first I wrote the

1. m'avaient contraint

2. avons réduit au silence

3. juré

4. Faute de quoi, c'est toute mon intrigue qui se serait délitée

5. s'est chargé de

6. ai moi-même étouffé

7. l'ai attaché

8. lui ai infligé pas mal de souffrance

9. J'ignorais tout autant

10. Pour être honnête

11. endurer la torture que représente un genou brisé

12. que l'on triture

13. non sans une certaine fanfaronnade

14. hors de ma portée

15. escargot caché dans sa coquille

16. l'appâter à découvert

17. histoire de le laisser s'amuser un peu

entry in the diary for Jones to find[1] the next day: HORNER 13. Just in case the clue was not obvious enough, I placed a bar of shaving soap in the same drawer; an odd item for a man to have in his desk[2], you might think, but I hoped it would put Jones in mind of barber's shops[3]. I also left the invitation to the party at the American legation somewhere he would see it.

The horrible murders at Bladeston House were enough to galvanise Scotland Yard into action[4]. With all the single-minded determination that I had come to recognise in[5] the British police, they decided to set up[6] a meeting and talk about it. Even so, I was pleased when Jones told me that I was to be included. My one great concern[7] was that Jones, or one of his colleagues, would decide to contact the Pinkerton Agency in New York, in which event I would be exposed at once as a fraud[8]. It was for this reason that I asked about the telegraph room. It would take days to send a message abroad and perhaps days for the reply but that still left me with a sense of unease[9] and little enough time to bring my plans to fruition[10]. Then, when Inspector Lestrade insisted on contacting the agency personally, I decided I would have to take action. Before I left the building, I knew exactly what I had to do.

It was I, of course, who ordered the attack on Scotland Yard the following day. Although everything I subsequently said was designed[11] to make Jones believe that he was the intended[12] victim of the explosion, it was in fact the telegraph room – a fortunate coincidence that it was next to his office[13] – that was the real target, ensuring that Lestrade's irritating message[14] would not be sent

1. l'entrée dans l'agenda que Jones trouverait
2. le dernier objet que l'on s'attend à trouver dans un bureau
3. mettrait Jones sur la piste d'un barbier
4. exhorter la police londonienne à agir
5. Avec cette détermination obstinée que j'avais décelée chez
6. organiser
7. plus grande inquiétude
8. aussitôt démasqué
9. me chiffonnait malgré tout
10. pour exécuter mon plan
11. ai dit ensuite était destiné
12. visée
13. heureuse coïncidence qu'elle se trouve près de son bureau
14. pour m'assurer que le message contrariant de Lestrade

for some time to come[1]. Perry carried the bomb into the building while Colonel Moran waited for him in a brougham. Just before the explosion, I went through the charade of drawing attention to them[2], even risking my life beneath the wheels of an omnibus. It was important that Jones should see[3] that they had come in a brougham – I had chosen that type of carriage on purpose[4] – for I knew that he would use every means at his disposal to track it down[5]. Perry and Moran told the driver to take them to the American legation but, just as at Bladeston House, they did not in fact go in. It was enough that they had been close by.[6]

I was quite surprised that Jones so readily agreed to ignore the sanctity[7] of diplomatic immunity and to place his career at risk[8] by entering the legation in disguise, but by this time we were such close friends and he was so determined to find Clarence Devereux – particularly following the loss of life at Scotland Yard – that he would have done anything and it was he who unmasked Coleman De Vriess. I expressed the necessary amazement[9] but in fact had very quickly guessed as much myself[10].

From this point on, Jones took charge of the investigation and I had little to do but to follow[11], dutifully playing Watson to his Holmes[12]. We had visited the Bostonian together and it had been interesting for me to meet Leland Mortlake for the first time. However, the real advantage of the raid was that it had allowed me to plant yet another clue[13]. The Scotland Yard detectives had been singularly incapable of working out[14] what HORNER 13 meant, even when I had reminded them of the shaving soap and had suggested that

1. ne partirait pas de sitôt

2. noyai encore le poisson en attirant l'attention sur eux

3. remarque

4. véhicule à dessein

5. tous les moyens à sa disposition pour remonter jusqu'à lui

6. Il suffisait qu'ils s'en soient simplement approchés.

7. se résolve aussi facilement à violer l'intégrité

8. risquer sa carrière

9. ai feint un étonnement de circonstance,

10. en étais très rapidement arrivé à la même conclusion

11. il ne me restait plus qu'à le suivre

12. m'appliquant seulement à jouer les Dr. Watson

13. encore un indice

14. de deviner

it might refer to a druggist[1] or some similar establishment. No wonder Holmes so frequently walked all over them![2] I had therefore picked up an advertisement[3] for the barber's shop which I slipped[4] amongst the magazines in Pilgrim's room, even as I pretended[5] to examine them. Jones found it and once again the game, as he would have put it, was afoot[6].

His unravelling[7] of the Chancery Lane business was, I have to say, quite masterly, worthy[8] of the great detective himself, and I had no argument with the trap that he devised[9] at the Blackwall Basin. If only Devereux himself had come to inspect the plunder[10] that John Clay had supposedly removed from the Safe Deposit Company, how much more easily the whole thing would have ended. But he did not. Edgar Mortlake slipped through our[11] fingers and Devereux remained out of our reach[12]; I realised that he would need further goading,[13] another setback[14], before he would deliver himself into my hands[15].

The arrest of Leland Mortlake provided exactly that. It was a little sad, but not surprising, that Jones should leap to the conclusion that a blowpipe had been used[16], when the poisoned dart was discovered in the back of Leland's neck. He had, of course, been witness to a similar death, described by Watson in 'The Sign of the Four'. In fact, I had been carrying the dart all the time and simply slid it[17] into my victim's flesh as I steered him away from an overzealous waiter[18] when we were leaving the club. The tip was covered with anaesthetic ether[19] as well as strychnine, so he would have felt nothing. I would have liked him to suffer more. This was, after all, the man whose

1. cela fasse référence à une droguerie
2. Pas étonnant qu'Holmes leur ait si souvent volé la vedette !
3. à cette fin, récupéré une réclame
4. ai glissée
5. tandis que je feignais
6. comme il l'aurait dit lui-même, il se tramait quelque chose
7. résolution
8. des plus magistrales, digne
9. n'émis pas la moindre objection au piège qu'il avait imaginé
10. butin
11. nous a glissé entre les
12. hors d'atteinte
13. il faudrait encore davantage le contrarier,
14. se mettre en travers de son chemin
15. me tombe entre les mains
16. tire la conclusion hâtive qu'on s'était servi d'une sarbacane
17. la glissai
18. tandis que je l'éloignais d'un serveur trop zélé
19. d'éther au pouvoir anesthésiant

loathsome company Jonathan Pilgrim had been forced to endure[1]. But his death was a provocation, nothing more. And it most certainly worked.

I could not have foreseen that Devereux would respond by kidnapping[2] Jones's daughter. Even I would never have stooped so low[3], but then, as I have said, we played by different rules. What was I to do when Jones came to my hotel with the news? I saw at once that to accompany him would place me in the gravest danger but at the same time it was clear that the game was reaching its climax[4]. I had to be there. Once again, luck was on my side. Perry happened to be[5] in my hotel room. The two of us had been in conference[6] when Jones arrived. I was able to tell him of this latest[7] development and to make arrangements for my protection.

Both Perry and Colonel Moran were outside the Joneses' home, waiting in a hansom, when we left that night. You may recall that when I stepped into the street, I called out, as if I were addressing the kidnappers. In fact, my words were intended for[8] Moran, letting him know our destination and giving him time to reach it ahead of[9] us. So when we came to Dead Man's Walk, he was already there. He saw us knocked unconscious[10]. He and Perry followed us to Smithfield meat market and, although it was a close call[11], they managed to find us just when it mattered most[12]. It was when I was face to face with Devereux, by the way, that I came closest to being unmasked[13]. He had guessed that Jonathan Pilgrim had been working for me and that he was not a Pinkerton's man at all. He began to deny that he had ever written[14] the coded letter that had begun all this

1. dont Jonathan Pilgrim avait dû souffrir l'horrible compagnie
2. anticiper que sa réaction serait d'enlever
3. ne serais jamais tombé si bas
4. arrivait à son apogée
5. se trouvait justement
6. étions en pleine conversation
7. dernier
8. destinés à
9. avant
10. qu'on nous avait assommés
11. bien qu'il s'en soit fallu de peu
12. nous en avions le plus besoin
13. ai bien failli être démasqué
14. avoir jamais rédigé

and, had I not interrupted, the truth would surely have come out. I threw myself at Devereux for that simple reason – to bring any further discussion to an end[1] – even though it cost me the injuries that I subsequently received.

I am almost finished. Another drop of brandy and we will get there.[2] Now ... where was I?

All my efforts had been directed towards extracting[3] Clarence Devereux from the legation and when we arrived for our interview with Robert Lincoln, both Colonel Moran and Perry were already in place, one on a nearby rooftop[4], the other in the street, now disguised as a costermonger[5]. They have, all along, been superbly efficient[6]. It is true that Moran is interested only in the money that I pay him, while Perry is highly disreputable[7], an underage[8] sadist, but even so I could not have chosen two better companions.

And Jones! I think by the end he had actually guessed – perhaps not who I was, but certainly who I was not. All along he had been aware that something was wrong. His problem was, he simply couldn't work out[9] what it was. His wife had been right about him. He was not as clever as he thought and that was to be the undoing of him[10]. Ironically, she had been the wiser[11] of the two for she had mistrusted me[12] from our first meeting and even, at the very end, voiced her suspicions out loud[13]. I feel sorry for her and for her daughter, but there could be no alternative. Jones had to die. I pulled the trigger[14], but I wish even now that it could have ended another way[15].

He was a good man. I admired him. And although in the end I was forced to kill him, I will always think of him as my friend.

1. couper court à la discussion
2. Encore un doigt de Cognac et nous y serons.
3. avaient été mus par la volonté de faire sortir
4. toit
5. marchand des quatre-saisons
6. se sont montrés, de bout en bout, redoutablement efficaces
7. peu recommandable
8. mineur
9. n'arrivait pas à mettre le doigt sur
10. c'est ce qui a causé sa perte
11. plus maligne
12. s'était méfié de moi
13. a fait part de ses réserves à voix haute
14. ai appuyé sur la détente
15. en fût autrement

TWENTY-TWO

A Fresh Start[1]

I took out my own gun. Jones looked at me and I think I saw shock, dismay and finally resignation pass through his eyes.

'I'm sorry,' I said, and shot him in the head.

He was killed instantly, his body falling sideways[2] as his walking stick tumbled to the ground[3] one last time, rattling against the paving stones[4]. Everything had to happen very quickly for I knew that there were many Scotland Yard men nearby. I climbed down from the curricle[5] and walked the few steps to the Black Maria which had stopped in the middle of the road. Both the driver and his companion were dead. The constable who had been positioned at the rear was still clinging onto[6] the door as if it was his duty to keep it shut[7]. I shot him in the back and watched him crumple[8]. At the same moment, Colonel Moran fired[9] a third time and the policeman standing next to Perry spun round[10] and fell. I saw Perry scowl[11]. It was one less person for him to kill.

I climbed onto the Black Maria, pushing one of the dead men out of the way[12]. I was vaguely aware of pedestrians pointing[13] and screaming but of course none of them approached. They

1. Un nouveau départ
2. sur le côté
3. heurta le sol
4. claquant sur les pavés
5. fourgon
6. à l'arrière, se cramponnait encore à
7. la maintenir fermée
8. dos et le regardai s'écrouler
9. tira
10. tournoya
11. faire la grimace
12. qui était en travers de mon chemin
13. passants qui nous montraient du doigt

would have been mad to try[1] and I had counted on their fear and panic to give me time to make my escape. Perry hurried over, wiping his knife on a rag[2], and climbed up next to me.

'Can I drive?' he asked.

'Later,' I said.

I whipped[3] on the horses. They had already calmed down – but then the police would have trained them[4] to make their way through[5] noisy protests and hostile crowds. With Perry beside me, I directed them a few yards up Victoria Street, then pulled on the reins to force them into a tight turn[6]. This was another mistake that Athelney Jones had made. He had deployed his men along the route that would take us to Scotland Yard, but I had no intention of going that way. As we completed the turn[7], Colonel Moran appeared in a doorway, his face flushed[8], the Von Herder airgun already returned to the golfing bag[9] that he carried over his shoulder. He climbed onto the back of the Black Maria, as we had agreed[10].

Another crack of the whip and we were hurtling past[11] Victoria Station and down towards Chelsea. There were more crowds at this end of the street and they were aware that something had happened but could not tell what it was. Nobody tried to stand in[12] our way. We rattled over a pothole[13] and I heard Moran swear[14]. Part of me wondered if he would still be there when we reached our destination and I have to say it rather amused me to think of him being hurled off in one of the suburbs[15]. At the same time, I wondered what our passenger must be thinking. He would have heard the shots[16]. He would have felt the carriage turn[17]. It was quite likely that he had

1. le faire
2. accourut, essuyant son couteau sur un chiffon
3. J'abattis mon fouet
4. la police les avaient sûrement entraînés
5. à se frayer un chemin parmi
6. à prendre un virage serré
7. Après le tournant
8. dans une porte cochère, le visage empourpré
9. fusil à air comprimé déjà rangé dans le sac de golf
10. comme prévu
11. Un autre claquement de fouet et nous passions à toute allure
12. se mettre en travers de
13. heurtâmes une ornière
14. jurer
15. l'imaginer projeté à terre dans un faubourg
16. avait dû entendre les coups de feu
17. véhicule tourner

guessed what had occurred but the doors were locked and there would be nothing he could do.

We passed through Chelsea and into Fulham – or West Kensington as its residents insisted it be called[1]. When we reached the hospital, I handed the reins to Perry who guided the horses with a happy smile on his face. We were proceeding[2] more slowly now. It would be hours before the gaggle[3] of inspectors at Scotland Yard could mount anything that resembled a search[4] and there was no point drawing attention to ourselves. I called out to Colonel Moran and received a grunt by way of reply[5]. It seemed he was still hanging on[6].

It took us the best part of[7] an hour to reach Richmond Park, entering through Bishop's Gate which I had chosen as it was not actually intended for public use. I wanted an open space and the park seemed ideal for what I had in mind. We drove into the largest field we could find with views all around us, the river concealed by the rise of the hill[8] but the village clearly visible and the city far beyond[9]. It was a glorious[10] day, the spring sun finally shining and only a few puffs[11] of cloud floating above the horizon. At last we stopped. Colonel Moran climbed down and walked round to the horses, at the same time stretching[12] his arms.

'Did you have to go so damned far?[13]' he demanded.

Ignoring him, I went to the back and opened the door. Clarence Devereux knew what his fate was to be[14]. Even as the glare of the sunlight burst into the interior, he huddled away[15], hiding in a corner, covering his eyes. I did not speak to him. I climbed inside and dragged him out[16]. I

1. tiennent à l'appeler
2. évoluions
3. la brochette
4. mettre sur pied quelque chose qui ressemblerait à une battue
5. grognement pour toute réponse
6. tenait encore le coup
7. presque
8. qui disparaissait derrière la colline
9. dans le lointain
10. magnifique
11. bancs
12. étirant
13. Y'avait pas plus près ?
14. avait deviné le sort qui l'attendait
15. Dès que la lumière du solei pénétra dans le fourgon, il se recroquevilla
16. l'en extirpa

was certain that he carried no weapon and once he was in the open, he would be helpless, no better than a fish on dry land. Finally, I signalled to Perry who led the horses over to a clump of trees[1] where a second carriage stood waiting. I had, of course, concealed[2] it there earlier. It would now be his task to unhitch the horses and then to reconnect them[3]. We had a long journey ahead of us, all the way to the south coast.

I stood there with my enemy grovelling on his knees[4]. I knew that he could feel the breeze upon his cheeks. He could hear birdsong and understood well enough where he was even if he didn't open his eyes. I still had the gun that I had used to kill Athelney Jones. Perry, too, was armed. There was little chance that we would be disturbed by strollers for the park was huge[5] – two thousand three hundred and sixty acres[6], to be precise – and I had deliberately chosen an area that was remote[7]. Nor did I intend to be here long.

Moran stood beside me, examining our prisoner with his usual blend of cruelty and contempt[8]. With his bald forehead[9] and huge moustache he did rather unfortunately[10] resemble a villain out of a pantomime, but he was quite unaware of his appearance or perhaps indifferent to it. It struck me that although he had not been a pleasant man when we first met, he was getting worse, more irascible, as he grew older[11].

'So what now, Professor?' he asked. 'I imagine you must be quite pleased with yourself[12].'

'It all worked out very much as I expected,' I admitted. 'There was a moment when, despite everything, I thought the minister was not going to give his secretary over to us[13]. Why do these

1. fis signe à Perry qui conduisit les chevaux près d'un bosquet
2. caché
3. détacher puis d'atteler à nouveau les chevaux
4. qui rampait à genoux
5. des promeneurs tant le parc était immense
6. mille deux cents hectares
7. isolé
8. le mélange de cruauté et de mépris qui le caractérisait
9. front dégarni
10. malencontreusement
11. de plus en plus colérique avec l'âge
12. content de vous
13. nous livrer son secrétaire

people have to be so officious[1]? Fortunately, the late[2] Inspector Jones was able to circumvent this with one last display of genius[3]. I will be forever grateful[4] to him.'

'I take it … this nasty little man[5] … you're going to kill him?'

'Of course not! Do you really believe I would have gone to such extremes had that been[6] my intention? I need him very much[7] alive. I have *always* needed him alive. Otherwise my task would have been a great deal[8] easier.'

'Why?'

'It will be some years before I can operate again in England, Colonel. First, I have to rebuild my organisation and that will take time. But even when that is done, I have a problem …'

'Sherlock Holmes?'

'No. He seems to have left the stage[9]. But as surprised as I am to admit it, I must learn to beware[10] of the police.'

'They know who you are.'

'Precisely. It won't take them very long to work out[11] what happened – even Lestrade might be able to bring the pieces together[12]. And they've all seen me.'

'You've sat amongst 'em[13] and they've seen your face. You've killed one of their own[14]. They'll search for you, high and low[15].'

'Which is why I must leave the country. The *Vandalia* leaves the port of Le Havre for New York in three days' time[16]. Perry and I will be on board and Mr Devereux will come with us.'

'And then?'

I looked down at Devereux. 'Open your eyes,' I said.

1. font-ils autant de zèle
2. regretté
3. contourner cette difficulté dans un dernier éclair de génie
4. reconnaissant
5. J'imagine que… ce vilain petit homme
6. pris tant de risques si ç'avait été
7. tout ce qu'il y a de plus
8. considérablement
9. avoir quitté la scène
10. qu'il faut que j'apprenne à me méfier
11. comprendre
12. assembler les pièces du puzzle
13. avez participé à la réunion
14. l'un d'entre eux
15. remuer ciel et terre pour vous retrouver
16. dans trois jours

1. génie du crime

2. se balançait d'avant en arrière en gémissant

3. le restant de ses jours

4. ruisselaient de ses yeux et son nez coulait

5. articles

6. de mes propres yeux

7. Même si j'avais tendu

8. tirant une grande malle-cabine

9. Il y va ?

10. fortune

11. représentants de la loi

12. Vous et moi régnions chacun sur notre empire.

'No!' He was a criminal mastermind[1], the greatest evil to have emerged from America. He had almost destroyed me. But at that moment he sounded like a child. His hands were pressed against his face and he was rocking back and forth, moaning to himself.[2]

'Open your eyes,' I repeated. 'If you wish to live, you will do it now.' Very slowly, Devereux did as I said but he remained still, staring at the grass, too afraid to lift his head. 'Look at me!'

It took him a huge effort but he obeyed and it occurred to me that he would continue obeying me for what remained of his life[3]. He was crying. The tears were streaming from both his eyes and his nose[4]. His skin was completely white. I had read certain papers[5] about agoraphobia, a condition that had only been recognised quite recently, but I was fascinated to see its effect at such close quarters[6]. Had I handed[7] Devereux my revolver, I am not sure he would have been able to use it. He was paralysed with fear. At the same time, Perry reappeared from behind the trees, dragging with him a large steamer trunk[8]. It was in this that Devereux would be making his journey.

'Is he going in?[9]' he asked.

'Not yet, Perry.' I turned to Devereux. 'Why did you have to come here?' I asked him. 'You had wealth[10] and success in America. The forces of law[11], both public and private, were unable to reach you. You had your world and I mine.[12] What made you think that by bringing them into collision you would cause anything but harm?' Devereux tried to speak but could no longer formulate the words.'And what has been the result? So much bloodshed, so much pain. You have caused the deaths of my closest friends.' I was thinking of Jonathan Pilgrim but also of Athelney Jones. 'Worst of all, you have forced me to descend to your level, using methods which frankly I found distasteful[1]. That is why I feel nothing but hatred for you and why one day you must die. But not today.'

'What do you want?'

'You wished to take over[2] my organisation. Now I will take over yours. You leave me with no choice for, thanks to you, I am finished here[3]. I therefore need to know the names of all your associates in America, all the people you have worked with, the street criminals and their masters. You will tell me everything you know about the crooked[4] politicians, the lawyers[5], the judges, the press, the police – and about the Pinkertons too. England is a closed door for me for the time being[6] but America is most certainly not. The new world! That is where I intend to re-establish myself. We have many days of travel ahead of us. By the end of it, you will have given me all the information I need.'

'You are a devil!'

'No. I am a criminal. The two are not at all the same … or so I thought, until I met you[7].'

'Now?' Perry asked.

I nodded[8]. 'Yes, Perry, I am already sick of the sight of him[9].'

Perry fell on Devereux with glee[10], binding and gagging him[11], then bundling him into the steamer trunk and closing the lid[12]. Meanwhile, I spoke again with Moran.

1. me révulsent

2. vous accaparer

3. car, à cause de vous, je ne suis plus rien ici

4. corrompus

5. avocats

6. Les portes de l'Angleterre me sont fermées désormais

7. en tout cas c'est ce que je croyais, avant de vous rencontrer

8. opinai du bonnet

9. je l'ai déjà trop vu

10. se jeta joyeusement sur Devereux

11. pour l'attacher et le bâillonner

12. puis le poussa dans la malle-cabine et la referma

1. espère

2. en haute estime

'I trust[1] that you will come with us, Colonel,' I said. 'I am aware that you do not hold the country that is our destination in particularly high regard[2], but even so I will have need of your services.'

'Will you pay?'

'Of course.'

3. Je ferai payer mes services le double

4. à l'étranger

'My fees will be doubled[3], if I'm to work abroad[4].'

'They will be good value even at that price.'

5. file en

Moran nodded. 'I'll join you in a month or two. Before that, I'm slipping out to[5] India, to the mangrove forests of the Sundarbans. I've heard there are plenty of tigers at this time of the year. You'll leave a message for me in the usual place? Once I'm back, I'll wait to hear from you.'

'Excellent.'

6. nous nous mîmes à trois pour soulever

7. à présent verrouillée

8. descendîmes la colline en direction de la Tamise

9. prés

10. ni aux nombreux succès que me réservait à n'en pas douter l'

11. insondable

12. réfléchissais

13. que je souhaitais depuis longtemps déjà

We shook hand. Then the three of us lifted[6] the steamer trunk, now well secured[7], and placed it in the carriage. Finally, Perry and I climbed up together and, with the boy holding the reins, we set off down the hillside, heading for the River Thames[8]. The sun was shining. I could smell the meadows[9] all around and at that moment I was not thinking of crime, nor of the many triumphs that surely awaited me in[10] America. No. For some unfathomable[11] reason, my attention had turned to something quite different. I was considering the[12] different solutions applicable to the Korteweg de Vries equation, a mathematical model I had long been intending to[13] examine but for which I'd never had the time.

We bumped over the grass and came to a track. Perry was sitting happily beside me. Our guest, in his trunk, was in the back. And there was the river; a crystalline twist of blue in the soft green fields[1]. With the different variables – *x*, *t* and ø – spinning in my head, I made my way down towards it[2].

1. lacet de bleu cristallin au milieu de prairies verdoyantes

2. qui tournoyaient dans ma tête, je m'y attelais enfin

THE END

La collection Yes you can!

Les faux débutants

M.C. Beaton *Agatha Raisin and the Quiche of Death*

Michael Connelly *The Black Box*

Michael Connelly *The Burning Room*

Michael Connelly *The Drop*

Ken Follett *The Modigliani Scandal*

Mary Higgins Clark *A Cry in the Night*

Mary Higgins Clark *A Stranger is Watching*

Mary Higgins Clark *Loves Music, Loves to Dance*

Mary Higgins Clark *Where are the Children?*

Anthony Horowitz *The House of Silk*

Nicholas Sparks *Message in a Bottle*

Les intermédiaires

Harlan Coben *Caught*

Harlan Coben *Play Dead*

Harlan Coben *Stay Close*

Harlan Coben *Tell No One*

Harlan Coben *The Woods*

Ken Follett *Paper Money*

Anthony Horowitz *Moriarty*

P.D. James *A Mind to Murder*

P.D. James *Death Comes to Pemberley*

La collection Yes you can!

Douglas Kennedy *The Big Picture*

Stephen King *Finders Keepers*

Stephen King *The Green Mile*

John le Carré *A Most Wanted Man*

Yann Martel *Life of Pi*

Les avancés

Paul Auster *Leviathan*

Paul Auster *Oracle Night*

Julian Barnes *The Sense of an Ending*

Michael Cunningham *By Nightfall*

Michael Cunningham *The Hours*

Helen Fielding *Bridget Jones's Diary*

Helen Fielding *Bridget Jones: The Edge of Reason*

Elizabeth George *A Great Deliverance*

Stephen King *Misery*

Les classiques

Jane Austen *Pride and Prejudice*

Arthur Conan Doyle *The Hound of the Baskervilles*

Francis Scott Fitzgerald *The Great Gatsby*

Mary Shelley *Frankenstein*

Oscar Wilde *The Picture of Dorian Gray*

Virginia Woolf *To the Lighthouse*

HARRAP s'engage pour l'environnement en réduisant l'empreinte carbone de ses livres. Celle de cet exemplaire est de : 500 g éq. CO_2
Rendez-vous sur www.larousse-durable.fr

PAPIER À BASE DE FIBRES CERTIFIÉES

Imprimé par Jouve (France)
Dépôt légal : mai 2017
317408-01/11031977-mai2017
N° 2536477X